M000195967

Where the Pieces

Fall

Lost Hearts 1

Blue Saffire

Perceptive Illusions Publishing, Inc.
Bay Shore, New York

Blue Saffire/Perceptive Illusions Publishing, Inc.
PO BOX 5253
Bay Shore, New York 11706
www.BlueSaffire.com

Publisher's Note: This is a work of fiction. Names, characters, places, and incidents are a product of the author's imagination. Locales and public names are sometimes used for atmospheric purposes. Any resemblance to actual people, living or dead, or to businesses, companies, events, institutions, or locales is completely coincidental.

Ordering Information:
Quantity sales. Special discounts are available on quantity purchases by corporations, associations, and others. For details, contact the "Special Sales Department" at the address above.

Where the Piece Fall: Lost Hearts Book 1/ Blue Saffire. – 2nd ed.
ISBN 978-1-941924-78-5

Why hide who you are? We're all special in our own way. Never let the words of others define you. When you hide your light, it still comes through. After all, secrets have a way of coming out in the wash. You'll never be able to keep secret that you're just amazing.

−Blue Saffire

Broken

Caleb

I look around the room at everyone. I want to run for the door. This is all so overwhelming, but there's one thing gluing my ass to this seat. My family.

I'll put up with anything for the one woman that *saw* me. Or at least, I once thought I would. Now, I don't know if I can. That's why I'm here.

My gaze sweeps the faces in the room from under my lashes, once again. This is probably going to be harder for me than any of the others in this room. I've listened to the two before me. I've watched them figure shit out right before my eyes.

It won't be that easy for me, not at all. It doesn't matter that I've made my way to the professional baseball league, or that I have a gorgeous, sexy as hell wife, that I love the fuck out of.

I'm a failure. My life is imploding right before me, and I can't stop it. This is my last resort. My cousin Dakota said it was now or never, this is my only option, so I'm here.

"This is good. I think we're making amazing progress in this group. So, who's going to be our Braveheart, today?" Dr. Winsor's brown eyes land on me. As if she knows I'm going to be the next one to speak up.

The new guy next to me tenses. I shift my gaze to the Native American looking guy in the seat beside me. If I let him go now, if I allow him to jump ahead of me, I may never come back. I've already waited long enough. I need to fix my life; it can't wait any longer.

"I'll go," I murmur. My voice rumbling through the room. I take a deep breath.

Here goes nothing.

I wrinkle my brows trying to get my brain to form the right words. Pursing my lips, I start to squint. Some habits never die. I pull on the focus I've learned to control through playing baseball. No one is going to do this for me. I can't rely on anyone else. Sucks, but I have to push through.

I start. "My name is Caleb, Caleb Perry. I'm thirty-one. I was born and raised here in Texas," I pause and clear my throat. "I've always been different. Not that it's a big deal to me, but to others around me, it has been the bane of their existence."

"It took me a long time to understand what made me so different and an even longer time to feel okay about being different," I admit.

My southern drawl is heavy on a good day. Right now, I don't want to do this, so it's extra thick. The pain in my voice is evident, even to my own ears.

I get lost in my thoughts, as I continue to talk. I muse on how different I've always felt. Until one day, one day, I just didn't anymore. I guess that's why I fell in love with *her.*

She was different too. She was shy and content with hiding in the background, away from everyone else. It was one of the first things I noticed about her. She was hiding in plain sight.

I notice things. I have to, and at the same time I can't help it. I have to process everything to get the little things. It's what made me see she was special.

I saw that she would understand what I needed. What I wanted so much. *"Normal"* people take a lot for granted, but they don't understand how hard something as simple as love can be for me. Love isn't concrete. It's not something you can measure or explain. It's not something that can be mocked or mimicked.

I don't do well with things I can't mimic. I need a reference, a learning point if you will. I need the controlled model of the desired outcome.

Mama says I'm just extra special, and to do great things, I can't be like everyone else. When it's convenient Mama also likes to ignore how different I really am, and she points it out when it's not. I have been different for as long as I can remember, but that has never stopped me. My family wouldn't let it.

Most people look past it all because of the way I look. I guess you would say that I'm handsome. But Mama, she says I'm gorgeous. With my blue-grey eyes and sandy blonde hair, I've stood out most my life, but as soon as I reached six foot seven, I stood out like an apple in a pumpkin patch. People are either in awe of my good looks and massive size, or they are wary enough to walk the other way.

It's funny to think of a guy as huge as me trying to hide, but I do it every day. Always surrounded by others, but hiding just the same. They all see what I learned to show them, but she saw right through it all and noticed me.

It's the real me that no one else sees or understands. No one, but *her*. She's the one thing I treasure in my life. She's the one person I've ever wanted to change for. Yet, she's loved me for me from the beginning.

Yes, she loves me. We have our own love. It's complicated, unlike any other, and at times a lot to swallow. Not many can understand the world through my eyes, but she has been the first to try.

I mean truly try, without asking me to hide or to change. Nicole is the glue to my puzzle pieces, but I've been shitting all over the glue and the puzzle it's holding together.

Nicole's leaving me. I did this, it's not her fault. Let her tell it, she still loves me. I can see it in her eyes, she does, but she's starting to think I don't have room in my head to handle our love. That's not it.

"No, I love my wife," I choke out to the group. "I'm just scared as fuck. Shit got real for me, and I'm not handling it well. I let others make decisions for me and now, I've pushed my heart, my breath, my life—away."

"Okay, Caleb," Dr. Winsor says. "So now, tell us how you think you got here?"

CHAPTER ONE

Lost

Nicole

Ten years ago…

What was I thinking? I should've arrived a day early like my mother and father suggested. Right now, Dad would have a good laugh at me. If he could only see me trying to find my way around this campus. Mom would just shake her head at us both and ask for directions.

That's not me. I will drown before I ask for help from one of these strangers. Seriously, I live in my shell.

It took a lot of convincing for me to transfer here in the first place. Sure, my last school wasn't the best experience and I'd been unhappy, but I figured I could make it through two more years.

My dad, on the other hand, believes I tried things the way my mother and grandfather wanted me to. In Daddy's words, "Now, you deserve to see if a change will bring you happiness." You see, my mother and grandfather wanted me to attend an all-black college. Go figure. My dad is white, born and raised in Washington State. His mother and father, my grandparents, are both Scandinavian. At first glance, my mother looks like a good old Georgia peach, with her cocoa brown skin, bright brown eyes, full lips, and plentiful curves.

Look closer at the family tree and you will find that my granddad, mom's dad, is African American. Despite all granddad's pro black talk. Lectures on supporting black owned, being enriched in the culture, and going to a black historical college—his wife, my grandmother, mom's mom—is Asian American.

I say all this to say that I have never fit into the neat box my mother and grandfather want to put me in. I never fit into the whole black college scene with my light brown, almost hazel eyes, pin straight, brown bob, and bronzed chocolate complexion. Nope, I get stares and someone is always asking what am I? Like I'm not human.

Forget that I am painfully shy. Let's focus on the fact that I have always been treated by the black kids like I've been tainted by aliens and white kids could only see my color and send me packing to "be with my own kind."

This has been the story of my life, so I've learned to hide in the background and be there, but not be. It's just…it's been a lot harder in college, believe it or not. I think in my early adult life, I have been made more aware of how different I am. Everyone treats me like some spoiled rich brat, with a white daddy that would ensure I never wanted for anything in the world.

Sure, my mother and father have made a great life for themselves. Also, both sets of my grandparents are well off, but I still work hard for my grades. I want to make my own place in the world.

That's the way I was raised. My family has never denied me anything, but I have always had the truth of—hard work and smart work—drilled into me. I work for what's mine.

I think what became the final straw for me in my last school was the fact that it wasn't just the students that had a bias against me. A few professors had made my life hell. Unfortunately, in order to finish out my literature and art programs, I'd have to deal with the same professors more than I would've liked.

So, here I am, on a new campus for the first time, a week into the semester. I peek down again at my schedule and map that I have in a death grip. I frown at the traitor map and press my lips, as my feet carry me forward. Suddenly, I crash into what feels like a solid wall.

But walls don't have arms, right?

Ignoring my bag, books, and map that have fallen to the ground. I look up into intense blue eyes, fanned by thick blonde lashes. The thick trunks that rescued me from falling backwards abruptly release me. Standing in front of me is the biggest white boy I've ever seen. I mean he is huge. My eyes widen as I let them take in over six feet of tanned grizzly.

Wow, is he gorgeous. I'm not usually impressed with blondes or with blue eyes, but his are unique and not in the least the highlight of his beauty. Those full lips count for a whole lot.

I can't help noticing the fullness of the soft looking pillows, as his beard calls all types of naughty attention to them. The beard is another feature I wouldn't normally find attractive on anyone else. Slightly darker than his thick blonde locks, the scruff on his face is full, but not overgrown or hanging off his face.

My gasp rings in my ears, when I watch his muscles flex under his tight black t-shirt. I lick my lips and look back up at his face, which I have to crane my neck to gaze up at. His lips are pursed and he's squinting down at me. It's an adorable expression that makes me blush and turn away to my fallen books.

"S-sorry, ma'am," he murmurs and bends to retrieve my things.

I'm not sure what's wrong with me because I shiver as his rumbling voice rolls through me. I bend to stuff my fallen items back inside my bag. I chance a peek at him again, before I answer.

This time he seems to be trying to look anywhere but at me. It's as if he is searching for someone to come and rescue him. I laugh internally. Like this big dude would need someone to save him from little old me. I have to be more than a foot shorter than him.

"I think it was my fault. I'm the one that should be apologizing," I say with a small smile.

He shakes his head. "Practice ran over. I'm late for class. Dakota is going to have my ass," he replies with a heavy southern drawl, still looking around. His eyes snap to me as if an afterthought. "S…sorry, excuse my language ma'am."

By now, he hands me my books as we both stand. I accept my books. Tilting my head back to look him in the face as I thank him.

"Nicole, my name is Nicole, thank you."

He reaches for the back of his neck, still looking a bit lost. "I have to get to my psych class. I…I'm late," he squints again and bites his lip. Damn, if that twang isn't sexy as hell, coming from his deep voice. "Sorry, Nicole."

My eyes drop to my books and I realize he may be able to help me and since he is here….

"Oh, I'm trying to find the psych building. This map isn't helping. Can I follow you?" I ask shyly.

I have no idea what has gotten into me. I could've just followed him there without asking, but there's something about him I can't put my finger on. I don't want to let him go yet. Not until the nagging in my brain sets me free.

"I…you…you want to walk with me? Or I can point it out to you if that's what you would like," he offers, and his cheeks flush under the cover of his golden beard.

"I think we could walk together if that's okay," I speak the words before thinking.

I remember him mentioning a Dakota and blush. Maybe his girlfriend wouldn't want him walking with another girl. He seems to be a bit nervous. I hold up the schedule to show him where I'm headed.

"I mean, if it's a problem, you can just show me. This is my class here."

I rush the words out, feeling awkward, but he shakes his head as his eyes seemed to clear. As if just having a sudden thought, he reaches for my books. Taking them from me, he wraps my small hand in his huge one. Next thing I know, we're walking in the opposite direction of where I'd been heading.

I should be in a panic, having this huge stranger leading me by the hand with almost a possessive grip on me. I don't though.

I feel safe, almost like for this moment, I'm his precious cargo and he's going to make sure I arrive safely.

We make it to class as the professor enters the lecture hall, through another door close to the front of the room. Too bad our arrival seems to be more interesting to the rest of the class. Gasps and murmurs break out around the room. I peek up at my guide and he gives me the first sign of a smile since we crashed into each other.

"Perry," a gorgeous blonde hisses, as she appears at his side. "You're late. Come on, I have our seats."

He turns that smile to me as he hands me my books. "Sorry, Dakota," he murmurs and gives her a boyish smile. "This is your class, Nicole. Here are your books, sorry again."

Then he's off to the front of the class with the pretty blonde. I feel left behind and embarrassed for the silly feelings buzzing in the hand he held. I bite my lip, as my skin continues to tingle from where our skin touched.

I can be so foolish. I should've known someone as gorgeous as him would have a girlfriend that's equally as devastatingly beautiful as he is. I shake off my feelings and my thoughts and move to find a seat.

It would be a lie if I said my eyes didn't try to find Perry more than once. Well, I assume that's his name since he never told me, but that's what the blonde called him. When I do find him in the front, I notice that he and Dakota are indeed sitting together and she keeps leaning in to whisper to him every once in a while.

She even turns in her seat once, and our eyes connect. She gives me a small smile, then turns to whisper something else to Perry next to her. I don't know how to take that or the questioning looks and glares that I'm getting from other girls in the class.

I'm feeling sick already. I want to blend in here as best as I can without being noticed. I want to finish these next two years without being reminded that I don't fit in. I sigh to myself.

Good luck with that. This is the same pony, Nicole, different saddle.

CHAPTER TWO

Normal

Caleb

"Who's your new girlfriend?" Dakota wiggles her brows at me.

"I don't have a girlfriend, Dakota," I reply and look at her confused.

She laughs at me and nudges my ribs with her elbow. "Oh, come on. Who was the pretty girl you came into class with? Was she the reason you were late?"

"No, coach wanted to talk to me after practice. Cameron couldn't wait around for me. He had to meet up with Kay. I thought I could take a shortcut to class and I ran into Nicole. I almost knocked her on her ass. She was lost, so I helped her find the class," I reply.

"Oh, shit. I'm sorry, Caleb. I forgot Cameron asked me to meet you at the field after practice," Dakota makes that face she makes when she is sorry or guilty about something. I know that one. I see it a lot.

"I'm not a baby. I know how to walk to class," I grumble.

"Sure, I almost bulldozed a girl on the way, but I made it."

"Oh, my God, was that a joke," Dakota nudges me. "Cameron was right. You being on the team is having all types of influences on you."

"Well, that's what mama's plan was right," I frown and watch as Dakota's face turns into a pout. Her eyes are far away. I purse my lips and fight not to squint. I'm not sure what she's thinking. That frustrates me.

"You know, Aunt Jemma wants the best for you and so does Uncle Kyle. They may not show it the way the rest of us do, but they mean well. Don't you like college and playing on the team?" She says after a few minutes.

I shrug. "I love my classes and I really like that you and Cameron are here with me. Everyone knows playing is like breathing to me. It's the only time I can just be me and I have it all figured out."

"I still don't get that. You're so amazing, I would think that playing would drive you insane," she pauses and shakes her head, "but watching you. It's like you said, you would never know, you know?" Dakota says while tilting her head and studying me.

"I couldn't do it without you guys. Your mom and dad, Cameron, and Thomas, you all have helped me figure a lot out. I just wish…do you think I could have what Cameron has someday?"

My mind turns to the girl I almost ran over. She was the prettiest girl I've ever seen. Her pretty brown skin, her hot body, and those eyes. I swear I could spend hours learning to read those eyes, trying to figure out everything they would tell me about her. I love how her hair cups her face.

I blink several times to focus. If I don't, I know I'll get lost in my thoughts of her for hours. I wouldn't mind that, but I want to hear Dakota's response.

Dakota looks up at me and I realize she is bewildered. I know the look from when I tutored her in math.

"Cameron and Kay," I elaborate. "Do you think a girl could love me like that?"

Dakota's eyes take on what I think of as a gentle look as she gazes back at. She reaches for my face, but pauses and drops her hand to her side. I watch her lips turn up.

"Yeah, Caleb, I think the right girl is going to come along and she's going to get you and you're going to be able to let her in. Absolutely, handsome, you'll have what Cameron has and so much more, because you deserve it," Dakota chokes out and I note the tears in her eyes.

I think about my cousin's words, but my mind shifts back to the girl. "She was pretty, wasn't she?" I ask.

Dakota gives me one of those smiles she has when she is about to get me in trouble. "Yeah, she sure is," she smirks and laughs.

"Perry," I turn as I hear my name called by one of my teammates. "Hey, man, what's up?"

Hamilton is a good guy from what I know. He also makes me nervous sometimes. Of all the guys on the team, I think he is the one that has figured out that I'm different, that I'm hiding something.

I would probably be worried if he wasn't a shit pitcher and one of the strongest hitters on the team. He's no threat to me and I'm no threat to him, because of that I don't so much mind that he's so perceptive.

"Hey, Hamilton," I answer back a bit stilted.

"Hey, Dakota," Hamilton says, as he turns his attention to my cousin.

I watch as his face takes on a look I know too well. It's the way I look at steak and how Cameron looks at Kay. He looks like he is ready to devour Dakota right here on the spot.

"Hi Hamilton," Dakota purrs back, as she blushes to her roots.

Aw hell, I know Cameron wouldn't like this one bit. I step in front of Dakota, blocking Hamilton's view. I cross my arms over my chest, making sure that Hamilton can see all my muscles flex. Yup, I have his attention now.

"Would you like to stop eye fucking my cousin?" I say it just as I've heard Cameron say a million times to a million different guys.

Dakota gasps behind me and I turn to look over my shoulder and give her a wink. I'm quite proud of myself right now. I know this is what Cameron would've done, and I think I'm handling it very well.

Dakota's blush deepens and she scowls at me, shaking her head, but I know she's on the edge of laughter. I can see it in her eyes.

"Really, Caleb," Dakota groans. "Leave that shit for your brother."

"Cameron isn't here," I say innocently. Cameron and Dakota are always looking out for me. I can do the same. I got this.

"I'm not so sure about that," Dakota murmurs to herself.

"Lighten up, Perry, Dakota is way out of my league," Hamilton says, but winks at Dakota.

I just shake my head. Maybe I didn't do as good a job as I thought. When Cameron does it, guys usually don't look at Dakota while he's around. I'll have to work on that one.

"Whatever," I shrug. "You wanted something?"

"Oh, yeah," Hamilton chuckles. "Always direct, that's why I like you, Perry. I wanted to remind you about the party next week and I won't let you beg off of this one. You owe me."

I groan. I hate parties. They're way too much work for me. I'm left exhausted from the effort after an hour or two. The music, the persistent girls, and it's not the ideal situation for me to be in control.

Control is important to me. Having control allows me to hide. Parties aren't on my list of things I enjoy, because they add too many factors I can't control or handle.

However, Hamilton is right, I do owe him. He's the closest thing I have to a friend, outside of Cameron, Thomas, and Dakota. He saved me a few more times than I would like to admit.

The team's assistant coach hates Cameron and especially me for some reason. He's always giving us a hard time when the coach isn't looking or when Coach Snider isn't around.

One practice assistant coach, Robinson, purposely split me and Cameron up. Sending Cameron into the weight room, as a punishment for something bogus. Then he leaned into me like nobody's business.

Riding my ass until I almost snapped. Hamilton stepped in, taking the attention off me, just as I was about to explode. Since I hit puberty, I tend to lash out violently when I'm not coping.

I have to say I've gotten a lot better the last few years. Thanks to Cameron and Dakota.

Hamilton has become a friend without me realizing it. I guess I owe him this party, despite as much as I don't want to go. I'll just have to make an appearance and then I'll get out of there as fast as I can.

"Yeah, sure I'll be there," I reply.

"Great! What do you think about this calendar assignment being forced on the team?" Hamilton asks.

"Not sure how I feel about it," I answer honestly.

I haven't had time to process the information. I was running late for class because Coach wanted to talk to me about some charity calendar, every team member is required to do. He wanted to offer me options.

I appreciate Coach looking out for me, but I know the team would want to know why this is mandatory for everyone except me. I know I will probably regret it later. However, I more than plan to do my part like the rest of the guys.

"I was just heading over to the art building to see which of the photo geeks I can get to take some shots for me. I think they're getting some type of incentive for helping out or something," Hamilton shrugs. "You want to head over with me? The sooner we get it over with, the better."

I look over at Dakota and she gives me a small smile and nod. I take a second to run the look through my mental Rolodex. I nod as it registers that she is encouraging me to do this.

This is what I want, to be treated like I'm normal. To have friends and not feel like a freak or like I'm out of place. I take a deep breath and nod my head at Hamilton.

A part of me is screaming for me to run and hide. Talking to Dakota or Hamilton is one thing, but talking to strangers from the photography class is another. Not that Coach didn't warn me that I would have to, I just didn't think I would have to do it so soon. I had figured I could let Cameron or Dakota handle it for me.

Coach had suggested I team up with my brother for my calendar shoot, but I want to do my own. I can't always count on Cameron for everything. So, I'm going to do this myself.

Well, as on my own as I've ever done anything.

The thought floats through my head, as Dakota falls in step with me and Hamilton. We set off for the art building and I try my best not to meltdown.

You can do this Caleb. You can be normal.

CHAPTER THREE

I want You

Nicole

"Hey, there, roomy," Taylor calls after me, as I once again stand in the middle of campus, frowning at my traitor map.

"Hey." I sigh in frustration, not meant for Taylor.

"Give me that," she laughs, taking my map and crumpling it. "This damn thing is backwards. I swear they printed it as a cruel joke for freshmen. Where're you headed?"

"The art center, I have a photography class," I say, as Taylor wraps her arm around mine.

"Well, you're in luck because that's exactly where I'm going," Taylor beams at me, then reaches in her bag to pull out her camera.

I groan, then curse under my breath. I'd forgotten my camera with all of my rushing this morning. I'm not starting off too great here.

"What's wrong?" Taylor asks, as she picks up on my frustration.

"I forgot my camera in the room," I huff.

"Don't worry about it. There's this big contest, charity thing that all of the photographers and the baseball team are being paired up for," Taylor chirps, with a dreamy look in her eyes.

I look at her and wrinkle my nose. "What?"

"They're going to pose for us in all their glory and we get to capture their Godliness. The calendar that brings in the most for the charity wins and the photographer gets a trip to Paris. I think the jocks get something out of it too."

"Seriously, that sounds amazing," I say excitedly. I wasn't expecting something like this.

"Yes, getting to drool over all those abs is right where I want to be. Eye candy and a trip to Paris, what more can a girl ask for?" Taylor giggles. I think I can learn to like her. "I think it's mandatory for the team, but it's optional for our group. But like, who wouldn't want to do this?"

Me.

I wouldn't mind winning the trip. However, as the assignment starts to sink in, I don't think I want to spend time shooting pictures of some jock.

It's just not my thing. I like landscapes. Not that I don't shoot people. I did my brother's engagement photos and pictures of my new niece and nephew, the cutest twins ever.

That's the thing though, I only shoot friends and family. Unfortunately, being as shy as I am, doesn't help with directing people into position for the perfect shot.

No matter if I get to hide behind the camera. I'd much rather shoot a bunch of kittens, than do a shoot with people. Although I keep this opinion to myself.

Turns out, I was walking away from the art building after all. It was right behind me. I shake my head, agreeing that that map is a joke, some kind of prank on poor unsuspecting students.

I'm surprised at how happy I am to have Taylor in my photography class. We'd talked briefly last night. I know the funny redhead, with freckles sprinkled across her light brown face, is an art major. If I'm honest with myself, I found something refreshing about Taylor.

She's a petite girl like me, but where I'm full and curvy, she's lithe with a shapely figure. I love her long red locks with her sweeping bangs. They make her—with her bright brown eyes— look like a model, instead of the one behind the camera lens.

I noticed more than once since the first time we met that her brown eyes have sparkled with mischief. Taylor is the type that can talk you into a happy mood with just her smile alone. Her happiness is infectious.

Once in class, we take our seats at a table toward the back of the room. Taylor takes two packets from the center of the table and slides one in front of me. I look at the school logo printed at the top and smile.

Dad had made it clear that I could go wherever I wanted. As long as it made me happy. I decided on moving to the Midwest. Texas couldn't be further from Atlanta for me. My eyes move to the title on the packet, *Give Back*. I tuck my hair behind my ear and opened to the next page.

I have to admit that I'm becoming more interested. Mom is big on giving back, and I've done a lot of charity work. As I read through the packet, it's clear that this is being done for a good purpose.

Each photographer and athlete will work together to come up with a calendar for one of the charities of their choice, from the list provided. All proceeds will go toward that charity. In addition, some big corporation is donating a trip. The photographer that brings in the most money for their charity will receive a trip to Paris for two.

It's a pretty cool idea. I'm still not sure I'm willing to do it, until my eyes landed on a charity that is near my heart. I suck in a large gulp of air, as my mind starts to wonder. I'm a million miles away when a squeal breaks through my reverie.

"Oh my God, this can't be real." Squeals the cute, pixie looking girl that just sat down next to Taylor.

She's pretty with her pointed nose and full cheeks. I would normally wrinkle my nose at someone with blue hair, but this girl makes her blonde pixie cut work with its blue tips. Her tanned skin sets the blonde and the blue off.

"I just saw Caleb and Hamilton and some of the other team members heading this way. So, I know it has to be real."

Taylor throws her head back and laughs. "You're worse than me," Taylor giggles. "Joelle, this is my new roommate, Nicole. Nicole this is Joelle, the only other cool person in the arts program."

Joelle pouts, "That's not true. My brother isn't so bad."

Taylor rolls her eyes. "Okay, okay, Jonah isn't so bad," Taylor relents with a smile. "Jonah is Joelle's twin. He's like a literary genius and his paintings are awesome too."

"Nice to meet you," I say to Joelle, with a small smile. She beams back at me, as she gives me a curious once over.

"You're gorgeous," Joelle claps her hands together. I frown and blush at the same time. "No, really, you're," she gasps and grabs Taylor's hand. "I think I found my subject."

Taylor looks over at me and gives me an apologetic smile. "Jo has this idea in her head. She just hasn't found the right model, as of yet. Well, until now. Sounds like you just became her victim."

"Oh, no, I don't think that would be a good idea," I say quickly.

"Oh, come on. Your eyes, they look like you're hiding a million secrets or something. Jonah is going to freak when he sees you. I know he's going to want to paint you," Joelle gushes.

"That's so not going to happen," I snort.

"Oh, come on," Joelle pouts prettily, causing me to genuinely laugh, as I shake my head at her.

"What the heck, I knew everyone was going to go nuts about this assignment, but there's a line of jocks outside the class." Says the newcomer to our table.

"I stand corrected, once again. Nicole, this is Maribel, now you have officially met everyone you need to know," Taylor introduces the beautiful girl that's now looking at me with a friendly smile on her face.

All of these girls are pretty in their own way, but seem so down to earth. Maribel towers over all of us. She has to be five nine, at least. Her chocolate brown eyes are friendly and light up her pretty brown face.

I love the confidence I feel coming off of her. I wish I felt as comfortable in my own skin, not that I don't think I'm pretty. It's never been a lack of confidence because of my looks that keeps me shy.

I've just never been one to need attention centered on me. I'd much rather hug the wall and observe. I'm a great observer, or so I've been told.

"Nice to meet you," I say to Maribel.

"I would say nice to meet you, too, but I want to go to Paris and you're now one more camera in my way," Maribel says with a smile to take the bite out of her words.

"Oh, you don't have to worry about me. I'm not sure I'll even participate," I shrug.

"Are you kidding?" Taylor and Joelle say in unison.

"No," I shrug again.

Before they can jump me with questions—like I feel they're about to—the professor calls class into session. I'm relieved. I don't want to have to explain myself.

The professor explains that the baseball team will be interviewing us to see who will give them the best chance to win the competition. While he's talking, I keep my head down, doodling on the paper in front of me. As much as I would love to help a charity, I don't think this whole thing is for me.

My attention is dragged away from my drawing as I feel warmth beside me. The air seems to be sucked out of my space, causing me to take notice of the chairs scraping the floor and the eerie silence that is now at my table. I look around the table to see the girls all looking past me in awe.

I look up to find none other than Perry staring back at me with those startling blue eyes. *Wow, they're not just blue. They're blue-grey.* I feel like I can't breathe, as I get lost in his stare. *What is wrong with me?*

I never have this intense of a reaction to guys. I take in how close he is to my personal space and try to tell myself that that's the reason for my response.

I shift in my seat to gain some personal space back, but I stop when his eyes narrow into a squint and his lips purse together. Something about the action triggers something in me. I tilt my head to stare back at him. The trance is broken as the pretty blonde from earlier appears at his side, placing a hand on his shoulder.

Perry looks over at her, as he flinches, but immediately moves his big frame a few steps back from me. Dakota, as I remember him calling her, pulls over two stools and the two of them sit next to me. I frown, a little unsure of how to take any of this.

"Hi," Dakota sings as she holds out her hand.

I stare at her hand for a few seconds before reaching out to shake it. "Hi," I mutter.

"I'm pretty sure your pictures could look like shit and Caleb would still want you to work with him. But your professor said we should at least look at your work before deciding to work together."

I looked at her, confused for a moment. Taylor nudges me in the side and clears her throat.

"The athletes are supposed to interview you," she whispers to me. Then to the two sitting before me she says. "She wasn't paying attention. She doesn't want to participate."

A blush blooms as shame for not paying more attention in class rises. I look at Perry and Dakota. He's staring at me again.

It's making me so uncomfortable. Why would he stare at me like that in front of his girlfriend? What is more baffling, is that she doesn't seem to care that he's doing it.

Perry clears his throat as I look on confused. Dakota looks as if she's going to speak again, but his words cut her off. "I want to work with you."

"I…um…I really hadn't planned to do this. I work with landscapes and things. I think you'll have a better shot with someone else," I stammer.

He shakes his head at me. "No, I don't think so. I want you," he says with no expression at all.

I have no idea how to read this guy or his girlfriend. She's looking at him just as stunned as I am. She quickly snaps out of it and turns to me.

"Would you reconsider?" Dakota pleads, throwing me for another loop.

"I...," I start to chew on my lip, as I think of the charity that stood out to me. Perry is gorgeous, I'm sure I can take some great shots of him and the calendars would be a cinch to sell out. "I'm sorry. I just don't think I can."

"What if we paid you?" Dakota's eyes brighten up with the request.

I snort and shake my head. "I don't need your money," I snap.

I'm insulted. Do I look like I need their money? I stiffen in my seat, ready for them both to leave me alone.

"Dakota," Perry groans.

"What? I'm just trying to help, Caleb," Dakota pouts.

I furrow my brows, as she calls him by a different name from the one I assumed was his. Perry or Caleb, whatever his name is, seems to study my face for what feels like hours, before he purses his lips and squints at me. A few more moments pass before he stands.

I notice him shaking his right hand as his eyes cloud over. "Think about it, okay," he says simply before turning and leaving out of the classroom, leaving a stunned Dakota sitting with her mouth open. She remains until he's out of sight, then turns to me as she stands and gathers her things.

"You'll think about it, right?" Dakota pleads, biting her lip nervously.

I'm more than confused with these two. I nod at her, not sure what to say and watch as she rushes off—to find her boyfriend I suppose. I hope she plans to tell him how not cool he is for looking at me that way with her sitting there.

"Oh, my God," Joelle bounces over to me, after she finishes her interview. "Caleb. Freaking. Perry. I can't believe you turned down Caleb freaking Perry. I mean the fact that the guy even spoke to you is enough to agree to do it."

"What?" I murmur.

"Caleb is always all brooding and no one gets close to him, other than Dakota and his brother Cameron. And trust me, every girl on campus has tried," Joelle fans herself. "That boy is seriously hot, brooding and all."

"I photograph landscapes," I say lamely.

Joelle lifts a brow at me and shakes her head. I wrap my arms around my middle, feeling exposed and out of place. "He has a girlfriend, what does it matter if I don't want to take his pictures?" I say bitterly, now feeling like I'm being attacked.

Joelle lifts her hands in surrender. "Whoa, where are you getting your information? No girl has been lucky enough to hold that title."

I shrug. "I thought that…well, who's the blonde?"

Joelle falls into me, in a fit of giggles and wraps an arm around my shoulders. "That's Dakota, she's his cousin. I don't blame you. We all thought the same thing freshman year," Joelle says through her laughter.

"Oh," I reply, mentally kicking myself. Not that I would have taken the assignment even if I'd known.

CHAPTER FOUR

Crush

Caleb

I pace outside of the art building trying to get my shit together.
I don't know what got into me. When we walked into the
classroom and I saw Nicole, I just had one thought. *I have to
work with her.* I never thought that she would say no.

Girls are usually trying to pry their way past Cameron and
Dakota to get to me. As soon as the professor said we could start
the interviews, I forgot about needing Dakota, and rushed right
over to Nicole, before anyone else could get to her. *The look in
her eyes.* I'm not sure what it was.

Damn.

I push my fingers through my hair, totally frustrated with
myself right now. I'm still trying to process the whole situation.
Did she tell me no because she seriously doesn't want to be a
part of the contest or is it me? Did I weird her out?

"Fuck," I groan as I continue to pace.

"Hey," I hear Dakota's heels clicking toward me, but I'm not ready to talk to her.

The one thing I know about what just happened is that Nicole was pissed that Dakota offered to pay her. I hated to see her upset. I had to get out of there.

As confused as I may have been with Nicole's other reactions, I have become very familiar with anger. I didn't like seeing it on her pretty face. Those oval shaped light brown eyes didn't seem right angry.

"Caleb," Dakota tries again.

I whirl around and glare at her. "I wanted to do this one thing on my own, Kota. Just this once, I needed to do this on my own," I fume.

"I'm sorry. I was just trying to help. I could see how much you wanted to get her to work with you," Dakota says in a small voice, so unlike her.

"I...what just happened, Dakota? Did I fuck that up? Do you think she really doesn't want to be in the contest or did I freak her out?" I ask furrowing my brows and biting my lip.

"Oh, honey, you did awesome in there. Hell, you shocked the hell out of me," Dakota says, giving me a big grin. "You like her a lot, don't you?"

"Yeah," I nod. "That's why I can't fuck this up. Do you think she'll change her mind?"

"Relax, if she doesn't do portraits. We will get someone else and we'll figure out how to get you on a date with her."

I nod and stop pacing. "Okay, okay," I murmur.

"Let's go get something to eat," Dakota offers.

Food, I can do. I'm always starving. I follow my cousin as my head stays filled with thoughts for me to filter through.

We arrive at one of our favorite spots right off campus and I'm still lost in my musings. I'm annoyed with myself because I can't freeze out the thoughts, to focus on anything else. I clench and unclench my fists, as I follow Dakota to a booth in the back. Once we're settled in our seats, Dakota levels her eyes on me. I purse my lips in frustration. It occurs to me that I'm blinking rapidly. I take in a deep breath and focus on my cousin's eyes. Dakota gives me a smile when the blinking stops.

"Wow, I haven't seen you like this in a long time. Then again…Nicole is very pretty," Dakota tilts her head to the side. "She's not what I thought your type would be. I mean, I'm so used to Cameron picking your hook ups."

Dakota stops talking to roll her eyes. Cameron usually does have a big hand in who I hook up with. I've never considered a type.

I know what I like, I think. Breasts, I fucking love tits. Other than that, maybe I'm not sure on my type, but Nicole. I love her eyes and her ass. The way it sat spread against the stool in the photography class, my eyes were glued to it as I made my way over to her.

"Why is she wrong?" I blurt out and wrinkle my brows, as I squint at Dakota.

"Oh no, I didn't say she's wrong," Dakota's face changes and I wonder what I've done to make her angry. "Promise me something, Caleb. If you and Nicole do hook up, you'll never let anyone tell you it's wrong to be with her. If you like her, if you end up falling in love with her. Never ever let anyone tell you that it's wrong."

I process her words and nod. "So, she's not wrong for me?" I murmur.

"No. Honestly, I think you two looked adorable next to each other. It's the girls that you and Cameron usually choose that I think are all wrong for you. Nicole...she's...perfect. I think she'll be perfect for you."

"But you only talked to her for a few minutes," I knit my brows further.

"Trust me, I'm right about this one," Dakota smirks.

"Right about what?" Cameron says as he appears and slides in next to Dakota.

"Where's Kay?"

"Dude, I can go places without her," Cameron grumbles in his southern accent.

"You're fighting again," I state not needing him to answer. It's nothing new.

However, if I'm right, something has changed. Cameron and Kay have been fighting for years, since they started dating in junior high school. Although, lately I've picked up on new emotions and more intense tension around them.

"Can we order some food? I'm starving," Cameron waves the waitress over.

We all place our orders. Cameron and I order enough to feed a small town, while Dakota sits shaking her head over the amount of food the two of us can consume. It's always this way.

Dakota eats like a bird and Cameron and I devour a ton. I guess that could account for us being so large. Cameron and I are only mere inches apart, me being the taller one.

"What are you right about?" Cameron turns his attention to Dakota to ask once more.

Dakota shrugs, but has a smile on her lips. "Caleb has a crush," she coos out.

Cameron turns his eyes toward me and lifts a brow. "Really, on who?"

"I think she's new," I reply to my own summations in my brain.

"New and gorgeous. And he let her touch him," Dakota says, as she makes this goofy face.

"Wait, touch him like how?" Cameron says, with what I assume is shock written on his face.

"They were holding hands," Dakota sings.

"We needed to get to class. It was the best way not to lose her in my rush or to knock her over again," I frown.

"Knock her over?" Cameron asks, as he studies my face.

"I almost knocked her on her ass. I wasn't looking where I was going," I reply.

Cameron turns back to Dakota. "So, what does she look like? Did he get her number?"

"We're not talking about her and stop talking about me like I'm not sitting here," I scowl.

Cameron's head snaps in my direction. He looks me in the eyes, but doesn't say anything for a long moment. Then his face breaks into a smile.

He nods. "Okay, little brother. You're full of surprises today. Heard you want to do your calendar alone. You have a little girlfriend and now you're barking out commands like you found your balls. Nice."

"Whatever, Cam," I grunt. With a straight face, I say. "I've always known where my balls are. You shouldn't be mad mine are bigger than yours. I promise, I won't show Kay."

"Oh, shit," Dakota bursts into a fit of laughter. "Oh, my God. That is the second good one today. I love it."

Cameron just sits with his mouth hanging open. I smile and pat myself on the back internally. I've wanted to work on my humor so badly. Everyone loves Cameron. Over the years, I've come to believe it's because of his humor and charm. I'm working on that.

"You little shit. That was fucking awesome," Cameron finally laughs out. He reaches across the table and slaps me on the shoulder. "Real fucking proud of you, Bro. I couldn't have delivered that shit better. But watch your mouth or I'll kick your ass."

I sit and stare at Cameron's face. Maybe I went too far, but as I look in his eyes, I shrug it off. He is returning my teasing, that's all.

As if reading my mixed up mind, Cameron's smile broadens. "I'm teasing, Cal. That shit was funny. I'm proud of you."

I nod my head on the outside, but my chest swells on the inside. I love my big brother. He always does his best to make sure I fit in. I know someday he won't be there, so I'm getting ready for it.

"Now, back to this girl. You want some help," Cameron locks eyes with me again.

"No, no, I think I got it," I say feeling more confident.

"All right," Cameron nods and changes the subject.

CHAPTER FIVE

Stolen Kisses

Caleb

It's been a week since I first ran into Nicole. I haven't had the courage to walk up to her like a normal guy, and ask her out. Well, honestly, the team just returned from a three-day road trip, for an away game.

So, I haven't had time to try to talk to Nicole or to find a different partner for the contest either. While I've been nearly obsessed with how to ask Nicole out, I haven't given much thought to what I will do about all of the rest.

Cameron has offered, more than once, to let me in on his calendar. Just like Coach had suggested, but a part of me is still holding out hope for Nicole. I keep hoping that the week has allowed her time to change her mind.

I've just finished working out at the team gym with Cameron. Now, I'm grudgingly taking a shower in our apartment. I wish I could stay under the hot spray, rather than have to get out and get dressed for this party tonight.

Stepping out of the shower, I look in the mirror at my wet hair. It has gotten pretty long in the last few days, brushing my shoulders in the back and meeting my cheekbones on the sides. I use my fingers to push the damp strands off my forehead. I make the decision in my mind to wear a baseball cap to the party in hopes to hide.

I get dressed in a light blue t-shirt, with a grey V-neck sweater over it, and a pair of dark blue jeans. I tug a pair of tan work boots on my feet and shrug. Concerning fashion, Dakota has been a pain in my life for longer than I'd like to admit.

I pretty much know what will keep her happy now. I'm glad to say it's the one thing I have picked up better than Cameron. According to Dakota, I just have a natural swag. I'll take that, since I have to work so hard at everything else.

Once dressed, I walk out to the living room of our apartment. I find Dakota sitting on the couch, looking uncomfortable. Kay and Cameron look as if they've just had another one of their fights.

I ignore the tension and let them think I just don't get it. Sometimes, people's assumptions about what I pick up on and what I don't, works in my favor. I let this one seem to fly over my head, so that we can get out of here and get this over with.

"You don't have to go to this party if you don't want to," Kay says, as I shove my keys in my pocket.

"Really?" Cameron growls.

"What Cameron? This is stupid. He doesn't have to prove anything to anyone," Kay hisses back, her green eyes narrowing.

"I don't have to prove anything to anyone, but I want to go. Hamilton asked and I'm going for my teammate," I say, with a shrug and open the door to leave. "If you guys don't want to come, it's fine."

"Thank you," Cameron exclaims. "Now do you see? This is his decision. I didn't push anything on him."

"Fine," Kay snaps and storms out of the apartment ahead of everyone.

"Dude, this is going to be a long night," Cameron sighs and pats me on the back.

I heave a heavy sigh and shake my head. We pile into his car. This being a long night could suck. I just want to show my face and come back home.

~B~

Nicole

I can't believe I let Taylor and Maribel talk me into coming to this party. I could strangle them both right now. This is so not my thing.

I feel like I stick out like a sore thumb. I haven't seen Maribel or Joelle for the last two hours. Then, Taylor keeps dropping random guys off to—*"get to know me"*—as she put it.

I haven't wanted to get to know any of them and it has probably shown. I'll admit that this last guy is kind of cute, but that makes it worse. I can't stop blushing and my bronzed brown skin has done nothing to hide it.

I gulp a large breath of relief, as some newcomers to the party grab this guy's attention. I finally have a reprieve to frown at my stupid replies to our conversation. I can't believe I'm so lame.

"Cameron," cute guy calls out with a huge grin, lifting his beer in the air.

With me forgotten, he crosses the crowded room to greet whoever he's calling out to. A fleeting thought crosses my mind. He has made up someone just to get away from me.

I'm too short to see across the space, to see if there's truly anyone new, but I don't much care. I turn to head for a fresh cup of beer. I've been nursing the same drink for a while now. I push my way into the kitchen, totally relieved to get a fresh cup and find a stool to sit on to people watch.

"Hey, Nicole," Jonah says, as he walks up.

"Hey, Jonah," I say with my first genuine smile.

Jonah is very handsome, but the fact that he looks just like his twin, Joelle, somehow makes me feel at ease. They both have such inviting personalities. So different from my twin niece and nephew who are like night and day.

"I've been trying to make my way to you for about an hour now. Every time I go to make my move, you have a new guy at your side," Jonah says, with a teasing smile.

"Oh, please Jonah. I doubt you've been alone for longer than a few seconds once tonight," I laugh.

"But none of them were you, sweetheart," Jonah replies throwing an arm around my shoulder. He winks at me and I actually blush.

This is going to have to stop.

"So, what do you think about our resident jocks," Jonah says into my ear.

I shrug, trying not to think about Caleb. "I guess they're all right," I say nonchalantly.

"Oh, come on, you haven't started drooling over these guys like Jo and the rest of the girls yet?" He teases.

"Nope," I say, but squirm on the stool.

I'm lying. I haven't been able to get Caleb's eyes out of my head. I won't admit it to anyone else, but I've felt a pang of disappointment each time I've noticed him missing from class this week. I only found out yesterday that the team has been away for a game.

"So, does that mean I actually have a shot?" Jonah raises a brow at me.

I throw my head back and laugh at his silliness. Jonah places a hand over his heart, giving me a wounded look. It only causes me to laugh even more.

"Oh, please, Jonah," I laugh out.

~B~

Caleb

I wasn't expecting her to be here, and I sure wasn't expecting to see her talking to some guy. I can't even explain the feelings I'm having right now. I want to throw a baseball right through the guy's face. I don't like that she looks so…relaxed with him.

"What the fuck?" I hear Cameron growl in my ear, before he punches me in my arm.

I turn toward him, blinking back my confusion. "What?" I growl back, holding my arm.

Cameron steps in closer and gets in my ear. "Dude, you're fucking clicking. What the fuck is wrong with you? If this is too much, we should go," Cameron says, in a strained voice.

Clicking. It's the sound I make in the back of my throat, when I'm over stimulated. I haven't done that shit in years. I blink a few times, before I realize I'm blinking repeatedly.

I purse my lips. "No, I wasn't," I argue.

"Dude, yes, the fuck you were," Cameron snaps.

I turn at the sound of laughter from across the loud crowded room. She's laughing with him and she looks so gorgeous. I realize that I'm losing my shit, just before I feel the sting of Cameron punching me in the arm again.

"Pull your shit together, Cal. Fuck, Kay was right," Cameron groans and pushes his fingers through his hair.

I don't stop to ask him what he's talking about. I know why I am losing my shit, and I'm done waiting to figure out what to do about it. I need answers. I need *her*.

I turn away from Cameron and start straight for her. The crowd parts for me and that's when it happens. I watch her eyes lock with mine, as I move to her.

I have no idea what I plan to do at first, but I know what my mind tells me to do when I reach her, and I do it. I walk upright between her legs, placing one hand on her waist and the other I use to tip her head back. Her eyes widen, but I don't stop to process what that could mean.

I just lean in and capture her lips with mine. I literally growl at my first taste of Nicole's soft plump lips. My fingers on her waist tighten and I open her mouth with my tongue. My heart almost leaps out of my chest when I feel her tongue move to meet mine. I hope like hell I am doing this right, as I deepen the kiss almost devouring her whole face.

Nicole tastes like beer and something sweet. I've never tasted anything so good. I push my fingers into her hair and she opens up to me a little more. I think I have truly lost myself in her. I start to groan and suck on her lips.

That's when her hands land on my chest and I feel her push at my hard muscles. At the same time, I feel a strong hand on one shoulder and a smaller one on the other. I cringe at the contact, but surprisingly Nicole's touch is soothing, unlike the others.

I take a few steps back as Cameron pulls at me. I turn to him to see...*what is that*... shock, frustration, anger? I look over to my other side and Dakota's look I understand.

I fucked up. I look back at Nicole, with her flushed cheeks and swollen lips. I purse my lips and start to squint. Control, I need to gain control.

"Help me," I plead with Cameron in a whisper. "I want her. Help me."

"Shit," he sighs. He leans in to whisper in my ear. "I guess she's the one Dakota's been telling me about?"

I nod, knowing that Dakota, true to her word, has been trying to figure out how to get me a date with Nicole. I haven't been able to get her off my mind since I nearly ran her over. I've sent Dakota text messages everyday I've been away asking about Nicole.

"Please," I murmur to Cameron.

He nods his head in understanding and turns on the charm like only my brother can. If anyone can help me, Cameron can. He's the one that has always gotten me close to girls. Not the way I want to be close to Nicole, but close in a way that won't bring me trouble when it counts.

~B~

Nicole

What the heck just happened?

I mean, one minute I'm talking and laughing with Jonah. The next I'm locked in a stare down with Caleb as he crosses the room. I had no idea he was even here at this party.

I didn't have time to process that fact either. By the time I did, he was eating my face. Not that I am complaining about that part too much. I mean, *wow*, he can kiss.

Things that just shouldn't be wet, are soaked and wet right now. Although, I'm totally confused, I'm also aware of the electricity that is zipping back and forth between us. I mean from the moment his eyes locked on mine, I was in a trance.

Watching his huge, powerful frame move toward me was like watching a big cat stalk its prey. I was totally distracted by his broad shoulders on display under his tight sweater and t-shirt. His jeans cling tightly to his powerful thighs and his eyes look sexy and mysterious underneath his baseball cap.

I'd be lying, if I said that I wasn't drooling as I watched him make his way to me. It was as if the crowd parted for him, and his smooth swagger allowed him to glide his way over. I marveled at how his large body moved through the crowd so gracefully.

Wait, I don't think graceful would be the right word. It was more like his body moved with an unspoken confidence. Like for him, moving is as easy as breathing.

He moved as if everyone else was an afterthought. As if they would just allow his presence to take front and center. As I watched, that's exactly how it happened.

I was so enthralled I hadn't known what to expect. I hadn't realized he intended to kiss me. Not until he was standing right between my heated thighs, with his hand on my waist and one on my face. I started to protest, but his full lips crushed mine before I could get my thoughts together.

I was a goner the moment his lips touched mine. That sexy groan that came from the back of his throat, turned me on like nothing has before. His lips tasted of heaven, like he had been eating caramel and chocolate with a faint hint of mint.

I was so consumed with sipping from his intoxicating flavor, and the mouthwatering scent of his cologne or body wash. It never occurred to me that we were making out in the middle of a crowded party. I mean, I have only spoken to this guy twice.

It wasn't until the bite of his large fingers tightening on my waist and the pull of him sucking on my lip, that I started to remember our surroundings. I could have kissed him all night, but I knew I needed to stop the madness. I placed my hands on his chest, gently pushing him away.

I can still taste him on my lips and my cheeks are tingling from the burn of his beard. I bite my lip as I blush, finally taking in the others now standing around our little scene. Dakota is standing beside Caleb with a smirk on her lips.

Then there is the spitting image of Caleb, standing on his other side, as they whisper to one another. My mouth pops open when both gorgeous faces turn toward me. Wow, Caleb is a sight all on his own.

However, looking at who I assume to be his brother, and him at the same time, is enough to give anyone's heart palpitations. His brother looks just like him, only clean shaven and his hair isn't as long, but still the same blonde color. Caleb looks to be a few inches taller than his clone. His brother is just a bit leaner standing next to him.

When his brother turns to me, I notice the biggest difference between the two. The smile on Caleb's brother's features is open and charming. It lights his entire face, as if he smiles like this all the time. I blink to clear my head as his voice pulls me from my musing.

"So, you must be Nicole, I don't think we've officially met, yet. I'm Cameron, Caleb's older brother and twin," he says reaching out his hand.

"H…hi, ni…ice to meet you," I stammer in shock.

"No, I think it's my pleasure to meet you. My little brother here may have had too much to drink," Cameron says with a grin. "I apologize for his drunken blunder. It's just you have left quite an impression on him," Cameron pauses and shrugs his large shoulders.

"I guess the alcohol has brought his true feelings for you to the forefront. I hope you don't hold it against him."

I frown as I take in Cameron's words. I didn't taste alcohol on Caleb's breath. I look over into his eyes and they look clear to me. I do notice that he looks...nervous, unsure, confused maybe.

Then there is something else. I tilt my head to the side, as I watch him. He's pursing his lips and squinting at me, but it's not at me. Now that I'm paying attention...it's like he is looking past me, anywhere but at me actually. The more I stare, the more I start to get the feeling that there is more to him making that face.

I've heard girls on campus talk about him and the cute faces he makes. All the girls think his pout is the hottest thing, but I know that look. I've seen it on much younger faces. I've come closer to having an understanding of that face in recent years.

I gasp as realization hits. There's no way. I mean, Caleb is in college and on the baseball team. Wait, I know I sound so stupid, even in my own head. Olivia has come so far after her diagnosis.

She's such an amazing little girl. My brother, Harris, is lucky to have her. My niece wasn't the perfect child her mother wanted, but Harris has been the perfect father. Even after Kelis left him, when Olivia was diagnosed with autism.

So, I know that look Caleb has on his face. I know it, although my brain is struggling with it. Is it possible that this huge bear of a man is so much more than the great looks or the athlete everyone sees him as? So much is making sense to me now. I have never seen Caleb without Dakota, since the morning he ran into me.

The shyness I picked up on the few times we've interacted. Even when I've watched him from a distance, and he thinks no one else is watching, I've noticed. Watching him next to his brother now, shows me that the confidence he gives off is mimicked from his twin.

I've watched Liv do the same thing a million times. She mimics what she perceives as socially correct or the people she perceives as good role models. Sometimes, she mocks traits from characters from TV shows for weeks at a time.

If I hadn't seen my niece do it, I may not have put my finger on it. Heck, if I hadn't known better, I would've just chalked it up to being a twin thing. I wish I could say that I am less confused, but now I wish I knew the real reason Caleb kissed me. I know from Liv that things aren't always so simple.

Did he think I would shoot his calendar if he kissed me? Why does he want me to shoot it in the first place? Could he sense I would understand him?

Olivia has clung to me since she could walk, maybe even before. I had been the only one that could get her to go to sleep for months after she was born. It drove Kelis insane.

I spent a lot of time at Harris's place back then, excited that my favorite brother had finally had a baby girl. He and Kelis had Harris Jr. in their teens, but Harris had begged Kelis to try again once they were married to give him a little girl.

I think she resented him for having to have another baby. Then she had the twins and for baby Olivia to not be perfect in her eyes, sent her running. Harris would do anything for Olivia, Keith, and Harris Jr.

Even move back home with our parents at thirty-four. Just so he could have the support to deal with all of Liv's needs. It crushed my heart to see all Harris had to go through.

I look at Dakota and notice her protectiveness toward Caleb. I laugh to myself for ever thinking that they were a couple. I can see traits of their relation now.

I don't blame her for being protective, I'm that way with Liv. My mind is racing, but I know I should respond to Cameron. I look back at Caleb and blush.

"It's okay…I…um, I kissed him back," I say, in all but a whisper.

This time a real smile crosses Caleb's face, making him look all the more like his brother. He even looks younger. However, it's Cameron that speaks once again.

"Hey, listen, I was wondering if you've considered working with Caleb on the calendar?" Cameron asks with that panty dropping smile in place.

I shake my head and look between the three cousins. Three pairs of blue-grey eyes are trained on me. My eyes land on Cameron and I sigh.

"I really don't do many portraits. I mean, I don't usually photograph people. Just my family," I shrug my shoulders. "I was honest about you having a better shot with another photographer."

"Something tells me you would do a great job," Cameron says and winks at me. "Come on, Nicole. My little brother would love to work with you."

"Why me?" I blurt out without thinking.

Cameron shrugs his shoulders. "Why not you? Besides, every other girl on campus would have said yes immediately, and then suggested my brother strip naked for them to ogle and put on display. Something tells me you will do something with more taste."

I pause to think about his reasoning and then something hits me. Dakota and Cameron are not only Caleb's protection, they're like his ambassadors or spokesmen or something. Caleb has yet to say a word.

I remember the shocked look on Dakota's face in art class, when Caleb spoke to me. It's clear this is something out of the ordinary for him, which peaks my curiosity further. Why is this so important to him?

I think of the charity in the packet from class. It would be great to help those families. I think of Olivia and how hard things were for Harris in the beginning and even now at times.

"I'll do it under one condition," I relent.

"Name it," it's the first thing Caleb has said directly to me, since that day in photography class.

I look up into his intense blue-grey eyes and draw in a deep breath. "I get to pick the charity," I say.

"Oh, well, Caleb kind of had one in mind already," Dakota replies, seeming a little hesitant.

"It's fine," Caleb says looking a little crestfallen. "Which charity would you like to work for?"

"Luther's World," I say as I watch the stunned look appear on all three of their faces.

Caleb looks away, but not before I see the solemn look on his face. Dakota looks sad and disappointed. Cameron narrows his eyes at me.

I quickly figure out that they all think I've picked the charity because I figured out Caleb's secret. Yes, I've figured it out, but I would've chosen Luther's World regardless. It's a charity for families with autistic children. Like Liv and the children my mother works with at her early intervention clinic.

Not wanting Caleb to feel self-conscious, I quickly explained my choice. "It's a charity dear to my heart. I saw it on the list. It was the only reason I had ever seriously considered taking the assignment."

He turns back to me. His eyes searching my face for a few moments that seem like hours. "Okay," he simply replies.

I release a breath, I hadn't known I was holding and nod. "Okay," I smile up at him. "So, I guess we should exchange numbers so we can get started on the ideas and the shots for the calendar."

He pulls his phone from his pocket quickly and hands it to me. I tap the screen, but there's a lock on it. I turn it back to him.

"It's locked," I smile.

"Oh, sorry," he murmurs and quickly taps in his password, then turns it back toward me.

I program my number quickly and send a quick text to my phone before handing it back to him. "I texted myself, so that I'll have your number," I tell him.

"Maybe you should give me your number too," Dakota gives me a friendly smile. "I can help you guys out with the planning."

"No, I can handle this," Caleb says, before I can respond.

"Oh, okay," Dakota nods, but the proud smile on her face doesn't go unnoticed.

"Thanks, Nicole," Cameron says with a smile and another wink.

"I just hope we can raise some money," I reply shyly.

"Have you looked at this guy? You'll be sold out," Cameron laughs. "Anyway, now that that's settled, we'll get out of your hair."

Caleb's head snaps toward his brother and a look passes between them. Caleb's expression is close to desperation as he tries to convey something to his brother, without words. Cameron shakes his head and laughs, but turns back toward me.

"Actually, we're getting ready to get out of here, maybe get something to eat. Would you like to come with?" Cameron asks, turning up his smile a few megawatts.

I'm still not sure what exactly Caleb wants from me and there are so many other questions running through my head. I'm not sure going to hang out with them all is the best idea.

"I was thinking about heading home. I wouldn't want to ruin you guys' night, with having to worry about me," I answer.

Caleb steps closer to me. "Please, it would make me happy if you would come with us," his deep voice rumbles through me.

What is wrong with me?

I chastise myself, as a shiver runs down my spine. How could I not be turned on by such a masculine voice? Even so, I look at the raw vulnerability in his eyes. It's that same look that makes me cave. Just like I do every time Liv gives me that same look.

"Um…okay," I relent.

"I thought you said you weren't into jocks," Jonah teases from beside me. It's the first time I remember it's not just the four of us standing here. "It's okay, I knew you were way out of my league anyway."

I laugh and shake my head at Jonah. He is a sweet guy, on top of being a super-hot nerd. Stepping down from my stool, I move to give him a hug.

"Whatever, you'll be on the arm of some lucky girl before I get out the door," I say, as I lift up on my toes to hug him.

Before I can get in a good hug and move away, I feel a large arm slip around my waist pulling me back possessively. I turn my head and look up to find Caleb staring down at me. My whole body heats up, the moment my back connects with his hard body. To my surprise, I just melt back against him.

Cameron clears his throat with a chuckle. "I guess we should get out of here," he shakes his head and starts off into the crowd.

I wave to Jonah, who lifts a brow as he looks between Caleb and me. Caleb's arm remains around me as he leads me through the crowd. As we step out of the house with Dakota still beside us, I remember I didn't come to this party alone.

"I should let my friends know I'm leaving," I say taking out my phone to text Taylor. By the time I'm done, Cameron emerges from the party with a pissed off looking brunette on his arm.

Her eyes widened when she sees me standing with Caleb. "Oh, my God, is she the girl," the green-eyed brunette turns to Cameron.

"Kay," Caleb groans.

"Okay, should I be scared. I feel like I should be scared," I turn and look up at Caleb.

His brows furrow as he looks down at me intensely. "I would never hurt you," he says so sincere and sweetly.

I instantly feel guilty. It's clear he missed my sarcasm. Liv has a hard time with my sarcasm as well. At least, she did for a while. Now, I think she lives to piss Harris off with her witty comebacks. It shocks us all at times, after knowing her struggle with it.

Feeling like an idiot, I place my hand on Caleb's chest and look up into his eyes. "I know, I feel safe with you," I reassure him.

I hear a gasp behind me, before I hear Kay mutter. "He let her touch him, without even a flinch."

"Shut up," Cameron growls out.

It's too late, I have already heard her. I quickly remove my hand. I'm reminded of Timmy. He couldn't stand to be hugged or touched when he first came to my mother, but with time he started to accept his own mother's touch.

Eventually, he was willing to accept her hugs. Again, I have to wonder what's wrong with me. I'm clearly getting into something that's over my head. I should just go home.

Caleb reaches for my hand, searching my face once again. "I like it when you touch me," he says, as he wraps his huge hand around mine.

I'm instantly comforted by the warmth of his fingers around mine. I watch as he studies my face to ensure that this is okay. I smile back at him and slide my hand in his until our fingers are laced together, as much as my tiny hand will allow. I squeeze his fingers in reassurance, then turn to the others.

"So, where are we going?" I ask to break the tension.

"There's this diner not far from here. Caleb and Cameron love their food. We can go there," Dakota suggests.

"Okay," I shrug and look up at Caleb with a smile.

His eyes flicker down to my lips and butterflies fill my tummy, as I remember the kiss from inside. I mentally shake myself, forcing my feet forward to join the rest of the group.

I'm being so stupid. I could never have a relationship with Caleb, and I'm sure not going to just sleep with him. There are so many things wrong with all of my thoughts.

In my defense, he is insanely hot and I have only assumed he's a little different. *I could be totally wrong, right?* I had some drinks tonight. Clearly, I'm not thinking straight. Heck, I'm walking with a group of strangers to a restaurant. So not like me at all. Nicole Waltersson would never kiss a random guy or go off with random people to some diner.

Caleb squeezes my fingers gently, bringing me out of my head. I look up to see him smiling down at me. Yeah, I just had too much to drink. There's no way I could be right about this. Just look at him.

CHAPTER SIX

Time Alone

Caleb

I can't believe Cameron pulled this off. I'm so nervous, I think I'm going to be sick. I thought Nicole would've snatched her hand away from me, but she held it all the way here. God, I want to kiss her again and I almost have.

Each time she looks up at me, I feel my heart pounding in my chest. The walk here was like the longest ten minutes of my life. Dakota and Kay spent the time asking Nicole questions I felt like I should've been asking to get to know her.

I know they mean well, so, I'm not too annoyed. This is my family wanting to see me happy. I'm just happy to get to know anything about this gorgeous girl sitting beside me.

I know that she's from New York, she has three brothers and two sisters. She's the baby of the family and it sounds like her father means a lot to her. I would even say they're close from the words she uses when talking about him. Nicole has tons of nieces and nephews. She seems to be fond of them, too.

Although she used to attend college in Georgia, something about that time made her unhappy. I picked that up, it's the first time I was able to get a read on her. I can't tell you how happy that made me. I usually take a long time to be able to read new people.

I haven't said much since we arrived at the diner. I have this feeling that Nicole has already figured me out, or if she hasn't she will soon enough. There's this look she gets in her eyes when she looks at me, as if she can see right through me.

I want her to. I don't want to hide from her. I want Nicole to know me.

No one knows how it feels to see and hear the world on my own frequency, to process everything in shattered pieces that I have to put together, to understand and be understood. I want to share how that feels with someone, and everything inside me tells me that I can do that with Nicole.

"Your milkshake looks so good," Nicole turns to me and says with her beautiful smile.

"It is, would you like some," I offer, as my eyes lock onto her lips for the millionth time.

"Only if you want to share," she says, as her cheeks take on a glowing color. I love when they do that.

I reach for my cup with the milkshake and place the straw to her lips. Once again, my attention is drawn to those lush pillows. She takes a pull from the straw and makes a little moaning sound.

I shift in my seat as my pants tighten. My attention is pulled away from Nicole, as I hear Cameron chuckle across the table. I want to flip him the bird, but I refrain. I'm trying to make a good impression.

Cameron knows this is hard for me. He's just being a dick. I'm so used to Cameron doing all the work for me and me just closing the deal, but I want more from Nicole.

A quick fuck isn't going to do it. I want it all with her. I want to touch her and I want to be touched by her. There's no way I will be satisfied with taking her from behind and rushing off after, like my dick is on fire, leaving Cameron to smooth things over.

I've never felt this way before. Something about Nicole's touch soothes me. I've learned to deal with being touched by my family, but they know I have limits and I still flinch no matter what, but not with Nicole.

I scowl at Cameron, but turn back to Nicole, just in time to see the straw slip from her lips and some of my milkshake lingering on her mouth. Just like at the party, I let my instincts guide me. I bend my head to suck her bottom lip into my mouth. I pull away when I hear her gasp, feeling like a jerk, but the smile on her lips relaxes me a bit.

She shakes her head at me then tilts it to the side thoughtfully. She does that a lot. I just watch. I want to learn her.

"You, Caleb Perry, are going to have to stop that. What if I have a boyfriend somewhere?" She says.

I frown and glare at her. "Do you have a boyfriend?" I ask, pissed off at the thought of another man with his hands on her.

"No," she says with a grin. "Why Caleb, are you jealous?"

"Yes, very. I want to be your boyfriend and I wish I didn't have to stop kissing you," I reply.

Her mouth drops open at my direct words. I don't know any other way to be. She'll always get the truth from me.

Snickers pour out from my brother and cousin. I look at them and kick myself. I know I probably should have replied differently, but I'm honest and to the point, if nothing else.

Nicole tucks her hair behind her ear and straightens in her seat. "I...I... I think I had too much to drink tonight to respond to that," Nicole says, with a tiny laugh.

"So, then you guys should go out on a date," Dakota chirps.

Nicole starts to chew on her lip. "I don't know," she whispers.

"What's there to know? Caleb clearly likes you and it seems like you like him. Why not go on a date?" Cameron jumps in, turning on his lady killer smile.

"Well, we have a working relationship now. It may not be smart to start dating," Nicole answers.

"But you two make such a cute couple," Kay whines.

"I was thinking the same thing," Dakota nods, looking between the two of us. "Come on, Nicole."

"Can I think about it?" Nicole asks, as she peeks up at me through her lashes.

I don't want her to think about it, but I know it's the right thing to say at the moment. "Sure," I say, not sure if I hide my disappointment well.

"It's been a long night. I think I should head home," Nicole says, as she pushes her plate of fries away. She goes to pull money from her pocket, but I stop her. No matter how different I may be, my Mama still taught me to be a gentleman and it stuck.

"I got it and I'll walk you home," I say, as I pull out my wallet and toss a few bills on the table.

"You don't have to," she replies, so softly, I almost don't hear her.

"Yes, I do," I say, as I stand and reach for her hand. If I can't kiss her, I sure do want to at least hold her hand.

"We'll catch up to you," Cameron says.

I know my brother. He is giving me some time to be alone with Nicole. Without Dakota and Kay thinking they're being helpful.

My heart is pounding again, as we walk out of the diner hand in hand. My mind races with all the things I can say, but I don't know if I can get any of it to come out right. They're jumbled and in pieces. I feel Nicole squeeze my hand and I look down to see her smiling up at me.

"Caleb," she says. "Is there something I'm missing? Something I should know?"

I swallow hard. This is it. I want her to know everything, but now that it's time to tell her, I'm not sure I can. I feel myself becoming overwhelmed, but I have to push through this.

Cameron and Dakota won't always be there. That's something I have been thinking about for a long time, since before I ran into Nicole. I want a normal life or as normal as I can get. It's not likely that Cameron and I will get drafted to the same professional baseball team.

I have what it takes to go pro. Cam does too, but there has been a lot of talk of me playing in the big leagues. I want it. I want it bad. It's the main reason Cameron and I agreed with Dad that we should hide the truth.

"It's okay, you know. I won't judge you," Nicole says gently, then stops and turns toward me. "I think I understand, but...if you don't want to tell me, it's fine."

I rub the back of my neck with my free hand, trying to put the words together, but I can't. I feel so lost. Maybe this is a bad idea.

I mean, what would a girl like her want with someone like me. I can't even answer her simple question. What kind of future can I give her? This was so stupid of me.

"Oh, I'm sorry," Nicole says. I'm so lost I can barely focus on her face. *Shit, I'm clicking.* "Come here, honey."

Everything in me goes silent as her small hands tug at my shirt and she lifts up on her toes to kiss me. I'm too stunned to kiss her back at first. When my head clears, she's all I know.

I grasp the back of her neck and wrap an arm around her waist, lifting her closer to me. I kiss her with the hunger that's been bottled inside me for much too long.

I have never been this at peace, this close to anyone. I growl into her mouth and deepen the kiss. I never want to stop kissing her.

The feel of her hands in my hair has me hard all over. The only thing that stops me from kissing her is the small whimper that escapes her lips. I pull back quickly and look her over with wild eyes.

"Am I hurting you?" I ask in panic.

"No," she pants. "But maybe we should stop. I didn't mean to take things that far."

I nod and place her on her feet. We stand staring at each other for…I'm not sure how long. I watch her eyes soften as she looks at me, and I know.

I know she knows. Without any further words, she tugs at the fistful of my shirt she has her fingers wrapped around, and starts for her dorm again.

CHAPTER SEVEN

Mixed Up

Nicole

I must be out of my mind. I feel like such a jerk. Hell is making a special place with the name Nicole on it. What was I thinking last night? I mean it was clear Caleb was having a freaking meltdown, right in front of me.

I shouldn't have asked him to tell me anything. I sure shouldn't have kissed him when he was so vulnerable and freaking out. I just didn't know what else to do.

He looked so lost, but when he started to make that clicking sound, while grinding his teeth. I knew I messed up. I only meant to kiss him to calm him down, but then he took over the kiss, and I was the one that was lost.

What girl wouldn't be, with over two hundred pounds of solid, six foot and change, muscled mountain pressed against her? I blame it on my lack of experience with the opposite sex.

My inexperience is coming back to haunt me. My twisted mind is letting my deprived body take over.

I punch my pillow and berate myself again. All I can see is the disappointment in his eyes. When we arrived at my dorm and I only hugged him goodnight, he looked crushed.

I wanted to kiss him, but I knew it was so wrong. I'm so confused. I had hardly any sleep because every time I closed my eyes, I saw Caleb in ways I shouldn't be seeing him.

Having enough of trying to sleep and failing, I toss the covers. I need to channel this energy. Tugging on some track leggings and a tank top, I decide on a run. I haven't been running since I arrived on campus, but I think a good run will help to clear my mind.

I drag into the bathroom to freshen up and pull my hair from my face with a clip. Some days, I regret the bob I've cut my hair into. I miss a good messy ponytail.

I step from the bathroom and look over at Taylor. She's still knocked out with her mouth hanging open. It reminds me that I need to find my earplugs.

She came in way after midnight, so I don't think she will be moving anytime soon. I grab my phone and keys and set out on my run. My thoughts go right to Liv. I have always wished for a normal life for my niece.

I know life will be more challenging for her, but I hope that one day she'll know love, friendships, and a life full of happiness. Mom has worked so hard with her. I think a lot of it is out of guilt that she didn't push Harris and Kelis to do something sooner. She had her suspicions, but Kelis was in denial and my mother never pushed until she was sure.

Olivia has flourished with mom's help, and a change in her diet. She's one of the lucky ones, to have so much support. The thought makes me think of Caleb. After his meltdown, I'm quite sure I'm right.

It seems he has just as much support as Olivia. I mean a brother and cousin that stay by his side, and from what I can tell they have been doing a great job. I don't think anyone here at this school knows about Caleb, unless they want them to.

I wonder what that's like for him. I know being autistic doesn't define him. It's just with Liv, it's one of the first things my family tells newcomers. So, they understand to treat her with care.

Maybe that's why Caleb chooses to keep it a secret. If everyone knew, he wouldn't get to be just a student or just an athlete. He would always be defined by his autism first. That autistic student, or that autistic guy that plays baseball—would more than likely be how everyone would address him.

Is that not what I am doing? A week ago, he was just a really hot, mysterious, brooding guy. Now he has made it clear he would like to date me, and all I can think about, is the fact that he has autism or some probable dysfunction.

I stop in my tracks, disgusted with myself. All I can see is his disappointment, as he turned to leave last night. I would be crushed if Liv was rejected like that.

I wipe away the tears that slip from my eyes. Volunteering at mom's clinic, I've seen high functioning clients and their families come back to thank my mom. They share with her how great their lives are now.

Some have started families; others have their own business. Some of her old clients you wouldn't even know their diagnosis, until you spend real time with them. I have no reason to believe otherwise about Caleb.

On the contrary, from what I've heard, he's like a God at this school and on the baseball field. I'm the one being a complete jerk. He only wants to go on one date.

If we have nothing in common or if it doesn't work out, I can walk away. At least then I can say I was open, that I tried. It's not like I'm not attracted to him as a man.

I mean the way he kissed me. I could feel my whole body charge with the energy swirling between us. I'm not doubting the fact that there is something going on between us.

However, there is the part of me that feels like I'm taking advantage. I mean, look at Caleb. He is gorgeous. That face, that body. I can't help but think that he wouldn't be interested in me if his world wasn't fuzzy or mixed up, or whatever is going on in his particular head.

Mom has taught me that every individual is different. What if what makes Caleb different, is what has him so interested in me.

Damn it, I just don't know.

I'm so lost in my own thoughts, I don't realize that my feet have carried me to the baseball field. I step over to the bleachers as my eyes land on one of the most awe-inspiring visions I've ever seen. Caleb is standing on the mound in his tight uniform pants and a cutoff t-shirt.

I knew he was muscled, but to see his tanned arms exposed as his muscles ripple and play underneath his skin, brings my fantasies back with a vengeance. I could watch his tight ass all day. His big body looks so fluid. I can see every cut in his long arms, every bulging muscle in his thighs, but that isn't it.

The focus in his face takes me back to the first time Liv sat at a piano and started to play from memory. It's breathtaking.

He looks as if he is in his own world as he is singularly focused on catching and returning the baseball.

I blink and think of my niece. That serene look that is only there when the music is flowing from her hands. As if being transported to a place, where the world looks perfect and everything makes sense.

That's the look I see on Caleb's face as I watch him on the field. I would have given anything to see that look on his face last night. The confidence that would have reassured me that a goodnight kiss was okay.

"Hey, if you're going to stare at my brother like that, you better be here to agree to that date," Cameron calls, as he walks over to me with that cocky smile.

"Hi, Cameron," I laugh and start to fidget, as I imagine how gross I look this morning.

"What did you do to my brother last night?" I flush and drop my head. I feel so ashamed. I wouldn't blame Cameron if he has Dakota kick my ass. "He wouldn't shut up about you, although, I can't blame him."

I sigh in relief. I thought this was going a whole other way. "I think your brother is sweet," I say with a smile.

"Sweet on you, yeah," Cameron smiles. He nods toward the field. "I haven't seen him this focused in a long time. Whatever you did, don't stop. I think you're good for him."

I start to chew on my lip and my thoughts from my run rush me. What would one date hurt? I look out at Caleb and lick my lips, as I track a bead of sweat down his bicep.

"He told me you figured him out," Cameron says nearer to my ear than I expect. I hadn't noticed him come closer. "I don't know what you're thinking, but I don't want him hurt. If you can't handle him, don't go there. He has never tried to date before, but he wants to with you. Don't hurt him."

"I...I don't know what I want," I say honestly.

"Yeah...you do. I see it in your eyes. Caleb isn't in this by himself, just make up your mind before he figures out how to read your face and knows the truth for himself. When he sees what I see in your eyes, he will become relentless. Right now, he's unsure, but when he can read you, he's coming for you," Cameron finishes with a sly smile.

I'm speechless. I look up at him, not knowing what to say. Cameron leans in again, this time with his voice lower.

"My brother is autistic, not stupid and he's definitely a man. You're a beautiful woman, Nicole. When Caleb wants something, he becomes as focused as the man you see out on that field. Trust me, after last night, he is focused on reading you and your feelings for him."

With that, Cameron turns and jogs out to the field. He whispers something to Caleb on the mound that has his head whipping in my direction. The smile that appears on his face startles me. It isn't the innocent one I've come to know, but a more confident and sure one, much more like his brother's.

~B~

Caleb

"Look who's watching you," Cameron whispers in my ear.

I had assumed it's a scout, but it's even better. When I see Nicole standing there, in tight running pants and a tank top, I can't help the smile that consumes my face. Even from this distance she looks amazing.

I want to rush off the field and scoop her into my arms. I spent most of the night analyzing every part of my time with her. From the kiss at the party, to the moment I turned to walk away from her at her dorm. When I processed it all, while lying in bed, I had been confused on a few things.

Now, I'm starting to see things differently. She's here and she's watching me. Suddenly, the look in her eyes takes on new meaning. Cameron may be right about my chances.

I had a little talk with my brother this morning. I have more confidence that I can make Nicole mine. Seeing her standing here now, I know I can.

I also know I need to talk to her. I need to say what I couldn't say last night. I think about the way she didn't run from me, but kissed me. I have hope in my heart that she will accept me as me.

"Hey Perry, get your head out the clouds," Assistant Coach Robinson snarls.

I would love to hit him with a ball one day. I shake off that thought and push thoughts of Nicole to the side, just for now.

CHAPTER EIGHT

First Date

"What are you smiling about?" Taylor asks me while throwing a piece of bread at me.

"Nothing," I shrug and place my phone back on the table.

Caleb has been text messaging me since this morning. He has asked me if I made up my mind about the date at least a million times. Cameron's words have been playing on a loop in my mind.

While I think the right thing to do is go out with Caleb and give him a fair shot, I don't want to hurt him. A date would just get his hopes up. Then what?

What if things don't go well? I don't know if that will hurt him. Cameron is right, I do want to see where things go with Caleb. Despite everything, I've never felt the way I feel with him with anyone else, and we've barely spent any time together at all. My phone buzzes again.

Caleb: *I'm an amazing cook. I could cook for you. We could watch a movie. Romantic comedy, I would love to watch your eyes sparkle while you laugh.*

These are the types of messages I've been getting all day. I smile at the text and bite my lip. I don't think I will be able to hold out much longer. How can I? I text him back quickly.

Me: *Is Cameron telling you to say all this?*

His reply comes back just as quickly.

Caleb: *No. He actually told me to leave you alone, but I can't. Can we have dinner tonight?*

Me: *Sorry, already had plans for dinner. Out now.*

Caleb: *With a guy?*

Me: *No, not with a guy. Stop being so jealous.*

Caleb: *I can't help it. You're gorgeous.*

Me: *OMG. Caleb, I'll call you later.*

A few minutes go by without a reply. I figure he is just waiting for my call, so I put down the phone and look up. Taylor has a mischievous smile on her face. I can tell this isn't going to be good.

"Okay, spill, rumor has it you were sucking face with Caleb at the party and don't lie to me. My source is golden," Taylor says, practically bouncing in her seat.

"Ugh, yes, we kissed, but it's complicated," I groan.

"What could be complicated about being the lucky girl that Caleb freaking Perry finally sucks face with? Do you have any idea how many girls hate you right now? I, being on the list," Taylor says with a mock scowl.

I laugh. "Oh, stop, aren't you into that guy...what's his name," I try changing the subject to her.

"Ugh, Freddie, I'm so over that one. Now back to Caleb. That's him isn't it. You've been rude texting since we sat down, and with the biggest smile on your face," Taylor says with a pretty pout.

"Yes, it's him," I say as another text comes in. I had planned not to reply, but as I sneak a glance and see his text, I snatch up my phone.

Caleb: *Are you mad at me?*

Me: *No. I just don't want to be rude to my friend. I will call when I get back to my dorm.*

Caleb: *Okay. I want to see you. Can we go for coffee after your dinner?*

I stare at my phone chewing my lip again. I want to see him too, but once again Cameron's voice rings in my ear. I slump in my chair not knowing what to do.

"What is it? What just happened?" Taylor says with concern.

"He wants to meet up tonight, for coffee," I wince.

"Why aren't you texting, *hell freaking yeah!* It's just coffee. Okay, just coffee with the hottest guy on campus. Wait, the hottest single guy on campus because if Cameron ever breaks up with Kay I'm so on that," she wiggles her brows at me.

"You, Taylor, are a mess," I laugh.

"And you love me. Now text that hottie that we will be done here in a half and you will meet him in forty-five," Taylor commands. Before I can obey my phone buzzes again.

Caleb: *Sorry, Nicole, I'll back off. You can call me later if you want.*

Me: *I want to see you too. Meet you at the coffee house on my side of campus in forty. Is that okay?*

Caleb: *Yes, I'll be there.*

~B~

Caleb

"Maybe she changed her mind," I grumble to Dakota, as I look at my watch.

Nicole is only two minutes late, but I am already freaking out. I wanted to come alone, but Cameron and Dakota insisted she come along. *In case someone approaches you before Nicole gets there*, was their logic. They had a point, so I made Dakota promise to disappear the moment Nicole arrives.

"Nope, there she is," Dakota smiles at me.

I look toward the door and sure enough, there's Nicole. She looks so beautiful. Her hair is framing her heart shaped chin, framing her brown face, highlighting how gorgeous she is.

She's wearing a tight pair of black jeans and a figure hugging yellow leather jacket. On her feet, she has on black-heeled boots. I love her in heels. Last night had been the first time I saw her in them. I could certainly get used to the look.

I stand nervously as she makes her way to me. I'm so nervous, I pay little mind to the fact that Dakota has gotten up and made herself vanish as promised. Nicole stops right in front of me, looking up into my eyes with a smile.

"Hey," she breathes, before lifting on her toes and pecking me on the cheek.

"Hey," I murmur back, pulling her into a hug before returning her kiss, with one on her cheek. "You look amazing."

"You don't look bad yourself," she replies, as she steps back out of my arms.

Removing her jacket, she reveals a tight yellow t-shirt, before taking a seat. I sit back in my seat and search her face. She's smiling up at me and it makes me feel warm inside.

I wonder what she's thinking about me. Has she figured me out? Will what I'm about to say ruin us? *Us*, can there even be an us?

"What are you thinking about?" she asks, as she reaches across the table and wraps my hand in hers.

A split second later she releases my hand, snatching hers back. I reach for her small hands and entwine my fingers in hers. I run my thumbs over her smooth skin.

"I told you, I like it when you touch me. I do have some sensory issues, but for some reason, I don't have them with you. I knew you were different that day I almost ran you down. When I pulled you close, I felt something," I stop talking when I feel my cheeks heat.

"Is it just touch?" she asks softly.

"No, but I've learned a lot of coping mechanisms. Sounds used to be overbearing. I used to hate certain fabrics or clothes in general," I shrug, but I keep my eyes on our entwined hands.

"My aunt and Uncle, Dakota's parents, helped a lot when I was younger. Cameron and his best friend, Thomas, had their unique ways of helping," I laugh. "And that helped me outgrow some of my habits and self-stimulation. My sensory issues are still there, they're just not as loud as they used to be. Now, I just mostly have issues with social queues and at times processing.

"It's just like…I always have things going on in my head, everything that you can block out without effort. Sometimes, I can't, and it makes processing things different for me. Or causes me to just shut down.

"I may miss something because I'm working with more information than everyone else. At least, that's the best I can explain it," I shrug again.

"So, you're on the spectrum, just high functioning?" She asks in a whisper.

I think I just fell in love with her. I don't feel like she's embarrassed by me. I know what that feels and looks like. Nicole looks like she's just trying to understand me, like I am trying to understand her.

I nod. "My doctors call me an anomaly. While there was a time that I fit neatly on the spectrum, under Asperger's, I now defy a lot of my initial diagnosis."

Nicole nods her head, then tilts it. I think I understand this one. She does it when she understands something or is looking to connect her thoughts. I smile at her and she smiles back.

"What?" she asks with her pretty smile.

"You do that," I point to her tilted head. "A lot. I think you do it when you're seeing something clearly, like you're connecting thoughts."

"Wow," Nicole laughs.

I look down at our joined hands. "My parents… they never really wanted to accept my diagnosis. So, my dad would drill into me to focus and to learn people. It was overwhelming at first. I spent a lot of time in trouble.

"Then, Cameron realized that I loved movies, so he would sit with me and help me read people in the movies. Eventually, I started to translate it to real life. I still struggle with humor a bit, but since I've been here and on the team, I have gotten better, I think," I look up into her eyes. She's watching me again with her head tilted.

"What do you want from me, Caleb? Help me understand us," Nicole says before biting her lip.

"I want you. I want you to be mine. I want what Cameron has, but I want it with you. I…I…," I shake my head, when the words won't come out right.

"I've been taught to hide for as long as I can remember. Then one day, I ran into this beautiful girl and I felt like maybe it was time to stop hiding. At least, from this one girl, I thought that she could be my safe place.

"The one I trust. The one I could someday love and cherish like Cameron does Kay. Even when she drives him crazy."

"But why me?" Nicole asks. I can see the moisture in her eyes. I purse my lips trying to understand if I've hurt her somehow. "I just need to know why me? I...you make me feel ...I don't know. I've never felt this before and everything you've just said. I think every girl would love to hear that, but why me?"

I relax and try to think of the best way to explain. "You light me up from the inside, just when you're in the same room. When I look at you, the pieces fall into place. The world is quieter; your touch makes all other touches feel less offensive.

"Most of all, when I look at you, I feel like a man. I've been coddled all my life, by one person or another, but with you. I feel like finally someone sees me."

"Really? Because there are girls all over this campus that would love to jump your manly bones," Nicole says, with a laugh.

"But you're the only one I want inside of," I counter.

Nicole's mouth gapes open and her cheeks turn a deep purple. "Caleb," she gasps.

I drop my eyes back to our hands. "I messed up again, didn't I?" I murmur.

She reaches across the table and lifts my chin with her fingertips. "When have you messed up before?"

"When I kissed you last night," I say.

"I don't believe you have messed up yet. You're honest. When you want something, you go after it. When you feel something, you say it. I think I like that," she says and then I'm stunned.

When she stands and leans over the table, crushing her lips to mine, I think I'm dreaming. I cup her face to hold her to me and kiss her back. It's a kiss full of passion, but not half as long as I would like. She pulls away quickly and sits back in her seat.

"Maybe we should order something before they throw us out," she says with a grin.

"We could go to my place. We have coffee there," I offer.

Nicole laughs and shakes her head. "If that came from anyone else, I would think you were trying to get me to your place for more than coffee."

I study her face and process her words for a moment and I laugh too. "That's not a bad idea. Nicole, will you go on a date with me?" I ask for the millionth time today. Yet, happy this time it's in person.

"I thought we were already on a date," she says with a smile.

I nod. "I want to take you out again. I want to show you; I can do this. I can be your man."

Nicole's eyes light up. "Okay, Caleb. Show me what you got."

CHAPTER NINE

Just Being Us

Nicole

I haven't been able to stop smiling all week. Caleb is like a big old sweet teddy bear. After our coffee date, he took me to the movies that next night. It was one of the best dates I ever had.

I wasn't surprised when Cameron and Kay tagged along. I get that Cameron is protective over his little brother. I think that's where Caleb gets his possessiveness over me.

Not possessive in a creepy way, but Caleb is watchful and protective when we're out. I think he likes to keep me close in case he reads something wrong at first glance. I can understand that.

However, on our date, Cameron being there seemed to relax Caleb. I watched him turn into a different person from the guy that I had coffee with. Not in a bad way.

Whether he notices it or not, Caleb doesn't second-guess himself as much when his brother is around. They're the epitome of twins. Moving in sync, finishing the other's thoughts.

I have wondered repeatedly, if Caleb has done better than most because of his twin. I did, however, pick up on Caleb's struggle with humor. Although, that doesn't stop Cameron from being humorous.

While Caleb may struggle with picking up sarcasm, he is good at tossing it back out. I love that. He has caused me to double over in stitches a few times, and the way his eyes sparkle with joy each time tugs at my heart.

So far, we've been on a date every night this week. Tomorrow will be the first night we won't be going on one. Only because Caleb has a game. I haven't been able to turn him down for a date, not that I want to.

I feel foolish now for my initial reservations about dating Caleb. It hasn't been easy or perfect, but we are making it work. Through frustrations and all.

One source of both our frustration has been text messaging. Caleb tends to take my response time to heart when I take too long to answer back after he's said something he's unsure of.

For example, just this morning he texted me just before I jumped in the shower. I replied to his first text, but I was in the shower before I saw the second.

Caleb: *Good morning, gorgeous.*

Me: *Good morning, handsome.*

I proceeded to my shower with a smile on my face. When I returned, I found a string of texts from Caleb, going from sweet to frantic.

Caleb: *I miss you.*

Caleb: *Was that too much?*

Caleb: *I'm sorry, Nicole. That's too much too soon.*

Caleb: *Baby, are we okay?*

Caleb: *I hope I didn't freak you out.*

Caleb: *Fuck, I'm fucking this up.*

Each message was a minute or less apart. I had to call him to squish the storm he was creating in his head. The phone rang once before he picked up my call. I couldn't help smiling, when I heard his voice.

"Hello, I —," I cut him off right away.

"Babe, I miss you, too. I was in the shower. I didn't see your messages, until just now," I giggled.

"Oh," he sighed. "I'm sorry."

"Hush, Caleb. You did nothing wrong. I'll see you in class. Later, okay," I said with a smile in my voice.

"Nicole," he called before I could hang up.

"Yes."

"Thanks, darlin'."

"For what?" I asked in confusion.

"For trying with me," he said, blowing another hole through my heart.

He's been doing a lot of that. Blowing clear through my heart. Making it impossible not to care for him. Impossible not to fall for him.

So, yup, I, Nicole, have had a perpetual smile on my face for this entire week. Not even the snarling girls on campus have been able to dampen my mood. Oh, they're snarling all right. Caleb and Cameron walk me to all of my classes, when they're not at practice.

Caleb is not shy about holding my hand as we walk the campus. Having Cameron and Dakota around has just become the norm. I'm used to it.

"You know, your lips are going to fall off if you keep smiling so hard," Taylor teases.

"Oh God, I thought it was just me," Maribel says. "I keep getting asked out by these lames and here miss itty bitty cutie comes and steals my man right from under my nose."

"Does Caleb know about this?" I giggle.

"I was working up the nerve to tell him. He can be scary sometimes, you know?" Maribel says as she fans herself. "That's what makes him so hot."

"I can't," I roll my eyes and zip up my camera bag.

"So, you're going to his game, right?" Taylor asks.

"She's his girlfriend, she has too," Joelle sings, with stars in her eyes.

"We're just dating. There are no titles. Besides, I'm not sure if he wants me at his game. He hasn't asked me," I shrug.

All eyes grow large and look over my head. I can feel his warmth before he stops behind me. My cheeks hurt from smiling, when I feel his arm wrap around my waist and my body tugged back into his.

"I missed you," he murmurs into my neck, as he buries his face there.

I turn to face him, craning my neck to look up at him. I swear I get lost in those blue-grey eyes. Caleb takes my bags, and I wrap my arms around his waist.

"I missed you, too," I purr up at him.

He dips his head and pecks my lips. His eyes remain on my lips and I know he wants more. I also know that if he is going to walk me to my dorm he has to be quick about it, so he's not late for practice.

I move to his side and take his free hand. It's then that I notice my friends looking dreamy eyed. Then, I take in Cameron standing with his arms folded over his chest, while shaking his head.

"What?" I shrug.

"If I'm late for practice. I just want you to know, I'm kicking your boyfriend's ass," Cameron grumbles with a smirk on his lips.

"She's not my girlfriend, yet," Caleb says, but clamps his mouth shut, as he notices the girls watching him.

"You guys would make such a cute couple," Taylor gushes.

"I'll see you guys later," I sing and wave as I tug Caleb along with me.

I feel Caleb looking down at me, causing me to look up and smile at him. When I see the intense look in his eyes, I wrinkle my brows. I can nearly see the gears turning in his head.

"What?"

"You don't think we would make a cute couple?"

I smile at him. "Yes, I think we would make a cute couple. I just didn't want my friends badgering us. We'll do things when we're ready," I chirp.

He nods. We walk in silence the rest of the way to my dorm, but I can feel him thinking. I try my best not to rush him. I will never forget the time he had that meltdown, because I pushed him before he was ready.

Cameron stops in the common area on my floor, while Caleb walks me to my dorm room. I open my door and reach out my hand for my things. Caleb hands them over, but he inches me into the room by crowding my smaller body.

I step back, allowing him in. He looks so nervous, I'm not sure what he is about to say. I watch as he clenches and unclenches his fists.

"I...," he closes his eyes and blows out a breath.

I move closer and wrap my arms around his waist. I remember when he told me my touch calms him. When his eyes open, he looks at me with so many emotions warring.

"Just spit it out. It's just us," I say softly.

"I want you to come to my game. I want you to come see me play. Tomorrow night, will you come to my game?"

I beam up at him. "Of course, I will."

His hands go to the sides of my face and he devours my lips. I feel like he's trying to drink from the soul of my soul. I moan and he groans, pressing his hard body into mine.

We only pull apart at the sound of the knock on my door. I know it's Cameron. They're going to be late for practice if they don't get going.

"Fuck," Caleb grunts as he places his forehead to mine. "We're still meeting at our coffee shop later, right?"

"Oh, okay, if you want to. I didn't think we were going to."

Caleb nods. "After my dinner at Coach's house. I'm going to miss you like crazy."

"The sooner you go, the sooner it will be later," I giggle.

"You're lying, but I'm leaving." He smiles.

It's such a beautiful smile, I'm bereft when it falls from his face and he turns to leave. Cameron knocks once more as Caleb reaches for the knob and pulls the door open. I smirk as Cameron looks in and wiggles his brows at me.

"Let's go," Caleb says and pulls the door closed behind him.

I sigh. Suddenly, nerves and anticipation take over. I'm going to my first game as Caleb Perry's...*what?* I frown. I think I understand how Caleb felt on the walk over.

I touch my whisker burned lips. With kisses like that, Caleb needs to have some type of title in my life. I grin as a few thoughts take root. I'll have this handled before the night is out.

For now, I have to put together an outfit for our date tonight and another for Caleb's game tomorrow. No matter my status, I want to be representing my boo tomorrow night.

~*B*~
Caleb

I've been a mix of anxious and unsure all day. Or maybe I can explain it better as being nervous. I like Nicole a lot. I crave being around her.

It drives me crazy when Cameron starts to tell me I need to give Nicole space to breathe. I try not to text her all the time, which is starting to look like a better idea every day. I thought I totally fucked up this morning.

Reading a text message is worse than trying to read people for me. Long pauses between messages, or the way things are worded can trip me up. It's happened with Nicole more than once, but she handles it without freaking out on me.

I know I'm falling for her. My Mama has always told me I wouldn't understand love, so not to get my hopes up of ever having a wife or a real girlfriend. That shit pissed Cameron off. That's when he started to take it upon himself to hook me up with girls.

Cameron wanted to know my limits and we found them all right. For a long time, I've thought my mother to be right. Not anymore. Now I know. I know I have feelings growing for Nicole.

I won't tell her though. I don't want to scare her off. That leads me to my current anxiety. I want to make things official. I hate not knowing that Nicole is mine. I want to be able to call her my girl.

I know we've only been going on dates for a week, but I only want her. I've been amped up since this morning, when Nicole told me she would come to my game. I want to be able to introduce her to my family as my girl.

I pull the tie from my neck and climb into the car with Cameron. We've just finished having dinner at Coach's house. Coach Snider is an old high school friend of my uncle and dad's.

He's like a godfather of sorts. He has known me since I was a baby. Coach Derrick Snider has done everything he can to help me adjust here at college and on the team. He often has Cameron and me over to see how I'm doing and what he can do to help.

"You know Coach is right," Cameron says as we pull out of Coach's gated community.

"Yeah," I sigh. "I get what he's saying, but I don't want to become a gimmick and I don't want you giving up anything else for me. You're good on your own."

Cameron snorts. "Fucking right, I am," he says with a grin.

I turn my eyes to my brother. "You're joking about this," I say as more of a statement. "We both know you're as good as me, but you don't want to play ball. You only play because of me. You've never wanted to go pro. That's even more reason not to try this."

Cameron shrugs his shoulders. "Can I be honest with you, Caleb?"

"Only thing I understand, Cam," I reply.

"I've lived my whole life trying to be there for you. Doing what I had to for my little brother. You're right. I don't necessarily want to play ball in the long run. But honestly, I've been in your shadow for so long, I don't know what I want to do," Cameron glances over at me for a second then looks back at the road.

"My shadow," I murmur, as I filter in all his words. "I've always felt like I'm the one living in your shadow. Trying to do things the way you do them, because that's the right way. The way Mama and Daddy want it."

"Caleb, you're the most incredible person I know. You could never live in my fucking shadow, because you're such a better man than me. So, if this is what you want. If you need me to play, so you can play, I'm all over that shit."

I shake my head. "No, Cam, that's not what I want. I want to play, but I want to do this on my own. If a team wants us both, fine. If you decide you want to go pro, great, but not because of me.

"I think it's time we both do the shit we want. No more living for Mama and Daddy. We live for us. No more stealing from each other to please them," I say with clinched fists.

"I knew she was good for you," Cameron says after a long pause.

"What?"

"Nicole, she's good for you. You've changed in this short time. She's right for you. That's something I've never been able to figure out for you. I'm glad you're doing this, dating," Cameron's eyes flickers over to me. "You hold onto her. Relationships are hard, but that one right there. You fight for her, even if it means fighting your own head."

I just nod as I take in his words. We're silent for the rest of the drive to the coffee shop. The little shop has become our spot. Or at least, I think of it that way.

My heart knocks hard in my chest as Cameron and I sit waiting for Nicole to show up. This is technically my Junior year, although I'm several credits ahead of my degree. I have a lot of decisions to make. Cameron and I are being watched and there's been a lot of talk of us walking away from our college career this year.

To be honest, I should have been in the league by now. There's been interest in me since high school. We all just knew I wasn't ready for that then. My social skills were rough to say the least.

"Ah, fuck," Cameron groans beside me, as he looks up from his phone.

I follow his gaze to see what has his face looking like he smells something sour. When I find the source of the look, I understand it. Leslie, one of my old hook ups is headed our way.

I can't say I regret much. I'd never understood the concept until I started fucking Leslie. Not that she was a bad lay. It's the shit that has come with said lay.

Leslie got the rules, no kissing, no touching, and no commitments or conversation. What she has seemed to stop understanding is the no commitments and no conversation part. I'm not stupid. I can hold a conversation. Actually, that's one of the issues.

I'm extremely smart. Leslie is a complete airhead. The things that interest me go over her head. One time, Dakota had to run to the bathroom in the mall, and Cameron and Kay had taken off.

I stood with a physics magazine in my hand, reading an article I'd been waiting to get my hands on. I swear, Leslie walked up, pointing to my magazine. She started talking about physiques.

I remember standing there looking at her with more than my usual confusion. When Dakota came back from the bathroom, she laughed in her face. It was then that I figured it out, I was not the confused one.

"Hey, Cameron," Leslie chirps, she then turns her eyes to me and purrs breathlessly. "Hi, Caleb."

"I'm waiting for someone. You're blocking my view," I reply and blink at her.

Cameron chuckles and shakes his head. "For once, I can say I love that shit," he mutters under his breath. "Listen Leslie, this isn't a good time. We'll see you around."

Leslie pouts and gets ready to open her mouth, but I spot Nicole crossing the street outside the window. I stand and head out of the café. I don't even hear whatever it is Leslie says, or Cameron's response.

Nicole's eyes light up when she sees me and she tugs her scarf down from over her face. I open my arms and she leaps into them. I feel my heart burst as my arms envelope her.

Her small hands cup my ears and she pulls my face down to meet hers. I tilt my head so my baseball cap doesn't peck her in the face. When my lips meet hers, I feel the day wash away.

Everything that has been weighing on me feels like background noise. Background noise, that for once in my life I can filter out. I don't feel the pressure of hiding or of trying to be perfect. I stop thinking about all the stuff Cameron gives up for me.

I take my time kissing her soft, sweet lips, moving one hand to her hair to keep her with me. My fingers curl into the back of her locks, pulling a sexy moan from deep inside her. When I grow hard against her belly, Nicole pulls away.

A little smile is on her lips, as her breath puffs out before her face. "I missed you too," she giggles.

I place her on her feet and put a little distance between us. My eyes sweep over her. She's changed her clothes since this afternoon. She now has on a black pea coat and a thick grey knit scarf.

When my eyes land on her legs, peeking out from under her coat. I see that her thick shapely legs are covered in black tights, with heart designs. On her small feet are suede grey-heeled ankle boots.

"I missed you more than I think I should tell you," I murmur.

"Whatever, Caleb," she laughs and places her hand in mine. "Oh, my God, it was just eighty-three degrees yesterday. It's freezing out here."

Nicole gently tugs me toward the coffee shop. When I see her shiver slightly, I release her fingers and pull her little body into my side, wrapping my arm around her.

I bend to kiss the top of her head and she looks up at me with that smile. I love that smile. I give her a gentle squeeze, as we stop in front of the counter in the coffee shop.

"Can I have a hot chocolate and two lemon squares?" I say to the barista.

"Sure, Perry," the lanky guy behind the counter says.

I squint at him trying to place where I know him from. Before I can place him, he's off to get our order. I'm still fixed on figuring it out, when Nicole tugs on my dress shirt.

"You're a baseball star," Nicole says softly. "You may not know him, but he wants to feel like he knows you."

I look down at her as I grasp her words. When the barista returns, he places our order on the counter on a tray. I reach for my wallet, but he looks around and shakes his head.

"Nah, man, it's on me. You just pitch us a win tomorrow, Bro," he says with a hopeful smile.

I look at his name tag and nod. "Thanks, Bernie."

The guy's whole face brightens. "No problem. You and your girl come here all the time now. If you ever need anything, I'm your guy."

"Cool, thanks," I nod, taking the tray with my free hand.

I haven't released Nicole from my side. It feels too good to have her snuggled into me. I hate that I have to let her go so that we can sit when we get to the table.

Cameron is long gone, but my coat is still resting on the back of the chair I had been sitting in. I place the tray down on the table to help her take off her coat. Nicole sighs as she pulls away to take her seat.

"You're always so warm," Nicole says as she looks at my side with...I want to say longing. "If you didn't have a game tomorrow night, I would so talk you into going to your place so I can snuggle into your heat."

"Are the dorms cold?"

"My room is. Taylor has the place like a freaking ice box," Nicole wrinkles her nose.

"You're welcome to spend the night with me," I offer.

"Um, tempting. You probably make a good blanket," Nicole chuckles. "Nope, no sleepovers, yet."

My breath catches in my throat, as I slip her jacket from her shoulders. The figure fitting black dress beneath is covering everything, but not at the same time. I mean, the dress falls to her knees and reaches up her neck in a turtleneck style. It is just molded to her body in a way that accentuates all of her curves.

"You're gorgeous, darlin'," I bend to breathe in her ear.

Nicole looks over her shoulder and gives me that sweet smile. I pull her chair and watch her ease into it gracefully. I won't lie, my eyes are glued to her ass.

Clearing my throat, I place her coat on the back of her chair. When I find my own seat, she's giving me that sweet look again. I stare back into her light brown orbs.

"What?" I say when I can't read her.

"Look at you, ordering exactly what I want without asking," she grins.

"Do you want me to ask first?"

"Nope, you're doing just fine," she says. "How was your day?"

Her eyes remain on me, as she waits for my answer. I think over her question. All through dinner with coach, I wanted to know what Nicole would think about it all.

I lick my lips and sit back in my chair. I draw in a deep breath and look Nicole in the eyes. This is what I want, I want someone I can talk to and be real with.

"Coach Snider thinks we should play up Cameron and I being twins. It's not guaranteed that we will get drafted to the same team," I pause and look down at my hands.

"Cameron is good. He's really good. One of the best hitters on the team. Hell, in our division, but he doesn't love baseball the way I do. He plays because of me.

"I don't want to force him to play and I don't want to become a gimmick. A triple A team may eat that shit up. Two all-stars that are twins. Coach had stars in his eyes as he talked about Twin day and fans getting discounts or getting into games free if they're twins.

"All I hear is circus. I've spent my entire life trying not to become a circus. Now, I'm supposed to willingly do this," I shake my head. "I don't think it's what I want. If Cameron chooses to play, fine. But he has his own life. I can't hide behind him forever."

Nicole stares at me wordlessly for so long, I start to shift in my seat. When she tilts her head to the side, I relax. She's just putting it all together. I can understand that.

"I haven't seen you actually play, but you're so focused when you're just practicing. Who you are off the field shouldn't stop who you become on that field. I don't believe you and Cameron need to become a gimmick so that you can play," she pauses and rolls her lips.

"If this is what you want, Babe. If you want to play. You'll do it. I know you will. The rest you'll figure out too. You're amazing, Caleb. You don't have to play in anyone's circus. Your brother is amazing too, for doing this for you. I know it will all work out," she finishes with a big smile.

If I didn't love her before, I know I love her now. Everyone else is always telling me and Cameron how great an opportunity we have. Never once have they asked if either of us wants it.

I reach across the table and link our fingers together. Nicole breaks off a piece of one of her lemon bars and holds it up to my lips. I go with my instincts and nip her finger after the treat is in my mouth.

Her eyes drop to the table and her cheeks glow. When her gaze lifts to look at me through her lashes, I lean over the table to place a kiss to the corner of her lips. Nicole turns her head to press her lips fully to mine and I take over the kiss.

When Nicole breaks the connection, and pulls away, I groan. I wish we had gone to my apartment. These stolen kisses aren't enough.

Nicole looks me in the eyes and surprises me with her question. "Why baseball? What is it about it that makes you so focused, so driven?"

I sit back and look at her for a moment. I feel like I'm stripping bare for her. It's an odd feeling, when I've held my cards close for so long, but once I start to speak it all feels freeing.

"I'm not some cool guy at all. If it were up to me, I would be focused on my studies," I look away, not sure how she is going to react. "I do love baseball, but the part that makes me so focused when I play is the aspect of Physics. When I play, I'm almost singularly focused on the motion, force, and speed behind throwing the ball.

"Being able to time a hitter to the base and throwing a ball that out guns him. The ability to measure a hitter's swing and adjusting my pitch to out pitch him. I don't see the hitter up at bat.

"What I see is the formula of his speed, timing, and force. I see the energy that nature throws into that equation and I calculate in my head the speed, timing, and power I'll put behind my pitch.

"I took what I love and channeled it into baseball. Into pitching. My uncle is an astrophysicist. I got into his magazines, when I was little. Around the same time my dad put me and Cameron into T-ball.

"It all sort of clicked for me. My dad went nuts. He had finally found something that made me normal. Cameron and I have been playing ever since," I shrug.

"Wow," Nicole breathes. "You really are amazing."

"Amazing enough for you to go out on another date with me this weekend?" I ask and give my best attempt at one of Cameron's smiles that gets him anything from girls.

"You're just too handsome for your own good," Nicole laughs. She taps her chin. "I don't know if we can do another date, though. My boyfriend tends to be a bit jealous."

I frown and sit back in my chair. She told me she didn't have a boyfriend when I asked a week ago. Why would she kiss me the way she has if she has a boyfriend?

I get ready to ream her about honesty when the pieces fall into place. I practically knock the table over when I stand from my seat and rush to her side pulling her from her seat. My hands cradle her face in my hands.

"Are you talking about me?" I ask against her lips waiting for her answer, before I claim what's mine.

"See, humor isn't lost on you at all," she purrs against my mouth.

"You're going to be a challenge," I actually laugh, before crushing her lips with mine.

Nicole is a challenge worth taking. That I'm sure of. I'm never letting her go.

CHAPTER TEN

Game Time

Nicole

I'm so nervous. I have no idea what to expect at Caleb's game. I'm not that big on baseball, but I would watch Caleb race turtles if he asked me to. I'm just in awe of the man.

I mean, look at this place. We've been trying to get to our seats for like an hour now. I've seen more girls than I'd like to admit wearing number thirty-four jerseys.

I feel pretty lame wearing mine. If it weren't for the fact that Caleb gave it to me this afternoon, I probably would have snatched it off by now. However, he did give it to me. I'm the only one here wearing it that can say I'm Caleb Perry's girlfriend.

I beam to myself with that thought. Caleb was so happy last night. After walking me to my dorm, he gave me the longest, tightest hug goodnight. Not to mention the toe curling kiss right before.

"You're doing it again," Taylor sings.

"Doing what?" I ask, trying to stay close to my group as we push our way forward.

This is insane. Some of these people aren't even looking for their seats. They're just milling around socializing and getting amped up for the game. You can feel the energy coming off the crowd as they buzz about the twin Perry's.

I think about all that Caleb told me about what his coach wants to do to package the twins as one, but it seems not much work would be needed. People are just as excited about Cameron as they are Caleb. I see just as many girls marching around in number thirty-three jerseys. I wonder if away games are like this.

"You look like you're floating in the clouds. You haven't stopped smiling since you came back to the dorm from your date last night. Did Caleb lay down the D?" Taylor wiggles her brows, as she looks over her shoulder at me.

I feel my face flame. I swat Taylor's shoulder as I give her a wide-eyed expression. She just throws her head back and cackles at me. Joelle tucks her arm through mine and gives me a toothy grin.

"You would tell us, right? If Perry is giving you that good loving, we need to live through you. I want details. Stroke by delicious stroke details. That man is just fine," Joelle fans herself with her free hand.

"Oh girl, that pout," Maribel rolls her eyes and bites her lip.

"Who you telling," Taylor sighs. "I damn near cream my panties every time I see it."

"Okay, I think we all need to reel it back," I sass. I feel a pang in my chest for the truth of that pout. "That's my boyfriend you're creaming over and I'm not too sure I like it or want to hear about it."

Taylor skids to a stop, causing the people behind us to nearly run right into me and Joelle. We both look back with apologetic smiles. When I turn back around Taylor and Maribel are staring at me, with their mouths hanging open.

"Wait, yesterday you guys said you were just going on a few dates," Maribel narrows her eyes, as if I've been holding out.

"Yeah, Caleb said you weren't his girl, yet," Taylor says.

"Well, that was yesterday. Before we made it official," I shrug and shoo them forward.

We need to get to our seats. I look down at my phone to see Dakota is sending me, yet another text, asking me where the hell I am. Apparently, there are seats reserved for me and my friends.

I had wondered why Caleb texted me so early in the morning. Asking if I was coming alone or if I planned to bring friends, and how many. I'd shrugged it off and texted him back that the girls were coming along.

The girls. Two years at my old college and I never had girls. I've been here for two weeks and these three have become my little crew. When I spot Dakota, waving frantically at me, I count her into the mix.

"Damn, he's even more yummy in that uniform," Maribel groans.

My eyes follow the direction Maribel's head is turned. They lock on Caleb, he is on the mound with his coach and Cameron. They all seem to be locked in a deep conversation.

Something is off with Caleb's body language. I find my feet are moving without my command. I push my way forward, needing to get close and find out what's going on.

When I draw closer to Dakota, who is standing in a row of empty seats right beside the dugout, I see the worry on her face. I rush to her side and look up at her for answers. Dakota is just as tall as Caleb and Cameron, her eyes more blue than grey.

I see the relief that comes to those blue eyes as I get to her side. Dakota cups her hands at her mouth and starts to call Cameron and Caleb's names. She flails her arms in the air to get their attention.

I see the moment Caleb's eyes look up and he locks his blue-greys on me. He starts to move toward the bleachers, his focus solely on me. The crowd goes wild for him, totally unaware that something is going on.

I move to the fence separating me from the field. My fingers hook into the chain links. When Caleb reaches the barrier, I can see in his eyes, he is not okay.

Wordlessly, we move toward the left, where there's an opening out onto the field. I run my fingers across the fence as I go. Caleb lifts his hand to the metal between us, allowing his fingertips to graze mine as we move to meet at the opening.

When we clear the fence and I turn the small corner to stand before him, he immediately reaches for my hair and locks his fingers in my short bob. His lips are on mine in a passionate kiss that curls my toes in my ankle boots.

His free hand goes into the back pocket of my jeans as he pulls me up against his body. Caleb is huge compared to me. However, I've never felt like the perfect fit, more than I do right now.

All the cheering around us goes completely silent. It's as if you can hear a pin drop on the field. Caleb doesn't acknowledge any of it. He deepens the kiss and groans into my mouth. I grab his ears and kiss him back, uncaring of anything else.

Suddenly, applauds and whistles break out from the crowd. My cheeks heat, but as I try to pull away from the kiss Caleb follows. Tightening his hold in my hair, he holds me to him.

"That's my girl, claim your man," I hear Maribel call over the crowd of cheers and whistles.

Caleb finally breaks the kiss and presses his forehead to mine. His eyes look more focused and I can feel his body relax against mine. I look up at him questioningly.

"Well, will you look at that, ladies and gentlemen," a voice breaks out over the crowd, through the PA system. "Looks like another Perry is off the market. Those twins are nothing but eye candy now, ladies."

I giggle and turn to look at the crowd behind us. I shudder at the mixed reactions I see in the crowd. Caleb reaches to turn my face back to him.

"I didn't think you were coming," he breathes, as his eyes search my face.

"I'm so sorry, Babe. I was making my way through this monster crowd. I would have left sooner if I knew it would be like this," I apologize.

He nods. Then a smile breaks across his face. It's so gorgeous it stuns me for a moment.

"This one is in the bag. I have to win for my girl," he says with a determined smile, then pecks my lips. "You look hot in my Jersey, Nicole. I like knowing you're mine."

I beam up at him. "I like knowing you're mine, Caleb. Give them hell."

He winks down at me and it is so endearing. His eyes are the clearest I've ever seen them. I can tell he has honed in on that focus he draws from on the field.

With one last kiss and a squeeze of my ass, he releases me. I look up at him with a goofy grin, before I give a dumb wave. I inwardly kick myself, but Caleb doesn't care about any of that, as he backs toward the pitcher's mound without turning or taking his eyes off me until it's absolutely necessary.

I bounce my way back to my seat. I hadn't even realized I walked down three rows to get to the fence. I lose a bit of my bounce, as I make my way up the stairs, I catch the sour stares of some of the other girls. Even women much too old for Caleb glare at me, as if they've just lost a chance at being a cougar.

"Damn, I'm so jealous," Taylor breathes as she fans herself in her seat.

"That would make two of us," Joelle giggles.

"I'm just saying. I'm still holding out hope for his brother," Maribel sighs.

"Excuse me," Kay leans forward in her seat. When my girls turn to her, she gives a sugary sweet smile. "Yes, hi, I'm Kay, Cameron's girlfriend."

"Oh, so nice to meet you," Maribel says with just as sweet a smile. "I'm Maribel, Cameron's future wife."

My mouth falls open. Maribel says it with such a straight face. Taylor, Joelle, and Dakota all blink at her as if she's crazy.

"Oh, my God," Maribel rolls her eyes. "A girl can dream, can't she? I mean, seriously. You and I are worlds apart, sweetie. I'm not even Cameron's type. It was a joke."

Waving us all off, Maribel turns her attention back to the field. Dakota and I burst out laughing. A red-faced Kay only manages to shift in her seat, turning to look at the field.

I stifle my laugh as the awkwardness of the situation sets in. I do notice that Kay doesn't look as confident about her status. My brows furrow. I wonder what that's about, but Dakota grabs my arm and pulls me into my seat.

"I don't know what you did to him, but he's crazy about you," Dakota whispers in my ear. "I love you two together. You don't treat him...you know, different. Thank you."

"For what?" I turn to whisper back.

"For giving him a chance," Dakota says with a trembling smile. "My cousin is brilliant. People that know...you know, they tend to miss that. Did you know he tutored me in high school? I suck at math. Caleb is a math whiz. It's like he can pull numbers out of thin air."

"He told me about loving physics, but I didn't know he tutored you."

"I used to feel like such an idiot when it came to math. Caleb is straightforward about everything, so when he found me floundering with my homework, he gave it to me in a way I could understand. None of the extra confusing stuff." Dakota shrugs.

"He's amazing. I don't doubt what you're saying." I smile as I watch Caleb warming up on the mound.

"You haven't seen nothing yet," Dakota sings. "When the game starts, you're going to meet another side of Caleb."

I bite my lip and push to the edge of my seat. From the intensity rolling off of him with simple practice pitching, I know I'm in for a sight.

Dakota was right and I'm not disappointed. Cameron and Caleb have an amazing game. Caleb pitched his ass off. I have never seen such singular focus. The man is a beast on the field.

After hearing Caleb explain why he loves baseball, and listening to Dakota talk about him being a math genius, I could see it. I could see in his face that he was calculating the dynamics of every pitch, every player on the field. Caleb is simply a phenom.

He pitched a complete game, shutting out the opposing team. He also had a homerun. Cameron had four RBIs, hitting two homeruns of his own. I know one thing. If the two decide to go with their coach's idea to create some twin hype, they won't have much work to do.

Caleb and Cameron made that field look like Mount Olympus. The two of them were the gods overseeing the mere mortals. My throat is raw from cheering so much, almost in worship like all of their other fans.

I've never been in love with baseball. I used to watch with my brothers and my dad sometimes. Enough to learn to understand the game, but tonight, I've never been so excited while watching any sport.

I can't wait to give my man his praise up close and personal. My heart almost jumped out of my chest when Caleb took his hat off and pointed it toward me at the end of the game. He gave a curt nod, before rushing off the field with Cameron before the team could surround them.

I understood right away, Caleb wouldn't be able to handle the celebration the team was aiming for on the field. I wonder what excuse he and Cameron gave for running off. It pissed me off to hear a few murmurs about them leaving and being unsportsmanlike.

It's okay. Caleb may not have been able to handle his team's celebration, but we'll have one of our own. I'll make sure he gets to celebrate the right way. He deserves to bask in this accomplishment.

~B~

Caleb

I never doubted that we would win the game. However, I was going to lose my shit when I didn't see Nicole in the stands. I needed her here. This was our home opener and I wanted my girl in the stands to watch me.

Once I knew she was there everything was right in the world. I hadn't planned to hit today, but when I hit that homerun, all I could think about was shutting out the game. I wanted to show Nicole she could be proud of me.

"You're so freaking awesome," Nicole squeals, as she runs at me and jumps into my arms.

I catch her and hold her to me, as she wraps her legs around my waist. It's the best feeling ever. My eyes drop to her lush lips. I've been wanting to kiss her again since before the game.

Nicole presses her finger to my lips when I dip my head to move in for a kiss. I knit my brows in confusion, but she gives me a smile and wiggles her brows.

"We'll have plenty of time for that when we get to your place," she starts. "Dakota invited us all to your apartment to celebrate."

"Oh, wow, thanks, Dakota," Cameron snorts, but the smile on his lips show he's teasing. He throws an arm over Kay's shoulder and whispers something in her ear.

I turn my attention back to Nicole. "I'd much rather be alone with you," I say.

Nicole's lip pokes out. "But it will be fun. Besides, you aren't allowed to sleep over at the dorm. I thought we could have our first sleepover tonight."

This time when I dip my head, I'm able to capture her lips. I groan into the sweetness of her mouth. Fuck yeah, I want a sleepover. I get hard just thinking about it.

Nicole breaks the kiss and giggles, breathlessly. "I think your version of a sleepover and mine are two different things," she laughs.

"What's yours?" I ask, as my mind races.

"Me, in one of your t-shirts. Us talking. There's still a lot I want to know about you, Caleb Perry."

I groan and place my forehead to hers. "Yeah, baby, we have two different ideas of a sleepover. When Kay sleeps over there's nothing but fucking going on in Cameron's room."

Nicole bursts into laughter. She pecks my lips and starts to wiggle, so I release her back onto her feet. I hold her close as she slides down my front.

"You and I, are not Cameron and Kay," she winks. "We'll learn to do things our own way."

My heart swells. As much as I would love to get inside Nicole, her words are like gold to me. I don't know if she understands how much I want to be my own person. How much finding my own way means.

I don't say anything, as I lace my fingers with hers and we all leave the field. I'm content for the first time in...ever. Nicole does that for me.

I'll admit—once everyone gathers at the apartment—I do enjoy myself. I think it's mostly because I get a chance to watch Nicole with her friends. Or it could be that she made me feel like a part of the group.

Anytime I seem to be withdrawing, she pulls me right back. Maribel's sarcasm has been a challenge all night. Her complete lack of expression when she throws her zingers throws me entirely.

Cameron wears a smirk when he's giving me shit, most the time. Maribel gives nothing away when she's throwing jabs or teasing. Nicole helped me through it though. Giving gentle touches and squeezes of my hand.

That's when I wasn't too wrapped in Nicole. A few times I didn't care what anyone else was talking about. Nicole's intoxicating scent engulfed me in her world.

However, now, I'm nervous as fuck. My hands are sweating and I can't stop blinking. I'm a little thrown off by this change to my nightly routine, but I'm trying my best to hide it.

I have several things that I usually do before bed, but I haven't done a single one, because I'm solely focused on the bathroom door. Nicole disappeared behind it a half hour ago. The shower stopped ten minutes ago.

I want to check on her, but I don't want to weird her out. I lick my dry lips and look down at the time once more. Just then the door opens, Nicole walks out swallowed whole in one of my shirts. She looks adorable and sexy.

My eyes fall to her breasts. She's not wearing a bra beneath, and her nipples are pressed against the soft fabric. When my eyes move lower to her brown legs, I groan. I run a hand through my hair, then down my beard.

"It's a good thing you have a king-size bed," Nicole says, with a smile, as she crawls up from the foot of the mattress toward me. "God, how am I just realizing how huge you are?"

"You're just tiny," I say, as I keep my eyes on her.

She snuggles her small body into my side. Instinctively, I wrap an arm around her and pull her into me. I relax as soon as she is in place.

Nicole tips her face up toward me. "I guess I am to you," she laughs. "Is this okay? Are you okay with me being here?"

"No," I shake my head and grimace.

"Oh," Nicole gasps and goes to sit up.

"Don't," I say, pulling her back down. "I'm dealing with my shit. I want you here."

"I wasn't thinking. I should've asked you sooner," Nicole says in a small voice.

I dip and kiss her forehead. "I would have told you the same thing. I'm dealing with my shit, but I want you here. From time to time, I'll have to adjust for you. Like my Aunt Judy says, everyone has to adjust in life. We all have to learn to adapt. It's not that I can't, I just have a harder time doing it. But I'm willing, especially when it comes to you."

"Tell me, how I can help?" Nicole says, as she reaches to hold my jaw.

I close my eyes and soak in the feel of her fingers against my face. I don't understand how or why I'm so open to her touch. It just feels right.

"Just treat me like you would anyone else. Let me deal with me and my head, if it's ever too much, I'll let you know," I open my eyes and look into hers.

A few moments pass without either of us saying a word. I reach for her face and run my finger over her full lips. They feel so soft, I have to kiss her. I dip my head and kiss her gently.

When I pull away, she has that smile on her lips that takes my breath away. My heart squeezes. All of my anxiety melts to a low hum that I can deal with. I have my girl in my bed with me, nothing else matters.

"So, tell me, Caleb. Am I the first girl you've had in this bed?"

"Yes."

"Good answer," she yawns.

"If you weren't, were you going to leave?"

"Um, I don't know," she snuggles in deeper. "You're so warm, I don't want to move."

I smile, but I don't move. I'm stiff as a board. I don't want to do the wrong thing. Nicole said no fucking. She shifts her sexy legs, grabbing my attention and my cock jumps in protest.

"Cal," she whispers.

I return my eyes to her face. "Yeah, Baby," I reply huskily.

"Tell me your hopes and dreams. What does your perfect life look like?"

Her eyes sparkle back at me. I can't think of anything but kissing her. I hear her question, but I need to do this one thing before I answer.

I hold her face and kiss her like it's my sole purpose. In my head, my thoughts are screaming.

You, you're my hopes and my dreams come true. You're what I want. You're my perfect life.

CHAPTER ELEVEN

Birthday Wishes

Nicole

I've been working away all night in the kitchen at the apartment, baking cupcakes and cookies. It's Caleb and Cameron's birthday. They just turned twenty-one today at midnight.

I wouldn't let them eat a single goodie, until the clock stroke twelve. I swear you would think they were turning six, the way they've been whining. Cameron just ran off in his boxers, with a plate full of cookies.

I shake my head as Caleb sits before me, his blue-grey eyes large and pleading. I peel the wrapper from the cupcake I'm holding. I baked him vanilla mint cupcakes, with royal blue frosting.

I move to stand between his legs, as he sits on a barstool at the kitchen island. His hand automatically drops to my waist.

Lifting the cupcake to his lips, I make a last-minute decision to be naughty.

"Oops," I giggle.

I throw my head back and laugh, as I point at his face. I just smashed the cupcake into his nose and mouth. Blue icing is all over his nose, beard, and those sexy lips.

"Happy birthday," I sing through my laughter.

I couldn't help myself, I had to do it. Caleb has been a smart ass all day. Along with pleading for the treats I baked, Caleb and Cameron teamed up in teasing me about meeting their parents.

Caleb was the first to pick up that I'm nervous about meeting their parents. He made the mistake of pointing it out in front of Cameron, and they have been relentless since. I swear they have been like two big kids today.

It's been two months, since Caleb and I have been a couple. I've seen so many sides of him in that time. The most interesting one being his version of his twin brother. Caleb has a damn good imitation of Cameron down. It sometimes gives me a headache to be around the two of them together.

Cameron knows how to annoy the fuck out of you. When Caleb decides to be a carbon copy of Cameron, they'll drive you up a wall. Honestly, I love them both for it. On some of my worst days, they've made me laugh so hard, I don't even remember what pissed me off to begin with.

However, today they have gotten on my last nerve. Caleb deserved this and more. Meeting his family is a big deal to me, I'm scared out of my mind. Honestly, I thought I would've met his parents at a game by now. However, they haven't been to any of the ones I've been to.

I've met his Aunt Judy and his Uncle Rusty. They were very sweet and warm to me, which I sort of expected. Caleb talks about his aunt and uncle as if they're the ones that raised him.

They seem like very nice people. Dakota's mom and dad have never made me feel any type of way, when I'm around. Actually, his Aunt Judy thinks I hung the moon. She fusses over me every time we meet at a game.

However, when it comes to the thought of meeting Caleb's mom and dad, something keeps nagging in the pit of my stomach. The more I learn about them, the more I'm not sure I want to meet them. Unfortunately, I have no choice today.

Mr. and Mrs. Perry are throwing a party for the twins. Cameron said it's nothing big. Just family and a few friends, but from the look on Caleb's face when they first mentioned it, I'm not so sure he's up for it himself.

Caleb growling into my neck, pulls me from my own musing. I squeal, as I feel the icing on his face smear against my skin. Only to moan seconds later, when Caleb licks and sucks the skin into his mouth.

"I think you taste better than any cupcake," he murmurs.

"You sure about that," I pant, as he continues to rub frosting from his face, onto my neck and collarbone just to lick and suck it off.

"I want to be very sure," he groans. "Nicole, darlin'. I want to taste you for my birthday."

I gasp. As always, I get exactly what's on Caleb's mind. No filter, no chaser. We haven't had sex, not for his lack of trying.

I just think we need to build our relationship more before we complicate things. However, right now, as his tongue and beard brush my sensitive skin and his lips suck frosting into his warm mouth, a sister is having a hard time keeping control.

Caleb lifts his head to look in my eyes and the lust I see trapped in his gaze almost blows me over. He still has frosting on his nose, so I lean in and lick from the tip up the bridge. His hands on my waist tighten, drawing me closer.

"I'll let you taste me, but only if I get to taste you first," I say seductively. "After all, it's your birthday."

Caleb growls, standing to his feet, lifting me onto his waist. His strong arms band around me to hold me to him. I feel like a little doll in his arms.

"Wait, Babe," I giggle, as he moves swiftly to his room. "I think we should bring the extra frosting with us."

"What?" Caleb goes to reply, but I see in his eyes when he gets my intention. "Fuck."

I nod my head and giggle. Caleb turns back for the kitchen island and I scoop up the bowl of frosting I had left over. In a flash, we are inside Caleb's room with the door sealed shut.

I'm spending the night, so I'm already in shorts and a tank top. My tiny shorts ride into my cheeks as Caleb palms my ass with his huge hands. He keeps his eyes on mine, as if needing the connection to make sure I don't change my mind.

He gingerly places me in the center of the bed. I place the bowl down beside me and Caleb leans over me, taking my lips in a deep kiss. I can taste the royal blue icing the moment his full lips touch mine. I moan as the flavor of vanilla bean, caramel frosting bursts in my mouth from his lips and tongue.

Caleb doesn't break the kiss, as he reaches behind me and releases my bra, with ease. My bra gets tossed somewhere to the side. Caleb never once breaks our kiss.

He groans into my mouth as my hands palm his face. Caleb's hands glide up my sides beneath my tank top, until his thumbs are right underneath my breasts. His thumb flicks one of my hardened nipples, once, twice, three times, before pressing down on it like a button.

It might as well be. I feel like he has just turned on a fire between my legs. I whimper and Caleb pulls back, his eyes are dark, as he reaches for the waistband of my shorts.

I place my hand on his chest and shake my head to stop him. "You first, remember," I pant.

Caleb nods, as his mouth falls open and his eyes become impossibly dark. There's no grey to be found. I push him to turn on to his back, reaching for the bowl, moving it out of his way.

I place the bowl beside my knees, as I look down at Caleb's tented grey sweat pants. I know for a fact there's a huge dick in there waiting for me. We may not have had sex yet, but we make out and fool around enough. Not to mention, on the nights that I do stay over, for a sleepover, I usually wake up to his morning wood pressed into my butt cheeks.

I lick my lips, I want to taste him. I look up at his face to see the pained expression written all over it. He needs a release as much as I want to give him one. I may not be ready for full intercourse, yet, but I'm going to suck the life out of this one eyed monster tonight.

"Nicole," Caleb groans in a plea.

"Take off your shirt," I whisper.

He nods and tears it off over his head, tossing it aside. His chiseled body is perfection. His skin is tanned from practicing with his shirt off. It's like every muscle has a muscle. His pecks are perfectly formed showing off perfect dusk color discs.

I lean forward and flick my tongue over one of those enticing nipples. He groans and bucks his hips. I place my small hand on his chest and run it down to his hip. Pushing my fingers inside of his sweats, I reach for his length.

I bite my lip at my first touch of his silky steel rod. He's thick and one of the first things I notice is the pulsing veins against my palm. My hand isn't nearly big enough to wrap around him. Caleb reaches to push his sweats out of the way in impatience. My eyes widen as he comes into view in the flesh. *Damn*, I halt as my eyes and brain try to catch up with what I'm seeing.

"Shit," I whisper.

"Is something wrong?"

I turn my eyes to his, as his words come out in a husky, but nervous breath. I shake my head and lick my suddenly dry lips. I swallow and shake my head again.

"No, nothing is wrong," I breathe out. "You're just...wow, Caleb. You're big."

"That's good right," he asks innocently. His brows furrow as he looks at me expectantly.

I bite my lip and nod. "Yeah, Babe, it's good, but it's probably going to hurt like a bitch our first time. Not to mention, my jaw is going to be sore in the morning."

"We don't have to...," I cut his words off, when I stick my hand in the frosting and then rub it off, down the length of his shaft. "Nicole."

I silence him once again, as I dip my head and start to lick the frosting off. I lick up the underside of his length, smiling in triumph when his fingers grip the sheets. I lock my hands together behind my back and lower to wrap my lips around his crown.

"Fuck," Caleb bellows.

"Shh," I giggle up at him.

His face twists as he gives me a look. His expression is priceless. It says, 'are you fucking kidding?' I wink at him and go back to bobbing for icing.

I lick him clean, before covering him again and going in for more. Caleb's moans and groans are so sexy as they fill the room. His hips buck off the bed, as he thrusts up into my mouth. He tastes so good.

I let my saliva drip down his length to wet him up, then I bring my hands from behind my back. I use both to work him as I bob up and down. Caleb covers his face with one arm, as his other hand shoots to lock in the back of my hair.

"Fuck, I'm so close," he grunts through his teeth. "Stop, Baby. I'm gonna come in your mouth if you don't stop."

I don't stop. "Mmm," I hum back.

"*Fuck*," Caleb shudders with his release, as he comes down my throat, hot and thick.

I lick him clean and sit back on my heels. I watch in satisfaction as my big man's chest heaves up and down. Caleb pulls a hand down his face, as he catches his breath.

I turn to sit on my butt and move the frosting bowl to the nightstand, but Caleb pounces. I yelp as my back hits the bed, with a bounce. Caleb pushes my tank up over my breasts and looks down at me hungrily.

"Baby, you're so beautiful." Caleb pauses just hovering over me, with his gaze locked on my mounds. He stares for so long, I start to become self-conscious.

"Is everything okay," I ask, sitting up on my elbows.

"You're so perfect. More beautiful than I imagined, I feel like this is a dream and I'm going to wake up," Caleb says huskily, with a tortured expression on his face.

"I'm all yours. I'm not going anywhere. I want to be your dream come true," I say. "Happy birthday, baby. You wanted a taste, come and get it."

Like a string has been cut, his restraint breaks. Caleb palms my right breast and dips his head to pull my hardened peak into his mouth. I cry out and buck off the bed.

"Caleb," I gasp and lock my fingers around back of his head. "Yes."

As if him sucking my nipple for dear life isn't enough, Caleb snakes his hand into my little shorts. He sucks my breast harder, when his long fingers find my wet center. He grunts, as his fingers slide up and down the outside of my slick lips.

I spread my legs wider and throw my head back. I start to rock my hips against his fingers, aching for my own release. Caleb moves to my other breast and starts to feast on it.

My juices flood his fingers, just before he shoves them past my drenched lips. My mouth falls open wordlessly. Caleb lets my breast pop free from his mouth, before swallowing my silent scream.

His fingers are still thrusting, as my chest heaves and I start to build again. I look into his eyes and he searches my face. I don't know what he finds, but whatever it is causes him to pull his fingers from my wet sex.

Caleb grabs for the waistband of my shorts, this time I let him pull them down. I hadn't planned on having sex, but I also didn't think Caleb would blow my mind with just his touch. Caleb grins up at me as he dips his fingers in his mouth and sucks on them.

He groans around them, then he sticks the same fingers into the bowl of frosting, coating them with icing. He drags the icing down my inner thigh, collecting more icing to do the same with the other leg.

I pant as I watch him stare down between, my open legs. He reaches for his cock to squeeze it. He's hard and ready again. Caleb moves his big body down the bed and settles on his stomach. He then brings his lips to my inner thigh.

Slowly, almost at a torturous rate, he starts to lick the frosting from my skin. He cleans both thighs at his leisure. Then his tongue dips into my pussy and I lose it all.

Caleb nips, sucks, and devours my pussy lips, in between diving in with his tongue. He eats pussy like a fucking porn star. I start calling his name out, totally forgetting about the thin walls or anyone else in the apartment.

I want to know who is this man. This is not my sweet Caleb, eating my core like a pussy cannibal. I look down to see his blonde head bobbing. His eyes flicker up just then and he smirks, latching onto my clit.

"Fuck, *ah,*" I cry out. "*Oh, oh, shit,* Cal."

I come so hard my eyes cross. Just then Cameron starts to bang on the wall. I cover my mouth and giggle.

"Fuck off," Caleb calls out. I can hear Cameron chuckling in the other room. "Asshole," Caleb mutters under his breath, as he removes the bowl from the bed and pulls me into his arms and his warmth.

"Happy birthday," I whisper before I pass out.

CHAPTER TWELVE

Blown Candles

Caleb

I know Nicole is nervous about meeting my parents. Trust me,
I'm not looking forward to it either. My parents still treat me
like the little boy that used to have meltdowns daily.

I don't know how they're going to react to me dating Nicole.
I've been avoiding my parents since Aunt Judy slipped up and
told my Mama about my girlfriend. It's not like it's a difficult
feat.

My parents are always off on some vacation or socializing
with their rich friends. It's one of the reasons Cameron and I
spent so much time with Aunt Judy and Uncle Rusty when we
were younger. Mama and Daddy never had time for us, or
should I say me.

Cameron got left behind because he had a big mouth. Even
at five, he had no problem telling my parents that they had to

treat us equally or leave us both home. My brother refused to leave me in the dark like a dirty secret and he wouldn't allow me to be ignored.

I hate that my Mama wants to be involved now. I would much rather she act concerned from a distance. I have no desire to be at this party, but I have no choice. She'll make a bigger deal if I don't show up.

I think Nicole would've been hurt if I didn't invite her. All she's talked about for weeks was spending my birthday with me. I wasn't going to lie to her and not tell her my plans.

Honestly, I think my Mama is doing this on purpose. Throwing a party with too many people, at the same time as when I bring Nicole home for the first time. It was just supposed to be a small dinner before I confirmed Nicole would be coming.

My Mama does shit to make everyone uncomfortable. Cameron has been telling her since we were little that I'm autistic, not stupid. Yet, Mama does stuff all the time that would make you think otherwise. Aunt Judy swears, Mama is a trigger for me all by herself.

I won't fall for that trap tonight. I won't let this feeling I have be stolen. I feel like a man, a man with something to live for, someone to love. Having Nicole's body at my fingertips did that for me.

She trusted me with something so precious and I destroyed it—in a good way. I haven't been able to stop smiling since I woke up this morning, with Nicole tucked in my arms and her ass tucked into my groin.

All I want is to go home for a repeat. It's all I've been thinking about. Actually, a repeat and continuation. Although,

I'm not sure if Nicole is ready for that. She wants to wait for our relationship to grow.

I get that, but it doesn't stop me from wanting her. Now that I've had a taste, I want her so much more. I was hoping for more last night, but I think Cameron more than killed the mood and any chance I may have had.

I'd rather eat pussy all night than be here, truthfully. I wish the car ride could have taken another hour or two. I'm not ready to get out of this car. Well, maybe that's not the truth.

Cameron and Kay have something going on. They have for a few weeks now. I want away from the tension rolling off of them. A blind man could see they're about to blow soon.

I look at Nicole and squeeze her hand that's been resting in mine, on my thigh. I don't ever want to know what it's like to be mad at her or to have her mad at me. I like the way we are. I can handle the way we are. Cameron and Kay's shit would fuck me up.

"Let's get this circus over with," Cameron grumbles.

I sigh, thinking the same thing. I give Nicole's fingers one more gentle squeeze before opening my door and getting out. I hold out my hand to help Nicole out as well.

She looks up at me with a smile, but it's not one of her usual smiles. Something is different about it, and I'm not sure I like it. I pull her close and peck her on the lips.

I just need to be in contact with her, so I wrap her hand in mine and keep her close. I can feel her looking up at me. When she tugs on my fingers, I look down.

"We're a team, right? We can do anything together," Nicole whispers, again she takes another part of my heart for her own.

I can feel my life changing. It scares the shit out of me. I'm used to my routines, but since meeting Nicole, I've had to adjust more and more. Most of the adjustments I've surprisingly welcomed and handled.

Things like accepting her touch, rearranging my schedule to see her in between classes and after practice. Or changing my bedtime ritual, because she's been sleeping over. Things that a normal person takes for granted in a relationship has taken me time to process and get used to.

However, I'm no fool. I know there is going to be a time when it's not going to be easy. So, hearing her commit to this. Knowing she's not going to run on me, I know I'm in love with her. No one has to explain that to me.

"Yeah, we're a team," I say and wrap my arm around her waist. "I promise, Nicole. I'll do everything I can to make this work."

"I know, Caleb," Nicole smiles, then she frowns. "Is this going to be that bad?"

"I don't know. I've never had a girlfriend," I sigh.

Nicole nods. "Okay, we got this, babe. Me and you."

I smile down at her, but that smile fades as we reach the front door and it swings open. My Mama is standing there with a smile on her face. Well, until her eyes swing over to Nicole.

~B~

Nicole

This is not going to be fun at all. I can see it in the tension in Cameron's body. He's been tense all morning, since I walked in on him and Kay arguing in the living room, while Caleb was in the shower.

Those two seriously argue all the time. I like Kay, but I'm not so sure they're right for each other. Hey, none of that is my business, though.

However, there is one thing I notice the moment the pretty, tall, thin, blonde older woman, answers the door. Cameron goes from tense to damn near rigid. My eyes go back to the woman. The sugary sweet smile she had on her lips when she opened the door is lost the moment her eyes land on me. My stomach drops.

Instinctively, I move into Caleb's side. He squeezes my waist and pulls me in close, almost as if it were a reflex. I knew I had a bad feeling about this.

I knew something was wrong when we pulled up and Caleb started to blink rapidly. I didn't want to point it out to him. Besides, once he's stepped out of the car and wrapped my hand in his, he seemed to calm a bit.

I know I just promised him we're a team, but I'm ready to turn tail and run already. I take a fortifying breath, as I look up at Caleb. His face is expressionless, but as he flexes his fingers almost rhythmically on my waist I know he's not so calm inside. *I can do this. I have to do this for him.*

I want to be in this relationship. I chose it. I don't intend to run now. Caleb means too much to me.

I pull my shoulders back and place a smile on my face. I'm determined that this is going to be a great night for Caleb. I will handle whatever is thrown our way.

"Oh," the woman standing before us says. She runs her eyes over me, her gaze settling on how tightly Caleb is holding me for a moment too long.

As if she didn't just look me up and down, she turns to Cameron and holds her arms out. "My babies are full grown men now. Come give me a hug, honey," she purrs at him.

"Hey Mama," Cameron mutters as he walks into her embrace while allowing her to fuss over him. She kisses his cheek and brushes his hair back from his forehead.

I take the time to take her in. Their mom is pretty in her own right. However, I think she has played a bit with what she was naturally given. Although, it's not too overly done as I have seen many times.

Her eyes are blue, not blue-grey, but she has the same sandy blonde hair as the guys. I can see some of Caleb and Cameron in her face. She certainly is tall, which I noticed runs in the family.

Aunt Judy is her sister, from what I'm told. Aunt Judy and Dakota are tall and graceful. I always feel so small around all of them. I feel even smaller when Caleb's mother swings her gaze back in our direction.

She looks at Caleb longingly for a moment. Her eyes then go to my hand on his chest, before landing on his arm wound tightly around me again. I shift under her gaze removing my hand from Caleb's chest. I hadn't consciously noticed that it was there.

Something crosses over her face, but the shutters slam shut on her expression. However, they didn't shut fast enough. Her eyes read of longing and hurt. Before I can process the emotions I've read, she turns that sweet smile back on and addresses me.

"You must be Natasha. I've heard so much about you."

"It's Nicole," Caleb and Cameron grunt in unison.

"Oh, I'm sorry," she waves them off. "Well, aren't you the cutest little thing. I'm Caleb's Mama."

"Hello, it's so nice to meet you, Mrs. Perry," I say as brightly as I can.

"Oh, none of that. You can call me Jemma," she says, with a little too much cheer. She turns her attention to Kay and gives her a real smile. "Hello, Kay, you're looking as lovely as ever."

"Hi, Jemma," Kay smiles. "Thank you. You look great as well. That blue looks so nice on you."

"Why, thank you, Sweetheart. Y'all come on in here. Everyone's waiting to see y'all. They can't stop talking about my superstar boys."

I see Cameron rolling his eyes out the corner of my eye. Caleb blows out a breath and starts forward into the house. I groan inwardly, this is going to be a long night.

We walk into a large living area, that's filled with people. They're all laughing at whatever the tall blonde man just finished saying. His back is to us as we enter.

"Happy birthday," Aunt Judy and Dakota sing, drawing all attention in the room to us.

I gasp as the man that could never deny being Caleb and Cameron's dad, turns to face us. He's movie star gorgeous, just like his sons. He has to be six-three. His hair is golden blonde and his eyes are the same blue-grey as Caleb and Cameron.

Wow, for an old man he has kept himself well. His lips lift into a smile, when he settles his eyes on Caleb's hold on me. In that very moment, he looks just like his sons. I can totally see what the guys will look like when they get older.

Their dad looks like he works out as much as they do. His muscles are bulging in his pink polo shirt and straining against the soft fabric of his grey slacks. However, what makes me relax for the first time since we pulled up is the warmth in his eyes and his smile.

"Nicole," he booms. "Well, I heard you were a pretty little thing. I think they were being modest. My boy has good taste. Come over here and give me a hug, darlin'."

His voice fills the room and I can tell he is larger than life. I can't help my answering smile. I look up at Caleb, he smiles back at me and nods.

"I'll give her back, Cal," Mr. Perry chuckles. "He's holding onto you like you might run, sugar. What have you done to my boy."

With that Mr. Perry crosses the room and pulls me into a bear hug as Caleb releases me. I'm a little thrown off at first, Mr. Perry's greeting is so much warmer than his wife's. I wasn't expecting that. I finally return the hug after I snap out of it.

"Thank you, darlin'," he gives a choked whisper. "He's a good boy. I hope you take care of that big heart of his."

The last part of his words holds a small hint of warning. Although, when he pulls away, I can still see the warmth. I watch his eyes turn to Caleb, with the same longing in them that Mrs. Perry had.

My heart squeezes as I place the look. Caleb can't take their touch. Yet, here I stand and Caleb's arm is right back around me. I've placed my hand on his broad chest again, without realizing it.

Being at Caleb's side. Touching him in small gestures has all become so normal for me. I don't think twice about it. I have forgotten about his aversion to anyone else placing their hands on him.

My heart aches for his parents. To raise a child that doesn't want or can't stand a simple hug from you. In his usual role, Cameron steps forward into a bear hug with his dad. He holds on a little longer and I know it's because he is giving his dad a hug for both him and Caleb.

"You boys make me proud. Beautiful young girls on your arms. You're having the season of your lives, this year. I'm sorry I haven't been to a game yet," Mr. Perry frowns. "I told your Mama this morning that I'm staying put for the rest of the season. She plans one more trip, she'll be making it alone."

Mr. Perry laughs his words off and pats Cameron on the shoulder. Only, I can see in his eyes and hear in his words, he means what he has said. It's then that Mrs. Perry moves forward.

"Dinner will be served in fifteen. Boys, you should greet your guests," she says, as she gives her husband a disapproving look.

"They'll have plenty of time to greet everyone," Mr. Perry says. "Let the men breathe. They just walked in. Cal, take your girlfriend on the tour. Take your time, son."

I like Mr. Perry. I can feel Caleb vibrating with energy at my side. His father seems to know he needs a moment to readjust, before he's thrown into this little crowd.

Honestly, I feel like I need to take a moment myself. I think I have whiplash from the polar opposites the Perry's seem to be. Cameron and Kay follow me and Caleb as we turn and head out of the room.

It takes us about twenty minutes to walk through the massive house. When we arrive in the dining room, everyone's just sitting at the table. Caleb and Cameron take a moment to circle the table and greet their guests.

Cameron is a master at this. He uses me and his own body as a buffer between Caleb and the others. Introducing me as Caleb's girlfriend, and orchestrating just how the interaction plays out without anyone being the wiser. If I weren't observing so closely, I probably wouldn't have noticed.

Once we're all seated for dinner, Jemma talks lovingly of her superstar boys throughout the meal. No one else stands much of a chance to get a word in. At some point, I realize that's Jemma's intention.

Whenever someone does try to get a word in or direct a question toward Caleb, she would start in, rolling right over that person's conversation. By the end of dinner, I find it to be annoying and condescending.

Caleb can hold a conversation if he wants to. She's just not even allowing him to interact. I try not to boil over in anger. I can see Uncle Rusty, Aunt Judy, as well as Mr. Perry, all wearing the same annoyed expression.

Thankfully, after dinner, everyone spills out into the large backyard. Caleb finds a seat in front of the fire pit and pulls me into his lap. To everyone else, he might seem like he's aloof.

I know better. Something is bothering him. He's brooding more than anything right now.

"What's wrong?" I whisper into his ear, for only him to hear.

He shakes his head and looks around us. We're sitting far enough from others not to be heard. Cameron is nursing a beer in a seat across from us. Kay is with Dakota, talking to Uncle Rusty over by the pool.

Mr. Perry is telling a story to some of the other guests over by the outdoor bar. I reach under Caleb's hair and start to massage his neck. I move my hand into his hair and twist a strand around my finger.

"Come on, babe. You can talk to me. It's just me and you," I whisper.

His eyes lock on my lips, with a heavy sigh he opens up. "I get tired of being treated like I'm not here. She always does this.

I'm not stupid. I can speak for myself. I let them all baby me all my life and I hate it now," Caleb frowns.

More words gush forward as his face fills with irritation. "This is why Cameron followed me to school. You do know that I have a 4.0 GPA. I don't need help in my studies. I would have figured the rest out. So what if people find out the truth. I fucking hate the way they make me feel.

"Daddy," he shakes his head. "He tries to listen to me, but Mama, she just wants what she wants. That was embarrassing for me. You're my girlfriend. I wanted to show you that I could sit at a dinner and be a fucking person.

"She just took that all from me. I just want to go home. I don't want to be here," Caleb turns back to the fire pit to watch its flames.

"Look at me," I say softly.

He turns his head to me slowly. His eyes searching my face. I reach for his cheek and press a soft kiss to his lips.

"I know that you're a person. I watch you with Cameron and Dakota all the time. You've been hanging out with my friends, as crazy as they are. You've been hanging with the guys from the team more.

"Caleb, you are so amazing in my eyes. Never doubt that. I don't think your mother does it out of malice. I think in her eyes you're her baby. She wants to protect you. Now, whether or not she's going about it the right way is another thing," I give a small giggle.

Caleb just stares at me for a beat. I see when the light goes off in his head, but I'm not sure on which part of my words it shines for. From the way, he grasps the back of my neck and kisses me deeply, I have a feeling that they all resonate with him.

"You're everything to me," Caleb breathes against my lips when he breaks the kiss.

I feel the lump form in my throat. The raw emotion in his voice pulls me under completely. If I didn't know before that I was falling in love with him, I know it now without a doubt.

I open my mouth to tell him just that, but we both turn as the air shifts. Mrs. Perry is standing right over us, with a glare directed at me. She quickly paints a smile on her lips, no doubt so that Caleb doesn't have time to read her.

"Nicole, I wanted to show you those pictures, honey," she says as sweet as pie. "Do you mind coming inside with me?"

"Um, sure," I say.

I know she has something she wants to say to me. I might as well let her get it off her chest. However, I do want to make something clear to her. I turn and touch Caleb's face and press my lips to his.

Caleb threads his fingers in my hair and takes over the kiss. He kisses me as if this will be our last. When I pull back the fear and anxiety I see in his eyes tears me apart.

I lean into his ear. "You're everything to me, too," I whisper.

~B~

Caleb

It takes everything in me not to stop Nicole from going with my Mama. I feel like I'm going to be sick. I just know this isn't going to end well.

I'll never forgive my Mama if she takes Nicole from me. I think of when I wanted to enter a National science fair in the sixth grade. I was so excited about my project. Uncle Rusty and I worked so hard on it.

Mama went to the school and made a big deal, bringing up my IEP and what my limitations were. My teacher stood up for me, but in the end the principal let my Mama have her way.

I was crushed. For the first time, the kids at school thought I was cool. My project had earned me new friends. I was so sure that I would be able to make it in the contest. She crushed that dream without even blinking.

It wasn't about me. It was more about me embarrassing her in front of everyone, if I melted down from losing or the crowds that would be at the contest. Uncle Rusty had considered all of that. We were working on me handling it, but she didn't care about that.

I won't let her take Nicole the same way. As I come out of my memories from my childhood, I stand and go to find my woman and my Mama. I just hope I find them in time.

I move into the house like a bull on a mission, ignoring the few people that try to get in my way. These people are more than used to me not answering them. Even if they weren't, I still wouldn't give a shit right now.

I stop in my tracks as I hear voices inside my father's study. Or should I say, I hear my Mama's voice. I move to the cracked doors and listen. I freeze, I'm glued to my spot, when I hear Nicole answer back.

"What exactly are you trying to say?" Nicole's voice comes out hard.

My brows furrow. I've heard Nicole sound like this once before. I go to flip through my memory for when, but my Mama's words give me pause.

"What do you want with my son?" Mama demands the way she does when she wants Daddy to give her, her way.

"I'm in a relationship with your son," Nicole replies.

"Why? I know you know about him. Judy told me you know everything."

"Why wouldn't I be? Caleb is an amazing man. I enjoy being with him," Nicole says.

My mother scoffs. "Listen here, honey. I will not let anyone make a meal ticket out of my son. He may not be able to see you for who you are, but I see you."

"Excuse me?" Nicole barks. "Please, understand this. I now, nor will I ever need Caleb to pay my way. Don't let the brown skin fool you. I come from money and have my own."

"Then I don't get it. What do you want with my son? You're a pretty girl. Boys must be lining up to court you. Why my Caleb?

"Don't you get it? This can't go anywhere. He will never be able to be a husband. He will never be a father. He can't give you a future. So why play with his heart?" My Mama asks. If I'm not mistaken, I think I hear tears in her voice.

"Why would you say such things? Caleb is not a little boy. Trust me, he is more than capable of all those things and more," Nicole bites out.

"He may have the physical capabilities, but he won't meet your expectations mentally. Do you understand that? Do you understand what Autism is?" Mama huffs.

"More than you do," Nicole growls. I see Nicole turn to leave the room, but she stops and turns back to Mama. "He's brilliant. He's kind. He's just...he's everything we'll never be. That's why...in the last two months, Caleb has inspired me to come out of my shell. That's why. Not that I need to explain us to anyone."

With that Nicole turns and storms toward me. My heart swells to the point of bursting. When she exits the room, she looks up at me.

"Let's go home," she says in a small voice.

CHAPTER THIRTEEN

Reality Bites

Nicole

I'm exhausted, but I can't sleep. When I walked out of that study to see Caleb standing there, my heart broke even more than it had listening to his mother. She's labeled Caleb without giving him a chance.

He's so much more than some assessment tests or evaluation says. He isn't defined by some title on some spectrum. If he were, he'd make it a lie. Caleb continues to smash every stereotype, every misconception about who he is or who he should be.

I think I was more pissed off at her lack of knowledge of the awesome man her son is, than the fact that she initially tried to peg me as a trifling gold digger. I can't believe the gall of her. Why wouldn't a mother want to see her son happy?

I toss and tug at the covers around me again. I hadn't planned on spending the night here tonight, but I couldn't leave Caleb after seeing his face. We didn't even bother to wait for Cameron. Caleb got us a car and we disappeared without a word.

Mr. Perry had called a few times, but Caleb wouldn't answer. Eventually, Cameron called my phone to make sure we were okay. After that Caleb spent the rest of the evening with his head in my lap and his arms wrapped around me.

When Cameron and Kay did arrive at the apartment, Caleb got up and went into his bedroom for the rest of the night. Now here we lay. Caleb is snoring, which is a first. Me, I'm trying to stop stewing so I can go to sleep.

I feel myself on my way to drifting off, when Caleb's big body starts to shake hard. I sit up quickly reaching to turn on the light. When I turn back to him I see he is convulsing.

"Oh, my God," I gasp and move quickly to my knees. "Cameron, Cameron, help!"

The walls in this apartment are so thin, I know he has to hear me. I flail my arms not sure what to do. Caleb is such a large guy. I don't want to do anything that will hurt him or will get me hurt.

Cameron bursts through the door, the look on his face says this was what he expected to find. "Fuck," he grunts and rushes in to his brother's side.

"What can I do? Should I call 911?" I say frantically.

"No, it will pass. I knew this shit was going to happen," Cameron grumbles.

"Does he have them often?"

"No, he usually only has seizures when he is under a lot of stress," Cameron purses his lips.

I bite my lip and watch as the shaking starts to subside. I feel the tears on my cheeks, but I'm too stunned to wipe them away. My fear literally grips and paralyzes me.

"Where's Nicole?" Is the first thing Caleb rumbles, groggily.

Cameron had rolled him onto his side away from me while he was still seizing. When Caleb tries to lift and turn, Cameron places a hand on his shoulder to hold him still. I reach a shaky hand out to rub over his hair.

"I'm right here, babe," I say softly.

"What's wrong?" Caleb says to Cameron, a little disoriented. "Why are you in my room?" He turns his head toward me. "Are you okay?"

"I'm fine."

"You had a seizure, man. Nicole called for me," Cameron says gently.

Caleb swallows and gives a small nod of understanding. This time when he tries to move Cameron helps him to sit up slowly. Caleb's eyes fall to his lap and he blinks a few times. It's clear he is still recovering and finding his bearings.

I swipe at my tears quickly, as I keep my eyes on him. Cameron sits on the edge of the bed next to Caleb and ducks his head to look up into his brother's face. I watch as something silently passes between them.

Cameron runs a hand through the front of Caleb's hair and kisses his baby brother's sweaty forehead. It is the sweetest thing ever. I can see how much Cameron loves his brother.

"You'll be fine. Don't let Mama get to you with her shit, man. You know we're all here for you. Nicole's right here," Cameron chuckles. "If she can spend time with Mama and not run, she's a keeper."

Caleb turns his head to me and lifts his eyes. I smile at him through the tears I'm holding back. Caleb reaches for me, pulling me to him. I straddle his lap and he wraps his arms around me, burying his cheek against my breasts.

"I've got it from here," I say softly to Cameron. "Unless we should take him to the hospital or something."

"I'm fine," Caleb murmurs, as his hold on me tightens.

Cameron stands, placing a hand on my shoulder. He gives a gentle squeeze and winks at me. I give him a wobbly smile. Truth is, I'm still shaken. That scared the shit out of me.

"He should be fine, but I'm keeping my door open in case. Just holler for me if you need me," Cameron says, as if trying to soothe a child.

I nod and he leaves the room. I run my fingers through Caleb's hair. He seems to relax after a few passes of my hand.

"If you don't think you can handle being with me, I understand," Caleb says quietly.

I reach to touch his face and lift it. I look into his eyes, but he tries to dodge mine. I follow them until he locks gazes with me.

"No one is perfect, Caleb. We all have our flaws. What's important is that we're with the one we care for, and care enough to see their flaws as perfection," I say, as my thumb caresses his bearded cheek.

"The things my Mama said. She was—," he starts, but I cut him off.

"She was wrong. Babe, you can have whatever you want in life." I shrug. "I've watched you struggle from time to time, but you push your way through. You're stubborn and determined as fuck when you want something. I don't see that ever changing."

"Baby, I want you," he breathes.

"I want you too, Caleb. If that's what has you worried, you can stop it right here," I say, then kiss his lips.

CHAPTER FOURTEEN

Playing with Fire

Nicole

"Caleb, we need to work on this calendar, will you focus please," I giggle as I try to wiggle free of his arms.

It's been a few weeks since his birthday. Things have settled and he talks to his mom a lot more on the phone now. Well, she has started to call every day. I don't let it bother me. Caleb and I are happy.

Although, I would be a lot happier if we could get this calendar done. We've brainstormed ideas a few times, but we haven't locked anything down. I know we still have time, but I want to get this right.

"I missed you so much. I've been gone for four days, don't you miss me, darlin'?" he croons in my ear.

"Babe, yes, I've missed you, but we've put this off long enough. Caleb," I squeal, swatting at his hand squeezing my ass.

"What?" he asks innocently.

"Hands," I say, pointing my finger at him.

"Could you two take that shit in his room?" Cameron grumbles, but the smile on his lips takes the sting out of his words.

"Absolutely not, nothing gets done in there. Being in there alone with him...well, you don't need to know that, but no. We're staying right here and Caleb you're going to keep your paws to yourself," I fuss with my hand on my hip to show I mean business.

"Fine," Caleb heaves, releasing me and walking over to flop onto the couch next to Cameron. "But for the record, you can't wear shit like that and not expect my hands all over you."

My mouth gapes open, as I look down at my black leggings and one of Caleb's team t-shirts. He has given me a ton of them in my size. I look back at him, wondering if he really spoke or if that had been Cameron.

In the three months that we've been dating, Cameron's words have come out of Caleb more times than I can count. The fact that Cameron is sitting there now, trying to hold onto his laughter, goes to show he knows his brother has just pulled one of his stunts. I shake my head at the two of them.

"Caleb, if I wanted to date Cameron, I would've beat Kay up and took him," I tease. "I'm with you, so I would appreciate it if my sweet boyfriend would talk like he has sense," I hiss.

"Hey, the man has a point," Cameron says, wiggling his brows.

"Really?" I say, snatching up a pillow from the armchair and throwing it at the both of them. I stomp my foot in impatience. "Seriously, Caleb, the mock up for the calendar is due in two weeks. You're the one that had me sign up for this. We have to turn something in."

Caleb stands back up. Walking over to me, he pulls me into his arms and kisses the top of my head. "Fine, I liked the idea you had of me taking pictures with other people with Autism. I think it would be cool to show people, we look just like them," Caleb shrugs.

"Wait a minute," Cameron lifts his head from his phone. "What do you mean show people *we* look just like them? You're not coming out in a school charity calendar."

"Didn't know I was gay," Caleb says with just the right amount of sarcasm. I double over in laughter. He has been nailing humor lately.

"Yeah, he is just the regular funny guy nowadays. Daddy isn't going to like this idea one bit. Think of something else," Cameron snarls.

Caleb sighs. I know he is about to relent, but I can tell he's disappointed. Caleb loves being himself with me. I have accepted him for who he is, quirks and all. The more we talk, I can tell he wishes he could be himself with others. That was one of the reasons I made the suggestion for this idea. If we could educate others, then they would be able to understand Caleb is just another person.

What would be the difference if we waited one more day?

I think to myself, seeing the disappointment in his eyes. I wrap my arms around his waist and bury my face in his chest, breathing him in. Like always he smells so good. I peek up at him through my lashes.

"Okay, Big Boy, take me to eat. I'm starving," I say to my big teddy bear of a man.

"We're stopping at your dorm for you to change," he grumbles.

"Oh God, you with the jealousy, there is nothing wrong with what I'm wearing," I fuss, stepping back from him.

Caleb can be extremely jealous, I am learning. Just last week he actually got in a guy's face for offering to pay for my coffee at the coffee shop. Caleb had been talking to a teammate that stopped him when we walked in. I'd gone ahead to place my order. So, in all fairness the guy didn't know we were together.

It used to be amusing, how protective and sometimes jealous Caleb would get. Now it is becoming a little issue. One I want to nip in the bud. He has nothing to be jealous about. I don't even notice other guys.

"Nicole," Caleb growls.

"You know what? Fine," I snap. If he wants to have this out, he'll soon learn that I will always win.

I drive back to my dorm alone, to change to go out to dinner. Dakota texted us to say she was bored. Cameron texted Kay and now we're all going to meet at the restaurant.

I'm happy to see Taylor is home. I'm going to need help with my plan. Taylor is just the one to help me.

My oldest sister, Stevie, is always telling me I would have a more interesting life if I dressed to show off my assets. Last time I was home, Stevie insisted on a shopping spree to buy me a bunch of outfits that I would never wear. Tonight, however, Caleb is going to learn a little lesson.

There was nothing wrong with my outfit earlier. This isn't the first time that Caleb has gotten in his feelings over my choice of clothing. I want to show him the difference between what I wear and what he should be giving a fuss about.

I rummage around my closet until I get my hands on the emerald green corset with black lace overlay on the torso. A wicked smile stretches across my face as the perfect skirt comes to mind. After some digging, I find a cutoff denim mini skirt.

"Hey Taylor, will you be around for a bit? I'll need a little help getting ready," I ask on my way into the bathroom.

"Sure, doll, I'll be here," Taylor looks up from her laptop and says. "You're the one with the life and the hot boyfriend, not me."

"Whatever," I laugh, as I dash into the bathroom. After a quick shower, I put on my favorite lotion and slip on a lace thong. I quickly throw some curls in my hair with the wand and then brush it out into waves.

I throw on some mascara and lip gloss. It's the most makeup I ever wear, and I don't do it often at all. Stepping out into the room, I pull on my skirt then hold up the corset so Taylor can fasten me in.

"Thanks," I murmur.

"Wow, Caleb is going to go insane," Taylor fans her face, as I bend to slip my feet in my ankle boots and zip them up. She whistles when I stand to look in the mirror turning to inspect my efforts. "You have amazing legs. You should definitely wear more skirts."

I tug at my skirt, second-guessing myself for a minute. I want to show Caleb that he's being silly, but this is so out of my comfort zone. I wrinkle my nose and bite my lip.

"Thanks, I guess running track in high school paid off," I wince at my reflection. This would never be my first choice, but for tonight it's perfect. "Now to see how Caleb feels."

"Have you seen the way he looks at you, Nicole? It's like none of the rest of us exist. I would love to have someone's singular focus like that. Scratch that, someone hot as hell, like Caleb, to make me the center of their world like that," Taylor says dreamily.

"Yeah, I love him too," I say and freeze. I turn to Taylor with my mouth flapping like a fish. I hadn't meant to say it, but it's the truth. I've fallen in love with Caleb. He's amazing, not just as a boyfriend, but as a human being. I'm amazed by him daily. "Taylor, I haven't told him yet. Please don't say anything," I beg.

"My lips are sealed, but you do know he loves you too?" Taylor asks. I bite back a smile and nod. Caleb hasn't said it, but I'm pretty sure it's true. "I won't be waiting up for you," Taylor winks.

"Oh no," I shake my finger at her, as I grab my purse and keys and start for the door. "There will be none of that."

"Whatever," Taylor calls after me.

I've been at Caleb's a lot lately, which is why I have papers piling up. I promised myself I would spend the weekend in my dorm. Besides, sleeping in Caleb's bed is becoming more and more tempting.

Since his birthday, I've gone down on him a few times and he returns the favor eagerly. I just still don't think we should move to the next step yet. I don't know why, it's just something I've been telling myself.

It's not like Caleb doesn't want to. I can see it in his eyes that he does. Even after I have drained him with a blow job, he looks like a starved man ready to pounce.

I also get the feeling that he doesn't push for more because something is holding him back as well. I haven't asked him about it because of Caleb's unfiltered honesty. I'm not sure I want to know what's going on in his head concerning our sex life.

I swear, one blow in the right direction, he'll have me on my back, screaming for more. The chemistry between us is undeniable when we are close. If I knew what Caleb was thinking it would probably match my own thoughts and I would throw caution to the wind in a heartbeat.

Honestly, I, for one, just happen to be scared out of my mind. Not just of sex, but also sex with Caleb. My first experience was so terrible; I couldn't let him finish. I, literally, politely asked him to get off of me, collected my things and left.

It was an awkward situation to begin with. Larry had been my neighbor for as long as I could remember. We were both awkward in school and happened to become friends. It was my hair brain idea to try things together.

Don't get me wrong. I had a small crush on Larry. He was only one year older than me. He was just as willing as I was. We just didn't know what we were doing, causing an epic fail.

When it was all said and done, Larry never brought it up after, and neither did I. He actually left for college and found a girlfriend there. From what mom says, his mom sings about how happy he is all the time.

What if Caleb and I are no good at it? What if it wasn't Larry, but me. I'm terrified of disappointing Caleb. I'm terrified of Caleb being Caleb and coming out with the honest truth, that I suck.

I know Caleb is no virgin, not after the way he has handled my body. Then there are the insane jokes Cameron makes in reference to Caleb's skills. Although, I can't be certain how much of Cameron's joking should be taken with a grain of salt. He's always teasing.

If the way Caleb touches me when we're fooling around is an indication of what sex will be like with him...*phew*. Once again, I think it's all me just making up excuses in my head for not having sex at all. I have to fan my face just at the thought of what a single kiss from Caleb can do.

My phone chimes, causing me to move faster to my car. I check to see it's a text from Dakota. I send her a quick reply before pulling out of the parking lot and heading for the restaurant.

The restaurant isn't far from campus and I get there in less than twenty minutes. When I walk in, I figure I'm right on time. Everyone is standing at the hostess station. Well, all except Caleb. I don't see him right away. I walk up to Dakota, and tap her on the shoulder. She turns around and her eyes bug out of her head as she takes me in from head to toe.

"You look hot," Dakota squeals.

Cameron turns around and does a double take. "Oh, fuck," Cameron groans. "He is going to lose it. Nicole, what the hell, seriously?"

"What? He has to learn somehow. I'm not going to change my clothes every time he has a tantrum," I put my hands on my hips and glare back at Cameron.

"Come on, Nicole, I get it, but that," he points at me and circles his finger, as if trying to fit my entire outfit into his point. "He's not going to hold it together with you looking like that. You have to be kidding me. I'd fucking lose my shit if you were my girl."

I look at Kay in her tight tank top, tight jeans, and heels. I look back at Cameron and give him a pointed glare. He looks back at Kay and rolls his eyes.

"Trust me, we had words," Cameron purses his lips. He shakes his head and sighs before muttering. "You just love pushing him."

"No, Cameron, it's the other way around," I shoot back.

"Nicole?"

I spin on my heels and I'm struck speechless. I have never seen Caleb like this. I feel my belly drop and butterflies take flight at the sight of him. I guess I wasn't the only one that decided to change.

He isn't wearing his baseball cap, as he does a lot when we go out. His hair is falling into his forehead and eyes, making him look hot as sin. Caleb has on a blue button down dress shirt with the top three buttons open and a blazer. His thigh hugging jeans are belted with a huge Texas style belt buckle.

While my eyes are eating him up, he moves closer to me, placing a hand on my waist. He tugs me forward, eyes searching my face. I can't get my brain to catch up.

I'm supposed to have a point to prove here, right?

"We need to go home," Caleb says, his jaw clenched.

"Really, Caleb? You're being ridiculous. I'm not going home because you have this insane idea about what I have on. Nope, not happening, you will get over this jealousy thing, tonight," I growl at him.

He tugs me closer and bends to my ear. "This has nothing to do with me being jealous," he breathes, holding me close so that I feel his erection digging into my belly.

I look up at him through my lashes and my mouth forms an *O,* but no words come out. Caleb's eyes fall to my lips, then down to my cleavage. I watch as he sucks his lip into his mouth. I lick my own lips in response and he groans.

"You have no idea how beautiful you are, do you?" he asks as he squints and purses his lips. I want to kick myself, Cameron was right this wasn't the best idea.

I lift on my toes and kiss him softly on the lips. "Are you okay?" I whisper.

"I am now," he nuzzles into my neck.

Taking a step back and releasing me, he shrugs out of his jacket and motions for me to turn around. I frown at him and lift my brow. "I won't be able to concentrate on anything else if you are sitting next to me like that. *Please*," Caleb asks sincerely.

"Okay, since you asked nicely," I oblige him, turning so he can put the jacket over my shoulders.

Caleb slips the jacket on me then wraps his arms around my waist, pulling me into him. Brushing my bob from my neck, he places a trail of soft kisses against my skin. I squirm in his hold and cover his hands with mine.

"We're going to have a conversation about this," he murmurs in my ear. I should've known this wasn't over. "You're just too beautiful to fight with right now."

I snort, but don't get to respond as we're led to our table. We're seated and everyone falls into conversation. Our waiter comes soon after.

I'm surprised when Caleb orders for us both. He's a creature of habit, despite Dakota and Cameron trying to prevent him from getting into rituals. So, I'm not surprised that he has picked up on my habit of ordering the same three things, no matter where we go.

Once our food arrives, Dakota goes into a story about her mom and dad, that's hilarious. I love spending time with these guys. It's as if they complete my relationship with Caleb in some strange way. I feel Caleb's eyes on me and I turn to look up at him.

"What?" I smile up at him.

"You're beautiful and you're mine," he says, always speaking his thoughts out loud. Never a filter. I blush and smile wider at him.

"You know, I could say the same thing," I tease.

He shakes his head. Under the table, he reaches for my knee and squeezes it. His hand slowly makes its way up to my thigh and he keeps it there as he goes back to eating.

Needless to say, I can't focus on anything being said at the table, or the plate of food in front of me. I, somehow, manage to get through my fries and wash them down with some raspberry lemonade. Caleb is staring at me again, but I'm trying to concentrate on Kay, as she shares about her crazy coworkers.

"Hey guys, Thomas just text me," Cameron says. "He's at a bar not far from here. You guys want to go?" We all look at Caleb to see if he is up for it. "He said it's not loud, an old jukebox and a few pool tables."

Caleb shrugs. "Sure."

I'm in such awe of Caleb. It's clear that he's never very comfortable when we go out to bars and parties, but he does it for his family and friends. He puts in such an effort to make everyone else happy.

This time he catches me watching him. "What?" he asks.

"I love you," I blurt out, without thinking.

He doesn't say anything, and the table has gone completely silent. I drop my eyes to my lap. That was so stupid of me. Why would I say something like that now, not giving him time to process his feelings or mine? I wish I could crawl under the table and disappear.

My cheeks warm. Caleb places his fingers under my chin and lifts my head until my eyes are level with his. There's a huge smile on his lips.

"I love you like crazy, Nicole. You have no idea how much I love you. I didn't know I could feel this way, but I do," he swallows hard. "I've known how I felt for a long time, but it has been hard not knowing if you feel the same way. Darlin', you just put my mind and heart at ease."

Caleb's other hand moves from my thigh to the back of my neck, as he kisses me like his life depends on it. Cameron clears his throat, causing Caleb to release me. Dakota and Kay are giggling, with tears in their eyes. Cameron has a huge grin on his face.

"I've been telling you, man," Cameron says, reaching across the table to slap Caleb on his back. "She's been in love with you for a while now."

"Really, babe, you were stressing over this?" I ask in shock. "You should have talked to me."

"And say what?" Caleb murmurs.

I wrap my arms around his neck and lean into him. "You could've told me that you loved me and wanted to know if I felt the same way," I kiss him on his scruffy cheek. "Promise, we'll talk next time, okay?"

"Yeah, I promise," Caleb agrees and kisses my forehead.

We settle the bill for dinner and start out for the bar. I shrug off Caleb's jacket, when we get outside. He glares at me, but I don't back down. He takes the jacket, tossing it over his arm and wraps his other arm around me, tucking me into his side. I look up at him and smile. Caleb bends to kiss the top of my head.

We walk into the bar and I notice a few familiar faces. Some of them are Cameron and Caleb's teammates and girls from campus that have been glaring daggers at me for the last three months.

I'm used to it now. We see Thomas and Hamilton sitting at a table together, Hamilton with a girl sitting in his lap. There's nothing new there.

Caleb and I are bringing up the rear as Caleb keeps a tight hold on me. It has been so long since Dakota or Cameron have had to run interference, they don't notice the blonde that heads straight for Caleb. She places her hand on his arm and he flinches away, side stepping her.

It happens so fast Caleb knocks into me, sending me stumbling a bit. The girl totally ignores the move and goes to put her hand on his chest. I can feel my face heat with anger.

"Hasn't anyone ever told you not to touch things that don't belong to you?" I growl, as I swat her hand away and step in front of Caleb, crossing my arms over my chest.

"Oh, please, Caleb could do so much better. When you're ready to stop slumming, I'll be more than ready to help you upgrade," she purrs toward Caleb.

"You must have already had way too much to drink. That's the only way you can possibly think, by looking in any mirror, that you are an upgrade from me," I snap back.

"Whatever," the slut snarls. "I'll just catch you on the road as usual." With a nasty grin on her overly glossed, red lips, she turns to go back the way she came.

I spin on Caleb and glare at him. "What's that supposed to mean?" I ask him, keeping my eyes on his face.

He doesn't say a word, as he reaches for the back of his neck and starts to rub it. He won't look me in the eyes and now my heart is pounding. Caleb looks over my head at Cameron.

"Oh, no, he's not going to answer this one for you. I asked you. What the hell, Caleb?" I hiss at him.

Cameron steps to my side and wraps an arm around my shoulders. "It's not what you think and you are making a scene. Just calm down," Cameron says in my ear. I look up and glare at him before shrugging his arm off me.

"Keep him away from me," I say and walk over to the table to sit between Thomas and Hamilton.

I give a hug to Thomas and then act as if no one else exists. I'm beyond pissed off now. I've heard so many stories about the baseball team when they're on the road. I never thought I had to worry about that with Caleb.

How could I be so stupid? He's a man and he's not getting it from me. The fact that he didn't just deny any of what that slut said, has me burning with embarrassment and hurt.

Everyone else takes a seat at the table, but I refuse to look at Caleb. He doesn't lie, so the fact that he chooses to say nothing says a million words. I can feel my heart crumbling in my chest.

The next half hour passes with me avoiding and ignoring Caleb. Thomas and Cameron make sure that my cup is never free of beer; which I figure they're doing to get me to relax. I know eventually someone's going to try to get me to talk to Caleb.

Good luck with that.

Too much beer has me needing a trip to the little girl's room. I ask Dakota to come with me. Kay has disappeared to talk to some of her friends that came in a while ago. Cameron and

Hamilton have just set up a pool table. Caleb is still at the table, brooding, while his eyes remain on me.

I go into the bathroom, finish my business, and wash my hands, before Dakota finishes up. I'm finger combing my hair, when the blonde from earlier pushes her way into the bathroom with two friends. A redhead and a short bleach blonde. They stop in front of me, scowling at me.

"Hey, you know Caleb is just going to stew until you talk to him," Dakota says, as she pushes out of the stall. When she sees the girls, she frowns and moves to the sink to wash her hands.

"Can I help you?" I say to the little posse.

"I just want to tell you to your face," the blonde sneers. "You think you're something special because Caleb flaunts you around campus, but when he's on the road, you're the furthest thing from his mind."

"Shut the hell up, Leslie," Dakota barks. I look at Dakota shocked and hurt that she knows this girl's name.

I get an uneasy feeling in my stomach. I should just walk out of this bathroom, but my curiosity won't let me. I need to know what's going on.

"She should know. When Caleb needs a release, it's me he comes to. I know very well what it feels like to have his big cock shoved inside me. I know exactly how he likes it and what he needs," Leslie says, with a sneer on her lips. "Just remember, the next time he's on the road, I'll be right there with him."

I can feel my heart break with each word she says. I refuse to let her see me fall apart or give her one glimpse of my tears. I hear Dakota telling her off, as I push past Leslie and her friends, but I don't register the words. I just want to make it to my purse and get the hell out of here.

I never in a million years would've thought Caleb would hurt me like this. The man I just said I love you to, is the same man that is now ripping my heart out. I make it out of the bathroom and out into the bar area.

I have the table in sight. Just a few more steps and I can be out of here, but a guy that may have had just a little too much to drink stumbles in front of me. I go to step around him, but he touches my arm to stop me.

"Hey, beautiful," he slurs. "Want to dance?"

I look at the guy, then past him at the table where my purse and a pissed looking Caleb are. Against the voice in my head, telling me to get the heck out of here, I nod. Drunk Guy, places his hand on the small of my back and leads me to the makeshift dance floor. I don't even bother to ask his name or to look him in the face to take in what he looks like.

I just want Caleb to hurt as much as I hurt. I can feel his eyes on me. I don't have to look at him to know that he's pissed off. Caleb hates for any guy that's not him to put their hands on me. It took him a while to be okay with Cameron and Thomas giving me friendly hugs.

I regret my decision right away. Drunk Guy becomes grabby hands. I just want to get his hands off me and to go home. As I push at drunk guy's chest, my feet leave the floor and I feel a familiar, rock solid chest against my back.

"Keep your fucking hands off my girl," Caleb growls.

"She didn't say she had a boyfriend," Drunk Guy slurs.

"Because she's pissed at me right now, for something I didn't fucking do, and she wants to get back at me," Caleb says in explanation. Leave it to Caleb to tell it. "But she's putting your life in danger. Keep your hands off my girl."

I wiggle free and step out of Caleb's hold. "Stay away from me, Caleb. Better yet, why wait until an away game? Why don't you go fuck that slut now?" I toss at him.

"Wait, Caleb Perry, right?" Drunk Guy snorts. "Dude, I didn't know you had a girlfriend. Word is, you plow through more pussy than a porn star." I think I'm going to be sick. Suddenly, Cameron's jokes aren't just teasing anymore. I can't even look at Caleb. "Well, you mind if I get a piece of this one, if you made her your girlfriend, she must be a fantastic lay."

I hear the growl that comes from deep in Caleb's chest before his fist flies at the guy's face. I don't stay to see what happens. I run for my purse and then I fly out of the bar as fast as my heels will take me. Tears stream down my face and I can barely see.

I head the two blocks back toward the restaurant where my car is parked. I have no idea what I'll do when I get there since I have been drinking. I just need away from that bar. I only make it a block and a half before I hear heavy footfalls and my name being bellowed.

"Nicole," Caleb calls after me. "Nicole!"

I know I can't out run him in these shoes, but I try anyhow. One minute I'm running, the next I'm airborne and landing across his shoulder with an, *"oomph."*

"Put me down, Caleb," I scream as I beat my hands against his back.

"No, we need to talk," Caleb demands.

"I don't want to talk to you. Put me down," I grab a hold of the back of his blazer.

"Dakota take her keys," Caleb orders. I look up to see Dakota following us. I glare at her, daring her to come near me. "Keys, Dakota," Caleb snaps.

Dakota looks stunned at his command and rushes forward to pry the keys from between my fingers that are clutched around a fist full of Caleb's jacket. We get to my car and Caleb folds his large body into my back seat, taking me with him.

"Where are you taking me?" I yell at him.

"Home," he says simply.

"Good, I want as far away from you as possible," I say to the window.

"I'm taking you home to my apartment," he clarifies.

"Oh, no, you're not. Dakota take me to my dorm," I demand, as Dakota starts the car and pulls out.

I soon find out that blood is thicker than water, as Dakota ignores my request. She pulls up to Caleb and Cameron's apartment and Caleb gets out of the car. When I refuse to get out, he reaches in and pulls me out kicking and screaming. I'm over his shoulder again effortlessly.

"Put me down, Caleb, now," I scream, as I kick my feet and punch at his back.

His hand comes down on my backside and I yelp as tears well in my eyes. "Stop it, before I drop you. We're going to talk, Nicole," Caleb says firmly.

I look up teary eyed at Dakota. She's walking behind us with a mixture of sadness and shock on her face. I sniffle, but don't struggle any longer. Falling from over six feet up doesn't sound appealing. I'm beyond pissed now and my butt is stinging from that slap.

Dakota scoots around us to open the apartment door and Caleb marches inside with me. He heads straight for his bedroom. I start to protest once again, wiggling and pounding on his back.

"I'm not going in there. Put me down, Caleb," I cry out.

He continues to ignore me, moving into the room and kicking the door shut. Moving to the bed, he tosses me in the middle and climbs over me. I go to turn away, but he moves faster, fastening his lips to mine. I don't return the kiss and he pulls away to look at me.

My eyes grow wide as I look at his face. It's the first time I notice his lip is busted in the corner and there's a bruise forming beneath his beard. I gasp and cradle his face in my hand.

"Are you okay?" I ask. I'm so mad at him, but I never want to see him physically hurt.

"No, I'm not okay, Nicole. I love you. I've never cheated on you," he says, as his eyes plead with me to believe him. "I didn't answer you when you asked about Leslie because we've never talked about that part of my life."

"What part of your life?" I snap becoming pissed off again.

"My sex life. Leslie…we've hooked up before. I've fucked a lot of girls. Cameron makes it easier for me. He explains the rules to them. No touching, no kissing, and I'm not interested in talking after. Leslie…well, she was one that was okay with the rules and didn't ask questions. She didn't mind that I would only take her from behind, or that I pretty much walked out right after. So, she was a repeat.

"Things got messy after a while. She would show up at all my away games and she started spreading word around campus that we were together. Cameron and I agreed I should end it with her.

"Baby, that was freshman year. I haven't slept with her since. I started to feel like a dirt bag, so when Cameron would ask if I wanted to hook up, I would tell him no," Caleb bites his lip, as he watches me.

"Why couldn't you just tell me that? I was so humiliated in that bar. She made it seem like you two are still hooking up," I sob.

"Please Nicole, stop crying," his long fingers wipe my tears away. "I didn't want you to know about any of that. With those girls, it was just sex," he replies. "I hated the way Dakota would look at me when she knew I hooked up with some random girl. I never wanted to see that look from you."

I look down at his chest, as he hovers over me still. He tips my head back and kisses the corners of my mouth, hesitantly he kisses my lips. When I wrap my arms around his neck, he deepens the kiss, pushing me onto my back to lie beneath him.

He wedges himself between my legs and his erection rubs against my heat, shooting sparks through me. He continues to sip from my lips, as I grind my hips into him. My thong is useless at this point. My toes are curled in my boots and I can feel him growing harder.

He groans and breaks the kiss. "I want to fuck you," he groans. My eyes widen and he pulls back further. "Wait…that came out wrong, I want to make love to you, Nicole. I want to touch you and I want you to touch me. I need you, Baby."

"I want you too," I pant.

The raw need in his eyes burns through my anger and my restraint. This is probably a bad idea, but I can't hold back anymore. I need him too.

I see the moment my words sink in and he's back on me, kissing me with passion and hunger. His hands move to the button of my skirt, unfastening and then unzipping it. Soon my skirt is on the floor and I am lying there in just my corset, thong, and ankle boots.

Caleb looks down at me like he's not sure where he wants to go next. With a nod to himself, he moves down the bed and unzips my left boot pulling it from my foot. He kisses my toes, the arch of my foot, and then my ankle.

His lips and tongue make the trip up my leg, until he reaches the top of my inner thigh. Then he stops to repeat the same actions with my right leg. I moan and feel my juices increase as the sight turns me on more.

This time when he reaches my inner thigh, he presses a small kiss to my mound. He travels back up my body, placing a kiss on my lips. Parting my lips with his tongue, he sucks my tongue into his mouth. I groan and follow him as he starts to pull away.

I lift up on my elbows as he breaks the kiss and starts to kiss his way down my neck to my collarbone. He looks up at me as his lips meet the tops of my breasts, kissing one then the other.

Caleb follows each kiss with his tongue peeking out for a taste. His hands glide up my torso and palm my breasts through the fabric of the corset. I'm so turned on and wet, I feel dizzy. Suddenly, he pulls away again, in an instant, he flips me over onto my stomach.

I start to panic as I remember what he just said about only taking girls from behind and not allowing them to touch him. The thought fizzles away as his tongue darts out to lick my bare shoulder. He brushes my hair back off my face and kisses my temple. Gentle kisses trail down my face to my back and I moan.

Caleb is so smooth in his touch; I don't notice that with each kiss, he has gently unhooked my corset. It isn't until the fabric falls to the bed, allowing him to pull it from under me and push it off the edge of the bed, that I realize how swift he has been. Flipping me onto my back once again, as I let out a startled yelp, Caleb stares down at me heatedly.

"You are so beautiful, Nicole. I love you," he whispers.

I reach for him, but he stops me, shaking his head and steps off of the bed. He heads over to the bedside table and turns on some music. I am amused as JT's, *Until the End of Time*, comes through the speakers.

However, as I think of the thin walls, I understand why he does it. I don't know if Dakota is still here and I'm sure Cameron will be home to check on him soon. The fact that it is romantic is just a heartwarming plus.

Caleb starts to remove his own clothes and I marvel at the perfection beneath. My mouth waters over every defined and cut muscle covered with tanned, smooth skin. The light blonde sprinkle of hair on his chest tapers down his stomach neatly, pointing to one massive erection. I can't pull my eyes away from his gifted length.

I don't know why, but it looks so much bigger in this moment. My pussy may be wet at the sight, but my mind is screaming for me to run. He reaches in his away bag and pulls out a foil packet.

Instantly, I bristle, torn from the moment, as that skank's words come back to me. I curl into myself, crossing my arms around my legs. Caleb's watching me so intently, he picks up on the change and his brows knit together. He looks between me and the condom.

"I've never done it without one," he says.

I shake my head. "That's not the problem," I mutter.

Caleb moves quickly to the bed, sitting back on his haunches in front of me. He frames the side of my face in his palms, searching my eyes, before he dips his head and places a soft kiss on my lips.

"What's wrong?" he whispers.

"You just pulled that condom from your away bag," I say brokenly.

"Oh, darlin', listen to me," Caleb presses his forehead to mine. "Cameron has made sure I keep them in my bag for when I used to hook up. I've never slept with anyone here, so I don't have them in my drawer. I promise I'll stock up tomorrow. Right now, the ones in my bag are all I have."

I nod my head, not having words to express how I feel about that. Honestly, I'm not even sure. I try to pull myself out of my feelings, but Caleb does it for me.

He moves his lips to my neck and places a soft open mouth kiss to my skin in just the right place. I release my legs and let them fall apart to accommodate his big body. Caleb moves to take my lips in a kiss, hooking his arm around one of my legs, he pulls me down onto my back, as he kisses me deeply.

I moan into his mouth, as his rough hand glides up my thigh. The fire is back with a vengeance. His touch feels like it's everywhere, but it's just his slow caress up to my breast. He covers and squeezes my mound in his palm.

"Are you okay?" he breathes against my lips. "Are we okay?"

"Yes," I whimper.

"Do you still want to do this?"

"Yes, Caleb, please," I almost plea, as he pinches and rolls my nipple between his fingertips.

I think he decides to hurry up before I change my mind. Lifting the condom to his lips. He tears into it, rolling it on smoothly, as I scoot down a little lower.

Caleb loops his fingers into the waistband of my panties and pulls them down my legs, tossing them over his shoulder. Placing a heavy hand on my waist, he lines our bodies up, taking my lips once again.

I kiss him back, becoming lost in the feel of him pressed against me. Caleb breaks the kiss, moving to trail wet, sucking kisses, down my neck. When he reaches my collarbone, he stays there, sucking and kissing. Pulling away, he looks down at my body.

"So, beautiful, so sexy," he murmurs, lifting a hand to palm one of my heavy, aching breasts.

He bends his head to kiss between my breasts, then licks a path to my right nipple, circling it and sucking it into his mouth, hard. With a pop, he releases it to move to the other, repeating the same licking trail and toe curling suck.

Caleb nips at that peak and starts to kiss his way down my stomach. Pausing at my belly button, his tongue dips in, once, twice, three times, causing me to pant and shiver beneath him. Using his hands to spread my legs, he dips his head between them, pausing to look up at me, as if asking permission.

I nod and seconds later, cry out from his first long stroke with his tongue. He licks through my already soaked folds, before he sucks my clit into his mouth. I buck off the bed, but he uses his large arms to pin me back down, as he feasts on me. My fingers dig into the sheets as I try to ground myself to something.

The sound of his groans, heavy breathing, and the feel of his mouth, commanding my body's attention has my head spinning. I can barely take it, reaching my hand up, I thread my fingers into his hair. One of his big hands reaches up to roll my nipple with his fingers. I arch off the bed and cry out.

He laps me up to the rhythm of the music and my hips start to gyrate. I wiggle and squirm against his face as his tongue pushes in and out of me. My eyes roll, he is so good at this.

"Caleb," I cry out, as his fingers join his tongue.

With his large fingers, the feeling is so foreign and too much all at the same time, sending me over the edge. That doesn't seem to stop him, though. As my orgasm rocks my body, Caleb sucks my juices into his mouth still groaning.

When he pulls my sensitive clit into his mouth once more, a second orgasm slams into me. My thighs are shaking. I'm in complete awe and practically in a daze.

Caleb covers me with his huge frame again. This time when he kisses me, I can taste me on him. I gasp at my own taste, my thoughts roam to what he tastes like. However, he makes it clear that I won't be tasting him now.

Caleb drags the heavy weight of his hard cock through my folds, rocking against me. I'm totally distracted from the thought of him in my mouth. I tense at the feel of him pushing the first inch into me.

I look into his face, but he's not looking at me. I'm not too hurt by that as I see the effort he's exerting to remain in control and focused. However, it's one of the first times that I've wanted that connection with him, and I'm not sure whether I should push.

As if reading my mind, he turns his eyes to me. I watch as they clear and focus on mine, while he pushes in a little further, before pulling back out. His breath fans my face and he licks his lips. I can tell he is restraining himself.

"I love you," he rasps, and thrusts into me to the hilt.

I cry out and feel the tears slip from my eyes and roll back into my hair. My tight walls push at him in resistance. He's so big.

"F-fuck, Baby," Caleb stammers pulling out and backing onto his haunches. His face looks stricken and his eyes wild with panic. He winces at the look of discomfort on my face. "Nicole, I'm sorry. I hurt you," he says in a pained whisper.

I sit up reaching for his shoulders and slip my arms around his neck. "It's fine," I assure him and kiss his lips. When he doesn't kiss me back, I gently caress his face and stare into his eyes. "I'm fine, babe, you just took me by surprise. I haven't had much experience and you're large. Come, I'll be okay."

He looks as if he might protest, until I reach between us and start to stroke him. His head falls back and his mouth drops open. I lie back again. This time when I tug at his muscled arm, he follows. My hand falls from his girth and his hand slips under my hip, as he kisses me.

He's extra gentle as he rocks into me this time. Back and forth, he moves as I struggle a bit to get used to his size. His fingers flex beneath my hip, almost like encouragement to get used to him.

"You're so tight," Caleb groans, squeezing my flesh tighter. "Open for me, Nicole."

I moan and do as he says. I relax beneath him, drawing my legs back. He starts to slide in deeper and more easily, as my sex becomes increasingly wet and stretches for him. The discomfort gives way to pure pleasure and my head falls back into the pillow.

"Caleb," I cry out in ecstasy. "Oh, yes, yes."

He growls and picks up the pace. The long, slow drags of his heavy erection, turns into deep hard strokes that come faster and faster. I'm building to a sweet release, when he begins to roll and gyrate his hips.

I can't hold back any longer. The fingers of one hand are digging into his back and the other hand is locked into his damp locks. I've never in my life felt anything like this. Caleb is amazing.

He guides my body to move with his effortlessly. I feel so small, yet, protected beneath him. I ache for more and it seems like with each stroke, Caleb is intent to give.

"I want to feel you come on me," he rasps. "Come on my cock, Nicole. Don't hold back."

My body answers his words for me. I feel my sex clench around him and my juices gush. Caleb growls and releases me, pulling out. I yelp in surprise as he flips me onto my stomach. Tugging me to my shaky hands and knees, he plunges into me again from behind.

My mind is racing. I'm not sure I want to be taken this way, knowing that this is how he has been with every girl before me. Knowing that with them, this position was to prevent a connection.

No touching, no kissing, no connection.

I thought I was different. As if he can sense my panic and discomfort, Caleb reaches beneath my jaw, cupping my face and tugging my head back. I am bent back with my breasts thrust forward, while he pounds into me from behind.

His mouth covers mine, as he holds me into place, bent over my smaller body with his bigger one. The slapping of our hips fills the room. Only covered by the soft playing music and Caleb's groans and grunts.

"I love you so much," he moans into my mouth, not breaking our kiss or stopping his thrusts.

I can feel his pelvis slapping into my ass. The power of his thrusts, the plunging of his tongue into my mouth, has me tightening again. This is insane.

Is sex like this for everyone? Why did I think this would be terrible? Wow, Larry didn't know what he was doing.

My screams of pleasure are absorbed into Caleb's mouth, as his free hand takes a firm grasp of my hip, pulling my body into his. I'm super aware of how sensitive my body is. I can feel every sensation, even all the places his beard has scratched and left his sweet burns. Our moans become a unified symphony.

The music in the background has changed a number of times by now, but I can't tell you anything about it. Other than the fact that Caleb has changed pace a few times with the changes. His hips are working my body over, like a sweet dance choreographed just for us.

I feel him swell inside me, but he pulls out again. I'm on my back, stunned, but more than welcoming his next move. He leans over me, trapping one of my peaks in his mouth.

"Yes, please," I plea, not knowing what for.

A shiver rolls through me and I arch into him. In one swift motion, he scoops my right leg up and crosses it over his chest and onto his right shoulder, while he slides into me again. This time his pace is quick and jerky.

I cling to the sheets, as his body powers into mine. We're both dripping with sweat, but the glistening of Caleb's abs is an amazing sight. My mouth waters, as I watch him enjoy my body.

"Oh, God, Caleb," I cry out.

His jaw flexes as he grunts. He kisses my ankle, then nuzzles it with his bearded cheek. The sensation shoots a sweet tingle through me.

His hand moves to the insides of my thighs squeezing my flesh. His eyes drop to where we're joined together, his rock hard shaft, disappearing inside me rapidly. A look comes over his face, so determined, so focused.

"Mine," he bellows as he throws his head back. "*Nicole.*"

My name sounds, ripped from his chest, as I feel him pulsing inside of me. I release once again to my utter surprise, as I feel him release into the barrier between us. I can still feel the heat of his cum through the condom, causing a shudder to roll through my sex.

Caleb releases my legs and crashes beside me. He tucks an arm beneath me, pulling me to him. I snuggle into his chest, running my hand across his beating heart, as we both catch our breath. Caleb's fingers run through my hair and I'm the most content I have been in...ever.

I turn my head up to look at him. His eyes are closed, but a smile is on his lips. I bite my lip as I think of how to ask him what's on my mind. His eyes open and he searches my face. A look of worry enters his eyes.

"Are you okay?" he asks. "I mean, did I hurt you? Was I too rough?"

"No, but can I ask you a question?" I say quietly.

"Yeah," he says hesitantly.

"Well, you know I think you are amazing, right?" I start, but don't wait for an answer. "It's just... that was...wow. You were incredible. I felt like you were so in tune with my body and what I needed. I guess what I'm trying to say is...um...how?" I whisper the last word feeling a little ashamed for asking him.

He just looks at me for a moment. Then, with a heavy sigh, he pushes my sweat dampened hair from my face, kissing my forehead. I watch a few emotions flicker in his eyes.

"You know that Cameron and Thomas had a lot to do with helping me?" I nod and he continues. "I guess you remember when I told you that I watched movies a lot, to learn to read people. Cameron was the one to come up with that idea.

"It worked well enough, so when we were fourteen Cameron decided to introduce me to a new type of movie. He said it was sex education," Caleb snorts. "I should've known it was something we shouldn't be doing when he made me promise not to tell anyone."

"Wait, are you telling me that you watched porn?" I giggle.

"Pretty much, a whole lot of it, too." Caleb smiles at my giggle. "All kinds, but that wasn't enough for Cameron. When we were seventeen, he thought it was time I put what I learned to the test. There was this girl we grew up with. She was a couple years older than we were.

"She had a thing for Cameron, so he talked her into giving me my first blowjob. It didn't go so well. I guess it was a good idea that Cameron wanted to be there for the whole thing. It wasn't that I didn't like it," Caleb looks over my head and blushes.

"She was hot and she knew what she was doing, it's just that she was…hands on about it. Cameron picked up on it right away. He got her to get on all fours and I lost my virginity. Cameron got that I wasn't averse to the penial to vaginal connection and stimulation, just the touching and kissing. All in all, it turned out I learned a lot from Cameron's sex education."

I burst out laughing. Caleb tightens his arm around my waist. "What?" He smiles nervously at me and smooths a hand over my hair.

I try to stifle my laughter. "Penial to vaginal connection and stimulation, that is so something Caleb. You sound like Cameron so often, I love it when the real you comes out," I giggle. "You should sound like you more often."

"Cameron and I do everything together. He knows me best. Being like him is what I know." Caleb shrugs.

"So, you like sex," I say, changing the subject. I already know Caleb has done what he needs to adapt.

"Turns out, I'm quite insatiable," Caleb says with a shrug. As if hearing his words, his penis starts to harden and poke into me.

"I guess you are," I laugh.

"Ignore that," he murmurs. "You should get some sleep."

"I love you," I whisper just before my heavy lids shut and I lose consciousness.

CHAPTER FIFTEEN

Morning After

Caleb

I wake up to a sore jaw, slightly swollen lip, and throbbing cock, but the best part of waking up is lying across my chest. I can feel Nicole's little puffs of air caressing my bare skin. I haven't opened my eyes yet, because I'm afraid if I do, this will all have been a dream.

Last night was amazing. Sex has never been that way for me. I've never imagined that it ever would be. For the first time, in forever, I felt like everything in my world was just as it should be. I didn't have to hide, I didn't have to worry, and I didn't want to come out of my own skin.

I love Nicole. Her giving herself to me...I have no words that can describe how that felt. Feeling her wrapped so tightly around me was unreal.

I never want to let her go. If I could've had my way, I would have taken her again last night. It took everything in me to fall asleep and let her rest.

Nicole stirs a little and makes the cutest purring noise I've ever heard. My cock twitches and I groan. I have to get up and out of here, before I do something I know I shouldn't.

I understand the physical body, anatomy is very clear to me. I know I'm above average in size. I put a hurting on Nicole's tight little pussy last night. She'll need time to recover from me before I should enter her again, no matter how badly I want back into her sweet cove.

She was so tight, I don't know how I lasted as long as I did. The feel of her around me was mind numbing, literally. It's like everything grew silent to the point that her body was all I heard, all I felt, and all I could see.

Fuck.

My cock jumps, as I replay last night in my head. I want her so much. I shake my head at myself. I've waited three months to have her. I can wait again.

However, I'm no saint. I gently slip from beneath her warm body and swing my legs over the edge of the bed. I run a hand through my hair and take a deep breath. I almost lost her yesterday.

I was riding a high after she told me she loves me. I hadn't seen that shit with Leslie coming. Seeing that guy put his fucking hands on Nicole had me losing my mind.

I haven't felt that out of control in years. I beat that dude's ass until his buddies tried to jump in. That was a mistake on their parts. I would have been fine on my own, but my brother and teammates were there to have my back.

Cameron was the one to bring to my attention that Nicole was gone. He was just as worried about her safety as I was. After my brother waved me off to go after my girl, I took off.

Now, as I sit here and think of the position I put him in, I feel like an asshole. I didn't even text him last night to make sure he was okay. Exasperated with myself, I lift to my feet and tug on a pair of sweat pants.

I look back at Nicole sleeping in my bed one more time, before I head out of the bedroom. I need to put some food in my belly and talk to my brother. Hopefully, that will get my mind off of wanting to fuck all day until Nicole can't walk straight for the rest of the week.

If she thought last night was something, she has no idea. I've always wanted to try the shit I've seen in movies. I've just never been interested in trying any of it with the girls I've fucked.

I plan to try as much as Nicole will allow. God, I need to refocus my thoughts. I bite my lip as images of her tight brown body float through my head.

I go to the bathroom to relieve myself and brush my teeth before heading to the kitchen. I have thoughts of a naked Nicole dancing in my head the whole time. I swear, I can smell her scent mixed in with mine.

"That fucker sucker punched you good," Cameron's voice pulls me from my mental torture when I walk out into the common area. He moves in front of me and grasps my jaw, turning my face from side to side. "Oh, well, you look better than the two you beat the fuck out of."

I nod and purse my lips. I'm not happy with myself. "Sorry I didn't stick around to finish what I started," I grumble.

Cameron squeezes my shoulder and bumps his forehead to mine. "You did what was right. We had it. You needed to make sure Nicole was safe. That's all that mattered."

"Yeah, but I still should've made sure you were all right," I reply.

Cameron snorts. "Which one of those pussies was supposed to make me not all right?"

"Thanks, Cam," I nod.

"You're my baby brother. I'm always here for you. Things work out last night?"

I blush and turn for the kitchen so Cam can't see it. "Yeah, we're fine," I say quickly.

Cameron gives a deep laugh. "You know, we should start looking for an apartment with thicker walls. From what I heard, you guys are more than all right."

I groan and lean my head against the refrigerator door. "I thought the music would cover it up," I mutter.

"Nope, not when you're giving as good as a Perry does," Cameron chuckles.

"Shut up," I breathe. I get out some eggs and bacon to start breakfast. "You want some?"

"Yup," Cameron says, rubbing his bare stomach. "Hey, I wanted to talk to you about that calendar idea."

I sigh, knowing this was coming. I wanted to go with the idea Nicole and I talked about. I also know my family will hate every minute of it.

"What about it?" I say, acting as if I'm unfazed.

"Maybe you should do it," Cameron says.

I have to turn to him to look him in the face, to see if he's teasing me as usual. His expression is straightforward. He means this. I squint and purse my lips, as I try to figure my brother out.

"Listen," he starts again. "You may not need to just come out with it, but what if you could make the statement, without making the statement?"

"What do you mean?"

"The thing is, you want to show everyone that there's nothing wrong with autism. That you guys can do whatever anyone else can, right?"

"Yeah," I nod.

"Okay, so what if for each month, you do photos of you doing something 'normal,'" Cameron says, making air quotes. "Then, you can get some of the children from the charity to pose in the same fashion. It'll be a big fuck you to people's assumptions. They won't even know they're looking at two sides of the same coin."

"I like that," Nicole's voice floats to my ears.

I turn to see her in my t-shirt, looking sexy and glowing. I feel myself hardening just from the sight of her. She's so fucking gorgeous.

"You think we can pull it off?" I ask, as I think about Cameron's suggestion.

"Yeah, I have a few ideas already. I think it's a great idea," Nicole says with a smile lighting up her face.

"Okay, let's do it," I nod.

"Awesome," Cameron says, with a smile of his own.

"You want some breakfast, darlin'?" I say to Nicole, when she pads over and steps into my arms.

"You're going to cook for me too?" she purrs. "No wonder I love you."

My heart swells in my chest. Reaching for her face I bend to sample her lips. My hand moves to her ass of its own accord.

"Get a room," Cameron chuckles from behind us.

Nicole breaks the kiss and giggles. "Where's Kay?" she asks, peeking around me to look at Cameron.

I feel the moment something shifts in my brother. I turn to face him and see his frown. He crosses his arms over his chest and leans back into his seat.

"We decided to give things a break last night," Cameron mumbles.

"Oh, wow, really?" Nicole says, then wrinkles her cute little nose.

"Yeah, Kay and I have been together since junior high school. We're starting to see that we may not want the same things. Or at least, we don't want the same things for me," Cameron blows out a breath.

"I'm sorry to hear that," Nicole says softly.

"Was it because of me and the fight I started?" I ask, narrowing my eyes at my brother.

"We were at each other's throats before that," Cam shrugs. "Don't worry about it. I think a break will be good for us. Dude, I'm starving. Can you make some breakfast already?"

I purse my lips and nod. Leaning in, I peck Nicole on the neck and tap her on the ass, before turning to start cooking. My heart leaps into my throat, when Nicole walks up behind me, wrapping her arms around my waist, and pressing her cheek to my bare back.

I'm momentarily choked up by how much love I have for her. My focus goes to her wrapped around me, instead of obsessing over whether or not I'm the cause of my brother's break up. It's then that I realize I don't want what Cameron and Kay have. I want what Nicole and I have. This is what I've been wanting all this time.

~*B*~

Nicole

"Ugh," I groan as I climb onto Caleb's bed.

I'm so full I could burst. That's what I get for trying to hang with Caleb and Cameron during breakfast. I don't know what I was thinking. I'm so full everything feels like it hurts.

Caleb flops on the bed and laughs at me.

"You full?" he chuckles. "Come here. I'll rub your tummy."

He reaches for me and places me in his lap. I sigh as I place my head on his shoulder. He snakes his arm under the hem of his t-shirt I'm wearing and places his warm palm on my stomach. Caleb kisses my temple, as he gently strokes my belly.

"I could help you with your papers. You don't have to go back to the dorm," Caleb says after a long stretch of silence.

I think I was actually drifting off to sleep. I snuggle into his arms and smile. I know just what he's thinking. I don't want to leave either. What I really want is my food to digest, so I can pounce on him.

"How about we take a nap?" I yawn. "When we get up, we can think about my papers that you keep making me neglect," I tease.

"You nap, I'll start on your papers," Caleb murmurs against my temple.

"Nope, you have your own homework."

"Which I finished on the bus, on the way back from our game," he replies.

I gasp and turn my face up to him. "You did not finish that ten-page psych paper already."

He shrugs and pecks me on the lips. "Sleep, I'll get your notes from your tablet. Let me at least start it for you. If you don't like what I write, you can fix it," his voice rumbles through my sleepy body.

"No, you hold me while I sleep, and I'll think about staying over while I write my papers," I argue sleepily.

"You're aggravating me," Caleb growls.

I burst into laughter. "Why, because I don't want you to do work I should be doing?"

"Work, I've kept you from doing," he says with a poked out lip.

I giggle and reach for his handsome face. "What you can do for me is make a list of your favorite things to do, so we can brainstorm on the photo shoots for the calendar. I can work on my papers while you and Cam are at the gym tonight," I say. "And by the way, I'm just as guilty for me not doing my homework."

"Whatever," Caleb huffs.

"I love you, Caleb. You don't have to do my homework."

"Horses."

"What?" I wrinkle my nose at him.

"I love horses. Daddy used to take me horseback riding when my Mama couldn't get me to settle. I could ride on my own, before I could toss a ball."

I can hear the fondness in his voice. His eyes have a distant look, as if in his mind, he's on a horse in this moment. I smile wide, knowing exactly what I plan to do for the photos for the calendar.

"You're just a regular cowboy aren't you?" I tease.

"Maybe," Caleb shrugs. His southern drawl heavy. "I haven't been on my granddaddy's farm since he died. When I go riding, I go to a friend's stable. I haven't gotten my hands dirty on a ranch in years."

"Seriously? I was just joking. You used to be a cowboy," I giggle.

"I used to be a little shit head, with Cameron. Running around making more work for the ranch hands and our granddaddy," Caleb says.

"You know you just get sexier by the minute," I purr.

Caleb groans, sliding his hand from rubbing my stomach, up to cover my breast. "You should sleep," he murmurs, just before kissing me.

"Mm," I hum as I break the kiss. "Sleep now, sex later, homework sometime after."

"Hurry up and sleep."

I let out a laugh as my lids droop. I'm too full and sleepy to reply. I pass out against Caleb's warmth.

CHAPTER SIXTEEN

Taking a Loss

Nicole

I've had this sick feeling in the pit of my stomach all day. Caleb's team has an away game in Arkansas today. I saw him off last night. The team will be returning this evening, right after the game.

I wanted to go, but I have exams to study for. Honestly, I should have just gone. I haven't focused on a thing in front of me for hours, this sucks.

I look at the clock, for the millionth time, as I chew on the edge of my highlighter. It's only five minutes past the last time I looked. The game should be over by now, but it will be at least another hour before Caleb and the team arrive back on campus.

I heard talk about a big party being thrown for their return. I doubt Caleb will go. Although, Cameron has been partying a lot more since he and Kay have broken up. I haven't seen or heard much from Kay in the last month.

Tournaments are coming soon, so everyone has been high strung. Caleb's team needs this win to stay in the running. If they lose, they could lose their seed.

Caleb and Cameron are under so much pressure. Drafts are right in the middle of the tournaments and Caleb has high hopes. For Cameron, it doesn't seem like such a big deal. He has fun playing. Lose or win, he'll be fine with it. If he gets drafted, it's just more good times.

For Caleb, it would crush him if his team slips from their coveted spot, because he didn't do well or because he could've done more. If he doesn't get called up, again, his dreams will be smashed. I'm so nervous for him.

I hate that he is under such pressure and I hate that I didn't go to be there for him. Caleb insisted I stay behind to study. I love him for putting me first, but I wish I would have done the same for him.

I just have this really bad feeling. I try to shake it off and pay attention to the notes in front of me. I wish Caleb were here. He has become the best study buddy, when we actually study.

Not that I'm a terrible student. My grades were stellar before dating Caleb. However, I have seen improvement since we've been dating. Caleb sees things from a different view, which often helps to get to the heart of things and makes them stick better for me.

When I finally get lost in my notes and some reading, my phone rings. My brows knit when I see that it's Cameron. The feeling in my stomach grips me. I reach for my phone and answer right away.

"Hey. Cam. Is everything okay?" I rush out.

"No, Nicky," he calls me by his nickname for me, causing my heart to pound hard in anticipation. "He's fucked up right now. You think you can meet us when we pull in. He needs you."

"Oh my God, you guys lost," I gasp.

"Yeah, his head just wasn't in it," Cameron whispers.

I don't miss the hard edge to Cam's words. Something else has happened. I know it. Now, I'm so sick that I didn't go. I swipe at the tear that falls. I should have been there for him.

"I'll be there," I say with a fierce promise in my voice.

"Thanks, Nicky." Cam sighs before hanging up.

I jump up and pull on the thin jersey hooded dress I had on earlier in the day. I pull on socks and shove my feet into a pair of Converse. I know they won't be here for a while yet, but I need to be moving. I can't sit knowing something is wrong.

~B~

Caleb

I fucked up. I never should've taken my Mama's call before the game. I thought that just maybe she was calling to wish me luck. Daddy said she wouldn't be joining him for the game. Mama took off a few weeks ago on a trip to Greece.

Mama has been pissed at Daddy for not going with her. It seems everyone but my Mama gets how important the next month of my life is to me. This is my moment of truth. I'm either going to play ball or I'm going to find something else to do with my life.

I blew that game. It was all my fault. My Mama called me not to wish me luck, but to tell me once again about the bad decisions I'm making. Mama started out pretending she was okay with me dating Nicole.

Now, lately, every time I turn around, Mama has been repeating all the shit she said to Nicole in the study that day. My head has been a fucking mess. I know what I want, but I'm no longer sure if it's what I should want.

I love Nicole. I can't see my life without her, but I know I can't be a husband to her. I know I can never give her a family. Or at least, I think I can't give her those things. I've been talking to Cameron and Daddy about it a lot in the last few weeks.

My father and I have never been so close, but I can see him trying. Something has changed and my Daddy has been a different person. I can see him treating me differently.

Daddy said if I love Nicole, I need to hold on to her. Cam says the same thing. I just don't know if they're right or if I can. Everything is about to change again. If I get called up to the majors, I'll be leaving her behind.

Nicole is a Junior. She still has a year left in school. This is it for me. I graduate at the end of the month. In the same time frame, I could be drafted.

There's no telling where I'll end up playing. This shit is going to be hard. I hate being away from Nicole for a few hours. If I get called to a team away from Texas, I'm going to come unglued.

Just let her go, Caleb.

My Mama's words have been ringing in my head since she said them this morning. I haven't been able to focus on anything but them. What if my Mama is right? What if I should let Nicole go?

"Thank God," Cameron breathes behind me as we step off the bus.

I stop blinking and squint my eyes. My heart pounds the moment I lay eyes on her. With a hood pulled over her head, her dress clinging to her full hips and Converse on her feet, she is the sexiest sight I've ever seen.

I've missed her so fucking much, and I just saw her yesterday morning. It hits me hard that I don't stand a chance in hell of walking away from her. Just seeing her helps me find my center again.

When she pushes her hood back and runs at me, I drop my bag and catch her in midair. Nicole wraps her legs around me and buries her face in my neck. I squeeze her tight, needing her embrace more than she knows.

"I'm so sorry, baby," she whispers.

"I need you," I choke.

I do. I need her bad. I need to be inside her. I need to feel her around me. When I'm inside her, I know she's mine. Nothing else matters. I need that right now.

She looks me in the eyes and nods her understanding. I start for the gym. I'm not going to make it home. The rest of the team is heading to some party on campus to drink their woos away. I know just the place where we can be alone.

My bag forgotten. It doesn't matter to me if Cameron gets it for me or not. I head into the locker room of the gym. I make it as far as my locker, before I start to devour Nicole's mouth. The way she just yields to my desires fuels me.

I deepen the kiss, begging her with my mouth to stay with me. I need her to fight for this, the way my Daddy told me I should. I'm ready to give it my all and I need her to as well.

"Caleb," she cries, as I move to suck on her neck.

I press her back against the lockers and push her dress up her thighs. Her legs are still wrapped tightly around me. When I reach her panties, I pushed them aside to tease her already wet center.

The heat coming from her pussy drives me insane. I want to feel that heat around me. I reach between us and fumble to release my cock.

"Caleb wait," Nicole pants. "Do you have a condom?"

I look into her eyes and blink my lust away. "I think I have one left over in my...*fuck*. My bag," I grumble.

Nicole bites her lip, as she looks down at my throbbing erection in my hand. She licks her lips and my cock jerks. Her eyes lift back to mine.

"You've been tested, right?" She asks, in a soft shaky voice, before biting her lip again.

I nod slowly. "Yeah, and I've never fucked anyone without protection before."

"I'm on the pill. It'll be just this once," she says quietly.

The thought of nothing between us snaps my restraint. I lift her hips to angle her over my pulsing erection. Nicole locks her fingers in my hair, as I pull her down onto me.

"Ah," we cry out in unison.

"God, baby," I groan. "You feel so fucking good."

I reach to cradle more of her weight on my forearms, bracing her thighs over my limbs. She opens to me, as I thrust up into her hot body. Nicole buries her face into my neck, calling my name over and over.

I've never felt anything this good. Her juices are soaking me, as I fuck her into the locker behind her. I'm a savage in this moment, but I can't stop myself. The thought of losing her has broken something inside me, something only she can fix.

My arms release her legs and I shift to palm her ass. Her ankles lock over my ass, as I pound out every word of doubt floating in my head. We can make this work. I can do better. We can have a life together. I won't hurt her.

"I love you," I pant, kissing the side of her head as she keeps her face in my neck. "I love you so much."

~B~

Nicole

His words have never been so desperate. I can feel it in my bones, something is wrong. This is not how Caleb makes love to me. This is something else.

All I can do is ride it out and cling to him. Don't get me wrong. He feels so amazing. Caleb knows what to do with my body and he never fails to bring me pleasure. Even now, as his hands palm my ass to knead my cheeks with each pounding thrust, he's applying just the right touch with just the right roll of his hips and force of his drives.

"I love you, too," I whimper.

"You feel so good," he groans.

"You do too. Caleb, please!"

I didn't think he could ever feel better than before, but skin to skin. This is the next level. I'm so close already. I ignore the bite of the locker digging into my back. It is actually mixing with the pleasure as just the right amount of sharp pain.

"Fuck, Caleb," I moan-sob, into his neck.

"You're mine, Nicole. I can't give you up. I can't lose you. I'll fight with everything I have for you," Caleb says.

I'm taken off guard. His southern accent has become thick, which usually happens when he's frustrated or tense. I pull my face from his neck and look him in his eyes. There is a storm brewing in them. I can see the cracks in the plate. Someone has rubbed him raw about us.

I have two bets that I know who. I've seen him change when his mother calls. His father has been stopping by the apartment to hang out with the guys more. I can see Caleb loves that, but the calls from his mother make him tense and standoffish.

I hold his face, while he continues to rock into me. My walls tighten and clinch at him. I kiss his lips. Reaching to wipe the tears that slip free from his eyes.

"And I'll fight for you, baby," I say with love. "You won't lose me, Caleb. I'm right here."

He reaches between us and strums my nub. "I need you to come with me."

I bite my lip and nod my head. When he picks up the pace, I throw my head back against the locker. I reach behind me searching for purchase to anchor me.

I loop my fingers through the padlocks to either side of me. It is all I have. I grip the locks, as I cry out in bliss.

Caleb roars out his own release as my body shakes around him. I feel him shoot his hot seed inside me, causing me to come harder. His big body shudders, as he slumps into me. Reaching for the locker behind me for support.

"Don't move," he breathes into my face as he presses his forehead to mine.

"We're not moving until you tell me what happened on that field today. I want the truth," I huff.

Caleb nods, locking his arms around me. He steps back from the lockers and sits on the bench with me still draped around him, while still inside me. I can feel the mixture of our essence sliding down my skin.

"I lost the game. My head was fucked up. I couldn't get focused. I should have done better," he starts.

"Well, where was your head?"

"On our future," he murmurs.

I wrinkle my nose. "What about our future?"

"What if I'm not what you want? What if you decide you want a family? What if me going pro changes the way you feel about me?"

"What-ifs suck. We can't live our lives by them. We could sit here all night and come up with all the what-ifs that could scare us apart, but the reality is, we love each other. If we want a family, Caleb, we'll have one," I say with conviction.

"That's just it, darlin'. I don't want a family," Caleb says, with pain in his voice.

"What?" I gasp out, feeling like someone has slapped me.

He shakes his head. "I don't want a family. I can't handle something like that. I…I don't want to put my children through what I've been through. What if I pass this down?"

"Stop it! Stop it, now," I yell. "You could handle it if you wanted to. I hate that you feel like something is so wrong with you, that you would be hurting our children if they were like you. You're brilliant, talented, and so freaking amazing. You just haven't had enough of the right people showing you that."

"I don't want a family," Caleb says firmly.

I start to feel cold inside. I wiggle to lift from his lap and let him slip from my body. The position we're in is too intimate for this conversation.

I stand and back away from him, wrapping my arms around my middle. I don't know what to say. I do want children someday, but lately I've been seeing Caleb as my future.

If he seriously doesn't want children, that could be a problem. I don't know if I can give up on the maternal instincts I have. I can't look Caleb in the eyes because I'm afraid of what he might see.

For the first time, I understand his fear. I feel the tears sting my eyes, because I don't know how to change or fix this. I want to, but I don't know how.

"You're pulling away from me," Caleb chokes out.

My gaze snaps up to meet his, at his words. My mouth falls open, but no words come out. I can't think of what to say.

I clamp my lips shut, searching his eyes with my own. The plea in his blues causes my heart to ache. It's right then that I know I'm willing to give up my dream of a family for him.

I've fallen that hard. The fear I see in his eyes floors me. I know it's not just the fear of losing me, but the fear of not being what I need. The fear of not being a good husband or father, things others learn to grow into.

I step back toward him and wrap my arms around his neck. I press my swollen lips to his. Neither of us force the kiss further.

"I want what you want. I want us to be together. I'm ready for whatever that brings," I whisper, even as my heart aches with the loss that my words bring.

CHAPTER SEVENTEEN

Charity

Nicole

Things have been so busy around here. Caleb has barely had time to spend with me. His team has been killing in the tournament. After that loss, Caleb turned into a different man.

The transformation has brought on more interest as well. It's looking very likely that Caleb will get picked up and called up to a major team right away. I'm so happy for him.

I have awesome news. I hope this is just the beginning of what's to come. I didn't know I would be so excited about this, but we worked hard on our calendar and it paid off. We could hardly keep up with the orders.

Everyone loved the photos of Caleb and the kids. Caleb riding a horse with a little boy named Jack that has autism. Caleb on the baseball field with a little girl, named Jennifer, that has Asperger's. We were able to get her in her softball uniform for the team she actually plays for.

We got Caleb and Danny, the cutest little boy ever. Caleb's dad pulled some strings and we were able to take the photos with a real NASCAR and Danny's go cart all in the photo. Month after month, Caleb is in a photo with a kid on the spectrum doing something 'Normal.'

In December, the final photo is of Caleb and Cameron, surrounded by the children. Caleb and Cameron wore t-shirts stretched across their chest that said, *What's Different?* Just like Cameron said, people didn't get the message. They only saw Caleb standing up for the kids from the charity we chose to sponsor.

I think most of the calendars sold out because Caleb was bare chest in a few photos, but I'll take it. We raised the most money. Almost five hundred thousand dollars. Mr. Perry had a lot to do with that. He bought out our first batch.

I won the trip to Paris, our charity will be getting all the money, and I get to take someone to Paris with me. I know Caleb may not be able to go…but if he can. I don't want to get my hopes up.

"What has you smiling so wide, darlin'?" Caleb asks, as he walks up and kisses the top of my head.

I just got out of class, after receiving the great news. I'm bursting at the seams to tell him about it. I know it doesn't compare to the draft tomorrow, but it means something to me.

The pictures for the calendar came out better than I expected. A few of the families involved have asked me to do some work for them. This project has totally taken me out of my comfort zone. I have Caleb to thank for that.

"Other than seeing my big strong man," I purr, "The fact that we totally crushed the calendar contest would be an awesome cause to smile."

Caleb stares at me for a moment before a huge grin takes over his face. He wraps his arms around me and lifts me from my feet. I throw my head back and laugh.

"We did it, Baby? We raised those folks some money?" Caleb asks in awe.

"Almost five hundred grand. We sure did, Sugar," I add with a sugary sweet accent.

He places his forehead to mine. "Thank you."

I grasp his ears in my hands and kiss his lips. "You don't have to thank me. We did it together. You were awesome. Those kids loved you. I love you."

"Have dinner with me?" Caleb says out of nowhere.

I wrinkle my brows in confusion. We already had plans to hang out together. I figured we'd get dinner at some point.

"O...kay," I say and give him a curious look.

"No, you don't understand," Caleb licks his full lips nervously and looks away from me. "I want to go on a date. Something special. It's been a while since we've done that. Ju...just me and you.

"I want to do something nice. Things will be changing soon. I want to spend time with just the two of us before my world gets turned upside down."

Oh, my God, this man is so adorable. I dip my head to find his eyes and smile up at him. "What should I wear and what time should I be ready?"

He blows out a relieved breath. "As long as I can see and touch your legs, you can wear whatever you want," he says with a grin. "Can you be ready in two hours?"

"Yup, already done. Now walk me to my dorm, Handsome. I have a hot date," I sing.

We start for my dorm, but I stop in my tracks. I look around for Cameron or Dakota, but they're nowhere in sight. I'm so used to one of them being close by I hadn't noticed that Caleb walked up alone.

"Where's Cameron?" I ask.

Caleb furrows his brows. "I have no idea. He's been acting strange. Kay has been over the apartment a few times the last few weeks, but something else is going on. He stormed out of practice looking like he saw a ghost."

"Oh," is all I say.

Now that I think of it, Dakota did mention Kay and Cam getting back together. I wondered fleetingly if Kay knows about all the hooking up Cam has been doing in the time they've been apart. I shrugged it off as none of my business then, just like I do now.

"So, we'll celebrate our win tonight?" Caleb says with a small smile.

"Yup, we sure will. I have so much shopping to do before Paris," I gush, dreamily.

Caleb stops on a dime. "I...I forgot about that. You're leaving?"

"Well, yeah," I say softly. "The tickets are for after the semester is over."

Caleb's face clouds over. "*Tickets*, I can't go with you, Nicole. If I get drafted tomorrow, there's no way I can go. Who's going with you?"

"I...I don't know. I would love if you could, but I know that's not going to happen," I frown. "I can take one of my sisters. Or one of the girls. They all wanted to win and go."

"No," Caleb says emphatically.

I look up at him stunned. "What do you mean, *no?*"

"I mean, what I said, Nicole. No," he says as his jaw tightens. His lips purse, he starts to squint down at me, and his jaw works under his bearded skin. His blue-grey eyes are more grey. My mouth drops open.

He's pissed off at me?

"Explain this to me," I say placing my hand on my hip. "You are telling me, I can't go to Paris, and why is this?"

"Because I won't be with you. I won't know where you are or if you're okay. You'll be too far away from me and out of my control. No," he says firmly.

"Hold on, let me clear something up. You don't control me," I hiss. "I'm grown. I have been taking care of myself for a long enough time to be able to take a trip alone or better yet, with a friend or one of my sisters."

"No!"

I suck my teeth and roll my eyes. "Whatever."

"Don't do that to me," he growls. "Don't dismiss me. You're my girlfriend. Things go my way, you'll be more. I'm not letting you go off to Paris, while I'm stuck in a contract that has me here, playing all over the country, with no guarantee that I can come find you or take care of you."

I sigh and lose some of my anger. I move to wrap my arms around his waist. I know my man, so I won't dismiss his feelings.

"Okay, Big guy," I huff. "Can we talk about this later? I'm listening to your concerns. I even understand them to an extent, but I think we should talk about it. I want to go."

A long stretch of silence passes. Caleb purses his lips. I see him getting ready to say no again, but suddenly, he smiles and nods his head.

I don't like that smile. Caleb is not as innocent as everyone thinks. I eye him warily, but he just dips to kiss my lips.

"Come on, you have a hot date," he wiggles his brows.

I can't with Caleb. He has me wrapped around his finger and he knows it. When the hell did that happen?

Whatever, I'm going to Paris.

~B~

Caleb

Nicole isn't going to Paris. I know just how to keep that from happening. I already had plans, but they'll work in my favor now. There's no way my woman is going to the other side of the world without me.

It's bad enough that I have been scared out of my mind that the teams from New York, Chicago, and Atlanta have been the ones that have started to show the most interest in me in the last month. I want to play here in Texas. Close to Nicole, while she finishes her last year of school.

After that I'll go anywhere they want me to. I've been looking at apartments with my Daddy. If I get drafted here, I want to get my own place. That way Nicole can move in with me.

I have it all figured out. I just can't get drafted to a team away from home. Since that loss that was my fault, I've been focused on nothing else but making this work.

I haven't talked to my Mama in weeks. I don't need her poison in my head. I know what I want and I'm going after it.

"You're really going through with this?" Cameron asks, from his perch on the bar stool at the kitchen island.

I look up at him. It's not disapproval in his words. I relax as I gather that much. I continue to look at him to understand what his question is asking.

Cameron sighs and nods. "I mean, you love her that much. You're going to do this for you. Not for Mama, not for Daddy, and not because I told you to. I'm proud of you and impressed."

I lick my lips and nod. "Yeah, I'm going through with it. It feels right. We won that contest, she told me today. That means she's won that trip," I purse my lips as I get angry about the thought of Nicole leaving me all over again.

I shake my head to focus. "I don't like it. Not having enough say because she's my girlfriend and not my wife," I grumble.

Cameron shakes his head and laughs. "Dude, I'm sorry to tell you, but that ain't gonna change cause you're engaged. If she wants to go, she's going to go. This is Nicole. She's shy to the world, but she knows how to put that little foot down. You're playing with fire, Cal."

"Well, I'm willing to get burned," I huff.

"It's a trip to Paris, Cal," Cameron says and lifts a brow.

"Do you not see how I get about my woman? How easy it is for me to fixate on her and nothing else. If I'm here and I need to focus on baseball, she can't be there. I'm not ready to handle something like that," I explain, looking away from Cameron.

Cam lets out a heavy breath. "Okay, yeah, I see your point. Good luck. I mean that. This is what I've always wanted for you. For you to be happy," my big brother says.

"Yeah, but are *you* happy? What changed your mind? Why are you entering the draft?" I quiz, I've been wondering this all week.

At the last minute, Cameron announced he'd be entering. I was positive he was going to walk away and do something else with his life. Honestly, I thought he was going to go work for Daddy.

However, lately, it's like Cameron has been avoiding Daddy. I don't think he knows I've noticed, but something is going on. Something big. He looks…stressed.

Cam pulls a hand down his face. "I fucked up. I can't afford to work for Daddy. He'll want me to work my way up. I'm going to need a hell of a lot of money fast," Cameron groans at the end of his words.

I look at my brother and knit my brows. "What for?" I ask with furrowed brows.

We both have trusts that we've had access to since our twenty-first birthdays. We just turned twenty-one. There's no way he could have blown through all that money. Not the way the trusts are set up.

Cameron's face becomes dark. His jaw flexes. I don't think he is going to answer me at first. When his eyes look up to lock with mine, I see so much pain.

"Kay says she's pregnant," Cameron says through his teeth.

"Wow," I breathe out.

"Oh, it gets better. She's not the only one. Ma—, my friend I've been hooking up with. We sort of hooked up the first time without protection. It was stupid, we were both hammered. I…I don't know what I was thinking.

"This breakup was supposed to allow me to see what's out there, to see if Kay was the one or if I just thought she was the one cause that's what everyone has been telling us since we were in junior high.

"Now…I know for sure there's more than Kay and I'm pretty sure she's not the one. I was supposed to be having fun, but I sort of met someone I clicked with. I…I just don't know what to do now. I just know I have two mouth's I'm going to have to feed and I'm damn good at playing ball."

"So, are you and Kay back together?"

Cameron shakes his head. "I...we were going to see if we could make things work, for the baby, you know?" Cam shrugs. "Then, I found out about the other baby this morning."

"Shit," I whisper.

"Yeah, tell me about it. Even with my trust, we're talking two babies. If I get married, the way Kay wants to, that's just more money I'll be shelling out. You know Kay. She's just like Mama," Cameron sighs.

"I'll help out," I offer.

"Nope, you're about to have a little wife of your own," Cameron smiles at me. "Speaking of which, let's get this show on the road."

I blow out a breath. I'm suddenly nervous, but I know I have to do this. Life without Nicole is not an option and the best way to deal with my Mama is to send clear statements. This is as clear as it gets.

~B~

Nicole

I stand before my closet wanting to stomp my foot. Nothing seems right. Caleb asked for my legs on display and I plan not to disappoint, but I feel like I've worn all of this stuff before.

Tonight feels special. I tap at my lips with my fingertip, my eyes roaming back over to the selection of items from my shopping spree with my sister. I sigh and give up. I don't have time to go shopping.

I need to find something and get dressed. I start to comb through the items in my ignore pile and freeze on what looks like a simple black dress. I pull it from the closet and smile, until I turn it around.

I just remembered why it was in the don't-touch pile. The back of the dress plunges to my ass. The dress itself—if I remember correctly—falls just above the knee. I place a hand on my fleshy tummy.

My bulge tends to make me a little self-conscious, especially in form fitting dresses like this one. With the plunging back, there will be no Spanx underneath this thing. I shake my head in determination when I think of how Caleb loves to kiss and press his hands to my belly and anywhere else he can get his hands on.

I dip to the bottom of my closet for the Giuseppe shoes I've been keeping there for a special occasion. I look into the two boxes and decide on the gold ones for tonight. I'll wear the blue ones tomorrow for the draft.

I smirk at the idea of the dress I've set aside for that. I went shopping for it as soon as Caleb asked me to go with him. Placing tonight's dress on the bed and my shoes beside it, I run into the bathroom to pass the flat iron over my hair.

I want to look perfect. I sweep on some lip gloss and run to slip the dress on. I'm sitting on my bed, fastening my shoes, when Taylor walks in with a long face. The smile on my lips falls right away.

"What's wrong?" I ask in concern.

"Maribel is thinking about dropping out," Taylor whispers.

"What? Why?" I gasp.

"I don't know," Taylor shrugs. "She won't say. She's been so happy lately. Now all of a sudden, she's dropping out. I just don't get it."

"Where is she?" I ask, as I stand ready to comfort my friend and find out what's going on with her.

Taylor's mouth falls open as her eyes sweep over me. "Wow," she breathes. "You look amazing."

"Thank you. Where is she?"

Taylor shakes her head. "No, you have a date. Maribel is hard headed. She's going to do whatever she wants to do. We'll give her time."

"But—," I start, but Taylor lifts her hand to stop me.

"Listen," Taylor shakes her head and rolls her lips. She sighs and her shoulders sag. "You have become one of us. I know you care and I know you want to help, but I'm telling you, I've known Maribel a lot longer than you. She's going to do whatever she wants. Right now, all we can do is wait for her to tell us what this is all about."

I eye Taylor warily. My first instinct is telling me to grab my phone and text Maribel. She can tell me to get lost herself, but as I look into Taylor's eyes, I think better of it and decide to wait it out. For now, at least.

"Okay, fine," I huff as a knock sounds on the door.

It's Caleb. I know his knock. I cross the small space for my bag, before heading to the door. I turn back to Taylor briefly.

"Call me, if you guys need me, please, Tay," I say.

"I will," Taylor gives me a small smile. "Now go."

I rush over and give her a hug, as Caleb knocks again. This time with impatience. I smirk at Taylor and roll my eyes, as I pull away. I move over to the door to open it and my mouth hits the floor, as I find Caleb standing before me with his hand raised to knock again.

He looks amazing in a light grey suit. It's paired with a pale blue dress shirt that plays off his blue-grey eyes. The top three buttons of his shirt are loose, revealing that yummy tanned skin. He's wearing one of those huge belt buckles at his waist. My eyes travel down to his feet to find expensive looking dress boots. My eyes roll back up, taking him in inch by inch.

I've never seen him with his hair like this. It's pushed back off of his face, combed into submission by some type of hair product. I've never wanted to tear his clothes off more.

Wow.

"Wow, you two are such a gorgeous couple," Taylor breathes from behind me. "Like movie star gorgeous."

I snort. "Him maybe."

"You're kidding, right?" Taylor says placing her hands on her hips. "I don't know what mirror you've been looking in, but you are absolutely stunning. Have fun, you two."

"Thanks," Caleb murmurs, as he reaches for me and pulls me into his side. He buries his face into my hair and inhales deeply. "You smell just as good as you look."

"You too, handsome," I beam up at him. "Where are we going?"

"It's a surprise," Caleb gives a small smile.

When I notice his dimples pop, I gasp. "You shaved?"

He hasn't shaved it all off, but it's now low enough to see the two dimples in his cheeks. I've always wondered if his were as deep and cute as Cameron's. I think Caleb's are cuter. I believe my panties melt when his smile widens.

"Yeah, you like?" His eyes widen. "Do you?"

"Yes, Cal. You look very, very sexy," I purr.

I swoon when his cheeks turn red. I lift on my toes and he dips his head to kiss me. I feel the vibration of his groan when his hand meets my bare back. Caleb breaks the kiss and looks down behind me.

He sighs, grumbling something under his breath that I don't quite catch. When he tugs me into his side, he wraps his big arm around me. I melt into him, placing my hand on his chest and lean my head against him.

I think this is my favorite place in the world. Caleb's arms are everything and more to me. I feel safe and loved when I'm in his embrace.

When we get outside the dorm Caleb leads me to a Jaguar SUV. He pushes the key fob and opens the passenger side door for me. I look up at him with drawn brows.

I have never seen Caleb drive. I don't know why, but I've always assumed he didn't have a license. Cameron or Dakota usually drive him. I never thought that he had his own license or car.

"You thought I couldn't drive," Caleb says with a smirk.

"Sorry?" I say, biting my lip.

Caleb shrugs. "For what, my family babies me. I never have to drive, which sucks because I love cars and love to drive."

"Wait, that guy Ernie, at the race track. That was what he was talking about that day, at the photo shoot. You can drive a race car," I gasp in realization.

Caleb grins and leans to peck my lips. "Maybe. Get in. We're going to be late."

I smile and climb into the soft seats. My smile grows as Caleb rounds the front of the car and climbs into the driver's seat. Seeing how well he fits behind the wheel makes sense.

We're often entranced by the task of driving. I can see Caleb being amazing in a racecar. The focus, science behind the car and its dynamics. Yes, I can see it.

What I don't expect is the pang of regret. As we ride in the sleek SUV, I can just imagine Caleb driving our family to dinner. Only, he doesn't want a family and if he's what I want, then I have to respect that fact and accept it. That's what I'm signing up for.

I take time to let that truly set in for the first time since our talk in the locker room. I'd pushed that conversation aside. However, for some reason, in this moment, I can't seem to let the thought go.

I look at Caleb's profile. Reaching for his cheek, I run my hand over the small scar that's usually hidden under facial hair. Caleb reaches for my fingers and kisses their tips.

"When I was ten, I had a meltdown on Daddy's boat. Cameron tried to calm me down and it only set me off more. I slipped and cracked my face on the stair rail going down to the lower deck," he says softly.

I lean in and kiss his cheek. "Just one more mark of perfection," I whisper. "You're not perfect unless you have the scars to prove it."

Caleb pulls to a stop in a parking space, turning to look at me. His eyes search mine. He leans to place a soft kiss on my lips.

"You're the one that's perfect," he says against my lips. "I love you."

"Love you too," I say as I look up at him.

Caleb turns to get out of the car and I realize we are at our café. I furrow my brows. We're a bit dressed up for this place.

Caleb helps me out of the car and walks me across the street to the place that's like a second home. I'm more curious by the minute. The front windows are covered from the inside. I look up at Caleb in confusion.

He just continues to lead me to the front door. When he opens the door, he gestures for me to walk in ahead of him. I gasp the moment I step inside. Our favorite little café has turned into a gorgeous romantic scene for two.

Twinkle lights have been strung up all over—along the front of the register, in front of the showcases. Around the bar stool and other furniture. The tables have been rearranged allowing for a single table to be the focal point in the middle of the shop.

A candle is in the center of the table, that's covered in white linens. The chairs are even covered in white cloths with pale blue ribbons. The entire scene is breathtaking.

I turn to Caleb with tears in my eyes. "What? How did you do this? Where is everyone?"

"Bernie made good on his promise. His uncle owns the place. He did me a favor," Caleb says, as he watches my face.

I wrap my arms around his waist, as my heart swells with love for him. Who has a café shut down for dinner for two? I don't even understand how I've met this man and fallen so deeply in love with him. This all seems so unreal.

"Thank you," I say through trembling lips.

"You're welcome," Caleb murmurs. "This is our place. I wanted tonight to be special. This just seemed like the right place to start."

He's blinking, which tells me he's nervous. I choke down my emotions, not wanting to overwhelm him. This is just the sweetest thing anyone has ever done for me.

"Hey, let's sit and see what you've planned," I encourage.

Caleb nods and walks me over to the table. He pulls my chair and I sit. When Caleb takes his seat, Cameron and Bernie show up out of nowhere. Cameron pours some sparkling cider into the champagne flutes and Bernie places two steaming plates before each of us.

Cameron winks at me, before he turns to disappear again with Bernie trailing behind him. I focus on the plate before me, only to find my favorite. Lemon chicken with asparagus and wild rice.

It smells delicious. I look up at Caleb and beam. "You had them make my favorite. I didn't know they have a full kitchen here," I gush.

"They don't. I made it at home and Cam brought it over, while I came to pick you up," Caleb says.

Again, I'm in awe of this man. I shake my head as I smile at him. I lift my fork and knife. When I cut into the chicken, it's juicy and tender. It slices apart like butter.

I scoop up some rice and asparagus and lift it to my mouth. When the flavors burst into my mouth, I can't help the moan that escapes my lips. The chicken just melts in my mouth and the rice and vegetables are cooked to perfection.

"You have to be kidding me," I groan. "Caleb, will you marry me?"

I start to giggle, but the look on Caleb's face, causes the laugh to die on my lips. He looks at me intensely, as if he's trying to assess my words for sarcasm or truth. He places his fork and knife on his plate and stands.

My neck cranes to follow him. He continues to look down at me with intensity. I don't know what's going on, until he moves to me and palms my face. In a fluid catlike motion, he bends to his knee.

"That was my question," he says.

He lifts a shaky hand from his suit pocket. My mouth pops open, when it all hits me full force. My mind starts to race.

"Caleb?"

He brushes his thumb over my trembling lip. "I've loved you from the moment I almost ran you over. I just knew you were what I've been waiting all my life for. Someone to see me, someone to love me," Caleb chokes.

"You're the most beautiful woman I've ever seen in my life, inside and out. You make me feel like the man I want to be. I know I can't give you everything you deserve, so I guess this is a bit selfish of me.

"I know that, but I love you, darlin'. I love you with everything I am. It would break me to lose you. I can't see my life without you. Please Nicole, give me a chance to try to be the best husband I can. I'll marry you tonight if you want."

Caleb pauses and take a deep breath. "What I'm saying is... yes. I'll marry you. Even if you're just joking, but I'm not when I ask...will you marry me?"

"Oh, my God," I whisper. "Caleb, I...I."

I don't know what to say. I know on the ride over, I had thoughts of the decisions I would have to make to have a future with Caleb. However, now faced with reality, I feel like I might faint.

This is real. The man before me has real feelings. I have to be sure this is what I want. I can't ignore the truth of our relationship or our situation.

Can I accept the man Caleb is? Can I truly say that I don't want children or that I'm willing to give up on wanting them? Can I say yes and mean it, knowing all of what that word means? Because if I say yes, there is no turning back. Not with Caleb. I wouldn't do that to him.

I look down at the ring and it's gorgeous. I mean, breathtaking. Two and a half carats, I believe with a halo of smaller diamonds. I wipe the sweat from my forehead and lick my lips.

"Nicole?" Caleb whispers. "You have to say something. I'm having a hard time reading you right now. I'm about to freak out."

"Sorry," I say, as my eyes flicker up to his.

When I look into those blue-grey eyes and see the disappointment in them, I know my answer. It's not a decision of pity. I don't feel obligated to give in because he can't handle the rejection.

No, the look in his eyes reminds me of the amazing man I've fallen in love with. He can't read my emotions or place my social cues as easily as others. Yet, here he is, putting himself out there, ready to accept whatever I hand him.

"Yes," I breathe. "Yes, Caleb. I love you. Yes."

Caleb blinks rapidly at me, until my words sink in and his eyes widen. He nearly tackles me, palming my face and kissing me hard. I wrap my arms around his neck and return his kiss with the same vigor.

Handclaps, coming from around us, pulls us apart. Caleb doesn't take his eyes away from me, as I peek around him to see Cameron, Dakota, and Mr. Perry. They all have bright smiles on their faces.

"Now, that's what I call well done," Mr. Perry says with a boisterous laugh. "Welcome to the family, little lady."

"Thank you, Mr. Perry," I laugh, as Caleb wraps his arms around me and buries his face in my neck.

"None of that. You call me Kyle or Dad," Mr. Perry says, with a broad smile.

"Okay," I say with a smile.

"Let's go kids. We'll let them have the rest of the night to themselves. Caleb, I'll see you on the plane in the morning."

Caleb breaks away from me and walks over to his dad. My mouth falls open when Caleb pulls his father into a bear hug. The shocked expressions on Cameron and Dakota's faces show I'm not the only one in awe.

Tears well in my eyes and I see Dakota wipe at hers. When Caleb releases his dad, Mr. Perry's eyes look moist. He pats Caleb's cheek and nods at him.

"You boys make me a proud father. You're both fine young men," he kisses Caleb's forehead. "God, I love you. You deserve this happiness, don't let anyone take that from you."

"I love you, too, Daddy," Caleb says, pulling his father in for one more hug. "See you in the morning."

"See you in the morning," Mr. Perry says through an emotion clogged voice.

"This may be pushing it, but can I get one of those hugs," Dakota says hopefully.

Caleb grins and opens his arms. Dakota rushes in and hugs him tightly. I didn't think this moment could be any more special. Caleb doesn't even flinch at their touch. He accepts Dakota's tight embrace, as if he does so all the time.

Dakota breaks the hug and looks at me. She wipes the tears from her cheeks. She points at me with a rueful smile on her lips.

"You, you're something awesome. He knew it the first time he saw you. I love you for loving my cousin so fucking much. Don't give up on him, we'll always be here to make sure he doesn't give up on you," Dakota says fiercely.

"Promise," I say, as I look at her through teary eyes. I look up at Caleb, as he returns to my side. I look him in his eyes and say it again. "I promise."

CHAPTER EIGHTEEN

My Mistake

Nicole

We should be happy. We should be celebrating, but I feel more like my heart is breaking. We all cried mixed tears of joy and uncertainty two days ago.

We'd all flown to Florida that morning to be there by two for the start of the draft. Mr. Perry provided transportation in his private jet.

I had mixed feelings when we arrived in Florida to find Mrs. Perry waiting on us in the Perry family villa. She was cold toward me the entire time, especially when Aunt Judy made a big fuss over my engagement ring.

I thought Jemma would swallow her own tongue. The sour look on her face was priceless. However, she seemed to get over it for the public when it came time for the draft. Yup, all smiles for the cameras.

Caleb and Cameron were drafted. It was the greatest moment of my life to sit beside Caleb as his name was called. There was so much nervous energy swirling in the room, I thought I'd be sick.

I was a nervous wreck the whole day, but not more than Cameron and Caleb. I truly saw the bond Cam and Cal have with each other. They had their own secret communication going on most of the time.

However, as we sat there and each one of them were called to their new teams, I watched them go from worried, to relieved, to awed, and finally to disappointed. Neither of the twins were called to Texas teams. Cameron was drafted to Atlanta and Caleb was drafted to New York.

It broke my heart to see them look like they were being torn apart. I don't think they've ever been apart. Kyle, the loving father that he is, was outraged once we returned to the villa.

He promised to call in favors and get the boys on the same team. In the end, Cameron told his dad he was happy for the change and he would make do. Caleb agreed, his only concern was me. He didn't want to be so far away from me.

I don't want to be so far away from him either. I know he'll be on the road most of the time, but that just makes it worse. I can't imagine going weeks or months without seeing Caleb.

When I started to talk about transferring to New York for my Senior year, Caleb wouldn't have it. I guess he and my dad are on the same page there. My father wants me happy, but he was unhappy to hear that I wanted to make the change because of *a boy*. His words, not mine.

That's why Mr. Perry flew us to New York, as soon as he found out my parents had no idea about Caleb or our relationship. My family wants to meet Caleb and Kyle felt it only right that they know his son, since he's the one I'll be marrying. He wasn't too happy that Caleb didn't ask my dad for permission to marry me.

Honestly, this trip is scaring the shit out of me. I don't know what to expect. My mom and dad didn't sound too happy to find out that I'm engaged to someone they've never met.

I didn't tell them much about Caleb, and I don't think that has helped matters at all. It actually seemed to piss my dad off more, if at all possible. I'm the baby in the family. My dad is super protective of me, and my happiness.

So, here I stand cringing in front of my mom and dad in the foyer of my childhood home. It's late, I'm tired, but we have to deal with this mess I've made. I hate that I've added just one more thing to our already heavy plate.

"So, you're the young man that proposed to my daughter without asking permission. And here, I thought you Texas boys had manners," My dad says, as he looks at Caleb through narrowed eyes.

I sigh, when I see the mirth in my father's eyes. He's only teasing. This is a good sign. I grin up at Caleb, who has tightened his hold on my hand.

"I...I'm sorry, s..sir," Caleb says. "I know I did this wrong. I should've come to you proper. My daddy isn't too happy to find out y'all didn't know about me first."

My dad rocks back on his heels and smiles. He laughs and holds out his hand. I squeeze Caleb's hand to reassure him and bite my lip, as he hesitates to return my father's handshake.

Caleb finally lifts his hand to take my father's. I don't miss that his grip on my hand tightens. I'm learning to understand more and more how much of an anchor I am for Caleb.

"I'm just giving you a hard time, Caleb. I can see those southern manners are in place," my dad says, with a warm smile. "It was Nicole that failed to mention she was off falling in love with a superstar pitcher."

"You know?" I ask in surprise.

I hadn't told my parents that Caleb is a baseball player, or that he just signed to play for a major league team. I wanted them to meet him as a person. I didn't want anything clouding or swaying their opinion of Caleb, before they got to meet the talented, sweet man I've fallen in love with, in person.

"The Perry brothers have been all the rave, sweet pea. Although, I was surprised to see one of them lift, my very own daughter, off her feet to lay one hell of a kiss on her on national television," My father says pointedly. "I was even more surprised to hear the TV announcer mention that my daughter was the fiancée of the youngest Perry brother, as the camera zoomed in on the rock on her finger."

I groan. Why didn't I think about all of that? I know my father follows baseball. I think it's still hitting me that I'm engaged to an up and coming baseball star. I never even thought about my parents seeing me on TV at the draft or about anyone saying anything about my engagement.

I'm not ashamed of it. I had every intention of telling my parents. There was just so much going on with flying out for the draft and letting the shock of Caleb going to New York set in.

Not to mention, I'm still in shock that I'm engaged. When my mother called me, and asked what I was up to, I spilled my guts. I never thought of the initial reason for the call.

"I'm so sorry you guys found out that way," I groan. Now I understand why my father was so pissed on the phone. "It literally happened the night before. I truly did plan to call you guys and tell you."

"Please don't be angry with Nicole. It's my fault, I was solely focused on getting her to agree to be my wife," Caleb starts, but my dad lifts a hand.

"I'm happy to see Nicole so happy," my dad says. "I just don't appreciate that I and my wife were the last to find out, and we still had to place the call to get the information from her mouth."

"Caleb, pay my husband no mind," my mom says with a smile. "He likes to tease people. Especially young men that come with the threat of taking his baby girls away from him. You're not the first to come to our home and get steam rolled. It's so nice to meet you."

"It's nice to meet you too, ma'am," Caleb nods.

I wince as it comes off a little stiff, almost robotically. Not that I'm embarrassed by Caleb. It's just I know that when his speech becomes more static, he's heading way out of his comfort zone.

"Mom, dad, between all of the excitement of the week and the flight, we're beat. Would you mind if Caleb and I freshened up and relaxed for the night before we get into greeting everyone and answering questions tomorrow?" I say, trying to buy us a chance to slip away.

"Sure, honey, you freshen up and come find me if you two want something to eat. Caleb, Nicole will show you out to the guest house," my mother says and looks at me, as if daring me to challenge her.

I know my parents and their rules. They used them on all my siblings before me. I roll my eyes, but I take the clue. Caleb and I will not be sleeping in the same quarters on this trip, engaged or not.

"See you in a bit," I say to my mother, as I wrap my arms around her neck. "I love you."

"Is your mother the only one you love? I'll be the one paying for the wedding after all. I think a hug will get you my black card," My father says with a twinkle in his eyes.

"Seriously, Dad?" I laugh, but hug him around the waist anyway.

My dad and my brothers are all tall, over six feet. I get my short genes from my mom. I rest my cheek on my dad's chest, happy to hear his heart still beating. My dad always has my back, I know this is going to be hard for him. Seeing his baby girl getting married is something he has always said would break his heart.

There was a time I would've told him he had nothing to worry about. I now know that not to be true. I plan to marry Caleb and break the heart of my first love, my dad.

Our bond is a tight one, which shows when he wraps his arms around me and holds me tight. I suddenly feel guilty that I didn't share my great news with him first. I'll have to make it up to him over the next few days.

Yup, I'll be the girl laughing at all her dad's lame jokes, like they're the funniest in the world. I'll also be on the golf course at six a.m. having a heart to heart, because that's our thing. Once again, my heart hurts.

My daughters will never have this. Not because their father wouldn't be able to give this to them, but because he's too afraid to even try. I just know in my heart that Caleb would make an amazing father. I've watched him with Dakota's little brother, Andy.

I pull away from my dad and try to cover my somber thoughts. It doesn't work with my dad. He looks me in my eyes and lifts a brow. My dad gives me that smile that says he'll fix whatever it is.

"We'll have to hit the course tomorrow. So, get some rest," my dad says.

It's his code for, *you're going to spill and I'm going to fix.*

"See you in the morning," I say, as cheerfully as I can.

Caleb grabs his bags and I walk him out to the guest house. He's super quiet, but I can feel the anxious energy rolling off of him. Couple that with the weight of this trip on my shoulders. I feel exhausted already.

"It's late. I'm sure things will be better in the morning," I say to Caleb, as we step into the spacious guest house.

Mom went all out in this place. It has a beachy feel, with all of the large windows covered in soft blues and white billowy fabrics. The soft furniture, accented with the same blues, some white, and beige. This has always been one of my favorite places. My little oasis.

"Your parents don't like me," Caleb says, dropping his bag by the door and going to flop on the couch. He drops his head in his hands. "I fucked this up. I should have come to your daddy first. I've been taught better. My Daddy said I should have met your family first."

"Your daddy is old school." I sigh and walk over to him. "You see he assumed you'd met my family. This is not your fault Caleb."

I run a hand over his hair, causing him to look up at me. I can see the wheels turning. I just wait until he finds the words he's looking for.

"Are you ashamed of me, of us? Why didn't you tell them we were dating at least? I know we got engaged quickly and have been running since.

"I just don't get it. My daddy thought that I'd met your family because I know so much about them. Why didn't they know about me?

"I understand you not getting a chance to tell them about the engagement. You've been with me almost every second of this rollercoaster ride," he purses his lips. "Why didn't they know about me?"

My gut turns. I hadn't meant to make him feel like I'm ashamed of him. In the beginning, I questioned me. I was ashamed of me. At first, I was ashamed for taking advantage of the situation. I know it sounds stupid, even to me, but it had crossed my mind.

Then, the more I got to know Caleb, I started to feel ashamed of me, for ever having those initial thoughts. There's so much more to Caleb and I almost missed out on that. I almost didn't bother to give him a chance.

"Am I shamed of us? Not ever. I've never been good at making friends in school. Forget having a boyfriend. I was so nerdy and shy. My parents did everything they could to try to push me out of my comfort zone. My siblings too.

"I transferred schools because even with my sister and brother's help, I just didn't fit in. I was tired of them trying to force their friends on me and just feeling awkward. My sister helped get me this one date and it was a disaster.

"I embarrassed myself by following everyone's advice but my own. When we started dating, I didn't know I would fall in love with you like this. I was sure I'd find a way to screw it up. Telling my family being just one way. Everyone would've had their own advice for what I should and shouldn't do in a relationship."

I move Caleb's arms from his knees, out of my way, so I can straddle his lap. Cupping his face in my hands, I wait until he gives me his eyes and his focus. I kiss him softly.

"You and I need each other, not what everyone else thinks. I should've done things differently, but I wanted to keep you to myself. You and the friends I've made back at school, you're all the first relationships I've made on my own, without feeling awkward or forced."

Caleb blinks at me. "So, you're not second guessing us?"

"No, babe, never. I love you, Caleb. I know this isn't going to be easy, but we'll figure it out. I still think the best thing would be for me to transfer to a school here," I say.

"No, no, Nicole. I could be traded in a heartbeat. Then what, you'll transfer to wherever I am then? No. You have one more year to go. You have friends now. My family's in Texas, you'll be in school with Dakota," Caleb shakes his head and blows out a breath.

I sigh. "Okay, fine. What about Paris? We might as well address that while we're at it."

Caleb turns his head away from me, toward the wall of windows. His jaw flexes and his nostrils flare. I place my fingers under his chin and turn his face back toward me.

"Why can't you stay the summer with me. We'll be married. We can do newlywed shit before you have to go back to school. You can come with me to my away games. Or you can fix up our apartment in Texas," Caleb grunts.

"We'll be married?" I frown. "What apartment?"

"Yeah, I want to get married soon. I'm getting us a place. Well, I sort of have it already. It's nicer than the one Cameron and I had. We sold that place and split the money. I got us a place," Caleb whispers, as his eyes search my face.

"Seriously?" I beam.

"Yeah. Did I do okay?" he asks, still searching my face.

"Yes," I squeal and throw my arms around his neck.

"I'll come home as much as I can. It's a two bedroom, so if you get lonely Dakota can come over. Or we can get a dog—," I place a finger over his lips.

"Shh, it's all going to be fine. My family's going to love you. You and I are going to plan our wedding. And you, my beautiful, strong man are going to go to the majors and take over," I purr against his lips.

Caleb captures my mouth and kisses me senseless. I say senseless because before I know it, I'm pulling my t-shirt over my head and grinding into his lap. Caleb's tight grip bites into my skin, as he holds me against him.

He breaks the kiss and looks down at my breasts that are heaving in the confines of my bra. He reaches one hand up, removing the restraint. My breasts bounce free, causing him to groan. He reaches for my right breast and dips his head to capture my nipple in his mouth.

"Caleb," I cry out, my head falling back.

I wiggle some more in his lap, as his growing erection starts to push at my soaked folds through my panties. I ache for him. It's not like we haven't been fucking like bunnies since we've been engaged.

Caleb has taken insatiable to a new level. We've had so much sex, I can't believe I can still take him, let alone want to take him. I can and I will, because I want him just as much.

Caleb's hands slip under my skirt and he tears my panties in half with both hands. He continues to rip the fabric until he pulls them from my body. His fingers find my wet core from behind and start to strum my wet lips.

I rock my hips over his fingers, moaning as his thick digits slip inside me. Meanwhile, his lips are still latched to my breast, as his tongue flicks up and down over my nipple.

"I need you," I moan.

I reach for his belt, loosening the huge buckle and tearing at the zipper of his jeans. When Caleb is free of his boxers and jeans, I reach for his length. He lifts his hips and pushes his pants down a little more. I pump him a few more times, rubbing my thumb over his precum.

When I can't wait any longer, I lift to line him up with my entrance. Caleb's hands grasp hands full of my ass, as he sucks harder. I go to sink down on him and he tightens his grip. My breast pops free from his mouth and he looks up at me.

"Condom," Caleb says huskily.

"No, I want to feel you. You're going to be my husband," I moan, as I sink down on him.

Caleb's head falls back as my body sucks him in. He feels so good. I moan while seating myself to the root. I can't sit still. I need more.

I start to ride him, not worried about my parents' rules, the world outside, where we will be in a few months, or all the what-ifs in between. We're all that matters here and now. There is nothing else.

"I love you so much, babe," I whimper.

I reach for his t-shirt and pull it over his head. I like watching his muscled body work with mine. As his tanned skin comes into view, I lick my lips.

I place both my hands on his shoulders for leverage and start to ride him harder. Caleb knows just how to push me over the edge. He brings his large palm to my breast and lifts it to his lips. He sucks it into his mouth, all while looking me in the eyes with those blue-grey eyes.

His eyes are dark with lust. More grey than anything else. I dig my fingers into his shoulders and my head falls back. Caleb groans and begins to thrust up into me, with each fall of my hips.

I'm so wet for him. The sound of him sliding through my juices fills the room. Caleb releases my nipple from his mouth and licks his way up to my collarbone. I shiver, feeling my climax approach.

Caleb moves his lips to my ear. "Come for me, darlin'. You feel so fucking good on my cock. Come for me."

"Ah, yes, yes," I cry out and gush all over him.

I expect him to chase his own release, but I'm startled from my sated bliss, when he flips me flat onto my back on the couch. Caleb hooks both my legs over his shoulders, moving in until we are chest to chest. He's so deep from this angle, I can feel my body building again.

Caleb works his hips into me, his face hovering inches from mine. His warm breath fans my face, allowing me to taste him, to breathe him in. I reach for my calves pulling my legs back to open for him more. Caleb anchors one hand to the edge of the couch cushion and digs his other hand in between the cushion and couch back.

His muscles bulge in his arms, as he picks up the pace. He lifts some of his weight off of me, throwing his head back, still thrusting into my body. It is a beautiful sight.

"Shit, Nicole," Caleb grunts.

I reach to push his damp hair from his face and tuck it behind his ear. I start to rock my hips into him from beneath. My eyes drop to the flexing muscles in his arms.

"Fuck," I whimper. "You're so sexy, babe."

"I don't know how I'm going to go four days without being inside you," Caleb grunts.

"You're out of your mind if you think I'm not going to be sneaking in here every chance I get," I pant.

Caleb chuckles and places his cheek to the center of my chest. His movements slow, they become thoughtful, more like each thrust is a sweet loving caress. Caleb lifts his head slightly to kiss the side of my breast.

He looks up at me, leaning in, he takes my lips in a searing kiss. My toes curl, as his tongue twirls with mine. His pace increases again. I pull my legs back further. I can feel him swelling, we're going over together this time.

Caleb's body shudders over mine, as he empties into me. I whimper out my own release. A shiver moves through me as Caleb's hands run up and down my sides. His head is back on my chest, as he catches his breath.

"Promise me we'll have a small wedding. I don't think I'm ready for more," Caleb murmurs. "Someday maybe I can handle it, but for now I just want you as my wife."

I close my eyes. Yet, another sacrifice I will have to make. My dreams of a big wedding crumble, as I nod my head and open my mouth to seal my dream's fate.

"Promise," I pant.

"I love you," Caleb whispers.

"Love you too, more than you know."

CHAPTER NINETEEN

Meet the Family

Caleb

I'm hungry as hell, but I don't want to move. After making love to Nicole last night, I just held her in my arms until she had to go back into the main house. My head has been a mess since.

I don't think her parents like me very much. I know they said they're just upset with Nicole, but I don't know them enough to know if that's true. Her daddy is the most difficult to read, and her mom. She looks a little too closely, but says way less. She's the one I fear.

I'm deathly afraid that they're going to come to the conclusion that their daughter is too good for me. That's why I'm trying to buy myself some more time. My stomach growls in protest, and I groan. I'm not going to make it much longer.

I swing my legs over the edge of the bed. I've been showered and dressed for an hour now. I've just been lying here, hoping

Nicole will come check on me, so I can bury myself in her, before I have to face this.

My stomach growls again, as I shove my feet in a pair of boots. "All right, all right," I mutter to my aching belly.

I trudge my way to the main house and enter through the sliding doors Nicole and I exited through last night. The smell of bacon and something sweet hits me as soon as I step inside. I slide the door closed and shake my hands out at my sides.

When I walk further into the house, the kitchen comes into view along with Nicole's mother. I chide myself mentally. I should've texted Nicole. I know she's probably sleeping last night off. I didn't want to disturb her, if I didn't have to.

I regret that decision now. It's too late to turn and hightail it out of here. Big brown eyes are staring back at me.

Nicole's mother is very pretty. She's darker than Nicole and her eyes are slightly more oval and have a more Asian look about them. They're also a darker brown. Where Nicole wears her hair in a sleek short cut, her mother's hair is pin straight, falling down to her waist.

I clear my throat. "Good morning, ma'am," I say, looking anywhere but at the big bright eyes looking back at me.

"Good morning, Caleb. You can call me, Joy," she says. "Come have something to eat."

"Thank you, ma'am…Mrs. Joy," I reply.

I move to the island, where she places a plate and glass. I sit and huff, staring down at my plate. I grind my teeth, when I catch myself blinking down at the plate.

"Is Nicole awake yet, ma'am?" I murmur.

Joy chuckles. "Yes, Caleb, but she has gone golfing with her father. They should be back soon."

I close my eyes and inhale. Shit, I should have texted Nicole. My leg is bouncing and my finger is tapping at the edge of the plate before me, but I can't stop. If I do, I don't know what I might do instead.

"Caleb, look at me," Mrs. Joy says. I lift my eyes. "Breathe, honey."

She reaches into a drawer and pulls out a stress ball, holding it out to me. I stare at the ball, reaching for it when I feel myself spiraling. I look around the room for the best escape.

"We're going to be family, honey. There's no need to run from me. Has Nicole shared with you about her niece, Olivia?"

I lick my lips and nod. I'm still weighing my options. I want to go and wait for Nicole to return. This isn't how I wanted her family to learn about me.

"My husband has spoken highly of you as a baseball player. Let's pretend you're playing now," she says softly.

My eyes snap to hers. I stare for a long time. She's not judging me. She's trying to help. I nod and squeeze the ball she placed in my hand.

"Awesome," she says when I stop the clicking in the back of my throat. I hadn't realized I started that. "Now, let's get some food on that plate, so you can feed that grumbling tummy. Would you like some bacon? I have eggs and waffles as well."

"Y...yes, ma'am," I pause and close my eyes briefly. "Mrs. Joy, I'd like all of the above."

With a grin, she brings over a platter at a time and fills my plate. I watch, as my mouth waters. I'm so hungry, I could eat this whole spread on my own.

"There's more where that came from so eat up. You can have as much as you like. Would you like orange juice or apple?"

"Apple, Mrs. Joy, thank you, ma'am," I reply after swallowing the eggs and bacon I've just torn into.

She pours the juice in my glass before making herself a smaller plate of food. She sits on the stool next to me and starts to eat.

I'm grateful for the silence. I haven't released the stress ball. It's going a long way, as my mind whirls.

Nicole...I need Nicole...Mrs. Joy knows...I've just lost my shit in front of the mother of the woman I love...where are you Nicole...They're not going to let her marry me.

I fucked up...Mama was right, I can't be a husband...too many clocks are ticking...I think Nicole wants babies...She's going to give that up for me...I'm selfish...there's a railroad somewhere around here...that's the second train that's gone by...I want more food...It's loud in here...fan...refrigerator...the rail is not that close...music in the other room...Mrs. Joy chewing...the forks hitting the plates.

Shut all of that out, Caleb...focus man...When is Nicole coming back...should I have another plate after this one?

I wish Dakota were here...Nicole is going to be hot when she gets older...Where is Nicole...I need her...Nicole should be back by now, right...I just need to hold her...Nicole loves me...I love her so fucking much...

I make it half way through my second plate when Mrs. Joy breaks into my maze of thoughts. I turn to look at her and she has a smile on her lips. I sigh, I can do this. I want to do this.

"Excuse me, ma'am?"

"I asked you to tell me a bit about you," she says and her smile grows.

"I was diagnosed when I was two—," she holds up a hand and shakes her head.

"Tell me about you, Caleb, not your autism. I'm sure Nicole has told you what I do for a living. I've learned a lot from observing you. None of that has caused my daughter to fall in love with you," she takes a sip of her juice. "I want to hear about you. What you like and dislike, what you do with your time. Who is Caleb Perry?"

"I love physics, ma'am," I smile. "I love Nicole and baseball. Those are the things that make me most happy. I want to play professional baseball and I've just signed a contract to do so here in New York."

"Yes, that is very exciting. Nicole has mentioned coming back home to be closer to you," Mrs. Joy replies with a nod.

"No, ma'am, she won't be doing that. She has school to finish. I'd be more comfortable if she stayed with her friends, in Texas, to do so. I'll be on the road a whole lot anyway." I shrug.

"This is true. How does Nicole feel about that?"

I look down and think for a moment. I think Nicole hates the idea of me being here and her being in Texas. I know if I asked her to, she'd follow me here.

I heave a heavy breath. "I don't think she likes it much," I say to the floor. I look up. "But her future comes first. Nothing is guaranteed in my career. I could be sent to a different team in a different state at the drop of a dime. I don't want to unsettle her life that way."

"Have you told this to Nicole?"

"Yes, ma'am, Mrs. Joy," I nod. "I'll miss her, but it's only right."

"I like you, Caleb. I think everything will work out just fine. You can hold onto that stress ball while you're here. I have them all over the house for our little Liv," Mrs. Joy says. "I'd hug you, but from the way you looked at my husband's hand last night, I'd say that's out."

"Yes, ma'am, but I'm working on that," I murmur.

"You're doing a fine job, young man. A very fine job."

~B~

Nicole

"So, your mother is right? Caleb is on the spectrum," my dad says, as I line up my shot.

I look up and drop my club to my side. I blow out a breath. Why do I ever think I'll get anything past these two?

"Yes," I whisper.

Dad whistles. He looks at me long and hard. "Do you understand what you're getting into here?"

"Yes, dad. I get it. It's not going to be easy and Caleb's career just may make it that much harder," I wipe at the tear that slips free. "I'll be giving things up, like a big wedding, a family. Yeah, I get that this is not ideal, but I love him, Dad. I really do."

"What makes you think you have to give up a family. Roy comes to see your mom all the time. He and his little family are doing great. Sure, from time to time it can be challenging for him. I'm not sure what all Caleb is dealing with, but I wouldn't think children were out of your future," my dad wrinkles his brows in thought.

I look down at my shoes and kick at the grass. "Caleb doesn't want children. He's afraid they'll fall on the spectrum too. He doesn't think he can handle a family," I say just above a whisper. "Daddy, can I be honest?"

"Yes, sweet pea. It's me," My dad says, placing a hand on my shoulder.

"I probably never should've started things with Caleb. I knew right away. I saw him. I should've walked away then. 'Cause now, Dad, I can't," I break into a sob. "I can't and I'm so afraid it won't be enough. I'm afraid that maybe one day, I'll look back and regret not having a family. But I know with everything I am, I *will* regret walking away from him."

My dad wraps me in his arms. "This is a tough decision, sweetheart. I can't tell you the right thing to do, only your heart can. But I do know love, it will make you choose the most difficult path for the ones you care about.

"You will bear the weight of the world to keep them from being hurt and you will let them go when you can do no more. Love isn't easy, baby, but it's rewarding and it's beautiful when you take a chance on it." With that my dad kisses the top of my head.

"Thanks, Dad," I sniffle.

"I'm always here, my baby girl." Dad smiles down at me. "Come on, let's get back to the house."

CHAPTER TWENTY

Big Leagues

Caleb

Seven months later...

I miss my family. I miss my brother and my cousin. I miss the fuck out of my wife. This is so much harder than I thought it would be.

I'm barely holding on. I've been in three fights this week alone. They're talking about sending me down to a Triple A team. I'm not coping. The only reason I'm still here is because I'm pitching my ass off.

I've become the angry mute. I'm the rookie the guys love to fuck with. They don't get that I'm different. Before I get that they're just teasing, I'm usually in a rage, beating the fuck out of one of them. I especially don't take well to the jokes about my wife's ass.

"I don't understand you, Perry," Coach barks at me. "You're a damn good player, but you go at your own team like they're your enemy. These guys josh each other all the time. What were you thinking out there?"

"She's my fucking wife," I grumble. "I didn't think his joke was funny."

"I've been watching you for months. I know you're a little different, son. Or could it be you're on something?" Coach muses out loud.

"I ain't on shit," I huff. "I...I...I fall on the Autism spectrum, sir. I don't get their jokes, because I don't pick up on social queues like other people do. Things get out of hand sometimes, because it's too late by the time I understand the guys' intentions.

"When it comes to my wife, I have a singular focus. I don't take time to understand whether someone is joking or not. My instinct is to protect my woman," I say.

"Well, I'll be," Coach says, running a hand down his face. He stares at me for a few minutes. "Now that makes sense. You'd think those assholes would learn to stop talking about your wife by now," Coach grumbles that part under his breath. "Well, fuck, son. If it didn't come from your mouth I wouldn't believe it.

"I have a nephew with autism. Shit, his mother has a hard time getting him to interact with his own siblings. You've been here hiding this for six fucking months.

"You're married to that pretty little thing," Coach holds up his hands, when I lift from my seat. "She's young enough to be my damn daughter. Sit the fuck down, Perry."

I huff and take my seat. "I'm on the spectrum, but I'm still a man," I say gruffly. "That woman has made me a better man. I won't tolerate them disrespecting her."

Coach nods. "I get it, son. I'll have a talk with the boys."

"I don't want them to know. I don't want anyone to know. I want to be known for my skills on the field, not by a word that isn't even adequate enough to define me. I used to think I wanted people to know," I shake my head. "I don't."

Coach nods and huffs out a breath. "I know how to have some decorum. Now that I know, I can help you, Caleb. I've been watching you struggle. You're the finest pitcher I've witnessed with my own two eyes. You have a gift, son.

"You played in college. This never came out. We have to be able to make the right adjustments to make sure you succeed here. Tell me what I can do to help," Coach implores.

"I need my wife," I say into my lap. I shake my head. I feel the tears sting the backs of my eyes. I look up at my coach. "I thought I could do this without her or my brother. I can't. I want her to finish school, but this shit is killing me."

Coach blows out a breath. "I have an idea. I don't know what to do about your wife. But I'll see if there is something else I can do."

"Thanks, Coach," I nod.

"Just stop beating my teams' ass, will you?" Coach snorts.

"Yes, sir."

CHAPTER TWENTY-ONE

Together Again

Nicole

I'm too pleased with myself. Caleb stood firm on not allowing me to transfer to a New York school. He just never said anything about taking courses online or taking a work study course.

Turns out I didn't need that many credits to finish my degree. I was able to take two courses online, over the summer, while in New York with Caleb. Caleb was so busy with the season, he didn't even notice.

For my final three classes, I was able to register for two online and the last one is a work-study. I just have to turn in a paper at the end of the semester. I'll be finished ahead of time.

I didn't tell Caleb, because I wanted to make sure I could pull it off. I just had to go back to finalize some things with my counselor. Now, I'm free to be with my husband.

Yes, I'm Mrs. Caleb Perry now. We married a week after spending time with my family in New York. It was a small ceremony with a few of our friends and family on Mr. Perry's yacht.

Taylor and Joelle were there, but Maribel had taken off by then. I still feel bad that I never reached out to see if I could help. I've texted her since, but after the first reply her number was disconnected.

That hurt. I thought we were friends. If Taylor hadn't told me to give her time, I would've been there for her. I hope I get to see her again someday.

Taylor and Joelle will be friends for life. I gave them my trip to Paris. They had a blast. I have plenty of pictures. Taylor met someone while there.

They seem to be pretty serious. I mean, he has followed her back here to the States. I'm happy for her.

I smile down at a text from Taylor. She and Dakota have been texting me non-stop since my plane landed. They want details on what I have planned.

Are you there yet?

I shake my head and laugh as I push my key into the lock of Caleb's hotel room. Caleb had a game tonight. When we spoke this morning, he didn't sound too good.

I tried to book a flight out to Seattle as soon as I could. Dakota was the one that called Kyle and asked him for the use of his jet. My father-in-law was more than happy to help. I'm so grateful to him. I miss my baby something fierce.

I was relieved to find out Caleb had his own room. His coach was in the lobby when I arrived, he nearly tripped over himself to get me a key to Caleb's suite.

I hear the water cut off in the bathroom as the door shuts behind me. "Hello," Caleb calls out. "Is someone here?"

Caleb comes storming out of the bathroom, wrapping a towel around his waist. "I'm tired of this shit! Whatever, they told you, I'm not interested, get the fu—," Caleb stops in his tracks. His mouth falls open. "Baby?"

"Hey," I smile and wave.

I know his team has been messing with him. They have sent girls to his room a few times. Caleb called me losing his shit each time.

Caleb bites his lip, as his eyes take in my trench coat, belted tightly at the waist. I see the lust that fills his eyes when they land on my six-inch heels.

"Oh, we're about to have some fun, big boy," I purr.

Caleb tears his towel away, revealing his saluting soldier. It's only been two weeks, but I miss him like crazy. I lick my lips as he stalks forward.

He wraps one arm around my waist, lifting me and slamming my back against the room door. My breath whooshes out, but Caleb's mouth is on mine before I gasp a breath back in. I lock my legs around his waist and grasp his ears in my hands.

"God, I missed you," he groans into my mouth.

His hand reaches for the belt of my jacket, pulling it apart. I turn from the kiss and gasp for air. "Babe, wait, you're ruining my surprise."

Caleb pulls away and looks at me with knitted brows. "What surprise?"

I unwrap my legs and slide down his hard body. I finish releasing the belt on my coat, peeling open the front, I smile up at him. Caleb's mouth drops open, once again and his eyes widen.

"The fuck, Nicole," he says.

I pout. "You don't like it?" I say, looking down at the hot pink, lace bra and panty set, I have on under my coat.

The bra is a cup size too small and the panties are the tiniest boy shorts ever. The black heels on my feet, only help to enhance the overall look. Caleb growls reaching into my coat to palm my ass. He tugs my body into his.

"You look fucking hot, darlin'. But you've been walking around like this for how long?" Caleb says into my neck.

He buries his face there and inhales. I close my eyes and relish the feel of my man, his beard teasing my skin. There's so much heat coming off his huge frame. I want to just wrap around him and never let go. It's not right to be as sexy as my husband.

"Just from the plane here," I say, when he starts to suck on my neck.

He pulls away and his eyes narrow. "What?"

"I dressed on the plane. Your dad flew me in on the jet." I shrug.

He cradles my face and backs me into the door with his hot body. His full erection pressing into my stomach. I shrug out of my coat, letting it fall to our feet. Caleb places his forehead to mine.

"Never, you hear me, sweetheart, never, do this again," he says.

"But, I wanted to surprise you. I thought you would like it," I whisper.

"I love it, but the thought of someone knowing what was under that coat. Or trying to find out," Caleb shakes his head, closing his eyes. "That's driving me insane right now."

"Okay," I nod. "Never again."

"Good," he nods.

His left hand moves down my neck over my collar bone to my breast. I arch away from the door into his caress. His large hand covers my breast, weighing it in his palm.

"Did your team win?" I whisper.

I didn't have time to check in on the game. Between my nerves, text messages, and wanting to get here as fast as I could, I never heard the final score. They were down by one, last time I heard.

Caleb shakes his head. "No, they brought me in too late," he breathes against my lips.

"Oh, yay, rough, dirty sex," I wiggle my body and grin.

Caleb doesn't make love when he loses a game, he fucks. Hard, dirty, and savage. I'm glad I changed my mind about getting a weave this weekend. Caleb likes to pull hair when he gets lost in fucking like a porn star beast. I hope he gets so lost, we don't find him until the morning.

Caleb chuckles and shakes his head. "Is that all right?" he asks in my ear, while simultaneously shoving down the fabric of my bra and pinching my nipple.

I don't get to answer. He wasn't asking for me to answer anyway. I know the drill. I'm about to get drilled. Add to the loss, the fact that we haven't seen each other in two weeks, Caleb is going to annihilate this pussy, and I can't wait.

I place my hands on his hips and let my palms glide around to his firm ass. Caleb deepens the kiss, pressing me against the door behind me. His free hand locks in the nape of my hair, tugging my head back.

Caleb peels his lips from mine and starts to kiss his way down my chin to my throat. His hands leave my breast and hair, settling on my backside. He kneads my cheeks as his lips continue to descend my body.

I'm panting in anticipation. I know he's just getting started. Caleb licks around my belly button, using his tongue to go lower. Dipping inside my panties with his tongue, he uses his teeth to pull the fabric away from my skin and down my hips. His fingers hook into the fabric to tear them the rest of the way down my thighs.

Caleb drops to his knees and I moan when he buries his nose into my folds and inhales. He slips his tongue into the front of my slit and wiggles it. I hook my fingers in his hair, rocking my hips forward, trying to get more of his mouth on me.

He chuckles and pulls away. He just stares at my mound. He stares so long, I reach to touch his face. His eyes lift to mine.

"Turn around," he says huskily. I slowly do as he says. "Hands on the door."

Caleb grasps a cheek in each hand. I look over my shoulder to find him dipping his head to take a bite out of my right cheek. I moan at the sharp sting. He sucks the flesh into his mouth, then licks a circle around the same spot, once, twice, three times.

Caleb slaps the same ass cheek. I feel my juices gush. He spreads my cheeks, before diving in. I reach to grasp the door handle.

Caleb hums into my sex, like a kid with his favorite flavor of ice cream. I widen my stance, poking my ass out more. I bite my lip and turn to rest the side of my face against the door.

Caleb finds his stride and I lose my mind. My hands slide up the smooth surface of the door, as I arch my back like a cat. My head falls back and I sing like my life depends on every note.

"Caleb!"

His name rolls off my lips so loudly, I shock myself. I go to clamp my mouth shut, but he wraps an arm around my stomach locking me to him as he latches on to my clit, rapidly flicking his tongue.

"Oh, yes, you ain't shit for this, Cal," I whimper as I crest.

Caleb lifts to his feet and bends to whisper in my ear. "You don't mean that, do you? I can stop anytime you want. I just want to make sure I'm clear on your wishes, darlin'," he breathes hotly.

"Babe, if you stop, we're fighting," I pant out.

He grasps my hips and surges forward, causing us both to moan out. He palms my sex, but doesn't move as I stretch around him, becoming reacquainted with his length and girth. My toes curl in my shoes.

He licks the shell of my ear. "I missed you so fucking much. I'm not dealing, baby." I whimper as he finally starts to move. "I need you with me."

"Shh, I've got you. It's going to be okay," I moan.

Caleb buries his face in my neck. Grabbing a hand full of my hair and sucking on my skin, while he pounds deep inside me. I clutch his wrist as he strums my over sensitive nub. He growls against my neck and starts to pound harder.

"I've been thinking about you all day," Caleb grunts. "Your gorgeous face, this tight pussy, I couldn't get you off my mind."

"I missed you, too," I whimper.

His hand that's not strumming my clit braces against the door. He nips at my shoulder, then drags his tongue from there over to my neck. I shiver as my pussy quakes around him.

"Ah, that's what I need. I need you dripping all over my cock. Again, darlin', give it to me again," he says in a sexy rasp.

My legs quiver beneath me and my heels titter as I try to shift my feet. Caleb pulls out and spins me in his arms. I'm wrapped around his waist before I can clear my head to take in the swift motion.

I lock my ankles over his ass, digging my heels in as he rocks his hips into me. Caleb presses both arms to the door, dipping his head between my breasts, as I lean back and stare at the ceiling, as if I can find help there.

He feels so good. Each stroke deeper than the last. He licks his way up from the center of my breasts to my throat. I squeeze around him, while grinding my hips.

"Dig your heels in deeper," he grunts.

"What?" I whisper in a daze.

"Dig your heels in, baby," he repeats.

I lock my legs tighter, digging the points of my heels into his ass harder. Caleb pounds his fist against the door. He presses me to the unyielding surface and lifts his thigh, planting his foot to the door for leverage. He's driving into me so deep my teeth chatter. It's like he is trying to climb inside me.

"Fuck, I feel you coming. I want it so bad," he breathes in my ear.

His big hands cover my backside, parting my cheeks. I'm startled when his long digits drag my juices to my forbidden hole and he starts to play there.

"Cal," I gasp.

"Shh, it'll help you come faster. Relax, I'll be gentle. I want to take you here later," he groans.

I shiver at the thought and come just as he slips his pinky in. My eyes widened. Who in the world have I married? Caleb's a bigger freak than I thought. I grin, in the midst of my own bliss. He's not alone.

Caleb keeps pounding, until he roars out his own release, punching the door beside my head. The heat of his seed sends aftershocks through me. I kiss his sweaty neck and smile in contentment.

We stand propped against the door for a few moments. When Caleb has his legs under him again, he turns and carries me to the bed, without pulling out. Tugging the covers back, he climbs onto the cool sheets and covers us both.

"What are you doing here?" He murmurs into my hair.

"I have another surprise for you," I yawn.

"Oh yeah, what's that?" He asks, combing his fingers through my bob.

"I'm moving to New York," I sing.

"Nicole, I know what I said earlier, but I don't want you messing up your shit for me." Caleb sighs.

"I'm not messing anything up. I took a few classes online over the summer. I can take the rest online and a work-study. I'll be finished earlier than I planned too," I turn my face up to him and beam.

He purses his lips and squints. I watch him and wait for it to sink in. He palms my face and runs his thumb over my swollen lips.

"I'm not good enough for you," he whispers.

"What?" I frown.

"Don't think I don't know what you've given up to be with me. I promise you, Nicole. One day, I'll give you a real wedding. One day, we'll have a stable life," he looks away and pauses. Swallowing hard, he continues. "I'll try to give you everything you want. Maybe...maybe we could adopt. Older kids, so I can't hurt them or fuck them up."

A tear slides down my cheek and my heart swells to the point of pain. "I love you so much," I choke out.

Our night of dirty sex goes out the window. This time, I take my time with my husband and show him how much his words mean to me. Though, I still think he'd be a great dad to our own children. I like his idea as well.

CHAPTER TWENTY-TWO

Oh No

Nicole

I feel miserable. I need to work on my paper for my work-study, but I can hardly think or hold my head up. I'm so tired. The weather has been back and forth here in New York, so I guess I have the flu.

This shit is kicking my ass. I couldn't even go with Caleb to his away game. He's been calling all day. I swear he's driving me crazy. I know he means well, but I can't sleep this off with him calling every five minutes.

It's the playoffs, he should be focused on pitching. I'll be fine by the time he gets home. I love that he cares so much, but truly, I'll be okay.

My stomach rolls and I groan. I don't ever get sick. I roll over on the couch and pull a pillow over my head. I just want to sleep the day away.

I hear keys in the front door of the apartment and pop up. I move too fast and regret it. Caleb shouldn't be here.

Who the hell is at our front door?

I swing my feet over the edge of the couch and reach for my phone. I pull up my brother's number. He lives the closest.

Before my brother can pick up, a tired looking Cameron comes strolling into view. My shoulders sag in relief. My brother picks up the phone just then.

"What's up squirt?" Freddy croons into the phone.

"Nothing, Freddy," I laugh. "Company just walked in. I'll call you later."

"Don't call, come over," my brother says.

"Maybe, I have so much homework. This work study isn't as easy as I thought it would be." I sigh.

"Yeah, I did a couple of those. They can be killer. If you need help, let me know, doo-doo bug."

"Ugh, don't call me that," I hiss.

"Whatever, doo-doo bug, later," he chuckles and hangs up.

I shake my head and place my phone down on the coffee table. I look up at Cameron curiously. I know he has keys to both our Texas apartment and this one here in New York. I just have no clue why he's here.

"What's up, big brother?" I smile.

"You tell me. Caleb is losing his shit. How are you feeling?" Cameron flops down beside me, reaching for my legs to pull them into his lap. "Have you eaten?"

"Wait, Caleb sent you? Shouldn't you be with your team playing somewhere or something?" I lift a brow.

"Nope, I've been here in New York for a few weeks. I'm in talks with Caleb's team. I'm on waivers and they're thinking about picking me up," Cameron shrugs.

"Seriously?" I say excitedly.

"Yeah," Cam rubs the back of his neck. "Atlanta wasn't working out and it looks like Caleb isn't dealing without me. His Coach wants to see if having me on the team will smooth things out next season."

"How's Kay?" I ask and bite my lip.

Cameron sighs and runs a hand through his hair. "Pissed. She hated Atlanta. Went back home after less than a month. She's been whining about me getting Daddy to call in some favors to get me back in Texas."

I watch Cam as he runs a hand down his face. I know there's more to the story. I've just been minding my own business. Kay was good and pregnant the last time I saw her.

"The baby will be here soon. Maybe things will get better then," I say hopefully.

Cam shakes his head. "Kay and I used to at least be friends. I mean we've always fought. It was our thing. It's just not cute or sexy anymore. She stresses me the fuck out."

"Have you guys thought about counseling?" I offer.

Cameron snorts, he turns to me and narrows his eyes. "You know, my father suggested that. I thought it would help, but Kay freaked out. I mean before we got married, she wanted to do everything we could to make things work for the baby. Now…." Cameron stops and sighs. "You don't want to hear this shit. How are you feeling? You didn't answer my question. Have you eaten?"

I groan as my stomach rolls at the mere thought of food. "No, I can't stomach the thought of food. I just want to sleep, but your brother has been driving me crazy with calls. I thought I would finally get some rest, since he's on the field," I mumble, pointing to the flat screen playing the game.

"He loves you. He just wants to make sure you're okay," Cameron chuckles.

"I'll be okay with some sleep. I swear, I just need a good nap," I whine.

Cameron looks at me funny. He tips his head to the side and studies me. I mirror him wondering what he's thinking.

"This may be none of my business, but have you and my brother been using protection?" Cameron says cautiously.

I blush at the question and start to reply, but pause. My mouth flaps for a few minutes, until I close my eyes and groan. I sag into myself. It's been months since Caleb and I have used protection. We stopped after getting engaged.

We'd both agreed. I'm on the pill and we're married now. Only…my bag was mixed up in the airport on the trip back to New York, after I surprised Caleb in Seattle. I didn't have my pills for three days. Three days where Caleb and I spent the entire time making up for lost time.

Shit, shit, shit.

I cradle my stomach with my arms wrapped around my middle. There's no way I'm giving up a baby I'm already pregnant with. Preventing having a baby is one thing.

I was willing to do that for Caleb. Killing our baby that's growing inside me is a whole different ball game. This is where I put my foot down.

How could I have fucked up like this? Caleb was just talking about starting with foster care in a year or two to see how things would go. From there, we were going to see if we should adopt.

Tears sting the backs of my eyes as I open them to find Cameron watching me closely. His eyes soften and he moves to pull me into a hug. He rubs my back as I release a small sob.

"It's going to be fine," Cam whispers.

"No, Cam, it's not. He said he didn't want a family. I didn't mean for this to happen. He is totally going to lose it," I sob.

"I know my brother. He may think this is something he doesn't want, but once that baby gets here, he'll come around. He'll love that baby, as much as he loves you," Cam reassures me.

"This is so messed up. I don't want him to hate our baby. I don't want him afraid of it either. Shit, Cam, how did I fuck up like this?" I cry.

"Shh, we don't know for sure yet. I'll run to the pharmacy and then we'll take it a step at a time from there," Cam coaches, kissing my forehead.

I sniffle. "Shit," I huff. "Thank you."

"Anytime," Cameron smiles. "My little ones will have a cousin to play with."

"Kay's having twins," I gasp.

Cam shakes his head and purses his lips. "No, Kay's not, but my other babies' mother is."

My mouth just hangs open as Cameron stands and starts out of the apartment. I stare at his back, stunned. Oh, he has some explaining to do when he gets back here.

~B~

Caleb

I'm tired, but I won't sleep until Nicole is in my arms. I've known my brother has been hiding out in New York for a few weeks now. His situation isn't getting any better. If you ask me, he's the most unhappy I've ever seen him.

I don't think he should've married Kay, but hey, what do I know. I'll tell you this. Something is off with Cam, and him hiding in New York proves it. My big brother hides from nothing.

I found out this morning that coach is trying to bring Cameron in next season. I haven't had time to process that or how I feel about it. I want Cameron with me, but I know he has a lot going on in his life. Neither of the mothers of his children are here in New York.

I have faith in Cam, though. He'll figure his own shit out. He has always helped to figure mine out. I'm just happy he could check on Nicole for me.

The team hadn't planned to fly out until the morning, but I needed to get home to my sick wife. I called in a favor from Daddy and he had the jet waiting for me. I wasted no time flying back to New York.

I lean my exhausted body up against the door and unlock it. I can hear the television playing in the living room. I pick up on Cam's voice murmuring something as I drag my ass in that direction.

I need to see my baby with my own two eyes. She hasn't been feeling well for days, but this morning she just didn't sound right. Not like my Nicole.

When I step into the spacious living room, the room seems to shrink. Nicole's eyes are red and puffy and her bronzed nose is tinged with red. I'm moving toward her before I can think about it.

"Do you need to go see a doctor?" I rush out. I sit on the edge of the marble coffee table, not even thinking about whether it can sustain my weight. "Tell me what you need."

Nicole leans forward and palms my face. She opens her mouth, but no words come out. She tries again, but tears start to fall.

"I'm sorry," she finally whispers.

I look to Cam. I'm not processing any of this well. I'm getting ready to freak out. A million things start to run through my mind. I suddenly can't filter out the extra noise in my head. Even Nicole's touch is setting me on edge. I ease away and feel like shit when her face crumbles and she starts to sob.

"Baby, I'm sorry," I whisper, unable to look at her.

I grip the edges of the coffee table I'm sitting on. I'm an adult. I'm not going to allow myself to melt down.

"Just give me a minute," I plead to no one in particular.

I focus on one item at a time, pinpointing it and shutting it down. It's something Aunt Judy helped me master when I was younger. I fade out all the extra shit I just don't need right now.

"Okay," I nod at Cam, I get the feeling he is going to be the next one to speak.

Nicole has curled into a ball and is still sobbing. It breaks my heart to see her like this. With shaky hands, I reach out for her. She comes into my arms willingly.

I exchange seats, sitting her in my lap when I take her place on the couch. For some reason, she seems so much smaller than usual. I start to rock, more to comfort me then her. I'm still right on the edge.

"Cal, I need you to listen to me. I'm your brother and I've never lied to you about shit. When I felt something wasn't right for you, I've told you. When I felt you needed to do something, I pushed you," Cam pauses and pulls a hand down his clean shaven face.

"You're both not making this better. Just spit it out, so I can deal with it," I grunt.

"I'm pregnant," Nicole whispers.

My head snaps toward my wife. She's looking up at me with the saddest expression I've ever seen on her face. My heart breaks into a million pieces.

This is why I said I didn't want a family. I can't take Nicole not wanting my child. I can't handle her not being able to love my baby like she loves me.

I nod and swallow, but my mouth is so dry, it's a fruitless effort. "And you don't want our baby?" I say stiffly. "You're crying because I'm the one that got you pregnant. You're afraid of our baby being like me."

"What?" Nicole gasps and pulls out of my lap.

She goes from sad to angry in a split second. It startles me as I watch it happen. I've never seen her looks so mad. She is shaking and her fists are balled at her sides.

"You said that bullshit," she points a finger at me. "I would never feel that way. I can't believe you. I've been crying my eyes out because I want this baby and I've been scared as fuck that you don't. This is our baby, Caleb. Ten fingers, ten toes, four eyes, no nose. It's ours and I will love it anyway God sees fit to bless it.

"Don't you ever fucking accuse me of not wanting a child that's as perfect as you are. I love you, just as you are. I married you, just as you are. You're not stupid, Cal, you have autism, so don't say shit to me that's not true and doesn't make a lick of sense.

"I'm your wife. This is our child. You're going to be an amazing father and that's that. I'm tired. Good night!"

Nicole storms off and slams the bedroom door. I blink after her, feeling like my head is going to explode. I rub at my chest.

Fuck, I'm going to be a father. One of my biggest fears in life. I hadn't admitted this fact to myself before. Truth be told, over the last few months, when I had Nicole in my arms at night, I'd sit up dreaming of a family with her.

Not the foster or adopted one I promised her a month ago. I've dreamed of what it would be like to watch her swell with our own child, like Kay. I can say I've truly envied my brother for having a child on the way.

They may not have planned it or have been together when they found out about it, but they have a family on the way. I've ached for that. To be normal and to know I can handle a family of my own.

Nicole deserves that. When I watched her with her family—with her nieces and nephews—I knew then I couldn't be selfish and take that away from her. It's one of the things I've been working on in my head and talking to Daddy about.

I want this baby too. As Nicole's words sink in. My chest begins to ache more. I was wrong. Nicole isn't like my Mama. She would never see our children as a burden or teach them to hide.

I fucked up.

"Well, shit," Cam mutters.

"I want the baby," I say to my brother. "I...I didn't think I did before. You know what Mama has always said. That I shouldn't have a family. I wouldn't be able to do right by them."

"Fuck that shit. Dude, you play professional baseball. Your coach took how long to figure out what was going on?"

"He didn't. I told him. I was having trouble with the team and I told the truth," I say.

"See my point? People don't know until you want them to. Which means you have control of this, not the other way around. You can't live your life for your diagnosis. You have to live your life and deal with autism when autism needs to be dealt with.

"It shouldn't define you. You define it. I'm so tired of everyone wanting to tell us what to do. You're super smart Cal. That baby is going to be so loved. Nicole loves the fuck out of you. She's going to love that baby just as much," Cameron reassures me.

I stare down at my palms. "Well, what the hell do I do now?" I sigh.

"Give her some time. She was really torn up when she thought you'd be upset that she's pregnant. I think you threw her. Give her some time to deal with that and the fact that she's going to be a mama," Cameron suggests.

I look up at him and he has a smile on his face. I furrow my brows. There's nothing funny about this. I have to fix this shit with my wife and I don't know how.

I was expecting to come home and find her with a cold, the flu—hell, not a baby. *A baby.* My stomach rolls and I jump up, heading for the front powder room.

Ah shit, I'm going to be a father.

CHAPTER TWENTY-THREE

What's Mine

Caleb

I woke this morning with a banging headache. My body sore and my mind racing. Cameron slept on the couch after we stayed up talking most of the night.

I'm glad I have my brother in my life. I know he has his own shit going on, but he was here for me last night. I know it would've been harder if he hadn't been here.

Nicole locked me out of our bedroom and I could hear her in there crying. That shit gutted me. I know it's probably not good for the baby.

I stopped trying to get her to let me in when she started to sob louder. I'll do whatever I can not to stress her or the baby out. My kid is going to have all the fighting chance it needs to be perfect.

Perfect.

Such an interesting word. All my life I thought it meant Cameron, or Dakota. Now, I hear it all the time, in reference to *me*. My wife thinks I'm perfect, but I'm not.

I hurt her. In more ways than one. I made her fear my feelings for our child. I placed pressure on her that she never should've felt. I won't forgive myself for that.

I blink at the ceiling of our guest room. I slept here last night, to give Nicole some space. I hate this bed. I hate it because Nicole isn't in it.

I want to wrap around her little body and feel her breathing next to me. I want to inhale her scent to calm me. I want to make love to her, without the fear of our future, because it's already set in motion.

We're having a baby.

Every time I've been inside her without a condom, I've worried this could happen. Honestly, I've secretly prayed for it on some level, deep down in my heart. A smile takes over my face.

A little girl as pretty as her mama. Or a son I can play catch with. I can handle that. Teaching my son the right way to pitch.

So, that's why Nicole's pussy has felt so damn good in the last couple of weeks. Her body is already changing with our baby. Her breasts do taste sore, but I just thought it was that time of the month.

Fuck this, I want my woman.

I want to touch her belly and talk to our baby. I sit up and toss my legs over the edge of the bed. The floor is cold against my bare feet, but I grit my teeth and bear it.

I can get warm in my bed with my wife. I pad to our bedroom and sigh in relief when I find the door open. A chill runs through me, when I step into the bedroom.

Nicole isn't here. I can feel it in my bones. I look around the room wildly, my stomach feels like it's going to drop out.

I run for my phone. Nicole and I have trackers on our phones. It's a precaution, in case I ever find myself in a situation I can't handle. Me shortening the leash my family has on me has caused Nicole and I to think of things that will compensate for the shit that could go wrong.

This is something I'm grateful for at the moment. I pull up the app and it shows Nicole's location. I try not to freak out. Just because she went to her parents' house doesn't mean she left me.

However, I'm not waiting around to find out. I rush to my closet, pulling on socks and some sneakers. I grab a hoodie and baseball cap. I'm on my way out the door, when Cameron stumbles out of the front powder room.

"Where're you heading, like you've got fire on your ass?" Cameron says, while scratching his belly.

"Nicole left," I say and keep walking.

"Cal." Cameron sighs. "She went to her parents' place to think."

"Yeah, well, I'm going to think with her," I toss back.

"Cal."

"No," I spin around. "She's my wife and she's pregnant with my baby. Whatever you're about to say doesn't matter.

"My wife left here not knowing how I feel," I pound on my chest. "She doesn't need that shit on her right now. She needs to know I love her and that baby.

"Am I scared? So fucking much, I might shit myself, but I'll walk through fire for her. I'll fix all my shit for her the best I can. I'm going to be a daddy, Cam. She has to know I want that."

"Did you just say you might shit yourself?" Cam shakes his head at me. "Do you know that was funny? Even more so, cause you said it with a straight as fuck face."

I roll my eyes. "Bye, Cameron."

"No, wait. I'll drive," Cameron calls after me.

I think about it for a second. "Nope, I'm driving. It will still some of this shit in my head."

~B~

Nicole

"So, you ready to spill?" my dad asks, as he places his crossword puzzle down.

I've been avoiding him all morning. I finally feel like I can eat something, so I came down for lunch. Mom just made it back from the clinic and she's making something to eat for the three of us. I haven't said a word.

I want to tell them about the baby first this time and I wanted to tell them together. If I would've hung out with my dad today, I would've spilled by now. Mom would be so pissed at me.

I sigh and look up at both my parents. They're staring at me waiting for me to speak. I smooth my hands over the napkin in front of me. I fidget in my seat for a few minutes.

"I thought I had the flu. Cameron came to check on me yesterday and suggested otherwise. Turns out he was right. I'm pregnant," I huff out.

"Oh, honey, this is wonderful news. You'll be finishing school in the spring. You already have a job at the clinic if you decide to work. Or you can write and take photos for your dad. So, why the long face?" My mother asks.

"Caleb and I had a fight," I whisper.

"Because he doesn't want the baby," my father states more than asks.

"No." I shake my head, "Because he accused me of not wanting the baby. I don't know what happened. I've never been so mad in my life. I just lost it on him. I didn't mean to. He must be so scared." I snort. "I am."

"Well, how does he feel about the baby?" My mother asks, with her brows drawn together.

I open my mouth, but I don't get a chance to speak. The house alarm announces the front door opening, just before Caleb starts bellowing through the house. My eyes go wide and I scramble to my feet.

When I turn to head for the door, a sleep messed, sweats wearing, Caleb is standing before me. He looks like he rolled right out of bed and raced here. He stumbles forward, dropping to his knees, pulling me into him by my waist.

"Caleb," I try, but he shakes his head against my stomach and squeezes me tighter.

He looks up into my eyes. "You didn't give me a chance to tell you how I feel." He places his large hand against my belly. "You two mean the world to me. I want our baby as much as I want you.

"I just, I never wanted to hear you say that you didn't want to have children with me." He lifts his other hand to place his finger to my lips when I go to talk. "Since I was little, my Mama told me it wouldn't be right for me to have a family.

"She told me I wouldn't understand how to love a woman. She said I'd ignore my children or get them hurt. She told me I wouldn't understand my manly needs and I shouldn't try." He chokes out.

"Then, I met you." His hands slide up and down my sides. "I know I understand how to love you, cause you call my name when we make love. You look in my eyes and tell me, you love me. You gave yourself to me, you're my woman and I know I please you.

"I understand my need for you just fine," Cameron clears his throat behind Caleb, but Cal ignores everyone but me. I blush all over, but I don't stop him. "I understand it clinically, I understand it physically, and I know how it makes me feel mentally.

"I understand that my love for you and those manly needs placed a baby in here," he dips his head and kisses my stomach. "I know one more thing, darlin'. You're mine and so is this baby. Just like I learned to shut out the screams of thousands of fans, to focus on a single pitch. I promise, I'll learn to focus to keep you and our baby safe.

"I'm sorry I didn't get to tell you how happy I was last night. I was already losing my shit before you said a word about the baby. You have to give me time sometimes, baby," he pleads with me. "I came to get what's mine, Nicole. Come home, darlin'. I'm sorry."

I stand stunned. My mouth hangs open, as I stare at my husband. I have no words. I'd only come over to think and share the news with my parents. I had every intention of going back home.

My dad stands on his feet, with his arms folded over his chest and a proud smile on his face. My mom has tears on her cheeks and Cameron looks like he wants to fist pump.

I have a mix of tears on my cheeks and a smile on my lips. That was Caleb's unfiltered way of letting me know how he feels and I wouldn't have had it any other way. Embarrassment and all, I love this man.

"I only came to think a little and tell my parents about the baby. I was going to head home after lunch," I say running my hand through his hair. My palms go to his face and bend to kiss his lips. "I'm sorry. I shouldn't have lost it."

My dad clears his throat. "How about we all have lunch and celebrate this new little one?"

"Come on, I know you and Cam are always hungry," I smile at Caleb. "And our little baby has me starving."

The smile that lights up Caleb's face takes my breath away. He pulls me closer and kisses my belly. Ignoring everyone, he lifts my shirt to get to my skin.

"This is your Daddy, I'm going to spoil you rotten. You're so loved, baby Perry," he whispers against my stomach.

I wipe the tears from my chin with the tissue my mother hands me. When Caleb lifts to his feet and pulls me into a hug, I finally feel like I can breathe. He wants the baby. We're going to be okay.

"I got some steaks for the grill. You want a beer, Cameron?" Daddy calls as Caleb sways me in his arms.

"Yes, sir, these two have driven me to drink," Cameron chuckles.

Caleb lifts me into his arms and I yelp. "Caleb, put me down," I giggle.

"Nope, you won't lift a finger or a foot, until our baby is born," Caleb says against my temple.

"Aww, my hero," I sing and giggle.

CHAPTER TWENTY-FOUR

All Falls Down

Nicole

Eight years and two months later...

I love my family. Our little girls will be eight this year and we have a seven-month-old son, Caleb Jr. My children are my world. I'm so glad we had them. My little girls are freakishly smart and Caleb Jr. is just adorable.

They show me something new every day. I love learning the world through their eyes. The girls are just as honest as their father. Not because of Autism, but because they are just like their father and their uncle.

Basically, my girls are smart asses. I swear some days I just can't. Monica told Caleb he needed to pull it together the other day. Caleb Jr. was crying because he needed a diaper change, Caleb had just come in from practice and I was in the bathroom.

At thirty-one, Caleb's shoulder has been giving him a problem. He had a bad day at practice and was already feeling bogged down. Caleb Jr.'s crying just sent him over the edge. When I found him and the kids in the living room, Caleb was sitting in the middle of the floor, with his hands over his ears, tugging at his hair. Our oldest, Monica, thinks she's the boss around here, so leave it to her to handle the situation.

"Daddy, Caleb needs changing and Mama's busy. We're not allowed to change him. So, you need to pull it together. You're the adult right now, you don't have time for a bad day. We need you, Caleb stinks," Monica said with her little hands on her hips. Her toffee colored face twisted up, her light brown eyes, screaming no nonsense.

I covered my mouth to keep from laughing out loud. My little girls are a mess. They love their Daddy and never like to see him having a bad day, but this was too cute because of what happened next.

Caleb lifted his head and looked our daughter in the eyes. He nodded and stroked her thick honey brown curls. He stood and walked over to the baby.

"Oh God, you do stink," Caleb said.

"Duh, Daddy, that's what I was trying to tell you. I don't know what Mama fed him, but it just ain't right," Monica groaned.

"Please, Daddy, my nose can't take it," Morgan pleaded.

Caleb huffed. "You two gonna help or complain," Caleb grunted.

"You want me to help with that?" Morgan frowned. "I love you, Daddy, but this is just too much."

After that one, I couldn't hold my laughter any longer. Caleb spun around to find me watching. The relieved look on his face was priceless.

He scooped the girls up, one in each arm, and dashed into the kitchen to get them a snack. I shook my head the entire time I changed my son. I laughed so hard that day, but I also smiled.

Our girls have been a light in Caleb's life. He didn't have another thought about practice, until the girls had gone to bed. Then he talked through things with me.

We've made our life work, I take care of the kids and he plays ball. I write for my dad's publishing company here and there. Caleb hasn't had to deal with the children on his own much. Over the last seven and a half years, with his schedule, most times he hasn't been around the children much.

It wasn't as easy to pick up and follow after Caleb, with little twin girls. When Caleb played in New York, I had my family to help me. It wasn't as hard on me, because someone was always there.

Since we've been back to Texas, things have been different. My father-in-law had a stroke last year. He hasn't been the same since. My mother-in-law has become a straight witch since finding out I was pregnant with the girls.

I can't count on them like I can my family. Dakota tries, but she has her own little ones now. She and Hamilton, *surprise, surprise,* married two years after we all graduated.

Dakota's little boy is five and her girl is four. They are a handful by themselves. Put them in a room with Monica and Morgan and you want to strangle the four of them.

The twins were pretty much a breeze to deal with from the day they were born. Then they started talking. Good Lord, if my son has half the mouth of those two, I'm going to sell him to the highest bidder.

I smile down at my little boy. I'll never get tired of looking at those dimples or seeing him blow bubbles at me. His hazel eyes twinkle as I coo at him. He was an even bigger surprise than his sisters.

I was four months pregnant before we noticed. Caleb was so proud to find out we were having a boy. He nearly passed out when we found out we were having twins, the first time.

Unfortunately, Caleb missed the birth of the girls by thirty minutes to be exact. He was sick over it for months. I'd been having false labor pains for two weeks, and when the real deal took place, Caleb couldn't get out of his game.

He made it for CJ though, and cried like a baby when his son was placed in his hands. I still remember it like it was yesterday. The sweetest moment ever.

"Mr. Perry, you can breathe now, your son is here," the nurse teased.

Caleb looked at her with wide eyes. He licked his lips and shook his head. I burst into laughter, when he finally spoke.

"I can't believe she let me touch her after our twins. Oh my God, Baby. That was incredible. He's so loud," Caleb swallowed hard, as the cries of our son filled the room.

The nurse came over and placed the baby on my chest. He quieted almost immediately. My son looked up at me with those hazel-blue eyes and I melted in his little palms. Caleb reached to run a shaky hand over our son's thick silky brown hair.

"You want to hold him?" I whispered.

Caleb's eyes flickered to mine, almost popping out of his head. It took him two whole weeks before he would hold the girls. I gave him a reassuring smile and handed our son over.

Caleb took him gently and tucked him into his chest. The awe and reverence in his face were just heartwarming. Caleb kissed our son's head and whispered something in his ear just for him.

"You will be the complete Caleb. The better version of me. The latter shall be better than the former," Caleb then said out loud for others to hear.

The older nurse in the room clinched her hand over her chest. It was clear she was holding back tears. The medical staff in our room were all aware of all of our family medical history.

The nurses had helped Caleb keep his shit through the delivery. He was so overwhelmed, but he refused to leave and miss his son's birth. Half way through, I had to bite the bullet and silence my pain, but it was worth it for the very moment that had us all in tears.

"So, that's his name?" I asked with a teary smile. "Will he be Caleb Jr.?"

"Yes, Darling, if that's all right with you. I want to name him Caleb Cameron Perry."

I giggled at the name, but I loved it just the same. "So not exactly a Jr.," I asked with a raised brow.

"No, baby, he's going to be the best of the men in his life," Caleb says, with his throat clogged with emotion.

"I like it, but I think he has some big shoes to fill. His Daddy is something amazing," I say softly, as I watch little Caleb start to fall asleep in his father's arms.

"Not as amazing as his Mama," Caleb whispered with so much love in his eyes.

Despite not having as much support here in Texas as we did in New York, we've been living in our own little bubble. We're happy, our children are safe and healthy, and we're making our dreams come true.

Cameron doesn't play baseball anymore, but he's still by Caleb's side as much as ever. Cameron has a position with

Caleb's team, as a hitting coach. Cam has changed a lot, but he and Caleb have been tighter than ever through it all.

"Daddy's going to shut them out," Morgan squeals excitedly.

"Look, he just did our thing," Monica giggles.

Caleb made up a simple gesture to let the girls know when he's thinking of them. I smile every time they get all excited to see him acknowledge them. He loves them so much.

I look over at our girls glued to the television as they watch their father play. This is what we do it all for. He's the world to them. I can't tell you how many times they have begged to have little parties with their friends to watch their father play.

"Look, Uncle Cam's going to talk to Daddy," Morgan points to the screen.

I grin. They brag about their Uncle Cam all the time as well. All their little friends are in awe of their father and uncle. Caleb has me go all out for their game parties.

It makes up for Caleb not being able to handle birthday parties, with all of their friends. My heart is sometimes heavy with things like that. The simple stuff other families take for granted that ours has to avoid.

We tried once. For the twins' fifth birthday. It was insane. We had the party at my parents' house. When Caleb disappeared into the house, my mother was the one that noticed. She found him hiding out in my old bedroom having a meltdown.

Mom and Caleb have a special bond. She helped him pull it together, even got him to play a game of baseball with a few of the kids. That he was able to handle—no contact, little talking, and his focus on the game blocked out the screaming kids.

However, he had his limits when some of the fathers wanted to get too close, reaching to pat him on the shoulder or back. I, too, had my limits when some of the moms thought Caleb's lack of spatial reference meant he was interested.

Yup, we haven't done that one again. Little miss, missy that tried to hand my husband her number, never tried me again either. Heifer really followed me because she thought I was going to give her a bag she commented on once at a play date.

Mom turned the other way, while my sisters stood guard as I handed out that ass whipping. It wasn't the first time I caught her behaving inappropriately toward my husband. He may not get it, but I do, and I don't play that shit.

Sigh.

I won't lie and say I don't miss New York and my family. My sisters and I laughed about that one for weeks.

"I think we need to go for a visit. What about you?" I coo to Caleb Jr.

His hazel-blue eyes twinkle and he shows me those gums and his one new tooth. His spit bubbles are his reply. I shake my head at my handsome boy.

"*Daddy*," the twins cry in unison, causing me to jerk my head up.

I rush for the remote to turn the sound up. Caleb is kneeling on one knee, holding his shoulder. It looks like he's screaming.

"This looks bad folks," the announcer says.

"Yes, we know Perry has been having trouble with that shoulder all season," the other announcer chimes in.

"Well, you know this could end the season for him. He looks like he's in a lot of pain. The club has been keeping talks of the shoulder as quiet as they could," the first announcer says.

"You're right. I believe they were going to try to trade him if they could. This won't bode well for a trade."

The first announcer speaks my fears right to my soul. He says the words that I don't want to hear, but are playing in the back of my mind. I close my eyes, not able to watch my husband like this.

"I don't think a trade will be an option. Sorry to say, but I think Perry is done. At thirty-one, he's been pitching longer than most, with the type of speed and precision he has," the announcer whistles. "I mean just look at him. He's really in pain. It may be his rotator cuff."

"Oh my God, please no. Caleb needs to play," I whisper to myself. "Please don't take this from him."

~B~

Caleb

My shoulder burns, but I'm not ready to call it quits. I can close this game out. My little sweethearts are watching at home. I can't let them down.

Two more hitters and I'll have shut them out tonight. I have to fight against this pain. This shoulder won't get the best of me. I'll finish this game and get some ice on it. I can do this.

I look my coach and Cameron in the eyes. "I'm finishing this game," I say for the second time.

"You're finishing your fucking career," Cam hisses at me.

"You're the hitting coach. I'm the pitcher. Why are you here?" I reply back.

"You little motherfucker. You're my brother. You little shit," Cameron snarls and gets in my face. "You know you're pushing it. Sit this one out asshole, before you end up sitting the season out."

"Fuck off, Cam," I bite out.

"Shit, Cal, Nicole isn't going to think you're a pussy for sitting out. Don't do this. You don't have to be superman," my brother huffs.

"It's not for Nicole. Monica and Morgan are watching. I won't disappoint my girls," I shake my head. "Their daddy is going to make them proud."

Cameron narrows his eyes at me. Then he closes them and groans. "Cal, you've been talking to Mama again, haven't you?"

I don't answer. I just stare past him at the field. I have, she's called me to the house to see my father a few times this week. She's still angry with me about the twins and now little Caleb.

"Listen, we have a game to play. Are you up to it, kid, or should we sit you out?" Coach asks.

"Are you kidding me? Why are you asking him? Sit his ass down," Cameron growls.

"He's about to shut this team out," Coach shrugs. "Why shake things up now?"

"Un-fucking-believable," Cam throws his hands in the air, then tugs at his hair. "Fine, your stubborn ass will do what you want. I don't have a good feeling about this, Cal, but you're not listening."

"I'm ready," I nod at coach.

"All right," Coach nods, "Let's finish this."

I need to pull it together. I asked Nicole to move back here to Texas. I won't move my family to Florida. That's where they told me they want to send me. I haven't told my wife they're seriously talking of trading me.

I know Nicole misses New York. My family isn't as helpful or close as hers. My little cousin Andy has been putting Aunt

Judy and Uncle Rusty through the ringer. Things aren't like they used to be.

In New York, I was sure that my wife was happy. Here, I just don't know. That's what has allowed my Mama to plant her shit in my head.

According to her, I'm not a good father. I'm failing as a husband. My focus is on baseball, where my attention should be. So why do I insist on dragging a family into it?

Nicole always looks so exhausted when I get home. I'm no help with the kids. Maybe my mama's right. Hell, I can't even attend my babies' birthday parties without being overwhelmed.

I close my eyes and shake all of that off. This guy can't hit curve balls, but he'll be expecting that. A fast ball will put this to bed. I strike him out, I'm one step closer to going home to my family.

I move back on my drive leg, lifting my left leg and my glove at the same time. I open up, planting my lift leg and cock my arm to release the pitch. I know right as its about to happen, I go to release the pitch and something in my shoulder explodes with it.

"*Arrr,*" I drop to my knee and bellow out. "*Fuck! No, no, no, no.*"

I clinch my shoulder and continue to scream in agony. It hurts so fucking much. There are people around me, someone is even touching me, but I'm in too much pain to even let that register.

"Shit, Cal," I hear Cam hiss. "*Shit.*"

I won't even look at my shoulder. I know what I'll see will just confirm what I already feel. I just ended my baseball career. I'm fucked.

CHAPTER TWENTY-FIVE

Always Here

Nicole

It's been seven months since the game that ended Caleb's career. He had to have surgery on the damaged shoulder right away. My mother flew in to be with the twins, while I flew out to be at Caleb's side.

One of my sisters was able to come along with me, since I hadn't weaned Caleb Jr. off of breast milk yet. That first three weeks had to be the hardest. Caleb has been pulling into himself since the surgery, which hasn't made things much better.

I hate seeing him like this. I know how much baseball means to him, but there is something more going on and he won't let me in. I've never been on this side of things with him. He has always said just what he has felt.

Now, I'm lucky if he says two words to me. He talks to his mother a lot. I can't fault him for that. She barges her way into our home almost every day with the pretenses that she's here to take care of him.

According to her, I need to focus on the kids. She can handle Caleb. I almost told her more than once where she can put that bullshit, but I've bitten my tongue because she's my children's grandmother and my husband's mom.

Not that she cares much about her grandchildren. I swear she watches my kids like they're aliens or something. I feel like she's watching them for signs of Autism. Like, I, as their mother have missed something she will see. My patience is so thin with that woman.

That's why I'm folding the mess out of these sheets right now. I need something to beat on, so I don't beat on her. How is she going to come in here and tell me that Caleb shouldn't hold his son?

I was sitting right there. Caleb had the baby in his lap, they were both fine. Caleb Jr. was on his way into a nap, as he leaned into his father's side watching some car show.

He was on Caleb's left side. Nowhere near Caleb's bad shoulder. I swear that woman drives me crazy. Throat punch is not the word.

"Nicole," I look up from the sheets I'm folding, in the guest room.

"Yes, Mrs. Jemma," I say, as nicely as I can.

"I was thinking. You have the children here. Your hands are full. Why doesn't Caleb come and stay with me and his daddy?"

I feel my face light up like someone set a match to it. This bitch done tried it today. Ten years ago, I didn't let her steam roll me and I won't be doing it today.

"Caleb is just fine here with me and the children. I don't see why he would need to stay with you. I would think you would have your hands full with *your* husband," I say, placing my hand on my hip and shifting on the bed.

This used to be my sanctuary. Where I came to write, pray, and hide from this woman when she comes to my home. At the moment, she has shifted the entire atmosphere.

Note to self, get some sage and exorcise this crazy bitch from your home.

She waves me off. "Kyle spends most of his time staring at the walls. I have plenty of time for Caleb," she says.

"Ugh, why can't you just let him be an adult. Listen, I'm not doing this with you," My patience has finally snapped. "I'm not having this disruption in my home. I would like it if you would leave. Come back when you can respect my home, my family, and my marriage."

"Well, I've never," she gasps.

"And you never will, not here you won't," I say, with narrowed eyes. "You need to stop being so trifling and start being a grandmother. You think my children don't notice you treating them differently. Get over yourself. Act like an adult and acknowledge my babies the way you should. I'm tired of putting up with your mess."

"Nicole, I have no problem acknowledging my grandchildren," she huffs.

"Right," I huff back. "That's why Morgan called your damn name, five times, before you answered her. I watched you. I don't get it, but I stopped trying to understand stupid a long time ago."

"I don't have to take this. Caleb knows what's right. He'll do the right thing," she snaps and turns on her heels to storm away.

My stomach sinks. Her words have an eerie feel to them that I can't shake off right away. I run my hands through my hair.

"I'm fed up," I mumble to myself. "Ready or not we are talking, Mr. Perry."

I storm out of the guestroom, heading for our bedroom where Caleb holds up most days. I don't know what that woman has been feeding him, but it stops now.

I walk into the bedroom to find Caleb staring down at his hands. My heart breaks. I know those hands worked hard to accomplish so much, and now, because of his shoulder, they seem useless to him. Or at least, that's what I think he believes.

I lean into the doorjamb, some of my anger melting away. I'm not used to seeing Caleb this vulnerable. He has always been ready to defy the odds.

"Monica said I'm not her fun Daddy anymore," Caleb says down to his hands, a little above a whisper.

"Yeah, well, Monica has been trying to make me beat her little ass all week," I say.

Caleb's head whips in my direction. I tilt my head at him and fold my arms over my chest. A smile tugs my lips.

"You and I know, I've never lifted a finger to discipline our little girls. A good look sends those two into act right mode," I laugh.

"It shouldn't be that way," Caleb growls.

"What way?" I furrow my brows and push off the doorjamb. I close the door behind me and walk fully into the room.

"I've spent our entire marriage on a baseball field. I've left you to raise our girls on your own. If things were different, it would've been the same way with our son.

"Why are you with me, Nicole? When have I done right by you? What can I give you now?" He turns to look at my face.

I climb on the bed and straddle his lap, palming his cheeks. I brush his long locks from his forehead and run my fingers over his beard. My heart aches for him, I'll do anything to take this hurt away.

"Babe, I'm with you because I love you. Every day I get to wake up to you and our beautiful children. You all make me laugh, smile, want to pull my hair out, but I wouldn't trade a single one of you.

"You have always done right by me. I've always had a roof over my head. I've never gone a moment without knowing how much you love me. You've given me three beautiful babies that I love to pieces and back whole again.

"You can give me what you've always given me. You can give me, you. You're all I ask for. We'll figure the rest out. Remember we promised each other we'd be a team. We'd fight for each other.

"This is it, buddy. You have to stand up for our family and know that we love you, whether you're playing ball, chasing a ten-month-old around the house, or reading your physics books for hours," I reassure him.

He looks away from me. "I haven't touched you like I should in months," I watch him swallow hard. "I haven't been your husband in the right way in seven months."

I smile as I place my fingers under his chin, turning his head in my direction. "Okay," I purr. "We can fix that."

I reach for the hem of my shirt and pull it over my head. "Nicole," he grunts out, sounding pained.

"Yes, baby," I say seductively, as I reach behind me and unhook my bra. "Don't worry about your shoulder. I'll do all the work."

I move off his lap to wiggle out of my sweats and panties. I'm not dressed very sexy to do house work, but once I'm completely naked in front of him, I don't think any of that matters. The lust that fills his eyes says a million words.

I tug at his gym shorts, looking him in the eyes, silently commanding him to lift his hips. I pat his thigh when he just continues to stare at me heatedly. After a few moments he obliges me, lifting up and helping me to pull his shorts down.

He springs free from his confines with precum already dripping from his tip. I lick my lips and inhale his scent coming off of his heated body. It has been much too long since we've been intimate. At first, we couldn't because of his shoulder, then it was just a matter of Caleb shutting me out.

He frowns, causing my heart to sink, as I think he is getting ready to deny me. "Who's with the baby, and the girls?" He asks.

I sag in relief. "My sister took them all to the park, and they're going for ice cream after. We have at least another hour," I say, squeezing my breasts and biting my lip.

"Shit, darlin', I miss you," he says hungrily. He reaches to tug his shirt off, awkwardly avoiding his shoulder.

"I missed you too," I whimper, as I slip my fingers between my legs. I play with my core, turning us both on, as he watches intently. "You want this, Cal? I want you."

"Come here," he says huskily.

I climb over to him to close the gap, but when I go to straddle his lap again, he shakes his head. Reaching for my waist with his good arm, he guides me over his lap, with my back facing him.

"Argh," Caleb groans, while I plant my feet between his open thighs.

I sink onto him, leap frog style, and lean forward on my forearms, arching my back when the full force of having him inside me takes over. He stretches me so deliciously, my mouth waters and I actually drool onto the sheets in front of me.

I pull it together, making a slurping sound that causes him to groan. He starts to massage my back, as I begin moving up and down on him. The feeling is so unbelievable.

I pick up the pace, when he grasps my ass cheeks in his huge palms. His groaning increases and he starts to move his hips. I grip the sheets and bite my lip hard.

"You feel so fucking good," Caleb growls. "I don't deserve you, darlin'."

"Yes. You. Do," I moan, grinding my hips to punctuate each word.

"Shit, Nicole," he calls out, as his hips move faster.

I punch my balled fist against the mattress. A yelp escape my lips, when Caleb shifts swiftly. He pulls my legs from beneath me, settling me on my side and lunging forward into my heat.

"Babe, be careful, your shoulder," I whimper-moan.

"I'm fine," he grunts, placing a hand to my belly and tossing his leg over the side of the bed for leverage. "I want this pussy so bad. You're going to come for me, baby. Nice and hard."

"Yes," I cry out, forgetting myself.

"You want this? You like it like this? I want to give it to you just like you like, baby," he says reaching between my legs for my clit.

"Oh my God, Cal," I gasp. "Just like that."

"I love you," he groans. "So much."

Caleb lifts my leg and tucks it into his side, as he continues to take over. He growls as he starts to hit my spot, and I begin keening. I gush around him, as I feel his hot seed burst into me, but he doesn't stop.

He plows through both of our orgasms, as if they never happened. He's so hard, his grip on my thigh is so tight. I think I'm going to lose it as he alternates between slow, deep, long strokes and fast, short ones.

"Cal, I'm coming," I holler.

His cheeks are red from exertion. They puff out and his head falls back. So, beautiful, always so beautiful, Caleb makes a gorgeous sight in the throes of passion.

"I feel you, baby. Stop holding back. I want it, give it to me," he demands.

I let go, not able to hold back if I tried. "Caleb," I scream my release.

"Nicole, damn, baby," he grunts through clinched teeth.

I sit up to support some of his weight, when his body goes to collapse. He wraps his uninjured arm around me and pulls me into his side, turning onto his back. I wrap my leg around his thigh and snuggle into him.

"Caleb," I whisper, after a while.

"Yes," he answers.

"I don't know what you're thinking, but I'm always here for you. Don't forget that. I've never run from you. I never will," I promise.

Caleb doesn't reply. He kisses the top of my head and runs his fingers up and down my back. We lay like that until we hear our loud children return.

I'm disappointed to see Caleb withdraw into himself all over again. At this point, I don't know what to do. I'll just give him time.

CHAPTER TWENTY-SIX

Too Much

Caleb

I'm a shitty father. I can't even handle my son's cries. Mrs. Joy has suggested that I start to find a safe place in the house. Somewhere I can regroup when I'm overwhelmed.

I'm broken inside. I can't figure out how to filter out all the noise anymore. Losing baseball has lost me my control. I don't know what to do.

Little Caleb is fourteen months old now. He fusses about everything. I know that's what babies do, but I don't remember the girls fussing so much. Then again, I wasn't around much when they were his age.

I just needed to get away. When Mama called saying my Daddy asked for me, I jumped at the chance to get out of the house. I don't think Nicole was happy about that, but she doesn't say much. Not after that one afternoon.

I miss making love to my wife, but I don't feel like I deserve her. Nicole does everything for our family, and she works from home. Let her tell it, she writes from time to time and is a freelance photographer.

In addition to taking amazing photos for travel and bridal guides for her father's publishing company, Nicole is a bestselling author. Her murder mysteries are amazing. I devour each one. If my wife decided she didn't want me anymore, she would be more than able to take care of herself and our children, without my help. Not that I would ever let that happen.

I hate that money is the only thing I have to give to my family. They'll never want for stability, but I lack everything else. Mama's right, it was selfish of me to marry Nicole and start a family.

"You can fix this, Cal," Mama coaches.

"How?"

"You know how. She's a pretty young woman. She's young enough to find a suitable husband," Mama suggests.

A suitable husband.

Those words sting more than she knows. The thought of another man touching Nicole sends my blood on fire. All of the noise in my head gets louder with the suggestion.

However, the words ring true in the back of my head. Way in the back, where the small voice is telling me I should provide better for my family. Even if that better is not with me.

"I don't know," I say.

"Yes, you do," Mama encourages. "I have the number to your Daddy's attorney. We can have him draw up the papers. It's the right thing to do, honey."

I purse my lips and squint. My head hurts. Maybe my Mama's right. I feel like I don't know my wife anymore. It's not her fault. It's mine. I shut her out and now I don't trust myself or my judgement.

"I flinched away from Morgan, yesterday," I whisper. "I've never had a problem with my girls touching me. Their touch used to help calm me. Just like their Mama. My head is so messed up."

"Exactly," I look up from my hands when my Mama's words sound off to me. There's a tight expression on her face for a moment, or at least I thought I saw it there.

She smiles.

She holds out a hand toward me, but drops it at the last minute. I look away. Mama's expression just reminds me of the look on Morgan's face, when I moved away from her.

"Listen, Cal, you have to do what's best for them. You know little Caleb is still young. What if he is diagnosed? Nicole will need someone that can help her."

"My son is fine," I bite out.

"Yes, he just may be. We didn't see it with you for almost two years," Mama says softly. "Two years from now, your family can have someone that will give them what they need."

I drop my head in my hand. "Okay," I say brokenly. "Do it. I'll move my things out. Just make sure they give her half of everything."

"What?"

"You heard me. I want her to have half of everything. No, the house is hers, the cars I bought her are hers, and she keeps the bank accounts I put in her name. Everything else, they can split in half," I instruct.

"You're doing the right thing," Mama says with a smile.

"So why do I feel like I'm breaking in two," I say hoarsely.

~B~
Nicole

I got a text from Caleb yesterday saying he was staying over his parents' house for the night. He had gone over to see his dad. At first, I didn't think anything of it.

Caleb has been having a hard time with the kids and being home with them on a regular basis. I know it's been a big adjustment. So, I just chalked it up to him needing a little time to himself.

My mother suggested we make a room for him to decompress when he needs to. She even mailed him some ear plugs, since he has the hardest time when Caleb Jr. is crying and the girls are being noisy.

Those helped some, but now I know Caleb's problem runs deeper than our children making noise. He doesn't want us. Or it may be me.

I thought I was being punked, when I was served with divorce papers this morning. I haven't stopped crying all day. I just don't understand.

What makes me so angry is that he won't even try to explain what the hell is going on. This isn't like Caleb. He won't answer my calls. He just texted me to let me know he's okay and won't be home again.

I pull up the app on my phone to see if Caleb's still hiding out at his parents' house. Once I confirm it, I get dressed and pull my hair into a ponytail. When I look in the mirror, at my jeans and rumpled t-shirt, I bite my lip. I run a hand over my messy ponytail.

I haven't worn my bob in years. I look hard at myself. I can't help but wonder if maybe I let myself go. Caleb hasn't touched me since that one afternoon. Most days, I'm in sweats and an oversized, baby stained t-shirt.

"I see what's running through your brain, like it's on a ticker tape. This has nothing to do with the way you look," My sister calls into the room.

"Then what is it?" I say angrily.

I know she's not the one to blame. She has been here for months, just trying to help out. Well, and hide out. My sister has her own relationship problems.

I see her shrug her shoulders through the mirror. "I don't know," Stevie says. "It's clear he's been having a hard time. If you ask me, his mother has been playing a part in all of this."

"But why," I sob. "Why would she work to pull him from his family? Do you know how much my girls adore him? Caleb Jr. goes crazy just trying to get to him whenever he hears his father's voice. Why would she do this?"

"I have no idea. That woman has issues. I think she's jealous of you and the kids. Caleb didn't used to have a problem embracing you all and focusing on showing you all how much he cares. I think that has made that bitch bitter," my sister muses.

"Oh my God. She has ruined my family for a *hug*? I can't bring myself to believe that," I shake my head as tears fall. "Caleb knows I love him. What is he thinking?"

My sister walks into my room, wrapping her arms around me. "Think about Liv. She's eighteen now. She has her first boyfriend. That boy loves her to the moon and back, but you and I have seen that some days she doesn't get that."

"That's different. Tate has been her friend since they were little. They're best friends. She's adjusting to what they've become. Caleb and I have been together for ten years.

"He pursued *me*. He made *me* fall in love with him. How does he just expect me to stop now?" I cry.

"Sweetie, I don't think he's thinking about that. I think he's hurt that the one thing he had control over was taken from him. I think he's trying to figure out his new role, just like Liv.

"I also think if you give him some time, he'll figure out this isn't what he wants. I've seen the way Caleb looks at you. I saw it when I first met him and it has only gotten more intense. That man loves the mess out of you," My sister says as she wipes at my tears.

"Then why is he divorcing me?" I sniffle.

"He's lost, Cole. When that man looks up and his Nicole is gone, he's going to lose his mind and be right on your doorstep," she smiles.

"So, what are you saying?" I whisper.

"I'm saying, running to his Mama's house isn't going to do you any good. She has probably talked him into hiding there, so she can block you," Stevie winks at me. "Trust me. Absence makes the heart grow fonder."

I nod my head. "Is that why you've been here for three months?" I say with a watery grin.

My sister rolls her eyes. "Maybe, but that's none of your business."

CHAPTER TWENTY-SEVEN

Letting Go

Nicole

I believe my sister was right. They say when you love someone, you let them go and they will come back if it was meant to be. I have three little children I have to think of. We can't keep going like this.

I love Caleb with everything I am. That's why I'm letting him go. If he wants a divorce, then, I'll let him have it.

I hope he sees the damage before it's too late. I don't want anyone else but Caleb, but I won't force anyone to want me. I'm tired. I can't keep fighting for us by myself.

It's been a month since I was served with those damn divorce papers. I've waited. Day after day, I've sat and waited for Caleb to come and explain.

He hasn't shown up, so it's time for me to go. I don't have the support system I need here, so I'm going home. I want to be with my family.

"Do you have to go?" Dakota says quietly.

I'm grateful to have her around when she isn't busy, but she has a family of her own. In New York, I'll have my Mom and Dad, as well as my sisters and brothers. The kids will have plenty of family to love on them.

Honestly, this move is for me. I can't be in the same State as Caleb and not be in his arms. I ache for my husband so much. Not just an ache in my body, but my heart and soul.

At some point, I lost myself in Caleb. I know I watched myself do it. I never had a chance to stop it. However, now, I'm taking my power back.

No man, not even Caleb should be allowed to destroy me like this. I won't let my little girls grow up thinking this is okay. I went from being hurt to plain angry somewhere along the line.

"I want to know why he didn't fight. We promised each other and he didn't fight for me," I whisper.

"You have to understand that Aunt Jemma has been feeding him a bunch of bullshit. She won't let any of us near him, because we'll talk some sense into him," Dakota huffs.

I bite back tears and ball my fist. It wouldn't be right for me to go beat my mother-in-law down. I hold my tongue.

"She's taking advantage of Cameron being away. He'll be back soon. Can't you just wait for him to come and fix this?" Dakota pleads.

"Caleb's the one that needs to fix this," I shake my head. "I can't do this to my girls. They ask for him every day. I...I don't know what to tell them."

Dakota nods her understanding. "You know, he's always wanted to fall in love and be normal. I just don't think he realizes that he got his wish."

"Dakota, he hurt me so much, but I still love him more than I can say in words. I…I just, I think it's all too much. Maybe we never should have married, or I shouldn't have gotten pregnant.

"I don't regret my children, but I think Caleb reached his ceiling. I couldn't love him through this," I say, with my heart crumbling in my chest.

I tape another box shut. The movers will be here in the morning. Stevie and I will be flying out with the children in the afternoon.

"This isn't over. I can't let it be," Dakota's voice shakes as she chokes back tears of her own.

"None of this is up to us. It's on Caleb. I can't make him love me," I shrug. "Dakota, can we talk about something else?"

Dakota clamps her mouth shut, swallowing whatever she was about to say. I'm grateful for her understanding that the subject is now closed. My heart can't take much more.

A few more hours pass, Stevie returns from the park with the kids. She had taken them so Dakota and I could get some packing done in peace. Those little monsters kept pulling things from boxes earlier.

Dakota says her goodbyes when Hamilton starts to ring her phone off the hook. I almost break down when she hugs me so tight, I can't breathe. I'll miss her and her two little ones.

Once she's gone, I walk the house and check for things I may have missed. I stumble on one of Caleb's gloves in the den. I lift it from the floor and hold it to my chest. I swipe at a tear and put the glove on my hand.

Of course, my tiny hand gets swallowed up. I smile when I see my name written in the palm. This is his old college mitten. I remember writing my name there. He had asked me to.

I run a hand under my nose, making a quick decision. This is my last attempt. I pull out my phone and text Caleb. This is on him now.

We're a team, right? We can do anything together.

~B~

Caleb

I stare at the text message on my phone. I wanted to answer it yesterday, but I don't know what to say. I run a hand through my hair. I needed a break from my Mama, so I drove out to my old high school.

This place held some of my greatest moments and some of my worst. I was so frustrated as a teenager. My seizures started in high school. This place stressed me the fuck out, but I had baseball.

Baseball helped people forget about all the weird shit going on with me. Hell, baseball made me forget to be different. I don't think I would've made it through without it.

I look across the baseball field, then back down at the ball in my hand. I want so much to rewind time. I would take back so much.

I'd start with, not always second-guessing myself off the field. I think I could've relaxed more as a teenager if I didn't question everything I did or said. As I sit here, I realize I stopped doing that when I met Nicole.

I worked my way through it all with her. Even when my Daddy had his stroke. I thought I was going to fall apart then.

When I started to question my role and what I should do, Nicole was there to see me through it.

For ten years, that woman has been by my side. I've loved her when I was unsure of everything and I know she loved me back. Nicole has been my voice of reason. She has never tried to change me. Only loving me for me.

I snort and blow out a breath. My Mama is already on my ass about me cutting my hair and trimming my beard. I don't want to think about any of that small stuff. I miss my family.

"Caleb Perry?" a gravelly voice calls out. "Well now, son, I thought that was you. Time sure does fly. I remember the first day you and your brother stepped onto my field. I swore neither of you were in high school, as big as you were."

I look up to find an older, withered version of my high school baseball coach. The same Stetson and cowboy boots. The same dark blue eyes and thick mustache.

Time does fly. I remember him being one of those that took time with me. Coach had helped me rein it all in and focused my talent.

"Hey Coach," I give a slight grin. I've nothing but fond memories of him.

"Now, that's the smile I remember," Coach nods. He ambles closer and takes a seat. "What's got you sitting here, looking like you lost your best friend, kid? Don't tell me it's all this mess over that shoulder, you had an amazing career, son. I was surprised to see you pitch as long as you did."

"I did lose my best friend. I'm getting a divorce," I mutter.

Coach Mc Rye whistles low. "I've seen that beautiful family of yours on the TV. You just had a boy, not too long ago. Am I right?"

I smile as I think of my son. Right about now, his cries would be music to my ears. I miss his chubby little toffee colored face. I miss burying my nose in his hair, while he falls asleep on my chest.

"I reckon a career ending injury will knock the stars out of these young ladies' eyes. They just don't make them like they did in my day," Coach sighs.

My jaw ticks. My situation isn't because Nicole was after my money or my fame. To Nicole, I've always been Caleb first. I just happened to play baseball.

"My wife has been by my side through everything. She loves me whether I'm playing baseball or not," My own words slam into my chest.

The truth stings me to my core. Nicole doesn't deserve what I'm doing to us. None of my family does. I just don't know what else to do.

"Forgive this old man, but I'm not understanding. You say she's your best friend and she's stuck with you through it all, so why the divorce?"

Swiping the screen, I look down at the text on my phone again, and tighten my grip on the baseball in my other hand. I have no idea why I'm getting a divorce. Mama wore me down. It seemed like the right thing to do then.

"I don't know," I breathe out. "I really don't know."

"You were always a smart kid. A jittery big fella, when we started out together. When I asked after you with the staff and started to watch you more closely, I figured it out," Coach turns to look at me.

I feel like he's looking for something again. Just like when I was younger. He's always had a watchful eye when it comes to me. As if he could see past everything, the noise, the consistent buzzing on my skin, and all the uncertainty.

"You're special, Perry, and I'm not talking about what you got going on in your head. I mean, you're a special person. I admire your determination. You never took no for an answer. You figured out how to make things work for you.

"You had a lot of support in your brother. I watched your aunt and uncle step in as well. Nice folks, I wish that knucklehead Andy would stop giving them such a hard time," he shakes his head and pushes his Stetson back, showing a shock of grey hair now running through the front.

"Folks like that should be able to enjoy life, with all they do for the community. Anyway, you had your family, but you still had this independence about you. It looked to outsiders like they were shielding you.

"But I think you were just working in the shadows on greatness. I'll never forget how you explained pitching to me from your view. The inner workings of your mind," Coach shakes his head. "Your phenomenal, young man.

"From what I'm observing, you don't want this divorce. I suggest you do like you did when you were a boy. Look at this thing from its natural science.

"Study the matter, find its motion, its behavior, look at the space and time you've been through. You and that little lady had your own energy, a force that kept you together. Find how the two of you behave in this universe and create the perfect pitch, son," Coach catches my eyes and holds them.

"Did I get it right?" Coach asks with a grin on his lips.

I blink at him. I remember when he asked me how I saw pitching. What I was thinking up on that mound? I had given him similar words, just in reference to baseball.

The pieces start to fall into place. I apply physics to my marriage, to my relationship with Nicole and it all starts to make sense again. There's an explosion in me, when I grasp it all.

Nicole and I are just natural science. I don't exist without her, she doesn't exist without me. We're what matters to each other.

Nicole and I revolve around each other. We set life in motion for everything we want around us. For ten years, we created our own time, moved through our own space.

She is my energy and I'm her force. Our children are just more matter that makes us stronger. I love each one of them.

Fuck, I need my family. I won't breathe without them. I've thrown a curve ball and almost ended the entire game.

"God, I hope I'm not too late," I gasp.

"Me too, son. Me too," he says and tips his Stetson at me. "I don't think you're done being great, Caleb. Not by far."

She makes me great. If I have Nicole, I can do anything. I'm great when I have her love.

CHAPTER TWENTY-EIGHT

She's Gone

Caleb

"You look like shit," Cameron grumbles from his seat at the kitchen nook.

"Thank you," I mutter. "When did you get here?"

"After I got a call, while in DR, only to hear that my little brother let his wife leave him," Cameron snorts. "You know she left, don't you?"

I make a sour face as the taste of bile rises in my mouth. "I went home to find my house empty and my family gone. Yeah, I know my wife left," I reply.

"What the fuck, Cal?" Cameron says in frustration.

"You left camp?" I ask.

"I'm here, aren't I? You know for the smarter one out of the two of us, I wonder about the shit you do," Cameron shakes his head.

"What do you want from me, Cam? I know I fucked up," I roar.

"We want you to fix it," I turn at the sound of Dakota's voice. She's in the entryway of the kitchen with her arms folded across her chest.

"I'm tired," I grumble and sit heavily in a chair across from Cameron.

"I bet you are. You've been having seizures haven't you?" Cameron accuses.

"Yeah," I furrow my brows. "I think so. I'm not sleeping much."

"Why put yourself through this?" Dakota asks, crossing the room and sitting beside me.

"Where's Mama?"

"Don't avoid my question," Dakota snaps.

"I think this shit snapped Daddy out of his zombie state. He's the one that called me. Haven't heard the old man sound so strong in a long time," Cameron looks away and pauses for a few minutes.

We all took my father's stroke hard—and the state he's been in since—even harder. Daddy usually doesn't say much. His left side was weakened, causing his speech to be unclear for a while.

"Your Daddy is just like you. His biggest problem is his pride, not his physical injuries," Dakota huffs, folding her arms over her chest. "He's pretending to be worse off than he is because of crazy ass Aunt Jemma. Your Mama can drive anyone to drink."

"Daddy got her to go with him to therapy so I could come talk to you. Why haven't you been answering anyone's calls?" Cameron snaps.

It's my turn to look away. I've been avoiding everyone's calls because I don't think I can handle anyone else in my ear. Between Mama and my own thoughts, I have too much going on already.

As I think about dinner last night, Daddy had joined us and he watched me the entire time. I hadn't thought anything about it. I thought he was just having one of his moments.

To now know he called Cameron, has a million and one questions running through my head. Daddy has always been an unusual man. At times, I wonder what my parents see in each other. They're like night and day.

"So, Daddy's been faking?" I turn back to Dakota and Cameron to ask.

Cameron shrugs. "I think so, to an extent," Dakota replies. "It's no secret Uncle Kyle has wanted a divorce for years. There's just some clause in their prenup. If he leaves, she can clean him out."

Cameron actually chuckles and shakes his head. "He's gotten her to stop talking to him for a year with this shit. He's on to something."

"That's crazy," I knit my brows.

"No, what's crazy is that you're getting a divorce," Dakota bites out. "This ain't right, Perry."

"As much as I love Mama, she ain't always right. I lost so much time with my sons listening to her. She doesn't always know what's best for us, as much as she wishes she does.

"You see how hard I've had to work for my family. At first, I let Mama put all types of stuff in my head. I know how manipulating she can be," Cameron frowns.

"You can't let whatever she's been feeding you ruin what you and Nicole have," Dakota pleads.

"What am I supposed to do?" I huff, tearing a hand through my hair.

"You have to show her you're sorry, saying it isn't going to be good enough. There's this group. It's a support group. A friend of Hamilton's runs it. She's a therapist. It's for men going through loss, those dealing with the decision to get a divorce or those who have the potential to fix their marriage before making that final step to end things.

"You know, Hamilton and I had a little rough patch. She helped him get his shit together. I think it would be good for you, Cal. At this point, if you want Nicole back, you have to do something.

"You need to fix what's going on in your head, so that whatever has gotten you to this point, won't tear you two apart again. Then you need to go after your wife and stop this stupid divorce," Dakota demands.

"That sounds just about right to me," my father's voice fills the room.

We all turn to see him making his way into the room. Our Mama at his side, looking shocked and confused. I look my father over and he looks the most healthy and alert I've seen in three years. The paralysis on the left side is still noticeable, but he looks more like his old self today.

"I've let the foolishness in this family go on long enough. I liked that young lady from the first time Caleb brought her home. She's good for him," Daddy starts, he eases down onto one of the bar stools at the island and turns his eyes on our Mama.

"Kyle, what's—," Mama tries, but Daddy sends her a sharp look.

"You've been jealous of that little thing from the moment you met her. She broke through to Caleb in ways none of us could. You just couldn't accept that," Daddy pulls a face and shakes his head.

"I know a hug from our son is like gold around here. Seeing him give that away so freely to Nicole stung my heart at first too, but I wanted my son's happiness, more than I envied a simple gesture that doesn't define his love.

"Caleb doesn't hug. He has a hard time being touched, but he has, in his way, always let us all know how he feels. You're dead wrong, Jemma, for trying to ruin the one relationship that has been easy for him."

Daddy's words are a bit sluggish, but they're hitting their mark. The room has fallen completely silent. You could hear a pin drop in between Daddy's words.

"Those grandchildren have enough going on in their lives without you and your harebrained schemes. I'm too old for this shit. If anyone is getting a divorce, it's the two of us. You stress me out. What good is my money if you kill me?" Daddy shakes his head.

Mama finally closes her mouth that's been hanging open. She gets in a huff and starts to speak, but Daddy holds up his hand. He shakes his head again.

"We've been nothing, but selfish. I've had a lot of time to think on that. We could have done better by our boys. I'm putting my foot down here.

"Caleb, go to this group. See if they can help you sort out facts from your Mama's BS. I wish I had the strength to speak up sooner," Daddy turns a sharp eye on my Mama.

"You've wasted years missing out on having a relationship with Nicole and our grandchildren. Fix it, or I'll have my lawyers prevent you from seeing a single dime in a divorce. Trust me, darlin', I've got a file thick enough to make it happen," Daddy says, with as much authority as he can muster.

He turns back to me, looking drained and tired. He gives me a small smile and a wink. I sit stunned, still letting it all sink in.

"Come on, Daddy. Let's get you in bed," Cameron says, as he stands to go help our father.

"Woman has lost her mind," Daddy mutters, while Cam helps him from the room. He chuckles. "Shocked the spit out of her, didn't I?"

My heart swells to hear the rumble of my father's laughter. It's clear that all just took a lot out of him, but he looks better for it. I look down into my lap. If my father has pulled on strength unknown for me and my family, then so can I.

"He's right," Mama whispers. "I am jealous of her. She's given you three perfect, beautiful little ones. You show them all affection I've been dying for. What I've done is wrong."

"You're damn right it is!" Dakota slaps the table. "My Mama is so pissed at you, she could spit. You had no right, Aunt Jemma. If he can't get his family back, I don't think I will ever forgive you."

"I won't forgive myself," Mama says in a whisper. "I'll do anything I can to help fix this."

I stand and walk over to my Mama. I pull her into my arms and hug her tight. "I love you," I whisper.

She clings to me and breaks down in my arms. I stand and hug her for as long as I can. Thoughts of getting my family back cancel out the buzzing in my skin. It's just a low hum as I allow my Mama to cling to me for the affection she has been craving all my life.

"Thank you, Caleb. Thank you so much. Now, let's go get our family back," Mama says shakily.

"If they'll have me," I whisper.

Why I'm Here

Caleb
Present
Back in the group session...

I come back to the present and look around the group. Dakota was right. I may have figured out that Nicole and I belonged together, but I still had a lot of shit going on in my head I needed to sort out, before I find my way back to Nicole.

"It doesn't matter that I've fathered two beautiful little girls and a son. It doesn't matter that I've had a nine-year professional career. I'm losing my wife," I choke out. "I'm failing at the most important thing to me."

"May, I?" The Native American guy asks.

"Sure, Hanson," Dr. Winsor says.

"It sounds like you just need to find your way back. You love your wife and she loves you," he shrugs. "Remember that love.

Remind her of that love. You sound as if you have given up, but I think you still have a family waiting for you.

"Your differences don't define you. You have done great things with your life. Why allow your challenges to guide you now? Be the man she married, not the man you've become."

"I'll have to agree," Dr. Winsor says. "You sound like you're just as much in love with your wife now as you were when you first fell for her."

"I love her more," I nod.

"Then go get her," the large blonde with the blue eyes says.

Trevor, that's his name. I stop to wonder why he still comes here. He sorted out his shit first out of all of the group. Our stories are miles apart, but after watching him find his peace, I feel compelled to listen to what he has to say.

"Is it that easy?" I blink.

"Yes," Tommy whispers. He was the second of our bunch to start to get his life back on track. "It is. Don't waste another minute. Life's too short. Remind her that you love her. Go get your woman."

Dr. Winsor smiles. "I know how hard it must have been for you to start today. Your wife is right about you, you're an amazing man, Caleb. I think if you put your mind to it, you can get your family back."

"I hope so," I mutter to my hands.

"So, the question is—why are you here, Caleb? What have you learned about yourself and your decisions?"

I sit and let her words sink in. I'm here because I want my wife back. I want to be with my children.

"I want my life back," I say aloud. "I learned I do have something to offer my wife. No one makes Nicole smile like me. I would know. I've watched her closely enough.

"She has a special smile for me and it's brighter than any other one she has. I fucked up. What I did was wrong, selfish, and not what a team player should do. I want my team back. I need Nicole back."

Dr. Winsor nods. "I want you to think about some things Nicole would like. Things you would do given a chance. As you all know, a part of this program is for me to talk with your significant others.

"I have been talking with Nicole via the telephone. I think you are ready to join us during one of those calls," Dr. Winsor says.

"No, ma'am," I shake my head. "Thank you, but I'm ready to go get my wife. I've wasted enough time."

She tilts her head at me, then smiles. "Well, I'm here if you two need me."

"Thank you," I nod.

~B~

Nicole

I'm disappointed that Dr. Winsor asked to reschedule our call today. I had some more things I want to get off my chest. Again, I'm grateful that she makes allowances for these calls.

She mentioned a while back that at some point, she would like to bring Caleb and I together on the calls. However, only after Caleb opens up. It's been a month since the warm sounding woman called me to inform me that Caleb had enrolled in her program.

I was shocked, but hopeful at first. Now, I don't know what to think. We have two sessions a week and she hasn't mentioned Caleb's progress or us coming together for a joint session yet.

I'm afraid he may have shut down on her like he did me. That wouldn't surprise me. What has surprised me were the phone calls from my humble sounding mother-in-law.

I don't know what's going on in Texas, but something has gotten into both Caleb and his mother. Caleb has sought out help and his mother has extended an olive branch of sorts. She even asks to speak to the kids.

The girls are excited. Apparently, both Jemma and Kyle want to spend time with them. I was wary in the beginning, but my mom talked me into giving Jemma a chance.

I'll be honest, though. It was hearing Kyle's voice over the phone that melted my heart. He sounds so good these days. I want the girls and Caleb Jr. to know the sweet man I grew to love.

"We're getting on a plane again, Grandma," Monica sings, at the breakfast table.

"Yes, sweetie, I know," my mother beams.

"I'm excited. I hope we see Daddy," Morgan chirps.

My heart squeezes in my chest. I don't know if they will see Caleb. Jemma never mentions him and we didn't talk about whether or not he would be around for the girls' visit this coming week.

"I miss Daddy," Monica says, her little smile falling off her face.

"Me too," Morgan nods and starts to push her food around on her plate.

I have a lump in my throat the size of a golf ball. I don't know what I am with Caleb anymore—angry and hurt aren't the right words. I've gotten over those. I'm settled somewhere between frustrated and missing him just like the girls.

"How about after you girls finish your breakfast, we go make some cards to send to your daddy? That way he'll know how much you miss him," My mother offers.

"Okay," the girls say in unison. I'm sure not half as enthusiastically as my mother was hoping for.

"Or, you two can come give me a hug and show me how much you miss me," a deep voice rumbles through the room.

No, scratch that. That voice rumbles through my body, awakening things I should be too furious to allow to awaken. Instead, I'm speechless as I hold my breath and my body stiffens.

"Daddy!" the girls squeal and jump from their seats.

I can't move. I don't turn to look at him. At this point, I'll fall completely apart if I do. I can feel his eyes on me. Even as I hear him talking to the girls.

"We missed you so much, Daddy," Morgan sings.

"Daddy, we've been staying with Gran and Pop, while Mommy looks for a new house for us," Monica says.

"We've been to a lot of houses. Mommy didn't like any of them," Morgan adds.

"Mommy said if we're good, we can see about getting a puppy at the new house," Monica giggles.

"I bet you girls have been sweet as pie. Look at you, you're all grown up. You're both just as gorgeous as your Mama," Caleb's voice slams into me again. "Here, Daddy brought you both some flowers."

I hear the crinkling of cellophane, but I still don't turn. I wrap my arms tighter around my son in my lap. Caleb Jr. just wiggles as he holds his hands out toward his father. I guess we all missed him.

I shudder when I hear Caleb's heavy footfalls begin to move my way. From behind, he plucks Caleb Jr. from my arms. I close my eyes as the sound of Caleb planting a big smacking kiss on our son, greets my ears.

"Hey, little buddy. Did you miss your daddy too?" Caleb coos to our son.

I think it's then that I snap out of my trance. I stand up, nearly knocking my seat over as I spin to face him. Only, I'm the one nearly knocked over.

The sight of Caleb leaves me speechless. While looking a bit leaner, he still looks good enough to eat. He has trimmed his golden beard close, revealing that little scar. His sandy blonde hair is pulled back into a low bun that's just so striking on him.

I've never seen his hair like this. He looks rough, sweet, and sexy all at once. He looks a little tired, but his intense stare sucks me in despite the circles under his eyes.

His white t-shirt still fits snug, stretching across his muscles and chest. The jeans he has on hug his thighs like a second skin, exuding the power this man holds. He's just mouthwateringly sexy.

"You just gonna stand there and stare at me? Or are you gonna come here and kiss me?" Caleb breathes.

I go to step forward, before my good sense catches me. I take two steps back when my mind catches up. I shake my head, as Caleb steps forward to compensate for my retreat.

He gets right in my space, placing a bouquet of roses on the table behind me and grasps my face. His thumb runs over my bottom lip, and my tongue darts out to follow the blazing path he leaves. Caleb passes his finger back over my lip, this time meeting my tongue on its withdrawal.

Caleb groans in the back of his throat. His hand slides to the back of my neck and he tugs me forward gently. I bite my lip, not wanting to cause a scene in front of the girls and my son.

Caleb presses his forehead to mine. "I'm sorry," he whispers.

"Girls, let's go wash up. We can play in the yard for a little while," my mother says, moving in to swoop a reluctant, fussing Caleb Jr. from his father's embrace. "Come with Gran, my sweet boy."

The moment they're all out of the room, my anger returns and I go to tear into Caleb. He has other ideas though. His lips capture mine and he devours my mouth. I can't help myself from clinging to the front of his t-shirt.

Caleb deepens the kiss and I'm confused and lost in him. I wrap my arms around his neck and a growl rumbles in his throat. His hands slide down to grasp my ass, squeezing me so hard, I lift up into his body.

When his bulge pokes into my belly, I grab onto my common sense. I turn away from his kiss, but Caleb only starts to kiss his way down my neck, with open mouth kisses. I barely stop myself from whimpering.

"I'm so sorry," he breathes against my skin.

"Caleb, I can't," I sob, pushing gently at his chest.

"I'm sorry, Nicole," he pleads. "I fucked up. What I did was so wrong. I was confused and hurting, baby, but I shouldn't have done this to you or our family."

"But you did. You broke your promise. You said you'd fight for us," I choke. "You didn't."

"Yes, I am," he says fiercely, still holding me tightly against him. "I'm here to fight. I'm here for my family. I want you to come home. I called the lawyer and told him to trash those papers. I need you."

"No," I shake my head, stunning myself.

Wasn't this what I wanted? Hadn't I waited for this?

I did, but now it just feels too late. I'm hurt too deeply to just roll over and let him back in.

I look up through my wet lashes. The stricken look on Caleb's face almost bows me over and makes me give in. I hold on, though, remembering the pain I've been in.

"Okay," he murmurs, releasing his hold on me. He nods to himself. "I don't expect you to make this easy on me. I fucked up big time and I need to work for your trust again. I understand."

He reaches for my hand, playing with my fingertips, before lacing his fingers with mine. He doesn't say anything for a while. However, his eyes are blinking and he's making that sound in his throat. I want to comfort him, but I don't want to send the wrong message and confuse him.

He shakes out his free hand and pulls himself together. He steps into me, until he backs me into the table behind me. He palms my face.

"Give me a chance to show you I'm worthy. Don't throw me away. Let me get this right," he pauses, purses his lips and squints. His country accent is thick as ever. "You need a husband, the kids need a father, and we all need a safe place to call home. Let me show you I can give you all of that."

"We had all of that, Caleb. We built all of that before," I shake my head. "You didn't want it."

"Yes, I did," he says brokenly. "I wanted you so bad. I just didn't think I deserved you. I thought someone else could give you better, but I can't breathe, baby. I can't breathe without you. Please, give me a chance to show you."

I close my eyes and lower my head. This is how he hurt me the first time. When it comes to him, I just don't know how to say no. Dr. Winsor said it doesn't make me weak, it just means Caleb is my weakness.

I have to decide how to handle that. I get to choose when I want to give in and when I need to put my foot down. I know this wasn't all Caleb's doing. Mrs. Jemma confessed to her sins the first time she reached out. Although, Caleb could've and should've come to me.

"Nicole," Caleb whispers with a plea. "I thought baseball was my center. The one thing that made me take control of my life. I know better now. Our love, our family, that's the force that drives me every day. I will never question or throw that away again. *Please.*"

"Okay," I whisper.

"Thank you, baby." he pulls me to him, lifting my face to his, he plants kisses all over my face before he takes my lips. "Thank you so much."

He goes to deepen the kiss, but I feel my resolve weakening. I step out of his reach, pulling my hand free from his. I wrap my arms around my middle.

"Show me. I never used to fear loving you. I do now, so you have to show me," I say softly.

"You got it, darlin'. I'll take all your fears away," he says the words so fiercely I want to believe him.

~B~

Caleb

"Daddy's here, he came to get us, Mama," Monica tries to whisper to her Mama as Nicole tucks her in. "I bet we find our own house now. Daddy will help."

My heart squeezes from my little girl's words. It's cute that she doesn't think I can hear her, while tucking in her sister on the other side of the room. It also stings like hell that I've done this.

"We'll see, sweetie," Nicole says softly.

I have to strain to hear her words. The uncertainty I've witnessed in Nicole all day has pushed me to the edge. I'm holding on so tightly to the last thread of hope I have. I can't give up.

Spending the day with my family solidified what I should've known all along. I belong with them. As noisy as they are, as busy as little Caleb is getting. I wouldn't change a thing about my family.

"You'll find us a house, right, Daddy?" Morgan whispers to me. Reaching out her little hand, she palms my cheek. "You were just having a lot of bad days. We still love you. You're back to our happy Daddy now. So, you can find us a house. I promise we'll be good. We'll even help to keep CJ from crying so much."

I swallow hard, but my throat is still tight with emotion. Nicole and these girls are my kryptonite. They shoot right for my heart. If I don't understand or get anyone else in this world, I know and understand my family.

"I have a lot of fixing to do, baby girl. Your Daddy made a mess. I promise I'm here to do everything I can to fix it, but it will take some time for Daddy to get through his bad days and to get through to your Mama," I try to explain.

Morgan lowers her voice a little more. "You can do it, Daddy. I have faith in you. You're my hero," Morgan whispers.

My heart bursts out of my chest. I scoop my little girl up and hug her so tightly, I'm probably crushing her little body. I'm gutted that I let myself be manipulated into thinking I don't deserve them.

"I love you, Daddy," Morgan says and kisses my cheek.

"I love you too, baby girl," I say back, kissing her forehead and placing her back into her bed.

I stand and cross the room to kiss my other little girl goodnight. Monica gives me a sleepy smile. I bend to kiss her forehead.

"Love you, Daddy. Pancakes in the morning, right?"

"Yes," I reassure her and her little smile returns. "I love you, sugar. I'll be here for pancakes in the morning."

"Okay, Daddy," she yawns.

"All right you two," Nicole says from the other side of the room, now standing by Morgan. "Go to bed. You can spend more time with your father tomorrow."

It's not lost on me that Nicole won't stay in the same proximity to me. I haven't been helping. Whenever she's close, I've had my hands on her.

It's been so hard trying to keep my hands to myself today. From the moment, I laid eyes on Nicole, I wanted to lay her bare and feast on her. She looks gorgeous as ever.

The simple grey t-shirt and short sweat shorts have been driving me crazy. I love her shapely brown legs. Those shorts haven't kept my imagination from going wild every time she's bent to help little Caleb with something or to pick up after the girls.

I'm starving for my wife. Whatever was going on in my head that kept me from touching her before has disappeared. I want Nicole with a vengeance.

I want to fuck her like we used to fuck after I lost a game. Those moments when she surrendered completely to me and my body's demands for her, but first. I want to take my time with her.

I want to kiss every inch of brown skin and devour her whole. I want her to remember my brand. I want to mark her in a way that takes her to ecstasy and back, over and over again.

"You coming?" Nicole whispers up to me, pulling me from my thoughts of ravaging her body. When she finally steps within my reach, my hands itch to touch her.

I nod and Nicole turns to leave the room. When we make it out to the hall and I close the door behind us, I reach for Nicole and pull her against me, her butt against my front.

I dip my head to nip at her neck. I miss my wife so much. I slip my hand into the front of her shorts and she gasps.

"I just want to make you come," I breathe in her ear.

"Caleb, my parents or the kids can come out here at any moment," she whispers.

I nip at her shoulder. "Then come into my room. I promise, I'll just make you come and then we can talk if you want or I can just hold you in my sleep. I haven't been sleeping without you. Let me hold you," I say against her ear.

I shove my hand further into her shorts, reaching underneath her panties. I feel her body tense against mine, but I don't know if that means she's going to deny me. I hold my breath, while stroking her button.

"Okay," she pants. "You can make me come. No sex."

"It's not about me," I reply, slipping my hand free and swiftly lifting her into my arms.

"Caleb," she gasps. "Your shoulder."

I peck her lips, moving quickly to the guestroom I'll be staying in. I use my back to close the door as gently as I can before placing Nicole on her feet. We don't get far.

I pull her back against my front, shoving my hand back into her shorts. I find her dripping wet for me. I groan and suck on her neck. My fingers circle her clit, once, twice, before pushing my fingers into her folds.

Nicole lifts on her toes, as I pump in and out of her. She so snug, my cock grows hard with jealousy, wanting so badly to be the one inside her. I push my other hand under her t-shirt, tearing down the cup of her bra.

"Cal," she moans, causing me to pump harder, while squeezing her full breast.

Nicole reaches for my hair, locking her fingers in my bun. I start to thrust my hips into her ass. I can't wait to taste her.

"Fuck, baby, you're so wet. I'm going to make you come, then I'm going to eat this pussy, until you come all over my mouth," I say.

"Cal, I'm so close," Nicole moans. "God, I missed your touch."

"I want to touch you everywhere. I love your body, baby," I groan.

"Cal," she whimpers, gushing all over my fingers.

I close my eyes and relish in the feel of her body trembling against mine as she comes all over my hand. I'm painfully hard inside my jeans, but I ignore it. I push Nicole's body forward toward the bed.

I spin her and toss her onto the mattress. She lands with a little bounce, as I pounce on her. I tear her shorts and panties down her legs. When her juicy pussy comes into view, I nearly go mad.

"I almost gave this away," I whisper to myself. "I have to be out of my fucking mind. This pussy is mine, darlin'."

I don't give her time to protest. I dive in and eat her center like it's my last meal. She so sweet, and smells so damn good. The fact that her hips are rocking into my face, her hands are locked into my hair, and her legs are wrapped around my neck, are only a bonus.

"Oh God, babe, right there," Nicole purrs. "Yes, right there."

"Mmm," I hum into her pussy.

She gasps and arches her back as I push two fingers into her and beckon her g-spot to life. I own this pussy. I may need to get my other shit together, but I know how to pleasure my wife.

"Caleb," she sobs, as her release slams into her.

Her belly quivers and her legs shake loosely around my ears. I lap up all her juices, wishing everything were this easy. I reach down and squeeze my aching cock.

"Caleb?"

"Yeah," I reply, moving her legs to my sides and climbing up her body.

I roll to my side and pull her into my arms. She snuggles closer to me, placing her hand on my chest. My whole body relaxes into contentment. It's as if my mind, body, and soul are aware of her.

"You hurt me, but I never stopped loving you. I need you to know that," Nicole says after a while.

"I know, baby," I sigh. "Let me take you on a date. Tomorrow night. I'll remind us both why we belong together."

"Sounds good," Nicole yawns.

"It will be."

CHAPTER THIRTY

Dinner For Two

Nicole

"Why am I so freaking nervous?" I say into the mirror, as I smooth my hands over the front of my dress.

The twins giggle from their seats on the bed. They've been in here trying to be grown, as my sisters and I get me ready for my date. I swear they're too smart for their own good.

They're sitting like little adults between their two aunts that are spread out on my bed. The smiles on their faces are so cute, which only makes me more nervous. I have to do the right thing for my children. They're in such expectation.

Honestly, so am I. Caleb has spent the day setting my body on fire, with just the simplest of touches. A hand on the hip here. A little touch to my back there. Even a hand on my ass, when we took Caleb Jr. for a walk.

All natural gestures before. Now, each touch has been like gasoline to a flame. I'm so hyper aware of him.

"You look pretty, Mama," Morgan gushes.

"Daddy is going to be so happy," Monica chimes in.

"Hey, why don't you two go see if Gran has a snack ready for you," my sister Wendy suggests.

"But we want to help Mama get ready," Monica pouts.

"I have an idea. Why don't you go see if your Daddy is ready?" My sister Stevie tries. "You can make sure he hasn't forgot anything important. He needs to get this perfect. You two go whip him into shape."

Monica gasps and claps her hands. "Come on, Morgan. Daddy has to get this right, so we can go home with him," she says determinedly to her sister.

They scurry off the bed and rush from the room. I clutch my hand over my heart, closing my eyes over the pain. I stumble over to the bed.

"I shouldn't make him work so hard. They miss their father," I gasp out. "What am I doing? We need to go home."

"Girl, please, Caleb needs to put in work. He screwed up and he knows it," Wendy crosses her arms over her chest.

"Sweetie," Stevie says, calling my attention. "Let him be a man. This is the problem. His family babied him for so long. He needs to find his own way. You making this hard is allowing him to be the man he needs to be. The one he wants to be for you."

I suck in a breath and nod my head. I stand again and move to the mirror. I bite my lip as I take my dress in. It was Stevie's choice.

"Are you two sure this isn't too much?" I sigh.

The platinum bandage dress hugs my body like a glove. The neckline dips low, right below my breasts, providing a healthy amount of cleavage. The color looks great against my bronzed skin.

The dress stops a few inches above the knee. The strappy blue ankle booties, give my legs some length. I may have three kids, but running behind my children has kept me fit.

"Girl, if you don't stop," Wendy rolls her eyes.

"I love your hair. If I would've had to look at that busted ponytail one more day, *girl*," Stevie drags out the last word.

"Shut up," I giggle. "Thank you, guys."

My sisters have been helping me all day. Stevie washed and blew out my hair, giving me a much needed trim. I look more like my mother with my hair flat ironed straight down my back.

"You're welcome. I've always liked Caleb," Wendy shrugs. "I think you guys can work this out."

"Think, girl, did you not see his face at breakfast this morning. I thought he was going to eat her alive, right at the table," Stevie cackles.

"*Yes*," Wendy fans herself. "The man can't even hide his desire for you. Shit, I think it's sexy."

"Exactly why I refuse to settle. I want to be looked at like that," Stevie huffs.

"Oh, here we go. Ramon does look at you like that. You're just too busy looking at everything but him," Wendy grumbles and crosses her arms.

"Excuse me," Stevie gasps. "What are you talking about?"

"You are so blind. You went running off to teach that fool, John, a lesson. Ain't nobody got time for him. You need to let John's behind move on to wherever he's been trying to float to," Wendy says as she looks at her fingernails.

"What does John have to do with Ramon?" Stevie blinks dumbfounded.

"Nicole, did she just ask me that?"

"I'm saying nothing. I just found out about John. I thought something different was going on," I shrug.

I had thought Stevie was running from Ramon. Not some other guy. I mean the two are always together.

"Newsflash, baby sister," Wendy sings. "Ramon is in love with you. If you would open your eyes you would see that."

Stevie blinks a few times before a rueful smile takes over her lips. She looks between me and Wendy, then bursts into laughter.

"My best friend, Ramon. The Ramon that's engaged, Ramon. You two have lost your damn minds," Stevie laughs.

"Oh, God," I groan. "She's so delusional."

"I know, right," Wendy shakes her head. "Stevie listen to me, honey," Wendy says very slowly. "Ramon is in love with you. Has been for as long as I can remember. If he could have you over little miss, missy, he would drop her like a bad habit. That's a marriage of convenience. If they ever even make it to the altar."

Stevie's mouth flaps open and closed a few times. "Oh, oh…oh my God. That's what he was trying to tell me. Oh, shit," Stevie gasps.

She jumps up from lying on her stomach across the bed. Wendy and I lift a brow at each other. Our sister shoves her feet into her shoes frantically.

"Where are you off to?" I chuckle.

"I…I have to talk to Ramon," she huffs and races from the room.

"Now that," Wendy points. "Is how you go get your man."

I throw my head back and laugh. "I can't believe she didn't know. Seriously?"

"Okay, now for you," Wendy says pointedly. "You don't have to torture him, but let Caleb work for it just a little. I think you guys will be better for it. He can't be letting his mother in his ear every time he can't cope."

"It's not like this has happened before," I bite my lip.

Wendy stands up and walks over to me. She leans her head on my shoulder, looking like my twin in the mirror. Wendy is just a little shorter than me with dad's hazel eyes.

I'm the only girl that didn't get dad's hazel eyes, but my own light brown color, almost hazel, but not quite. I cover my sister's cheek and kiss her forehead. Her gaze meets mine in the mirror.

"And after this, it won't happen again," Wendy says. "Don't be like me, Nicole. I let my husband walk all over me. I never gave him reason to be accountable for his shit."

"How are you holding up?" I say softly.

Wendy shrugs. "My husband was an asshole. He cheated, repeatedly. Then he died and left me with a ton of debt," Wendy's lips tremble, as she nods. "So, yup, I'm great. Never better."

I kiss her forehead again. "You're the best big sister in the world. You will find love, true love, and it will make up for all the bad."

"You're the best brat I could've asked for in a baby sister. Now let's go make that fine ass husband of yours drool," Wendy chuckles.

I shake my head at her, taking one last look in the mirror. I'm still nervous, but I'm ready to get this show on the road. I miss Caleb. I can't wait to see what he has in store.

Caleb

"Okay, Daddy," Monica starts. "You look very handsome. That's a start."

I look at the light grey suit, in the mirror. The white shirt and blue silk tie look sharp. Or at least, I hope they do to Nicole. I look down at my dress boots. It's not exactly what I wore to propose to Nicole, but similar.

I'm hoping the little details will work in my favor tonight. We've been dancing around each other all day. I can't seem to stay too far away from her.

"Wait 'til you see Mama," Morgan grins.

"Shh, don't give it away," Monica says to her twin. "Right...now Daddy. Did you get Mama some flowers?"

"There will be flowers when we get there," I reply.

These two are adorable. They mean business. They busted in here a few minutes ago, chirping about operation get Daddy back with Mama. If what I've done didn't sting so much, I would've found it heartwarming.

"Girls," I sigh and sit in between them on the bed. "I promise you I've got this. Daddy got your Mama to fall in love with him once. I'll do it again."

Monica eyes me warily. Morgan climbs into my lap and runs her hands down the front of my tie. I pull Monica into my side, kissing their heads in turn.

"I think you look handsome, Daddy. Mama doesn't stand a chance," Morgan nods.

"Thanks, baby."

"Come on, Daddy," Morgan says sliding off my lap. "Mama should be ready."

The girls grab one hand each, leading me out to the foyer of the house. I'm lost in their little chatter until the most beautiful woman in the world comes into view. I stagger to a stop and lick my lips.

"God, you're gorgeous," I breathe.

The others around us snicker, but it's just one of the things I register. I can't take my eyes off of Nicole. Her hair is so long and straight, falling down around her shoulders. The dress she has on…thank God, I'm taking her somewhere private for this date.

There's no fucking way I would let anyone else get a look at all that beautiful brown skin. I don't even want the driver getting a look at her to be honest. The way her breasts are pushing out of the dress has my jaw ticking under my skin.

"Nicole, darlin', that dress was made for my eyes only," I say.

More laughter fills the foyer. The girls drag me the rest of the way to their Mama. I release their hands as we reach Nicole. Cupping her face, I bend and devour her purple painted lips.

A few throats clear, causing Nicole to place her hand on my chest and gently push. I release her lips, staring down into her eyes. With her other hand, she reaches up to wipe my lips.

"You're very handsome yourself," she chuckles.

"You two get out of here before this goes from PG to something else," Wendy teases.

"I think it already did," Mrs. Joy laughs.

"Sorry, Ladies." I blush.

"You're fine. It's obvious you miss your wife," Mrs. Joy says.

"Yes, ma'am, I do." I turn back to Nicole and say. "Come on, you promised me a date."

Nicole gives me my special smile. My heart swells. I tuck her under my arm and start for the door. I won't lie. I've had a little help from Cam and my in-laws on this date. I hope it works out as I imagined.

I watch Nicole closely as we leave out of the front door. She stops abruptly when the rented Rolls Royce, Phantom, comes into view. I reach to brush her hair out of her face so I can see every nuance.

"Caleb?" Nicole whispers. "I...I...you."

"Remembered," I murmur. "Yeah, when you were in labor with Caleb, I asked you what our wedding would have been like, if we had one the way you wanted. You said you wanted to ride in a Rolls."

"Yeah," Nicole nods, as she blinks back tears.

"Come on," I smile and tug at her waist.

We climb into the car and I keep my eyes on her the entire ride. The small smile on her lips says a thousand words to me. I know Nicole. She's thinking, that smile means it's good thoughts. My hope is growing.

I'm sweating bullets by the time we reach the pier and board the rented yacht. Mrs. Joy and Mr. Gunner arranged the boat's rental, pulling some last minute strings for me.

The Manhattan backdrop is perfect as we move across the water. Nicole and I are having a private dinner on the main deck. It's a romantic setting with candles and lights all around us. Just like the night in the café, when I proposed.

Nicole's beautiful face is shining in the candlelight. She looks up from her plate of pasta and a smile illuminates her face even more. She tilts her head and starts to study me back.

"What's on your mind, Mr. Perry?" Nicole says, in her sweet voice.

"You," I say, after wiping my mouth with my napkin. "You've always told me how perfect you think I am. I don't know if I've done the same. I'm sorry."

"Um," Nicole tilts her head to the other side. "I don't know about that, but there's something I would like to know."

"Ask," I reply. "Whatever you want to know, I'll do my best to give you an answer."

Nicole places her fork and knife down. Her eyes search my face for a moment. Then, a decision fills her eyes along with tears.

"Where did I go wrong?" she chokes out. "We used to be able to talk to each other about any and everything. I gave you my heart. I was patient when you needed. Why didn't you trust me this time?"

I look down at the table, avoiding her eyes. I wrinkle my brows and blink rapidly. I should be ready for this. The group sessions with Dr. Winsor prepared me for this. I knew this moment was coming, but now my words are stuck.

I push to speak. "When I woke up from the surgery, you were lying next to me. You were so beautiful and peacefully asleep. I started to think about our life, without me playing baseball.

"I didn't know what I would do. I felt like I was losing everything. I would be home more, which would be a burden to you. It dawned on me how little I knew about raising our kids.

"My thoughts started to get the best of me. Then Mama showed up. She kept at me. Playing on all my insecurities."

"I still don't get it, Cal. You should've told me how you felt," Nicole says. I look through my lashes to see her face. *Sadness,* that's what I see.

"Baby, when I met you, I yearned so badly to be seen as a man. You saw me. All the shit going on in my head and what Mama was planting there, made me think that maybe I couldn't be the man you needed me to be.

"I didn't feel like I deserved to touch you, to have you. I didn't know how to explain the shit I was thinking. I forgot that you wouldn't judge me, or change me. I should've trusted you with how I felt."

"But a divorce?" Nicole's brows knit. "I told you repeatedly to talk to me. That I would be there for you."

I look back down at the table again. "Yes, you did, but my Mama made it sound so right. I would let you go and you could find someone to give you and the kids what y'all need."

"Okay, so what's different now? How do I know you won't second guess us again and take off running? I can't let you do this to our babies again," Nicole says with trembling lips.

I stand from the table and move to kneel in front of her. My hand covers her cheek. I run my thumb over her sweet lips.

"It's always been about me. What I can take, what I can handle, what I need. It won't be like that this time. You and the kids come first. You tell me where you want to live," I say.

"I don't think I want to go back to Texas," Nicole breathes out.

"Okay, then we'll find a place here, like the girls said," I nod. "You tell me if we're done having babies."

A smile tips Nicole's lips. "I like making them. I just don't know if I want to have any more yet. I think our three are a handful. Can we reserve that decision for next year?"

"Yes, darlin'."

"Good, and we'll decide together, when the time comes," she nods.

"Okay, together. Now, I have one more thing we need to get straight. I robbed you of a wedding. Our anniversary is coming. Do you have enough time to plan the wedding of your dreams for this year? Or do we need to wait for next year?"

"Oh, Caleb, we don't have to do that," Nicole shakes her head, as tears spill over.

I reach in my pocket, pulling out the ring box I've had with me, since I left Texas to come and claim my family. I'm going big or going home. I mean to show my woman, I mean business.

I open the box to reveal the four-carat emerald cut diamond ring. Nicole's eyes never leave mine, though. Her hands go to both sides of my face.

"I never want to see you give anything up for me again. I've had a lot of time to think about our relationship. You've sacrificed for me so many times.

"It won't be like that anymore. I'm going to lay the world at your feet. I'll swallow my own shit to give you and my family what you need and deserve. That's how the man I want to be would do things.

"That's how I'm going to do things from here on out. So, when are we having that wedding, baby?"

Nicole moves her hands to grasp my ears and tug me into her. She presses her lips to mine. I don't pull away, but instead, grasp the back of her neck and kiss her hard.

"I'll have to see if I can swing the wedding in such a short time. So, let me get back to you on that," Nicole says against my lips. Her tongue flicks out over my bottom lip. "Cal, you're making me fall in love with you all over again."

I take her lips in a searing kiss, wrapping my arm around her waist and standing. I shove the ring back in my pocket for now.

I head inside to the master bedroom that has been prepared for us to spend the night in.

Presumptuous of me, yes, but this is my wife. I'll be happy to spend the night with her in my arms, or with my face between her legs. Either will do.

I break the kiss long enough to see where we're headed. Nicole's dress is too tight for her to wrap her legs around my waist, so I tighten my grip, fastening her body to mine. Finding our room, I push the door open and step inside.

We're greeted by more candlelight filling the room. Music is flowing low from the sound system. Playing a mix Stevie insisted on.

Nicole takes hold of my ears, lowering her face to mine for a kiss. I sip from her mouth like it's the finest wine ever made. I groan when she purrs into my mouth.

Breaking the kiss, I start to kiss her chin, dragging my lips across her skin to underneath her jaw. She tastes so sweet. I feel like I'm drowning in her flavor.

Reaching down, I tug her dress up over her ass to free her thighs and hips. Instantly, her legs wrap around my waist. I grab her lush ass and start to knead it.

"Tell me what you want to do, darlin'. If you don't want my cock inside you, it's going to kill me, but we won't go that far. I can just make you come," I say.

"Caleb, don't make me freaking hurt you. If it were up to me, I'd sit on your dick for a straight week. We're fucking, Cal. Not making love, not having sex. We're fucking, hard," Nicole looks me in the eyes and pants.

I growl and pull her into my throbbing, pulsing, heat. Nicole grinds her hot pussy against my bulge, causing my eyes to nearly cross. I attack her sweet-scented throat again. I need to taste every inch of her.

The song changes and Nicole gasps. "Tank, I love this song. Babe, I've been masturbating to this song since you left. Please, I need to have you to it," she purrs.

My eyes grow wide, when her words sink in. "Fuck, I want to watch. I swear, I'm going to fuck the shit out of you. Show me what you did without me," I say huskily.

I'm so turned on at the thought of her making herself come. Images of her writhing under her own fingers take over my thoughts. Nicole slides down my front, breaking free of my hold.

I stand, watching her intently. She moves to the tablet remote for the sound system and fiddles with it for a few seconds. The grin on her lips causes me to study her more closely.

"You want to watch, sexy?" Nicole purrs.

I nod my head and start for her. Nicole shakes her head, holding up her hand for me to halt. I knit my brows, as I let my eyes travel over her body. She's exposed from the waist down, just a sheer, thin thong covering her most delicious secret. I lick my lips.

My head tilts. "Are you going to do it for me?"

"Yes, big boy, you're going to get your show. I just need you to do something for me too," Nicole's grin grows.

I lift a brow and blink. "What do you need me to do?"

"It's simple," Nicole says, but she doesn't explain further.

She moves to the foot of the bed. Slowly, she reaches behind her back and lowers the zipper on her dress. I swear the sound is intensified with my wanting. My eyes are glued to her as she wiggles free of the dress. I want to pounce, but hold perfectly still.

Nicole turns in a small circle, bending in half, before reaching up and peeling her panties down her legs. I watch the descent of the small piece of fabric. It glistens with her juices.

Nicole steps out of her panties, one foot at a time, then looks over her shoulder, holding the scrap of fabric up as an offering to me. I move closer and take them from her fingertips. I bring them to my nose and inhale, groaning at how damn good they smell.

I place a hand on her waist, but she bites her lip and shakes her head at me, yet again. I remove my hand as she reaches to remove her sexy black bra. I watch as my mouth waters.

Nicole tosses the bra, then deliberately climbs onto the bed. She flips to sit on her ass, throwing her legs out and up in the air, brown legs and heels on display. Her juicy pussy, open to my view.

She slides one hand down her center front. Past her breast, over her navel, to her pearl. I clinch my jaw.

My wife is trying to kill me.

~B~

Nicole

F***in With Me, by Tank, is playing on repeat. The moment this song came on, I knew I had to have Caleb to it. I'm not ashamed of the things I've done to this song while away from my husband.

They were all done with him in mind. Some of the hardest climaxes I've given myself to date were while masturbating to this song. Knowing I'll get to have this with him now has me dripping wet.

I circle my hips, as my fingers circle my clit. I keep my eyes on his face. He's focused on my every touch and caress. I grin, it's time for a little help.

"Caleb?" I whimper out.

His eyes flicker to mine. "Yes?"

"I need you to do something for me, babe," I say breathily.

"What?" he says.

"Strip for me." Caleb reaches to tug at his tie. I shake my head. "Slow down."

My own chest heaves with anticipation and arousal. He nods and uses both hands to slowly remove his tie. It slips to the floor, just before he shrugs out of his suit jacket, letting it fall slowly as well. His hands go to his shirt buttons next.

I keep my eyes on him, as I continue to tease myself. I cover my breast and squeeze, biting my lip. My head tilts to the side, as his bare chest comes into view. Caleb's leaner, but it seems to make his chest and ab muscles look more defined.

I lick my lips and moan as my fingers slip pass my pearl to my folds. I tease my own lips, then allow my fingers to slip inside, at the same time Caleb's shirt hits the floor. He reaches to unzip his boots and kicks them off one by one.

He starts on his belt buckle and pants, next. I suck on my lip, watching the way his bulge presses against the fabric. I start to gush, just from thinking of him inside me.

My toes curl in my shoes and I bend my legs at the knees. My thighs tremble from watching my man and my own touch. It doesn't hurt that the hooded look Caleb is giving me is to die for.

His pants drop with the thud of his belt buckle. He pushes his boxer briefs from his hips, causing his erection to bounce free. I whimper and arch my back, pinching my nipple.

Caleb gives up on slow, when he reaches to tug off his socks. Moving closer to the bed, he reaches for the tops of my thighs, tugging me down to the edge of the bed. He grasps my right leg, bringing my heeled foot next to his face.

Kissing my ankle right above my shoe, Caleb slowly releases the zipper and peels it from my foot. He does the same with the other foot, then runs his large hands over my calves.

Taking my right leg again, he starts to kiss and lick my ankle. "Don't stop," he says huskily, when my hand falls from my heat.

I nod my head this time, going back to stroking myself. Caleb drags his tongue from my ankle to the arch of my foot. He flicks his tongue up to my toes and sucks each into his mouth in turn.

He nips at the heel of my foot, before his tongue makes a trip down the back of my calf to the nook of my knee. He sucks the skin there into his mouth, then teases me with quick flicks of his tongue.

"Caleb," I cry out, as my body convulses in on itself twice.

He murmurs something intangible, against my skin and continues his assault. His lips caress their way to my core. His tongue peeking out here and there along the way.

Caleb inhales at my center, but bypasses my moving hand at my core, for my other thigh. He sucks my flesh into his mouth and hums. When he releases the spot, he circles his tongue there.

He moves his way up that leg to my ankle. I'm finished when he starts sexy patterns over my ankle, before sucking my big toe into his mouth. It's too much.

"I'm coming," I pant.

"Let me, help," Caleb says, lowering to his knees.

He knocks my hand out of the way and latches his mouth onto my wet lips. I start to convulse uncontrollably. My eyes roll to the back of my head. I throw my head back, lifting my back off the bed.

Caleb doesn't just help, he takes my orgasm to the next level. My fingers lock in his hair and I rock my hips harder. My body locks up, when the fullness of my release hits me. My heart is pounding in my chest, although it has skipped a few beats.

I release Caleb's hair and fall limply into the sheets. I'm mildly aware of my husband's hands slipping underneath me. He lifts me up the bed. I feel the mattress dip under his weight as he climbs on the bed above me.

"Baby," he whispers.

I blink my eyes open, just realizing they're closed. My hand cradles the side of his face. He dips his head and takes my lips in a passionate kiss. I meet his kiss, only to break it, to cry out.

"Ah."

Caleb growls as he pushes into my wetness. He hooks my legs over his forearms and intently does what I asked for earlier. He proceeds to fuck me hard. I cling to his sweaty back, holding him to me.

"I'm sorry, baby," Caleb grinds out. "I won't hurt you ever again. From now on, when you play with your pussy, it'll be for me to watch. Not because you need a release. That's my job, darlin'."

"Yes," I scream. "Yes."

He plows into me, rocking my body and the bed. He plants a hand on the headboard clawing at the cushion of the upholstery. I reach to wipe the sweat from his face. Caleb turns his head to capture my sweaty fingers in his mouth.

I clutch the sheets with my free hand. This man is killing me. I wouldn't have it any other way. I'm approaching nirvana. I can feel it coming.

"Don't black out on me," Caleb grunts.

My lips curl into a weak smile. My entire body tingles. *I will make no such promise,* is my last thought as my orgasm meets super nova proportions.

~B~

Caleb

I'm still hard as a rock. Nicole has passed out. I knew she would. I could feel it in the way her body tightened and convulsed around me.

I'm not done. I pull from her warm body and sit back on my heels. I reach for her waist and flip her gently onto her stomach.

Leaning over Nicole's body, I plant kisses on her thick thighs. Making my way to her ass. I take a small nip out of her cheek. When she doesn't respond. I take another larger bite. She makes a small whimpering sound.

With my fingers I spread her cheeks, using my tongue to explore her other hole. In my head, I need to reclaim my wife. All of her.

I feast on her until she's soaked in her juices and my saliva. I crawl over her body, trapping her thighs between mine. I slide my cock back inside her tight pussy. I grasp her waist in one hand and the sheets in the other.

I bury my face in her neck and curse. She's so snug. I start to slowly roll my hips against her ass. Nicole moans, but I know she's not conscious yet.

I want to take her hard, but I won't until she's awake. Then, I'm taking it all. I reach to brush my thumb against her puckered hole.

The moaning coming from beneath me increases. I move my face to her face and plant a kiss there. A smile spreads on her lips.

"I told you not to pass out," I whisper in her ear.

"It's your fault," she moans. I push the tip of my thumb into her ass and she gasps. "Babe, please."

"Please, what?"

"I missed you. Show me how much you missed me," she whispers back.

Her words send a shiver through me. I pull out of her wet pussy and line up with her other hole. Reaching beneath her, I start to play with her pussy. Slowly, I slide into her tight ring.

Nicole punches the bed. I bite down on her shoulder. I have to still. This woman is everything to me. Everything about her has the power to halt my world on its axes.

"Cal, don't stop, please," she pants beneath me.

I kiss away the sting of my bite and surge forward. I tighten my hold on her hip and the sheets. I'm not going to last long like this. Nicole lifts her ass up into me and I know I'm not.

I dig my toes into the bed and ride her hard. I can feel the tingling in my spine. This feeling isn't even one to be described. I don't know how I thought I was going to give this up.

I'm not able to do this with any other woman. Not just the connection I have with Nicole. Over the years, Nicole and I have tried so many positions. I've touched her in ways I know I couldn't with anyone else, and I've allowed her the same with my body.

I don't even think about what sex was like for me before Nicole. It was never like this. I can focus on chasing my climax. No distracting thoughts of my partner trying to touch me, or agonizing over the fact that I can't just focus on sex.

I don't want to let this moment go. A world without Nicole is a world that would ruin me. I don't want to know that world.

"I love you so much," I grunt. "You're my world."

"Come, Cal. It's okay, baby. I'm here. You can have me again. Come," Nicole encourages.

I roar my release, bursting inside her tight body. I've never, and I mean never, come so hard. I see stars and the room sways a bit, and not from the ocean.

My wife. I'll never doubt you again. You know me. You get me. I've got you.

CHAPTER THIRTY-ONE

Daddy Time

Caleb

"What are you guys doing here?" Nicole asks, when we step off the yacht. Her sisters are waiting for us with smiles on their faces.

We spent the morning making love. Not like the desperate fucking we did last night. Not that anything was wrong with that. It's just, I got to cherish her this morning.

After showering together, we dressed in the clothes I had sent ahead. Nicole teased me for my ambition. It feels good to be able to smile again. All of the anxiety has melted away.

I feel like I can do anything. I guess that's why I chose to be a little more ambitious today. I have another surprise for her. I plan to show her I can be a father to our children.

While I send Nicole for a day at the spa, I plan to take care of the kids. God help me. I'm most nervous about taking care of my son, but I have to do this. I have to do it for me. Nicole's brother Harris will be with me, but I plan to do as much on my own as I can.

I clear my throat. "There's a helicopter ride waiting for you. You and your sisters are going to get pampered today."

"What about the kids? I need to get back home," Nicole wrinkles her brows.

I kiss her forehead. "I'll have them for the day. Don't worry about it."

Nicole beams up at me. "Really?" she says.

"Yes, darlin', really," I pause and study her face. "Do you trust me with them?"

Nicole caresses my cheek, lifting to her toes to kiss my lips. "You're their father. Of course, I trust you. Have fun."

I nod. "You too," I murmur.

I see them off to the helipad, where their ride awaits, and then I make my way home for my kids. This should be interesting.

"Would you like some more tea, Daddy?" Monica asks excitedly.

I shift on the uncomfortable chair once again. I'm having a tea party in the back yard of my brother-in-law's house. Harris is inside with Caleb Jr., who's napping.

"Sure, sugar, go ahead and pour," I smile at my daughter.

"This is so much fun, Daddy. Can we have a backyard like this at our new house?" Morgan asks, with her eyes sparkling.

"If that's what you want," I shrug.

"I like New York," Morgan says, as she reaches for one of the cookies the three of us baked together. We made cupcakes too. I sucked at frosting them. Monica pointed that out.

"Me too," Monica nods. "Oh, Daddy! Do you think Uncle Cam will come stay here now?"

"I don't know about that," I reply.

The question gets stuck in my head. I've been without Cam before. It was hard, but I had Nicole there at those times to calm me. I don't know if another move is in the cards for my brother.

"We're going to Texas to see your Mama and Daddy. Are you going to come too?" Monica asks.

"I think I need to stay here with your Mama and get us a house. Daddy has a lot to take care of here," I say.

"Everything is going to be okay, Daddy," Monica says like she's the adult. "Mama loves you and you're the best daddy in the world. Even on your bad days."

My heart squeezes. I reach for my daughter, pulling her onto my lap. I bury my face into her hair and inhale. I love my family so much. Her words are just what I needed, without knowing I even needed them.

Morgan comes over and wiggles her way into my lap and the hug. I wrap my arms around my little girls and say a prayer. I know I won't be a perfect father. I'll make more mistakes than most, but I'm going to love my girls and my son with everything I have.

Morgan reaches to stroke my hair and looks up at me. "If you get sad again, Daddy, you don't have to go away for so long. We'll do quiet time with you."

"Yeah, and we can get a daddy room in the new house. CJ doesn't cry as much anymore, but you can still wear the ear thingies Gran sent and your special blanket," Monica adds.

I smile. This is why I know I can do this. This is why I should've realized it sooner. I have a support system. I always have. I think Nicole is right about staying in New York. Mrs.

Joy reminds me of all my options when I get too overwhelmed to see them.

I never took the time to use all the suggestions she gave me because my Mama was relentless in telling me I couldn't do this. Looking at my girls I truly don't believe any of that anymore. Seeing Nicole and myself in their faces, I know they are the best of both of us.

I want to be here to see them grow into the potential I see now. I want to give them the encouragement I wish I had as a little guy. I want them to have a daddy they can be proud of.

"No more sad Daddy," I murmur. "I'm not going anywhere."

I turn my head toward the house as precious infant giggles fill the air. Harris has just stepped out with little Caleb in his arms. Caleb's cheeks are red, as his head is thrown back in laughter.

Harris is tickling my son's belly, causing the joyous sound. He makes it look so easy. I remember being scared shitless when the girls were born. I'm the same with Caleb. I know those are just my old demons planted in my head from too far back for me to remember.

Even when I was little and became fascinated with a smaller child, my Mama would make me back away, as if I would hurt them. In my head, babies are breakable and I have the power to break them. Well, at least that's how I used to feel.

I look at my son now and ache to hold him and cause the same laughter. I've held Caleb plenty of times, but not without anxiety about it. I force myself to focus and push my anxiety down.

I think of Coach Mc Rye. Everything he said has made sense. I need to make my family my new sport. I know I can channel the same focus if I try.

The girls slide off my lap. Bouncing up and down, as they talk a mile a minute, telling Harris what a good time they're having with me. I stand and move closer to Harris to take my son.

Caleb nearly flings himself into my arms when he sees me. My heart swells. My son doesn't think he's in danger in my arms. In fact, as soon as I have a hold on him, he's fisting my shirt to pull himself up close to my face.

I chuckle when he leans in and slobbers all over my cheek. Tucking my face into his neck I blow a raspberry, and he releases that sweet laugh I was aching for only moments ago.

Harris pats me on my shoulder. "Never doubt yourself, Cal. You're an amazing father. You're a great husband too. My sister has always been happy with you.

"Having Liv and knowing how challenging life can be for you, I thought Nicole was nuts when I found out. I talked to her. Asked her if she knew what she was getting herself into," Harris smiles and shakes his head.

"She told me to mind my own damn business," he chuckles. "Then, she sat me down and told me how much she loved you and what she loved about you. My little sister is smart.

"I know she wouldn't make a poor decision without thinking it through, but when she spoke of you," he shakes his head. "Her face was lit up the entire time. I knew you meant the world to her, no matter what you two had to face."

I kiss my son's head as I take time to filter through the words Harris has shared with me. Nicole has been my day one. A man couldn't ask for a better woman.

"Thank you," I nod.

~B~

Nicole

I've been standing here for a half hour, without them knowing. Harris let me in just before CJ woke up. I told him I wasn't ready to disturb Caleb's day with the children.

I inhale deeply, as I watch my husband with our children. I don't know how he ever doubted himself. Just the fact that he's sitting in those tiny chairs with the girls and Caleb in his lap, says so much about the man.

What Caleb doesn't realize is that he's relaxed around the kids more often than not. He hasn't shown signs of one stem since I've been standing here watching.

It's because he's totally focused on all three children. It's in Caleb's instincts to protect and care for what's his, always. It's one of the things I love about him.

I watch Caleb Jr. looking up at Cal for his direct attention, while Morgan chews their father's ear off. I snort, when CJ reaches over and sticks his hand into a cupcake, just before smearing his fingers into his father's face.

I cover my mouth and laugh as memories come back. I will always have a secret love of royal blue icing. I back into a corner, as Caleb stands with the baby and starts for the house.

He comes inside the sliding doors grumbling at the baby. "You think this is funny don't you," he says. "You're just like your Mama."

I bite my lip to keep from speaking up. CJ coos up at his father and laughs. The two look so adorable together. Caleb wipes the frosting and cake from CJ's fingers, with a wet cloth.

"Da," our son coos.

"Don't try to butter me up. You're trying to make your Daddy look bad, Squirt. You know I'm trying to get your Mama to forgive me, don't you?" Caleb says to the baby.

I can't hide any longer, when CJ throws his head back and gives a sinister laugh, like a little brat, knowing he's causing trouble. I love that little boy. He has so much personality for his age.

Caleb's head shoots up at the sound of my laughter. His cheeks pink and I swear, I fall in love with him all over again. The look of love that fills his eyes when he sees me solidifies it.

"How long have you been standing there?" Caleb asks.

"Long enough," I smile. "You're such an awesome father, Cal."

His cheeks darken to red. "I've heard that a few times today," he says.

"Well, believe it, babe. You are. Caleb?" I say his name softly.

"Yeah, darlin'," he swallows, worry covers his face.

I smile brighter. "You're forgiven. Can we find a home for our family now?"

Caleb's head falls back. I watch as his throat works. When he lifts his head to look at me again, he swallows hard once more. He shifts CJ on his hip. I can see the tears in his eyes, as he nods his head.

"Yeah, baby, I already have two places to show you in the morning. I want my family under my roof," he replies and holds his free arm out for me.

I rush into his arms, wrapping mine around his waist. I squeeze tightly. The girls come out of nowhere and tackle his legs, wrapping themselves into the hug.

I reach for a wet rag and wipe the icing from his cheek. "You know, I was wondering if you have any leftover icing," I say, wiggling my brows.

Caleb growls softly, bending to peck my lips. "I suck at frosting cupcakes, but I think I can find something to do with that bowl of frosting in the freezer," Caleb smirks.

"Daddy really sucks at frosting cupcakes," Monica giggles.

"Well, you can't throw a baseball," Caleb teases back and I burst into laughter.

"Yes, I can," Monica pouts.

"Who taught you?" Caleb pokes.

"My Daddy," Monica lifts her head defiantly.

"He must be pretty darn good," Caleb grins down at our daughter.

Monica shrugs her little shoulders. "He's the best."

"Yup," Morgan nods.

"Well, since he taught you how to throw a baseball, I think it's only fair you teach him how to frost a proper cupcake. Don't you?"

Morgan and Monica nod with big round eyes. I know he's just made their day. He'll be learning to frost cupcakes as soon as they can get him in the kitchen again.

I look at my husband lovingly. This is what our family should be like. I love this man. My heart would be lost without him.

CHAPTER THIRTY-TWO

My Wedding

Nicole

One year later....

I'm standing at the end of the aisle, dress in a cathedral length wedding gown. It's white and covered in Swarovski crystals. I went with a sweetheart neckline and princess bottom. My dream dress.

I wipe away a tear as I look down the aisle and see my twin girls. They wanted to be my maids of honor, not flower girls. According to them, flower girls are for babies. At nine years old, those two think they are women.

My sisters, Dakota, and all three of my girls from college are standing with the girls, with huge smiles on their faces. They all look beautiful in the pale blue dresses I picked.

Taylor, Joelle, and Maribel have been there for me through the years. We've kept in touch, even when we've gone through our rough patches. If one of us tries to stray, the other three of us have gotten into the habit of banning together to track that straggler down.

Heck, Taylor and Joelle where at my front door to help me unpack and set up my new house the day the trucks arrived. Maribel and her pregnant belly showed up not too long after.

It took us about two weeks to find the right home. Caleb was so impatient to have us in our own place, he rented a suite for the month and a half it took us to find and close on a home. The former owners of the house wanted to hold out ninety days on the move.

Caleb offered extra for them to do it in thirty. In the end, I realized he was trying to free up my mind and time so that I could plan my dream wedding. All this man has done for me makes my heart soar.

Surprisingly, my mother-in-law had a big hand in planning this wedding. It's been a strained road, but we're smoothing it out. We have something in common. We'll both do anything for Caleb.

I think now the difference is that Jemma sees what's best for Caleb and his family. I think she sees what's best for her too. Kyle isn't having her mess. He has been recovering a lot more since he put his foot down.

He never filed for a divorce, but he sure did scare Jemma straight. Would you know, they bought a condo in New York to be closer to their grandchildren. They both look happier these days.

My eyes slide across the aisle to my handsome men. My little and big Caleb. Caleb Jr. looks more and more like his father every day, just a toffee colored version. His hair has even turned a lighter brown, almost blonde.

My son is tall for a two-year-old. I don't think he'll take after me in height at all. None of my children will. The girls are on their way to outgrowing me soon.

CJ looks up at his father with a grin. He reaches for his daddy's hand and says something as he squeezes it. Cal nods, I can see the tear that slips from his eye. He wipes it quickly, as Cameron leans in and whispers something to him, before barking with laughter.

I'm sure Cam just said some slick shit. I'll get the last laugh. I know who owns his ass. He better leave my husband be.

I smirk at my brother-in-law and he winks at me. I shake my head. Cam is a trip. My eyes move back to my husband. Eleven years of marriage. I've loved this man for twelve years and I wouldn't change a thing.

We're so much stronger now. I feel like we are unbreakable. This has been our story to write and write it we have. We are the Perry's, faults and all. We love and support each other.

The look in Caleb's eyes tells me he understands that now. I've been his since the day he almost ran me over. I was lost, but I didn't know I would be found for life.

I went to Texas wanting to find me, and I did. I found my voice and I found the love of my life. Caleb is the force behind my energy to move forward.

I look up at my dad. "Finally, we get to do this," I smile.

"This is just icing on the cake, sweet pea. You've been his for a very long time," my father whispers.

"I know, Dad, I know, but he's doing this for me. He didn't have to. I love him for it," I choke out. "This isn't easy at all."

I look around at our three hundred guests. I cried for days telling everyone this was selfish. Caleb curled me in his arms as I sat in the middle of the bed crying.

"I don't want to do this if it's not exactly the way you want it," Caleb murmured.

"But what if it's too much for you," I sobbed.

"I promise, I'll handle it or die trying. I won't allow you to scale back on a thing," he said fiercely.

Now he's standing up there, waiting for me, with a smile on his face. He's handling it, taking one for the team. This is for me, because it was my dream and he wants me to have it.

This is love.

"Come on, Dad," I sniffle. "I have a Hero to marry."

~B~

Caleb

Nicole is so beautiful. I can't feel, I can't see, I can't hear anything but her. She is my peace. All of the pieces have finally fallen into place.

I know I'm a good father. I take my girls to school and to softball practice. When Nicole needs to write, or go out to shoot some pictures, I handle little Caleb.

He's my little buddy. He's always getting me into trouble with his Mama. It drives Nicole crazy that I let him get away with too much.

What can I say? He reminds me of me and Cam. As Mama says. Boys will be boys. It's the one thing she's right about.

Well, that and what she said to me this morning. Mama came to check on me and my son as we got ready for the wedding. Her eyes filled with tears when she saw us. At first, I thought she was going to start some mess.

On second glance, as I studied her, I got it. My Mama was proud of me. Her words only confirmed it.

"You two look so handsome. I couldn't be prouder of you, Caleb," she sobbed.

I walked over and pulled my Mama into a hug. I try to do it more, and it's getting easier. I've dulled out the extra noises and sensations to a low hum these days.

"Thank you, Mama," I murmured. "Thank you for helping Nicole and thank you for understanding."

"I don't think I ever misunderstood, son," Mama shook her head. "I knew the moment I saw her, she was the one. That's what made me so jealous. Nicole's a beautiful, sweet, young woman, with the sweetest soul. I think that's why you cling to her. It's something peaceful about her."

Yes, Mama was right. I cling to Nicole with every breath. She's my perfect peace, and for her that makes me perfect.

So, today I stand here. I know there are hundreds of people here. I don't have a baseball in my hand to distract me from them, but I have my son, my daughters and my Nicole.

I'm just fine. I'll make it through today, because this is for my family. I even have a surprise party planned for the kids after we return from our honeymoon. My babies deserve it. I'd do anything for them.

"Caleb," Nicole whispers against my lips, after I'm told I can kiss my bride.

"Yeah," I pull away and look into her brown eyes.

She grabs my ears and pulls me back to her, placing her lips to mine. "One more baby," she smiles. "Please."

I growl and devour her mouth. Damn right, we can make one more. I get hard just thinking about it. Nicole breaks the kiss, giggling.

"Not, now," she laughs.

I bury my face in her neck. "I love you so much. Whenever you want to, I'm ready."

"See you tonight," Nicole winks and turns to the clapping crowd.

Well, damn. I forgot they were here. I wrap an arm around her waist and squeeze tight.

"My woman," I dip to say in her ear.

"Always," Nicole looks at me. "My hero."

Through Anything

Caleb

Three years later....

I swallow thickly. Life has changed a lot for my family. I love them even more than ever. We're perfect. I'm doing this today to prove that.

I kiss the top of my youngest son's head as he squirms in my arms. Tiger is two. He's my pride and joy. My son makes me proud of him every day. Not that the others don't. All of my children are amazing.

My oldest girls are a handful. I can't believe they'll be teenagers soon. They already act like little thirty-year-olds. I need to take breaks from them often.

Not because of sensory issues either. Those two will either have you in stitches from laughter or pissed off because they have no filter on their thoughts. Nicole says they get that honesty from me.

I look around at the room full of people. They probably will never understand my family or the love I have for my children. My eyes land on my Mama and Daddy.

I see the tears shining in my mother's eyes. For the second time in my life, I think they are tears of pride. I was surprised when she turned out to be one of the biggest supporters of what I'm about to do here today.

I clear my throat and move in closer to the table. It's time. This has been a long time coming, today will make a difference. I lock eyes with my wife in the crowd.

It's that special smile that gives me strength to do this. That woman sitting out there is my rock. Everything I do is for her and my children.

"Thank you all for gathering here today. My niece and I would like to share something with you. I think what we have to say is important," I look to my niece and nod.

Liv turns to the waiting room and leans into her mic. "My name is Dr. Olivia Clark. I'm a daughter, a wife, a neurosurgeon and I have autism."

People begin to murmur all around the room. I'm so damn proud of Liv. She's one of the youngest residents at her hospital. She's already receiving recognition in her field. Doing this today means a lot.

"I was diagnosed when I was eighteen months old. My mother couldn't handle it and left my dad to raise me and my two brothers, but I had a support system in my father and my family.

"My Aunt Nicole has always been one of my biggest supporters. When I said I wanted to study medicine, she was the first to root me on. Not that the rest of my family wasn't supportive. Aunt Nicole was just the one that didn't need to get over the shock or worry of me failing. She jumped right in," Liv nods and turns to me.

I know that's her way of saying she's out of words. Her comfort level has been met. I know the feeling. I'm right on the edge of coping.

I blow out a breath and find my wife again. I look across our family sitting with her and I gather strength from the little smiling toffee faces looking back at me.

"I'm guessing many of you already know, I'm Caleb Perry," I say and the crowd fills with laughter. Nicole smiles wider at me. I wait for the crowd to finish laughing.

"I'm a son, a twin, a husband, a former professional baseball player, and I have autism," I pause as the room erupts into a gasp and chatter takes over. I purse my lips and squint.

Tiger squirms some more in my lap, and I take a deep breath. I kiss his little head and he rests it on my chest. I nod, I can do this.

"For me, this has been my secret from the world. A secret I probably never would've told if not for this little guy here. Some people think my wife and I tempted fate.

"After having three healthy children, that all missed the spectrum, we still decided to have more. For a year, we thought we beat the odds again. Twins again, a boy and a girl, both developing just fine. Then a year ago, our son was diagnosed after we noticed some changes in him.

"We don't think we messed with fate at all. My son is just as perfect as his sisters and brother. He just has different needs. Right now, to be able to sit here in my lap in front of y'all, my son has in earplugs.

"Fourteen years ago, I met my wife. At that time, I never thought I'd have a normal life or a family. What y'all take for granted, I have to work hard for. Just talking to y'all today is a great effort for me, but I'll do anything to make sure my son has it better than I did.

"When my wife and I met, we came together to raise money for this very special charity, Luther's World. We were able to raise almost five hundred thousand, as college students. Today my wife and I would like to donate five million to Luther's World.

"We also want to announce that my mother-in-law, Dr. Joyce Waltersson, my wife, Nicole Perry, and myself will be opening a center for children with autism. They'll learn sports, writing, photography, and physics," I grin. "I love physics."

Nicole winks at me, when everyone laughs. I once explained to her how physics helps me understand us. That we became baseball for me. I wink back at my wife and continue.

"We know that most families and children aren't as lucky as we are to have a support team, and some families have a lot more challenges than ours.

"I've scared my wife plenty, over the years, with seizures and melt downs. We know that can be a daily occurrence for some. We want to help out in any way we can.

"So, we're inviting y'all out next month to support the grand opening of Tiger's House. All children are welcome. We find our other children aid in Tiger's development, just like my twin brother helped in mine," I nod.

I look out to see my brother. Cameron is finally happy and not living in my shadow or trying to cover me. I love my family and I wouldn't change them for a thing. Just like they would never change me.

ACKNOWLEDGMENTS

This is one from my archive. I needed to do this book just right and it has been half finished for almost nine years. If not longer. I loved Nicole and Perry from the time they appeared in my head. I knew they were special and couldn't be rushed. I'm happy with where their story went and how it finished.

Thank you all for your support and patience with me. This book goes out to all the lovely ladies that joined me for Blue's March Madness in 2017, in South Carolina. I hope you enjoy this book as much as I do. I had so much fun meeting you all.

Thank you to everyone for your love, encouragement, and support. I appreciate every email, post, and review. You are all the best.

God has shown his hand greatly, I just know this is only the start. Thank you, Lord. To You be all the Glory. I praise you for all you have done, continue to do, and will do in my life. Thank you.

Next!

ABOUT THE AUTHOR

Blue Saffire is a housewife with too much time to think and not enough time to herself. By some miracle, she has found the time to write books. Blue represents the secret author inside that some of us are too scared to let out.

Blue is a loving wife, who is itching to make her way back to city life. The burbs are not enough background music to the story of her life. Life throws Blue challenges daily and since her diary is no longer enough, she has decided it is time for a new outlet. Thus, you are gaining access to the mind of Blue Saffire.

So herein lay the thoughts of Blue Saffire, the author, the wife, and the woman. Enjoy.

Wait, there is more to come! You can stay updated with my latest releases, learn more about me the author, and be a part of contests by subscribing to my newsletter at

www.BlueSaffire.com

If you enjoyed Where the Pieces Fall, I'd love to hear your thoughts and please feel free to leave a review on Amazon Click Here. And when you do, please let me

know by emailing me TheBlueSaffire@gmail.com

or leave a comment on Facebook https://www.facebook.com/BlueSaffireDiaries or Twitter @TheBlueSaffire

Other books by Blue Saffire

Placed in Best Reading Order

Also available....

Legally Bound

Legally Bound 2: Against the Law

Legally Bound 3: His Law

Perfect for Me

Hush 1: Family Secrets

Ballers: His Game

Brothers Black 1: Wyatt the Heartbreaker

Legally Bound 4: Allegations of Love

Hush 2: Slow Burn

Legally Bound 5.0: Sam

Yours: Losing My Innocence 1

Yours 2: Experience Gained

Yours 3: Life Mastered

Ballers 2: His Final Play

Legally Bound 5.1: Tasha Illegal Dealings

Brothers Black 2: Noah

Legally Bound 5.2: Camille

Legally Bound 5.3 & 5.4 Special Edition

Where the Pieces Fall

Legally Bound 5.5: Legally Unbound

Brothers Black 4: Braxton the Charmer

My Funny Valentine

Broken Soldier

Remember Me

Brothers Black 5: Felix the Brain

A Home for Christmas

Coming Soon...

Road to Whatever Series (Perfect for Me): Ideal For Me Book 2

Brothers Black 6: Ryan the Joker

Brothers Black 7: Johnathan the Fixer

Other books from Evei Lattimore Collection
Books by Blue Saffire

Black Bella 1

Destiny 1: Life Decisions

Destiny 2: Decisions of the Next Generation

Destiny 3 coming soon

Star

For information on more of what's to come

Go check them out on BlueSaffire.com

Made in the USA
Middletown, DE
30 March 2023

27996541R00195